AF671277

FSC
www.fsc.org
MIX
Papier aus verantwortungsvollen Quellen
Paper from responsible sources
FSC® C105338

© 2024 Jakob Reul

Publisher: BoD · Books on Demand GmbH,
In de Tarpen 42, 22848 Norderstedt, bod@bod.de
Print: Libri Plureos GmbH, Friedensallee 273,
22763 Hamburg
ISBN: 978-3-7693-1711-4

Of Lilies and Daisies

The story of this publication is odd. I stumbled upon a deserted house, in which I found a pile of notes, from which I selected the below extracts. The notes are not dated, so I'm not certain that I'm doing the chronology justice. As to the author, I cannot claim to know their identity. Truth compels me to add that I find their writing neurotic, troublesome, and at times disturbing. However, I understand it as my editorial duty to publish it in its original form. My reader may be advised that, by all appearances, we are dealing with a deeply troubled soul, and we are not to read it uncritically.

To long for something that is so close, you can almost touch it. That's the poetic beauty I aim for. I just want to despair over my despair, and never move out of it.

To have it, is not beautiful. To not have it, is not beautiful either. To almost have it, that's perfect. One almost does, and yet one doesn't. It remains an idea, essentially.

The main body part of a spider is leg. That's what's so spooky about them. A leg needs to be a subordinate body part, not the main body part. It's not what God intended.

Take me into that land called oblivion. I will run there, walk there, creep there, if necessary.

Fading is disappearing, into the night, or to cease as one existed, unrecognized. Cease the day, as they say. Slowly I depart into the land called oblivion.

To fade means to disappear without being spotted. If you're spotted, you're no longer fading. You're leaving. It becomes an act, or an action. Departure has to be unnoticed. To slowly fade away. To leave, without being noticed. Or to know one is leaving, without anyone realizing. To be understood as being present, yet in a way you have left. This is what it means to fade. To fade from the situation, to fade away from them. They must never notice, or it becomes a thing of arguments, and discussions. It destroys the whole beauty of it. To fade away in plain sight of everyone. To be gone one day. That is beautiful. To feel the sadness you withhold from them.

Fading is the process of disappearing in plain sight.

A snow flake is a most beautiful thing. Incredible, how such beauty can be produced by nature in almost random fashion. Man is often used as proof of something higher, but I can do with nature alone to believe in man. A snowflake, on the other hand, is too beautiful, to have emerged randomly. If there is a God, it would be elegant to reveal the fact through the form of a snowflake. I would hide the Godliness of the universe into a slight and fading detail. A snowflake would be worthy, because it's small, so small that you really have to find it first, then look at it in detail, study it, and be in awe with it, fall in love with it, then take it to speculate on the hidden sense of the world. The snowflake offers a direct path to God, and I mean this quite seriously. Something so beautiful must indicate that there is more.

How can nature create such beauty as blue snow? Oh I forgot! It can't. That's only my mind playing tricks on me. I watch in awe, as my mind wanders. A little madness has never done any harm. The problem is it always escalates into a little more. One never stays ‚a little mad' for long.

The cold turns your sentiment into a matching climate. The air matches your sadness with her coldness. It's the loving coldness she only gives to those who acknowledge her. The air can be your friend if you befriend it.

It strikes me, that this is not nature. This is me. I'm projecting my misery into nature. Yet I can't help but to admire it. My misery is coming alive. A starry night. True beauty. When it's dark in the mind, the world becomes a picture.

If you only see the light, you will dread the night, for it gives you little to look at. The idea is to see another world when it's dark. Darkness is like silence, only for the eyes.

A physical canvas is white and the hands paint onto it. But the spiritual canvas is black. Most people leave it empty, for the dark is not conceived by them as something that can be painted on. Yet that's expressedly what the dark is for. The eyes are two-directional, this is often misunderstood. Our eyes are not just receiving, they're also transmitting. They reflect the world into ourselves, as well as ourselves into the world. In darkness we are everything, at light we're reduced.

We see what we seek.

To walk in the night. To be surrounded by it. The night is made for pride to fade. To sacrifice all vanity.

To pour out, to diffuse. To dissolve in the night, to become one with it. To see the things, unseen by day.

A bland soul can never sympathize. One has to know pain to relieve it. To relive it. That's the key. Oh what a beautiful thing it is when two miserable souls understand each other and their misery fades.

To not bring them down to your level. To bring yourself down to theirs. To join their misery, so they're not alone in it.

To soothe the storm by walking into it.

When one looks in the mirror and sees a grimace. My eyes collapse in my sockets, my smile is a grin.

I come alive in misery. I'm cheering for the loosing team. There is a peculiar joy in that. One would almost be disappointed if the losing team turned out to be winning.

There is something so shattering about being miserable on a beautiful day.

To live right on the edge of misery and joy is to feel alive.

My life is unique. It will either fail uniquely, or succeed uniquely. It will probably fail uniquely. But I haven't given up.

Writing is creating from imagination.

I think on paper now. For the longest time, I didn't consider it possible. I thought when I thought, and I wrote when I wrote. But it's different now. I don't think anymore, for only on paper I do. Only when I write, I start thinking again. My life has been transferred onto the sheet of paper.

Ever since I think like that, I have lost the ability to speak. I'm not unhappy about it. But I am surprised. My thoughts are in my words now, and without them, I hardly think at all. It becomes a fog of sentiment and reflection, but it's eerily imprecise. Which is odd, for my writing used to be like that.

My thoughts were sharp, my words were never. Now the roles have been reversed. If one writes a lot and speaks little, writing becomes what speaking used to be: the primary means of one's expression. Thought is affected too, for its major medium is no longer speech, but the written word. The writing acquires a precision which thought and speech used to have. I guess I live on paper now. Don't get me wrong, I like it. I'm just confused. I didn't expect this to happen.

When every word you say, is a word spoken by a stranger. Then you've navigated yourself into quite the situation.

This is a time that says: never give up. But giving up can be a beautiful thing. Fighting is tiring, it corrupts our souls. It makes us tough, yes, but it kills our innocence. Our youth is easily lost in this fight. To not fight, to accept, is a beautiful way of preserving yourself. Giving up is only defeat if we consider it defeat. It can be considered a win. For we are no longer tilting at windmills. To spend your life fighting is not a good way of living. It turns you cynical, and crude.

Acceptance is not appreciated in a society which always wants more. Fighting makes you miserable, who ever talks about that? It doesn't improve your life. It replaces it. Life becomes a fight, and that's not the point. There's nothing to win at the end of life. At the end of life, life is over. To consider life a fight is a reliable way of becoming miserable, and mean-spirited. Toward oneself and everybody else.

Acceptance is a virtue. People don't understand this, but this is to be expected, for we live in crazy times. If we were to accept more and fight less, we would be better off. To accept doesn't mean you become powerless or weak. Often it leads to real spiritual growth. When you keep chasing, without capturing, you should discontinue the chase. Or chase something else. When all people look in the same place, it's wisdom to look in another. Chasing, fighting, and for what? Don't chase what you can't get. It's a simple rule to life, but seldom respected. If you can't get it, stop chasing it. Chase something else. You should always choose what you chase, but you shouldn't always chase what you choose. Don't fight a losing battle. Fight a different one. It's much easier to manage expectations than to manage the world. You can be anything, truly anything, by managing your expectations.

One should not think, if only it could have happened. One must realize that it couldn't have happened any other way. To accept what happened because one understands that it was necessary. And to make peace with it. To be fine, and not even sad about the past. Not everything has come true, but you genuinely tried. To accept that some things are just not meant to be. Many things, in fact. You only see the heroes, you never see the failed heroes. But they exist in abundance. Once you learn acceptance, your view changes. You realize how much closer fighting is to failing. Failing spiritually. It's like an eternal immaturity. To try and solve the same math problem over and over. Never getting anywhere, yet one never stops trying. It's a bizarre way of living. It's stalling life more than actually living. It pushes life in front of you, as though you can only start living, once the fight is won. It never is, the fight continues, and one never starts living. When one learns acceptance, one sees it with almost clarity. Fighting is not living, it's a way of not living. The fight is never over, so life is never begun. It's a tragic existence. Acceptance is a way out. The road doesn't end there, it's the running that ends. It's a well-needed readjustment. Acceptance takes you home to yourself. ‚Never give up!', forget that advice. ‚Accept' is a much better advice.

Whenever I take a nap, my mind is so confused. It says, what's happening, are we shutting down? I say, yes, only for a while. Then it says, but it's the middle of the day, is this a drill? I say, no, it's the real deal. Then it says, so what am I supposed to do now? I say, just take five, and when I say five, I mean thirty. Then it says, so I'm going to feverishly think of the most absurd scenarios imaginable? I say, no, I'd rather you didn't. Then it says, gotcha! And then I take a nap and for twelve and a half minutes I feverishly dream of the most absurd scenarios imaginable. I never not regret taking a nap. It never relaxes me. After the nap, I need a nap, more than I needed it before. I should stop napping altogether.

Loneliness is the disease. Solitude is the cure. How beautifully paradox. The thing that afflicts you is the thing that will save you.

The aim is not to become like everybody else. The aim is to stay who you are despite the hardships. To change, but according to yourself, not according to others. To not let go of your afflictions for they show you the path.

To give up something which you never had. It still feels like a loss. Like in theory, if all the stars had been aligned, and the Earth had rotated at twice the speed, it could have happened. Even in moments of bliss, I would have been miserable. This is wisdom, to know that happiness was never an option.

Her glance was beautiful. I didn't think she would notice me. I was polite about it, I only looked briefly. It was then that she looked at me. I loved her in an instant. I'm sure she saw it. A girl like her must have seen many fools like I. But I felt bad about it. It must be unfortunate to be beautiful like her. Everyone calls you beautiful. It begins there, it ends there. They're not really looking at her. Nor was I. I was only seeing her beauty. I made myself not look at her, but this was even worse, for everything I looked at, still seemed so intense to me. I was intensively looking at the wall. You're not supposed to look at a wall, let alone intensively. It felt strange, so I escaped back to her. She still looked at me, and I felt like a fool. Only briefly, for then I was caught in her glance again. It was beautiful. And that was the end of it.

There was something about her glance, I cannot put my finger on it. It's the potentiality that makes it such a beautiful moment. It's not about reality, for you don't know her and she doesn't want to know you. In the exchange of looks, there is no word spoken. It can be anything, for it doesn't have to be something. You get a glimpse of hope, a moment of bliss, or a hint of something that could be, but only could.

Hoping is lying about reality.

How to help a grief-stricken soul? To cheer her up? Or to embrace her misery? The latter of course. Only a fool would cheer up a grief-stricken soul.

She was miserable. She was beautiful. I saw that from the start. I fell into her misery, like a seaman falling from a ship.

I fell into her misery. It was a beautiful place, for she was there. She lived in that place. I said to her, your misery is beautiful and so are you. She smiled a little, for I was a right fool again. I said foolish things, as we all do when we're in love. But I liked her misery. It was her home, and she invited me to it. It was an underwater palace. You had to dive to get there. Once you reached it, you could enter. It was a cave, devoid of water. Like a cave in the mountains, only in the water. Here she was sitting, on the top of the stairs. She was sitting on the top step, her head bowed down. I saw her when I entered. And so I approached. I walked slowly, for she was easily startled. When she was, she wouldn't talk anymore. You only startled her once. As I walked toward her, the world was silent. In this cave there was no sound. I could only hear my own steps. I walked on marble of sorts. She still didn't notice me. Her head bowed down. I walked up the stairs and sat down next to her. I would wait for her to look up. Sometimes it would take her a while, but eventually she would. She would raise her head and look me right in the eye. How beautiful she would be at that moment. I cannot describe her well. Her eyes carried a sadness which was beyond expression. She was more sadness than girl. Her glance was still. She was beyond hope. That's how she felt anyway. She looked at me, almost idly. How beautiful her idle glance. Her hair so long, like she was a princess from a foreign land. She was born and lived in dream. She never said a word. She registered me, but only just. I wonder what she saw when she looked at me. I did not make her speak. I don't think I would have succeeded. I waited for a smile that never occurred. She only ever looked at me. I loved her anyway. For I loved her beyond expression. It was here that our love was complete. When I whispered, she listened with intent. Her silent glance was her way of smiling. When I was there, she forgot her misery. I told her beautiful things. About the world and herself. She became calm, very calm. Her anxiety was gone, and so was her sadness. I know she knows this. I know she does. And yet she forgot it eventually.

One had to dive deep, all the way to the bottom of the ocean. Finally, one came upon a cave. The cave was not filled with water. It was an oasis of air, deep in the ocean. I entered this majestic place, which was sealed from the ocean outside. The cave was a hundred meters wide, and perhaps fifty meters high. The waters were shining through, as the walls of the cave were transparent. The sun came through, all the way from above. It was a bright, beautiful cave, with nothing in it, except for air and light. There was a stairway, in the middle, it was beautiful white marble. An ancient Roman looking stairway, flat steps, only a dozen or so. There she was, sitting at the top, bowed down, her legs tucked up. The only noise I hear is coming from my steps on the cave floor. I sit down next to her. She still doesn't move. And so I whisper to her.

I walked home. I had no hope, and no clue where I was. I tried to walk by memory, and that's never a good idea. One always ends up somewhere else. I took out my phone, just to realize I should have taken out my phone a long time ago. Of course I had forgotten to, for I had been in thought. I always sink into thought as soon as I'm by myself. Thought is my guidance, thought my undoing. Thought my elevation, thought my dismay. Either thought is my only friend in the world, or my worst enemy. One day I'll find out which one it is. It's always ambiguous when one listens to one's thoughts. You never know if they speak the truth. To be free of illusion. To be free in illusion. Life has broken me in two pieces, like the huntsman breaking his firewood. Life has humbled me. More than necessary. Honestly. Life has crushed me.

So I walked home. It was eerily quiet. I heard my voice talking to me. Where were you, it asked. Where were you, I replied. It said, you're still going to these awful people. I said, I have to. It said, why do you have to? I said, convention, I guess. It said, I'm not going there with you. I said, wait, who am I talking to? And it spoke no more. So I kept walking, and I became miserable, utterly miserable.

It was snowing, which I liked. I love the noise of a snowed in city. Shshsh. Chuchuchu. Krrrkrrr. Those are the noises. Winter is for the silent people. Let the happy people have their spring and summer. The winter belongs to us. If only we weren't even more miserable then.

I was happy in dream. I was so blissfully unaware. Anyone could have insulted me, I would have smiled gently. In my dream I wasn't a conqueror. I had nothing, and yet I had everything. The dream is what I miss above all, or the state.

A dream has to remain a dream. To long for something, without saying a word. To attempt fate only in theory, in practice to accept it. To swim out into the darkness, never thinking of how to return.

One should never try to turn dream into reality, as this is a safe way of destroying both. Dream will be degraded by being subordinated to reality, while reality will be degraded by being compared to dream. One must protect dream from reality, as well as reality from dream. Dream is to be kept within, while reality must be managed. Neither will we bring dream into reality, for this will quickly deflate the dream, nor will we bring reality into dream, for it will turn reality into the saddest endeavor. One should neither abandon dream nor reality. One must protect both in their respective realm. If one is lucky, one finds a way to be happy in both. One should not become a realist at the expense of no longer being a dreamer. One must be a realist while remaining a dreamer.

I saw a woman sitting on a bench. She was weeping. I did not approach her. But I imagined. Imagination is the better reality anyway. One is not so limited. I imagined talking to her about her grievances. I would ask her what she most desperately thought. What she most desperately sought. If only she told me, I could alleviate her pain. People die within, when they can't share their afflictions. But that's not how the real world works. She would have looked at me funny. My thoughts are for the departed.

If only I could have gone to her, and she would have told me what made her sad. I would have listened to her beautiful tales. Praying to every word she sang. She didn't even have to know my name. All I wanted was to be there for her. But I couldn't. I only looked at her, and let her be.

She was alone, and I couldn't help. I felt so utterly sad. I ventured, but only in thought. I wanted to know about her grief. And perhaps she would have liked. But perhaps she would have not. Sometimes grief wants to share, sometimes grief wants it not, and nothing is worse than interrupting someone's grief. All I wanted was to talk to that woman. I stayed away. And again, I felt like a failure.

To overcome sadness, one must be sad, entirely and throughout. I want to motivate people's sadness. I want to make them not happier but sadder still. Because that's the paradox. It often heals them.

I hate that things are the way they are. I don't understand why not everyone should be my friend. If only I could be the ears for their weeping hearts. I want to carry their burdens.

To be the one they can share with. To be a brother. To not give hope, but consolation. To conceive their thoughts. Not to leave sadness behind, but to persist in it. Not to overcome, but to succumb. To give up, finally.

To listen. To care. To be simple and kind. To give them faith, that relief is possible, and it will come surely.

To be the bridge they cross, over the angry river. To be the stars they look at, to rediscover their ways. To be the ears they need, to let go of their thought.

I wish I could have gone to that woman. I reckon she was around 45. And sad she was. She would have found it odd. The world is not made for people like I. One cannot tell a stranger one wants to die for them.

I saw a woman in the park, near the graveyard, and she was crying. My only wish was to go and console her. To sit with her, through the night, if necessary. To let hours pass, and forget you exist. To see her smile, through her agony, because you can only be sad for so long. To hear her out, when all is lost. The darkest night, the light will pierce, nothing stops thy blissful light. Let me be your silent companion.

Through the night, and through the tears, I found myself so drawn to her. My dream again came unto me. My dream again, I dream again. I dream again, this gentle soul, I couldn't help but love her so. Images, of Blake and Keats, I found again, beneath my thoughts. I saw her then, this beautiful, this beautiful, had found me thus. No words of mine have heard of thee, but you again, my everything. I loved her so. I loved her so. I loved her, loved her, loved her so. And only once I called her mine. And only then my sun would shine. And ever since, my sun has set, forever since my darkness came. My darkness is my everything. I cling to it, throughout the night, the night that never endeth now. I find myself in agony. In memory, I have her still.

I saw a woman in the park. All I wanted was to console her but I knew it wasn't appropriate. So I let her grieve in peace, and I escaped into my thoughts again.

Shallow nature of things. I want to return to the fog. I'm never myself when I'm with people. Who liberates my soul from my body. Depraved of substantial thought. For every word I utter I want to add an apology.

The sin is to be conscious. One never lives better than in times of oblivion. I turned myself into a sinner, when I took my dream into reality, and shattered it, like throwing the most beautiful marble against the rocks. I'm missing this marbling world of mine. Marbellous, it was marbellous. I wish I could go back to being the dreamer I was.

Her tender face, her pretty hair, her shameful eye, her palest skin, her world collapses, and her sins, my world collapses, ever since. I never get to dream of her, I flee the dream, to flee from her. True she was, and beautiful. The only one, I loved so much.

To abstain. That is the key. To not engage, to never mingle. To inhale. To absorb. To enter the fire, burning still. To not flee the dark, but to investigate it. Solitude is everything. One finally hears one's proper thoughts. I like to fall, head over heels, into dark, dark nothingness. Nothingness, I found in you, a most surprising fairytale. A tale of bliss and misery.

One can become the most courageous emperor if one is indifferent toward oneself. To dare the great, to never seize, to walk among the faithful lot. Among the shadows, I am home, among the shadows, I belong. Spare a tear, for those who are, long forgotten since.

Thy every word, within your thoughts, thy every thought is mine. Together, you and I we are, blissfully, oh blissfully.

To help an inflicted mind, one has to listen, and not in the common sense of the word. One has to listen with one's soul. One has to fall into every word they say. One has to dissolve in the moment. To truly help, one has to become them.

Only the heart can understand an inflicted mind. Where the heart is weak, the mind is generic. Every word is somewhat dry. Yet when the heart is right, there is no limitation.

To help an inflicted mind, one has to see them truly, and purely. In order to do that one has to self-abandon. One has to fall into the other like a crevice. One has to — not absorb — but be absorbed. One has to float in their words like a river. One has to look into their eyes like the night sky. One has to feel their warmth like a warm summer wind. One has to sense their emotion like one senses the earth.

I stayed when she left, in this prison of mine, this prison of mind, this prism of mind, breaks down the world, into rays and remorse, I dream, and I dream, indubitably.

To help an inflicted mind, only an inflicted mind can accomplish. An uninflicted lacks what is needed to unite what is two. Two becomes one, when one is abandoned, one or the other, has to be gone. A misery shared, there's bliss in despair, there is faithful reunion, of him and of her.

Thy memorable eye, thy memorable sigh, thy memorable word, thy memorable tear.

The sinking feeling when you fall into dream. I always have the reverse when I'm with people. I sink into shallowness. I fall from depth. I fall from grace. Every word I utter is one too many. The only good word is the word not spoken.

Never have I spoken a true word. I could, of course, but they would not. Begin to grasp. We would just be awkward together. I prefer to be awkward by myself.

I talked to them, and they were excited. About what? I don't know. I let it happen. Like a river running down, like the wind shaking the leaves of a train of trees, so their words sounded to my distant ear. Quite remote, I was never there.

They spoke and spoke, a little more, I couldn't bear.

He was happy. And I was happy for him. I'm not a cynic. I'm too indifferent for that. Life has not broken me, it has bored me. There is a difference. I want people to be happy, by all means. I just wish they didn't have to tell me about it.

Blissful melody. Like opening all windows on a quiet summer night. Wind carries me away, takes me away. Alas! Take out the trash. Leave the pieces. Leave me in pieces. Left me in pieces. Belief is virtue. No more virtue left in me then.

I always feel apologetic during and after every word I say. My urge is to explain myself — to myself. Why have I just spoken. And what. Every word feels wrong. So wrong, that I don't even care to explain what is right. Welcome to the abyss. You may want to leave this place. We all do.

When I, instead of a face, make a grimace, it's because I have spoken. Every word I say I want to chase with an apology. I have this vision to never say a word again. Or to deliberately say one last word, and then mute for the rest of time.

Absurdities, absurdities. The true absurdity is to carry on. I saw an abandoned house. It was in the forest. I went inside of course, as someone would who doesn't really care about what happens to him. I looked and explored. It left me underwhelmed. I pictured myself living there.

It's funny when you reach a point where you no longer care about your fate. It almost becomes exciting in its own way. I went into an empty house in the woods. It was deserted and clearly no one had set foot in it in a long time. Really it was more of a ruin. Naturally I felt drawn to it. I went in, and I saw what I expected. An abandoned house. I pictured myself living there, but it didn't lift up my spirits. I was still around, and that is usually the part that depresses me.

I walked around the house, and I pictured myself living there. I would do the walls, all over again, and how I would do this? In my imagination I can do anything. I would fix up the house, refurbish it. That's a good word. Refurbish. Here I would cook, and here I would sleep. Here I would think, and here I would read. I would go outside, too, into the beautiful forest. I would return to my beautiful house.

I walked around the house. The smell was not very homely, but not a bad smell either. It was the smell of an old house that hasn't been inhabited. I don't know how to describe that smell. I looked at the walls, and the floor, and then I walked upstairs. I didn't know if I could trust the stairs, but I didn't care enough to mind. I tried my luck and came out on top. The upstairs was beautiful, too. In my memory that is, for in reality it looked pretty shabby. Here I would talk to the imaginary girl I would love very dearly. Here I would tell her that all will be fine. Here I would tell her that eventually I will sell some of my work. Here she would tell me that this is ridiculous and it will never happen. I looked outside the window, which didn't have a window anymore. So I looked outside the window frame. I saw the evening sun flooding through the beautiful forest. The sunset is never more beautiful than in the forest. I had to make my way back. It became dark, and I respect the dark. One should never underestimate nature, for she is mighty indeed. Those who don't respect her, will soon be swallowed by her. When night is approaching, it's time to withdraw. I left the house, intending to go back. I haven't yet, but I'm planning to.

Today, I told a man that I thought a bumblebee was a bird. He almost went mad trying to convince me otherwise. I wonder how you could not sense that this is not serious talk. I'm always amazed by seemingly smart people not catching this sort of thing. It's almost a stupidity in itself. I know a lot of people who are not exactly geniuses but they would have realized that I wasn't serious. And I'm not saying people who know me. Even people who don't. For they have the instincts for it. They can tell when someone is joking. This statement, that a bumblebee is a bird, is so clearly nonsensical, that I can't believe that anyone would believe that anyone would believe that. I would instantly laugh a little, and so would my counterpart, in this example me. But they don't. They are smart people, and yet stupid somehow. It's strange, isn't it. I guess they may only exist in terms of truth and reality and the factual. They live on the surface, they don't have layers.

Friendship can be a curse as much as a blessing.

I always thought I knew what was best for me. Now I realize that what I considered best for me, wasn't even good for me.

One reaches a level where only misery consoles.

When misery is denied, it's often that we deny ourselves. We try to be who we are not, and arguably this is what created our misery in the first place. Misery is often the sign that the life we lead is not made for us. This is one of the paradoxical facts of human nature that makes us want to abandon all reason in favor of sentiment. Reason says we should be happy, but we feel miserable. Perhaps our reason is flawed.

Before the flower blossoms, it sprouts. Life is created from within. This is the breathtaking beauty of life. Life emerges from thin air, to which it eventually returns.

Misery is painful when it's contrasted with a reality we feel entitled to. Our thoughts make our misery worse, for they're a constant reminder of how we should feel. But who are we to determine this? We need to stop telling ourselves how to feel. The fear of being unhappy is a dangerous thing. It keeps us from learning and experiencing what we need to learn and experience. We should not deny our misery, or pretend we're not really miserable. Misery should be allowed in, like a guest that you welcome into the house. Misery shouldn't be left waiting outside. In that case, it will never leave, and your mind will always be occupied with it. When misery is not fought, when it's befriended, good things can happen. Misery is of temporary nature. But not if it's denied, in which case it sticks around in the unresolved form.

To master this craft of capturing the soul of another, by consoling their mind, is very delicate, and at times dangerous when misused. But it's powerful, and when used cautiously and respectfully, it's beautiful. People should not feel lonely, this is a great injustice. It's an ethical responsibility to console the sad. But support begins with understanding the other. One should not impose, instead receive. The grief of another alleviates when it's shared. The best way to help the miserable is to feel their misery. Find it within yourself. It begins with the sentiment. A misery expressed must become a misery experienced. Bear in mind, the miserable express their misery because they experience it. You understand them based on their expression, but you must work yourself back to the experience. The miserable person gives some of her misery to you. You take it, upon yourself, for it means that she loses some of it. You must help a person in misery, it's your ethical duty. Those who look away, contribute to the misery silently. Misery must be met with sentiment. Thought is only supposed to communicate the shared experience. Whose basis remains the sentiment. Where the sentiment is lacking, no commiseration takes place. Therefore when you meet a person in misery, try your best to feel their misery.

Since it's not your misery, it will fade soon after. But for now you must feel it. Your sentiment and words will resonate in the other person, and there they alleviate the pain.

Heavy thoughts. Light feelings. Recipe of demise.

There is something beautiful about walking in the night. When all is deserted, and the world belongs to you a little more. At day the skies are limited. At night these limitations disappear. You see infinitely. If your eyes were any better you'd see a little more. Why do we feel constricted at night, when it's day that constricts us? I look at the stars, and I find them beautiful. Isn't it beautiful that there are so many of them. Why would this scare us, when it's so fascinating.

It's beautiful to walk in the night. There is an element of privacy, which pleases us quieter souls. We shall be quiet, as quiet as night. We shall observe and reflect. At night, we are returned to ourselves. Night is our home, we are born from it. During day, we belong to the Earth. At night, we belong to the universe. Our glance is never stopped, it goes on forever.

I like the night, for it doesn't pretend. The night shows you the reality of things. You cannot pretend at night, for the night is omission. It removes the added elements. The night is a reminder of who we are not. It serves as our conscience, and many people can't stand that. The night takes away our illusions. We must trust our night personality more than our day personality. At night the external factors vanish, and the internal factors reappear. At night we realize who we are at heart. Night should lead you, not scare you. Day should scare you, if it scares you at night. Never fear the night, for the night is beautiful, and what is beautiful never lies.

Night omits the lies of day. When it scares you, what you become at night, you should be scared of day. Clearly you are living in a house of cards. Tear it down. Let night be your guide. When night begins, be extra careful, for it's here that the truth makes its way to you. The lies of day are revealed and ridiculed by the truths of night. Those who drown their souls at night, are corrupted. Their minds have become the yes-men of a world that glorifies the body and nullifies the soul. One should never betray one's soul in this fashion.

At night I find, my blissful fate, in agony, yet sympathy, to all the souls, abandoned are, a lonely soul is never lone. It's one of them, and two of them, and three of them, and four, and five of them, and six of them, and many many more.

Through the night, I find myself, reflecting in despair, yet find some little hope in there, in every thought I spare.

We must apply our minds to the dark. We shall wait for night, to start painting again. Thought paints best, when day has ended. The strongest minds are those who see their thoughts.

Thought should never be suppressed. The only thing that should be suppressed is that which suppresses thought.

As the world does, it steals our thoughts. Our prayers are pathetic, we pray for little things. We should think when others act, and when they speak, we should be silent. We are minds, not brains, whatever they say.

At night, we see it, all so clear. That thought alone should reign the world. Thought is something glorious, for thought and night, are siblings still.

Our thoughts go deep, our hearts undeterred. Our truest and truest, finally appears. The soul never cries, she whispers at best, and only is heard, when thought is at rest.

I always feel caught in a lie. It starts with me introducing myself by name. I always feels like I'm introducing a fake persona. Most people have one. I have hundreds. Ironically, the one I'm not is the one that introduces myself by name. How does one live so eccentrically. Bare a thought for me. It takes considerable strength to wear a mask that itches.

So he wears it and wears it, it's wearing him down, and all he can think of, is tearing it down.

I'm never myself when I'm with people. It's almost as though myself couldn't speak. When I speak, I speak as another. Myself has no voice. It only has thoughts.

To speak of things that shouldn't be, spoken of I mean, of things that no one cares about, the never ending spleen. To ask what you don't care about, to answer with a lie, and why a word exchanged it is, it's never any wise.

I listened to a guy talking about his band. I asked about their next gig. I hated myself when I did. Their next gig is on Monday, for those who were interested.

They had recruited a new bass player. Yes. He told me that. I have no idea why. I had known this guy for five minutes. But he figured this was a great piece of information, which would enrich my day. I briefly reflected on how I could return the favor. I could tell him about my favorite paper format. I reckon it's A5. A4 is overrated. It's not handy at all. A5 should have been the world standard. It's a lot cuter, too. Then I figured, I could tell him in what order I do my grocery shopping. Because, that's the interesting thing, I always start with the beverages, as I tend to forget them.

Reaching the heights. Tired in spirits. In other news. The eternal spiral.

What's the difference between diving and plunging? It's the level of control. In that sense, I should say I'm diving.

One who dives is in control. He enters the depths, yet in controlled fashion. One who plunges has lost control. He falls into depth. But where does control end. Is it a gradient, or a border? Does one lose control suddenly or gradually? I reckon, it must be sudden. It feels gradual, but as long as you control it, you're diving. Until you're no longer in control, and the dive becomes a plunge. This is of abrupt nature, so it's not a transition, but a transgression. There is a frontier between the controlled dive and an uncontrolled plunge. Yet this frontier is not visible. Often one only recognizes it after the fact. One gradually loses grip, while staying in control.

Until, suddenly, control is lost and one begins to plunge. Once control is lost, it's hard to regain it. This is why one must be careful that the dive doesn't become a plunge. Then again, when you increase the speed, when you dive faster and faster, you develop momentum, and this momentum increases the risk of a sudden loss of control. This is called playing with fire. One can dive into the depth of Earth, but similarly into the depth of mind. It's there that one discovers a world hidden from reason and abstraction. It's called immersion. One immerses in the depth of one's imagination. But this is still the controlled process of diving. There is a level of control which is maintained. At the same time, it only becomes exciting when control is given up. The exciting part about imagining is not the diving but the plunging. One should fall head first into one's fantasies. The reasonists are arsonists, they burn our imagination down. We must fight them by imagining harder. We shall turn the dive into a plunge. For only when we plunge into our images will the images become real. They become vivid and colorful, a second reality within. The true capacity of an image can only be released in the plunge. To plunge into one's imagination, is the ticket to one's madness. Yet it shouldn't be rejected based on that. A little madness is the ingredient that makes or breaks the artistic dish. One needs madness to be a genius, otherwise one remains a mere talent. Madness is just another word for genius after all. The mad are mostly the geniuses that don't create. But the creating madmen are the ones we aspire to. Madness begins when the frontier is crossed. The true power of the images is hidden to those who remain in control. Only when the images are allowed to take over, will they realize their full potential. But this requires a level of submission, and sacrifice, that cannot be reached as long as control is maintained. To plunge into the depths of mind is the privilege of madness. Control is a burden, it limits our potential. We must not worry about the consequences, for we are explorers and we explore our minds. There is so much to discover in our own thoughts, but we must be willing to let go of ourselves. Images are never stronger than during these moments of self-sacrifice. Only those who let go of the existing, will discover something new in the process. Divers are in control, and control limits us to what we already know.

To find something new, we must sacrifice the old. We must cease to be what we are, to become something better. To give up control, to live up to ourselves. To give up, to live up, in layman's terms. Who is layman and what are his terms? We must plunge, not dive, for diving is controlling, and the depths should not be controlled. The images will never be stronger than when they're in control. One must let the images think, instead of thinking the images.

Soil is light, air is heavy, silence is prayer, prayer my friend. I see a figure, coming toward me, wondering, should I hail them. The figures are so vivid, I can't bare the fact.

Spiders. They are well worded in English. Equally well in German, where they call it *schpinne*, with the hard German „sh" sound: shhhhhh-pinne! In Spanish it's called, *araña*, and that's great, too — arrrrranja! As always the bloody French step out of line. They call it araignée, pronounced arenyé, which annoys me. The word is way too beautiful. It sounds like the chef d'oeuvre of a symphonist, or the name of a young duchess born into a royal family. This is unacceptable, and I demand that the French find a better word for it.

The strange feeling of hearing yourself talk. Especially when you say things that you hear for the first time. You go: hmm, so that's what we say in public? I hear people talking about inner monologue, but what about inner dialogue. At what point does it become clinically relevant? I am probably past that point, so I consider myself a pioneer. I'm pioneering for the world of science. The item of science is myself, or I am creating life. Like Dr. Frankenstein. I read this book recently. Mary Shelley was 19 when she wrote it. I'm quite impressed by that, her style is beautiful. My style is deranged. Two schools of thought, I guess. One can be talented and one can be insane. In either case, it's important to nurture one's natural disposition. If one is insane one needs to become more insane. It's an artistic approach, I'm not sure if it leads anywhere. Fission is underrated. It's fun to have friends in your house, and your head is just an extension of your house. So it's like having friends around.

I heard myself talking again, and I learned quite a lot. For example that I'm into Persian food. I did not know that. So that's something I learned about myself today.

So yes, it was a good read. But I didn't know that Frankenstein created a second monster, after the first monster had killed Dr. Frankenstein's brother. Can we talk about this for a moment? This seems like an awful decision. If you create a monster that kills, should you create a second monster of the same kind? Now morals aside, I'm just not convinced of Dr. Frankensteins sanity. Maybe he was one of those pseudo-doctors who do their PhD in marketing and then call themselves doctor on their doorbell. Must have been one of those. Cause I want to believe that a doctor that creates a killing monster — would not create a second one. Be that as it may, he did, and since the story doesn't continue from there, I fully expect that Dr. Frankenstein created two serial killers. Then again, the manhunt must have been rather easy. On the photo fit, they could have just said: „We're looking for two non-humans, it's pretty simple actually, if you see two aliens with square heads, it's those two". Which leads me back to my question: why would he create a second monster? It's clearly a bad call. Another question I have is: do the monsters procreate? Can they have a monster child? I can't decide if I find it cute or terrifying if they could. I think I find it cute, though. Having a cute little square head monster around. I also wonder, they don't have friends, do they? So I guess my question is: who's coming to their gender reveal party? I said this jokingly, but this is the problem with me, I now feel genuinely sorry for the Frankenstein family. I am sad that they don't have any friends. I wonder how they manage the day to day. I guess they would be like Bonny and Clyde, which is nice. Is it a love story, though? It's pretty much an arranged marriage, isn't it? The male monster wanted the female monster, but did anyone ask the female monster what she wanted? How does Dr. Frankenstein sleep at night? Knowing that he created two killing monsters — honestly, I think the emphasis should lie on the „two" part. The first time was sort of an oopsie. It happened. But the second one? He really should have known better. I mean, seriously, the first one killed his baby brother. This seems like a serious lapse of judgement. I really want to double down on that (as did our dear Doctor), and say that creating one killing monster is bad enough, but creating two of them is inexcusable. In fact, he should probably be arrested for this. This guy belongs in a prison. It's what he did, and even more, what he's apparently capable of. He did it not once, but twice, and chances are, he will do it again. He will create more killing monsters. This is not something society should allow. I know, freedom and everything, but we need to draw the line somewhere. Here is a guy who is apparently able as well as willing to create killing monsters. Do I really need to explain why a guy like this isn't fit for society?

All roads lead back to myself. If only they didn't. I want to take another road.

In tiredness one makes the worst decisions. But what if one is always tired. It's hard to look at yourself objectively, when subjectively you are so tired. My mind always has a funny idea. Then it tells me its ideas and I laugh. Like a lunatic.

A picture well imagined is a picture well painted. You see so much with that inner eye. I love to see things that don't exist. To see what isn't real, is to see truly. It's a privilege to be delusional. An animal couldn't be delusional.

I love the pictures that are not real. They are my preferred thing to look at. It's beautiful to walk through one's imagination and see imaginary things. It's impossible to paint a pretty picture if you can't imagine it.

The pictures you paint were images first. When creation is not preceded by imagination, it lacks the imaginative element. It doesn't create images. It merely describes them. But true art creates images, not descriptions. As the words are uttered, the image emerges. If there is no image attached to the words, you can always tell. The words remain words. If the words were born out of images, then the images shall be reborn whenever the words are conceived.

When the form requires a medium, but the medium has no form. When formlessness and shapelessness are not expressible in proper form.

My words are spoken without conviction. One day I believe in one thing, the next day in the opposite. I cannot help but feel discouraged. All has slipped away from me. The convictions that I had collapsed into doubt. Doubt is my conviction now. But I don't even doubt. To doubt one has to care, and care I do not. I let it happen, more than anything. World is passing me by, like the clouds on a plane. I heard this expression the other day: „Explain it to me in plane English". And ever since I've been wondering. What is plane English? It feels like the English spoken on planes is pretty similar to the one we speak down on Earth. I could not wrap my head around this expression. Perhaps it means we should speak politely as if on a plane. Or it means one should speak English as if one spoke to a non-English passenger on a plane, i.e. we should use simpler language. Yes, that feels like it could be correct. So I guess to say something in „plane English" means to explain something in simple words.

I was at the airport the other day, and once again, I realized what I don't like about airports. It's the sheer number of people. It presents me with sheer terror. Flying is the safest means to travel, but perhaps it should be less safe? Then again, I wouldn't want to be on one of those unsafe planes.

Nature is my only bliss. It's myself that I can't seem to appreciate anymore. The feeling of letting go what has let go of me. The feeling of I. No complaints. Behind the horizon there is lurking an eternally long shadow. As I look down on the ground, I see my shadow disappearing in space.

To live in nature is so beautiful that one wonders why people live in cities.

My mind's not racing anymore. It's sort of creeping around. I find myself looking for a genuine thought.

Thought is the depth of speech. If there is no thought in speech, the words sound hollow. One hears it when there is no thought in speech, which is usually the case. That speech includes thought is the most seldom thing in the world.

Of all the vain things you can look for in life, truth seems to the silliest. I don't think I benefited from finding it. I would have happily stayed in the realm of false. I loved nothing better than these false truths of mine. I looked at them, in awe, for they were beautiful, and so true to me.

I believed wholeheartedly in my dreams. Who cares that they weren't true. They were true to me. I'd rather love the girl that I imagine than to despair over the girl that exists.

I want to believe again. Not in the real, but in the unreal. The unreal is so much prettier than the real.

To see the ideal, when looking at the real, to tip toe that balance, to never waver.

To believe in something, without wondering if it's true, is beautiful. To believe, wholeheartedly, in the untruth.

One doesn't impose on the ideal, for it's not real, and it's not supposed to be. As soon as one realizes the ideal, it becomes real, and therefore uninteresting. Perfect we are only, if and when we don't speak. Her as much as I. We are ideal. The only love I believe in is the silent one. The one that never speaks, the one that stays ideal. To enter the real is to burn through the love. The real is never any good.

The ideal is something one can believe in. Believing is not knowing, and the ideal is not reality, which makes it a double negative. To unknow the untrue, is to know the truth from inside. There is nothing like believing in a beautiful untruth.

The ideal can never become real. One has to be clear about that. One leaves the ideal where it is. In idle imagination.

To love the one that doesn't exist. To not love the one that does. And to never mix the two. Yet to look at the real and see the ideal. This is beautiful. I never want to leave this inner world of mine. If only I could unknow the things I have learned. I want to blur my vision, I want to enter the fog. When the mind is suspended, the soul comes alive.

I am not real either. The difference between her and me is that she is the real who portrays the ideal, whereas I am the ideal that portrays the real. The real me exists as little as the ideal her. I only love her ideal which doesn't exist. She sees the real me which doesn't exist either. Which means that we don't see each other. She sees a shadow, and so do I.

I live in thought, and there I perceive. But when she looks at me, she is everything. Yet of course she is not, and I know that. I want to love her for the ideal that she is not. To capture that moment, when she glances at me.

I was in thought today. When I looked up. By mere chance, she was looking at me. A girl so beautiful, I cannot describe. Her glance was everything. She was not real. None of it was. I made my point. She looked at me, as if she saw in me, another one like her. But she didn't, as none of this was real. I didn't care. I kept her glance, and I keep it still.

She was ideal. At that moment, she was perfect.

What beauty is to the world, the ideal is to the mind. The ideal is the height of mind. To reach up, this is what it comes down to. To become a painter in the mind.

Trembling is good. When the trembling stops, so does the music. Pure thought is either the best or the worst thing in the world. It depends on what you think about.

Trembling is a motion, that once started doesn't slow down. But to tremble is beautiful. There is nothing like a trembling soul. When the soul is steady and calm, it's not lovable. The soul needs to tremble, for trembling means she's breathing, and a soul not breathing is a soul not alive.

To be steady is to be ugly. Only the boring have a steady character. It's the trembling souls that sing the hymns of tomorrow. No, they hum them. They hum the hymns of tomorrow. A trembling soul thinks in melodies.

Tremble, hence, and tremble well. The soul is made for greater things.

Misery is a blessing, never forget. Only the miserable reach the heights of man. One never feels more alive than in times of trembling. The real tragedy is to feel no more. The Stoics are delusional. To tremble is the salvation of man.

I saw a girl trembling, she was trembling throughout. I have an eye for these things. Ever since her. A trembling soul, affects me instantly. I am at once trembling along. For if I tremble a little more, she might tremble a little less. Trembling dissipates when others tremble along.

I did not know who she was, or why she was trembling. It was beautiful, yet anonymous, as I know the difference between reality and ideality. That makes me a dreamer, not a romantic, for a romantic is one that constantly mistakes the two. I know where reality ends. One can live well, when one is willing not to realize one's ideals. To protect the ideal from the real. Only a powerful mind can play this game, but once started, it becomes addictive. One is limitless in the spirit.

Why she was trembling, I don't know. By all likelihood, it was something mundane, and nothing to worry about. Yet it wasn't the cause of her trembling, or even the circumstance, no — I was simply drawn to the fact.

My thoughts are written in delusion, albeit beautiful delusion. That's what it's all about. In illusion one says nonsense, but one feels good about it. I'm always amused by the sheer nonsense of it. When I speak real, I make sense, but how boring it is. When I speak ideal, it's all nonsense, but it's beautiful. If only one could make sense and speak beautiful at the same time. But this is impossible, because to speak beautiful is to be nonsensical. To be sensical would be to speak normally, not beautifully. Yet to believe in my ideal thoughts would be madness, and the only thing madder would be to believe in my real thoughts. One should not believe me altogether. Instead one should dismiss everything I say and call me a fool. It's what my neighbor does anyway.

I had an argument with a guy today. He said I was talking rubbish. He wasn't wrong, but that's not the point. The point is that he said I was talking rubbish. He looked at me, all smug, thinking he had hurt my feelings, but joke's on him, I don't have any. One shouldn't talk to people. It's never a good idea. One is always so confused afterwards. I never say my thoughts. What I think and what I say are distinct. I wonder if this is psychologically relevant. Then again, if I said what I thought, I would have had to agree with him, because I was talking rubbish. So it's good that I responded that, no, he was talking rubbish. I wanted to give him a taste of his own medicine. It was such a childish thing to respond that it confused him. It's like when a child asks you why the sky is blue, you ask it why the trees are green. It would be quite perplexed, because not just did you not answer the question, it wasn't even an answer but another question. I consider this an effective strategy to deal with nosy children. After all who are they to doubt the system? They should learn early that it's about accepting the world the way it is, not about changing it. Only idiots think they can change the world. Next time a child will ask me why the sky is blue, I will tell it that God made it blue. That will teach them a lesson. Free thought needs to be suffocated early. Where was I? Yes, the guy. He called me out, saying I was talking rubbish.

I was saying that the moon proves the existence of God. I was referring to the works of British logician William-John Hammersmith who had originally developed this theory in the late 19th century, which of course I made up on the spot, as I usually do, which would prompt some to say I'm a pathological liar, but that's not true, because my lying is not pathological, it's intentional. I lie by choice. I responded that, no, he was talking rubbish. Which confused him, because he hadn't really said anything. But since I said it with a straight face, he felt that the battle was on. He responded by saying that, no, I was talking rubbish. I was so close, really so close to saying No, he was talking rubbish, but I felt like it would have ended the conversation. So I said nothing. He then said, that the moon was created from debris of the Earth, and that it was scientifically proven. I was cheering inside, because I felt this could be the beginning of an exciting nonsensical debate, one of those I so utterly enjoy, for it's the one time in conversation that I get to use my head. I said that this cannot be proven. I said this with the matter-of-fact tone that actual idiots employ. He shook his head in disbelief and said of course it could be proven, and then he explained it with a bunch of pseudo-scientific arguments which I only half-listened to, as I was already planning what to say next. He had spoken for a good minute or so, it was quite scientific, he talked about the materials of the moon, he employed quite a few numbers, and I figured a good response would be to say this: Let's agree to disagree. But he got all worked up about it. He said, no, there is no discussion here, you're talking rubbish. I said, with stoic confidence, that if God didn't exist, the moon couldn't possibly exist either, and I was particularly happy with my choice of the word „possibly“, because it made my conviction sound so convincing. He said that God could not exist, yet the moon would still exist. I said, no, that's impossible. He said, why is it impossible? I said, because if God didn't exist, the moon wouldn't either. He couldn't believe it, and he was looking around in disbelief, trying to see if anybody else heard this. Unfortunately, there was no one around because I would have loved to play this game with a whole group of idiots. He said, there is no connection between the existence of the moon and God. I said, with a smug face, you should read Hammersmith then. He said, it doesn't matter if you found another idiot that shares your idiot beliefs. He got angry. I got angry, too, because what he had said last felt like a direct insult toward me. And Hammerton. Hammerton was also insulted, and I thought it was unnecessary to bring him into this. I said, that Hammertown had proved in a series of axioms that it was scientifically impossible for the moon to exist if God didn't exist, because otherwise, i.e. if God didn't exist, the moon wouldn't exist either and this is called Hammersen's Theorem, which is as accepted and proven today as Noether's

Theorem. This had the desired outcome, it put him right over the edge. He said that I was an idiot, and it was the stupidest thing he had ever heard. I said, that's a little harsh. I added that there was no reason to become insulting, and that we simply held two different opinions on an issue, and that in a society we must accept each other's opinions without condemning them. But he got up and left without a word. I was disappointed, because I felt I could have done so much more. For example, I could have said that if the Earth had two moons, there would be two Gods. This would have been perfectly in line with my reasoning. I could have also said that the moon was shining brighter than the sun, and that frustrated me. I would have loved to have him explain to me that the moon doesn't shine. I feel like there was additional potential surrounding the moon landing. I should have definitely come up with arguments why it didn't happen. All in all, I give it a 3 out of 10. I could have done so much more to keep this conversation alive.

The other day, I talked to a man in a store. I wanted to get advice on the products. I always dread asking sales people about anything. It's not that I don't get the information I want. It's all the other information that I don't want and that I get anyway. If only he could give me the particular piece of information that corresponds with the particular question I asked. Yet that never happens. One is always trapped in a situation. The sales man was all enthusiastic. Little did he know his enthusiasm was his most solid argument against purchase. He was excited, and I guess I should be less cynical and compliment him on his excitement. Yet I was annoyed by it. After all, we cannot change who we are. The product I inquired about (and here is where his enthusiasm becomes questionable) was a pan. I needed a pan for cooking. All I wanted was a cheap pan. All he showed me were the expensive pans. I wonder why, since I had specifically asked for a cheaper pan. He explained to me their heating behavior, or whatever words he used, he basically told me how quickly they got hot. I said that I favored a pan that would get hot quickly, because that would save me some time in the kitchen. He nodded enthusiastically. He understood what I meant and I gained confidence in the more expensive pans. I wanted to be favorable toward this kind man, yet at the same time I couldn't help thinking what a waste of intellect it is to become an expert on pans. Will he one day indulge in memory and think back to all the pans he sold.

In the same store a guy approached me, in one of the aisles. Something must have made him think that I was working there. Maybe I seemed competent to him. I learned that it's impolite to interrupt people, so I let him speak. He told me, what he was looking for. A pot of sorts. He had specifics, which surprised me, as to me a pot had always been a pot. For him it appeared to be much more. He spoke for 30 seconds straight. When he was finished I told him I didn't work there. He looked at me, clearly annoyed that I let him speak for that long. But I didn't make him speak to me, did I?

Whenever I enter conversation, my only thought is how to escape it. Conversation is not to be had, but to be fled. Once conversation has begun, it's hard to get out of it. The more people talk, the more they get into it, and at that point, all is lost. Never should one willingly enter conversation. If unwillingly you end up in one, only endurance and resilience will carry you through. But sometimes it's just not enough and conversation lies on our shoulders like a heavy weight. It's hard to pretend one is interested when one isn't. It's like falling asleep, while trying to stay awake. My eye sight becomes blurry, I can never follow for long. Not because I don't listen, but because I don't have to. One can sort of guess the rest of the story after two or three sentences.

Thinking and doing should never be mixed. The mind needs protection from the idleness of the world. Nothing corrupts the mind like applying it to the real world. Mind needs to detach. To say one thing, to think another, that is wisdom.

To speak earnestly, is a mistake. One gains so little from it. Thought is not something to be verbalized. It is something to dwell on in secret. Only a mind that keeps secrets is a mind worth caring for. One should never listen to people who speak from the heart. It's important to keep thought uncorrupted. Thought is sacred, and the world is not.

I have no intention of being understood. In fact, it is my particular goal to be misunderstood. When I'm understood it means my disguise has failed. This may seem like an original thought but it's not. I read it in Pessoa. His book of disquiet. I really don't know what to make of it. On the one hand, it's beautiful and highly readable. On the other hand, it's awful und unreadable. I have read many books, never has it taken me longer to finish one. I read it over a period of 7 or 8 years. This is how long it took me to finish it. I was both impressed and unimpressed by it. I'm sure Pessoa would be glad about this paradoxical statement. I assume he was also both impressed and unimpressed by it. There is something about that book, I don't know what it is. It is neither mundane nor poetic, but an odd mix of the two. One could say he describes the mundane poetically, but that's not it. The better way of saying it is that he describes the mundane, and then there's poetry. It's hard to capture his style. There is an element of Kafka in it. For the life of me, I cannot say if I love or hate this book. I almost want to say I do both. It's one of the best and worst books I've read. It's great because it's full of quality. It's bad because it was such a drain to read it. Nothing happens in this book. It's the premise of the book, yet the drain of it drains me particularly. It's like getting bored of watching a waterfall. Or walking through the most beautiful woods, but for too long and your legs get tired. Or like one of those deserts that taste incredible for three spoons, but then you still have the whole plate to finish.

Desire torments the heart. I'd rather be undesiring than desiring, for desire always aims for the unattainable. At least mine does. But to desire is also beautiful. So I'd rather be desiring than undesiring. Or I'm not sure. I want to desire, but I don't want to obtain what I desire.

It's beautiful to desire what you cannot obtain. It's beautiful because to obtain what you desire doesn't make you happy anyway. A wise man knows that desire is just the negation of what you have at this moment. Whatever you will have then, you will desire something else. It's human nature.

I'd rather despair than desire. To despair is beautiful, to desire is not. Desperation is the most beautiful state. It's so vivid and exciting. I wish I could always be desperate.

There is beauty in detachment. To get lost in yourself is exciting. I like listening to my own thoughts. They never bore me. I find myself to be good company.

Truth is limitation and one should never limit oneself. Therefore, logically, one should not pursue truth. Instead one should avoid it like the plague. What's the point of knowing the truth, if it takes away all the fun. It's better to believe in the untruth, and consider it true. It's not those who find truth that the world admires. It's those who put it in question.

The untruth never disappoints. The truth, on the other hand, disappoints all the time, and only a fool would seek it out.

Truth and dream do not coalesce. I just want to live in the dream's untruth, and never wake up to the truth of life.

Truth lacks intensity, which is why one should omit truth. Intensity is the only thing that matters. But truth degrades and deflates intensity. Truth is an abstract thing, and to become abstract is to die a death premature. It's important to stay away from anything resembling truth. „Beauty goes hand in hand with stupidity" — Virginia Woolf. One should always remain blissfully and beautifully unaware.

The innocent alone can capture the world's beauty. Truth consumes innocence, it doesn't leave it intact. Innocence is belief in the untruth, and loyalty to it. The innocent do not want truth, they want to be protected from it.

Innocence needs to be maintained, with the truth well outside the scope of things. There are plenty of people caring for the truth and let them deal with it. In innocence one is forever child. One never loses the intensity of youth. The intensive life is the only life worth living. But in order to keep the sentiment fresh, one needs to protect one's innocence.

Innocence is the purity of the soul. Life should not be lived, it should be stalled. We shall protect our innocence, that's the first and only responsibility we have. It is beautiful to remain innocent, and way beneath the threshold of maturity.

One should live intensively, not extensively, and that is to say, one should feel alive, yet never actually do a lot of living. This is the way to keep your innocence intact.

Intensity and innocence, to mix these seemingly opposite sentiments into one, it comes down to that.

Innocence is bliss. It needs to be protected. The innocent are eternally young. They never grow up, so they never grow old. Love is childish and so it should be. Innocence is not to be wasted on a troublesome world. The world has to be denied and dismissed. Innocence is a choice. One chooses innocence over everything else. Only a beautiful life deserves to be lived. And innocence is the way to keep beauty alive.

The beloved should eternally be what she was when love first awoke. The very feeling, its intensity, can be captured, but only if innocence is well and alive.

Innocence makes a soul beautiful. No one can resist an innocent soul. This goes for both men and women. There is no distinction in the soul. A soul is not male or female, a soul is only beautiful or ugly, innocent or corrupted. The soul, once ugly, will not go back to being beautiful. That's why it's so important to protect her beauty. Innocence is the way.

Beauty is the most delicate land, which only allows the innocent to enter. There are many young men and women who early on inhabit the land, but ultimately, they have to leave it, for they have depleted their innocence. This is an irreversible mistake, and it leads to eviction.

Innocence sacrifices the world to the soul, and the soul will be grateful for that. One gets a higher reward, if one is willing to abandon the world. One should never sacrifice oneself for the world, for this is the path to corruption.

Instead one should commit to oneself, and take upon oneself all misery arising. It's beautiful to suffer one's misery in style.

Innocence is the self untouched. One needs to make sure that the self doesn't get broken. The world is quite good at it. The self is protected by protecting one's innocence.

All things precious are destroyed by a world so ugly. A beautiful soul does not belong in an ugly world. It belongs in a beautiful world. It's the world of dream. There, and there only, good things can flourish. Beauty, innocence, and love. That's what it's all about. And thought. I forgot thought.

I stumble through life as though I just learned to walk. It's a slippery slope. One walks, without progressing. Today it snowed and the ground was slippery. I couldn't think, as I had to focus on walking. I hated that. The last time I had to focus on walking was as a toddler. I wish I still was. As a toddler, I would not think about any of these things. I wouldn't think, period. It was blissful. I would simply exist. The toddler life is the life. It only goes downhill from there.

I always hoped that one day I would realize my potential. Today I realize that a potential is better not realized. Instead of realizing one's potential, one should realize the absurd. It's about defining the most absurd scenario imaginable and doing everything in one's power to realize it. This seems counterintuitive at first, but I'm convinced that this is the way to go. To dismiss one's potential early on, and to choose the absurd, is unique. It's here that one truly starts to realize something. Otherwise one realizes what many others have realized before. Which means that one doesn't realize anything, one reproduces, or recreates. To define something absurd, e.g. to be an absolute non-success professionally and instead become the best at something completely stupid (and that is surely absurd) leads you on a path untaken. If anything, it's exciting. To dismiss your potential early on, which is often just a golden casket, and instead to go for something absurd. One should realize an absurdity, which one fills with life by dedicating to it.

One should never go for one's potential. It's a clear failure to do what millions have done. The earlier one realizes that potential is a devil, the freer one gets. Potential is not our friend, it's our enemy. All potential needs to be dismissed, and instead one should identify the most absurd possibility, and choose it. The more absurd the possibility, the more likely it is to be true. For the absurd is too bad to be untrue, and the fact that we understand it as absurd proves that. The absurd says to us: look, I am absurd, but at least I admit to it. Whereas the potential is a crook. He's selling us something we don't even need. It's tragic when it takes you fifty, sixty years to realize that. At that point, your potential has transformed into a reality, within which you no longer have anything to escape to, besides memories. Potential should never be realized, and instead one should realize the lowest available option. This alone leads you on a path untaken.

If one makes failure one's goal, then it's easier to succeed. It's an accomplishment to fulfill one's potential, so one should choose an easy to reach potential. The endorphins will be available more timely. It comes down to that. To set the bar low, for otherwise you may not be able to pass it.

One should go for the absurd. This sounds absurd perhaps, but I believe in it. It's failure to become like everybody else. No one in their right mind would question that. A potential is the shared vision of the many, and to realize this is not to realize oneself. Our potential has to be discovered, and it's more effectively discovered by choosing the absurd. On that road, you couldn't possibly be misled, since the road itself isn't leading anywhere. It's impossible to move to the wrong place, if the road has no destination. Just like that the absurd couldn't possibly lead you astray, as it doesn't lead you anywhere to begin with. Therefore, it's a measure of one's ability to set oneself free from the standards of the world. And nothing is easier than to get entangled in those.

One should always go for the absurd. The more absurd an option seems, the more likely it is to be true. Because if the absurd is even considered, it cannot be wrong. Why consider the absurd, if there is no truth to it. That would be illogical, and it must mean that there is some truth to it. This logic was of course completely absurd, yet it made you think and that's the point. If one chooses the absurd, one chooses to choose. And that's the most important choice of all.

One should choose the absurd. It's like jumping in at the deep end of choice. To choose the absurd, is like sharpening the knife by using it. One can no longer take the easy route now, for one has chosen the absurd, which leads to absurd consequences. But the consequences of one's choice lead to the mind being used and trained. The easy way makes it easy to forget that one has to choose and decide. The absurd doesn't allow for that, as it throws you into pandemonium, and there you have to learn to think for yourself.

To choose the absurd is therefore not at all absurd. It's quite ingenious. It's a way of stripping yourself from all external pressures and principles, which do not belong in you after all. They should be removed, the earlier the better. Only when the external elements are gone — and you will find out, to your surprise, that this is the majority of elements —, can the truth emerge. You will find yourself in the absurdest of situations, which is good, because now you can start to navigate. The absurd is that which liberates you from external circumstance, and therefore it should be selected.

Is it absurd to go for the absurd? Not at all. It's very smart actually. The earlier you start failing, the higher your chances of success. The youths should do everything in their power to avoid early success. As soon as the young find success in the world, they should let go of it, and move on.

The worst thing that can happen to an artist is early success. This will completely ruin him as an artist. His art will stagnate and never develop. There is nothing better than obscurity for an artist. Van Gogh, for example, desperately wanted recognition. Yet his early paintings were awful. He was shockingly bad at drawing people, yet all he wanted to do was painting portraits. It was good for him, that he never got recognition for it, for he would have continued to paint portraits, which he wasn't any good at. Instead he remained obscure, he turned a little crazy, and yes, he cut his ear. But ears are overrated anyway, eyes are more important. His eyes he still had, and he developed. So he began to paint what made him truly unique. His originality, ironically, was not original at all. It took him years to find it. He found it, within him, and his late paintings are the ones that made him a genius at last. None of this would have happened if he had been a success. Van Gogh had to become absurd to become a genius. If he had stayed ordinary and realized his worldly potential, he would have amounted to nothing artistically, and we would never even utter his name today.

To go for the absurd is to choose early on. Choice is what it's all about. Choosing wrongly is better than not choosing. Choice must always be made and prioritized. One needs to liberate oneself from the circumstances, which is done by having a proactive way about living and choosing.

To choose the absurd is to the set the rules straight early on. One doesn't choose the absurd because absurdity is the desired outcome. One chooses the absurd in order to prove that one is not afraid of anything.

Choosing the absurd means one is willing to choose. Nothing will stop me from choosing, and to prove this, I will choose the absurdest option. To prove that life and fate have nothing on me, and that the last thing I intend to do is realize my potential. Potential is a burden, and nothing else.

To choose the absurd shows strength. To be intelligent, yet to not choose the intelligent path, instead to choose the dumb path and see where it takes us. A smart person will learn so much on that path. To not go for the beautiful lover. Instead to go for the ugly lover, for chances are they have a much better personality. To not amount to anything. Instead to amount to nothing. It's nice to amount to nothing. One is so beautifully unimportant to the world.

Yet for those who find it absurd what I'm saying, this proves my point. When the absurd is chosen, life becomes unique. Of course one has little to show for, but at least it happened by choice. It's better to choose failure than to reach success by accident. To stumble into success is an embarrassment, and it's better to walk knowingly into failure.

The absurd is the best choice. One can be bright and brillant, but by choosing the regular path, one highlights one's deficiencies. Spiritually, it's such a loss to do what everybody else does. For the unique there is only one acceptable way: the unique way. And the absurd road is certainly unique, for no one in their right mind would consider it.

Only the chosen few choose irrationally. The absurd teaches us to rely on ourselves. Since in the absurd there is no reference we can use for orientation. Independence is not a result, it's a reward, or a decision. One chooses to be independent long before becoming it. Potential, realized or not, makes you dependent. That potential may be money, or a job, or family, or a house, all of this becomes your master. You are now in the hands of your potential. You depend on it, its achievement and possession. This is weak. It should not be encouraged, and it should not be pursued. Instead choose the absurd, for then and only then you can free yourself from your potential and become whatever you want.

To choose the absurd is to choose yourself. On this trip you only bring yourself. This is the ultimate choice. Scary as it may be at first. Never forget, you are by yourself anyway.

Boredom is the retirement home of the wandering mind. I'd rather succumb to illusion than to persist in this dull reality of mine. I wish I could plunge head first into insanity. But I can't even do that. My mind is too sound.

People say one should adapt to the circumstances. I disagree. I think one should fixate on one thing, and commit to it, no matter what. This is a way of taking ownership. To fixate something, and to live for the thing fixated. This schools the eye in ways unimagined.

To fixate is to observe. It enables you to drill into the heart of things. Fixation is the heart's decision to wander no more.

When one fixates, one doesn't see beyond, but beneath. And the ability to see beneath distinguishes the eye.

Fixation is abandonment of self. For only those who abandon themselves, can truly fixate. To fixate one thing, one must disregard every other.

Fixation is a way of seeing one thing, and one thing only. Yet this one thing has never been seen this way. It's to be a pioneer. One becomes the sole expert on a particular item, while becoming absolutely useless for everything else.

Fixation expresses the wish to fixate. The mind fixates what the heart dictates.

That's why one should fixate the right thing. It doesn't have to be an object. It can be anything. The mind decides. It can fixate a sentiment, or an impression, or an idea. Anything can be fixated, and herein lies the choice of the fixating mind. It must fixate, but what it fixates, it can choose.

The mind chooses what it fixates, and this is the element of choice. Yet when it finds something worthy of fixation, then it should fixate it with full attention. The object fixated doesn't have to be physical. A thinker should fixate an idea. A dreamer should fixate the dream. A lover should fixate the beloved. And a madman should fixate all of the above.

Only those who fixate have a chance of going deeper. To be a pioneer, one must do what nobody else does. And this is done first by not doing what everybody else does. This is how pioneering starts. To abandon the world, to fixate a particular thing. No superficial mind has ever changed the world.

To fixate is not to conquer. He or she who thinks that misunderstands the nature of fixation. Fixation is not taking. Fixation is giving. One gives the fixated object undivided attention. The fixated object becomes what used to be me. I only exist in relation to the fixated object.

Fixation is not conquering something. It's being conquered by it. To fixate is to capitulate. One capitulates to the fixated object. You are a servant to the fixated item. By capitulating to it, one conquers in a different way.

Those who fixate are different. Everything else is generic compared to their work. Their every word rings more truly. Their very gesture embellishes. Their very appearance makes everyone love. To fixate is to become devoted. And no one is stronger than the devoted mind.

I am constantly surprised by my own thoughts.

My heart is silent. I have gone for the unattainable. One too many times.

I hear a lot of people dwelling on their lost childhood. I cannot relate to this, which is probably a good thing. I don't want to go back to childhood which was as underwhelming as my adult life. All times I can think of were similar to this one. So at least I'm not tortured by memory.

There is something in a soul like mine. One should call me a strange mix of a young boy and an old man. I'm both characters in Hemingway's The Old Man and the Sea. Why is this book considered a classic? I read the whole thing. And when I say „the whole thing", I mean the booklet. I don't understand why it's considered a classic, as it seems pretty average. But maybe that's just me. I wonder if Hemingway is one of those writers who's considered a classic writer because no one has read him. Anyway, I am both the young boy and the old man. An intricate mix of the two. When I think of myself as old, I realize I feel pretty young. It's the other way around, when I consider myself young. My age evades me.

I always want to leave as soon as I arrive. I never feel like staying. Not that I can't find rest. I just get bored easily. It's my biggest social weakness. In a given social situation, there are three categories of people. One, the majority, which is succeeding at small talk. This I call the social bunch. Two, the minority, which is failing at small talk and always looks a bit helpless. This I call the awkward bunch. And then there's me, not making small talk and killing conversation with my indifference. There is something missing in me, a gene perhaps, or the social cells in my brain.

I am, for example, an expert on not registering somebody's name, when they introduce themselves. My head, in that moment, completely blanks out, so that, throughout the conversation, I'm always half-aware of the fact that I don't know their name. Which feels weird, when they tell me about their newborn, or their upbringing in rural God-knows-where. It feels like a strange mix of intimacy and anonymity. It's strange to know their child's name but not theirs. Even though I don't remember asking for their child's name. I feel like if I had asked this I would remember. Then again, I don't remember their name, so can I really trust my memory?

So the night progresses, and one is trapped in this endless loop of endlessly looping conversations, that are only interrupted by the occasional change of faces. One has the same conversation many times, and this is simply torture. None of this is newsworthy. Words can be said, but they can also be not said. I prefer the words not said. One should cultivate a culture of not speaking, for when one finally speaks up, it will carry more meaning. Both in terms of message, for the threshold of speech is higher, but also in terms of impact, for those who speak less are listened to better. This is an observational fact, or actually theory, because I don't know if it's true. Whenever I find myself playing the conversation game, which they all love so dearly, and I hate so dearly, I find myself in disbelief over the people who fail at it. I don't mean to offend anyone, but I genuinely wonder how you can be bad at small talk. It's so easy, just ask them anything, so they can pour out their nonsense. The hard part is not to start small talk but to end it. That takes a master indeed. Or a mistress. This was something I learned the other day: a mistress is a female master. I felt pretty bad, because in my head the word ‚mistress' had a different connotation. I then learned what a female dog was called, and I couldn't believe it either. I had used this word incorrectly all my life. When referring to dogs that is, not to women. There I used it correctly. That was a joke, I want to emphasize that. Back to my ramblings. I don't understand how you can fail at small talk. Just ask them what they do for a living, that will buy you at least five minutes. Ask them where they come from, another five minutes. I reckon I could teach people how to succeed at small talk. Perhaps this is a career path. I would have a lot to say on the matter, for I'm emotionally uninvested and this allows me to be objective. I think the most important thing is to not care. Those who care are vulnerable, so caring should be avoided. Generally in life, but particularly in conversation. One should be indifferent. Let's see, what else? One should ask open-ended questions that allow for conversation to flourish. For example: how do you feel about Mao's long march? This is, in my experience, a great conversation starter, because either they know about Mao and it becomes an interesting discussion, or they don't know about him and you can make up a ludicrous story. So win-win. One should ask questions that seem personal, yet they're generic. When they over-share details from their life, e.g. about their newborn child, one should aim to make the conversation more awkward to pay them back. One should ask strangely specific questions, like what was the birth like, or what was the birth weight of the baby. One should ask multiple questions about the decision process on the baby's name. Ask for alternative names they considered, and arguments that led in favor of one or the other. This is all valuable, for it teaches them a lesson: not to share stuff like this, for this is not a conversation topic. Not here, not now, not ever. You need to turn the situation upside down, yet with skill and patience. You need to finely balance the line between the appropriate and the inappropriate. Let's take another example, for in my lectures one gets fed a lot of examples. When someone tells you about their job, you ask them for the amount of toilets they have in their office building. You need to do this with a straight face signaling genuine interest. They will not realize that you're not serious, for they will find it unlikely that you're so openly antisocial. When they tell you about what their job includes, you must ask very specific follow up question regarding those daily tasks. For example when someone says they're operating a machine, ask them if they do it with the left hand or right hand. If they tell you their job includes paperwork ask them about their favorite paper format.

The rules of small talk dictate that one keeps it shallow and general. Therefore, naturally, one has to do the opposite. One should be very specific about a minor detail and ask repeated questions until the conversation partner gets as annoyed as you have been from the start of this conversation. It's called entanglement, and it's beautiful, for it brings the two of you closer together. Since all conversation is imposition, one plays the game best by taking it to its extremes. When someone tells you their life story, one needs to push this further, and ask for even more specific details, to a point where it becomes uncomfortable for the conversation partner. This is called: giving someone a taste of their own medicine. Next time, they will be wiser and not share these details. You're doing a service to mankind. It's ridiculous to show anyone pictures of your newborn. Newborns are objectively ugly, they're only pretty to your delusional eyes. Don't make us fake a reaction to this goblin baby of yours. And again, this has to be emphasized, no one made them share this. In fact one would have been more than pleased not to hear any of it. Once they talk about themselves, one needs to drill down into details, one step at a time. When someone talks about their vacation, it's an immediate „fire at will" moment, because nobody wants to know about other people's vacation. You should first ask about the destination. They will tell you. Then you ask about the amenities in the hotel. They will tell you. Then you ask about the hotel personnel. They will tell you this, too, while starting to get a little confused. Then you ask them if more men or women were working in the hotel. They will tell you, while wondering where this conversation is headed. Then you ask what the average height of the employees was and whether they believe it was representative of the country's average height. This is stupid, but clever, too, because you've lured them in. You are slowly becoming more absurd, not suddenly. If it was sudden, they would know that you're not serious. Their brains would pick up on that. It's the abrupt change from serious to unserious that creates the funny sentiment in the brain. If it's gradual, the average brain doesn't register it. Now they are trapped in the most awkward conversation, that they have unknowingly been in from the start. It's a behavioristic way of holding up a mirror to someone. It's the only way they will learn. They will now tell you if they think the hotel staff's average height represents the population's average height. Now here we come to a crossroads. There are multiple paths that can be taken, depending on your preference. You could now make up a story, why you asked this, and lecture about absolute nonsense, yet with a straight face. They will suffer, yet they cannot leave, so they join the hell which they themselves have brought upon the two of you. Such a story could be, that you recently saw a documentary about the correlation between population height and service staff height, the latter being lower indicating that they're smaller, shorter, connected to a sociological theory, originally based on darwinistic ideas, introduced and well explained by Mr Hammersen, a famous sociologist from 20th century Britain, that essentially service staff, due to being recruited from lower social classes have a lower average height, and therefore the discrepancy and deviation of service staff average height in comparison to population height indicates the developed or underdeveloped status of what's called the Hammerton index, essentially — long story short, for we don't want to be here all night — stating that the lower the discrepancy, i.e. the closer the average height of service staff and population, the more developed a country is, i.e. the higher the social transparency, or permeability, to use „jargon“, whereas on the other hand, the higher the discrepancy the lower the permeability, the more distinction and accordingly vertical distance between the different classes, which of course is absolute nonsense, but that's not the point, the point is you want to look at their stupid face while you're saying all of this. So that's one option. The second option and third, depends on whether you consider this conversation a sprint or a marathon. If considered a sprint, you just take it further, and make it even more absurd. For example, you ask them if they believe the hotel staff has dental care as part of their benefits, or if they think that the taller someone is the faster they rise up the ranks. At this point you essentially kill the conversation. The absurdity is not resolved, and it's coming to its natural conclusion. They either laugh it off, or answer particularly short, indicating that they no longer wish to have this conversation. Which is what you wanted all along, so that's a win. The other scenario is if you consider the conversation a marathon. In that case, you should ask something harmless, that will get them right back on track of not recognizing that you're a lunatic. E.g. you could say something like this: „It seemed like a great place to visit". Now they will continue their story, and you can re-start the absurdity any time. What is the point of all of this? As in every good story there are multiple lessons. First of all, you teach them how bad it really feels to be on the other end of this conversation. If they have any decency and social aptitude in them, they will learn from this, and become less obnoxious next time they talk to a stranger. Secondly, and this is more important, you get to entertain yourself. You exchange their entertainment for yours. Finally, and here comes the real upside. There is a chance they're just trapped in a social situation. If they are, an actual conversation may result from this. Through loosening the bonds of convention and conversation, one tests the waters and by any luck finds a little gold. If not, on the other hand, if they really are as boring as they seem, which is more often the case, then it's no loss, neither for you, as they provided nothing of interest to you anyway, nor for them, for they will continue to bore people forevermore.

Any road I take leads back to myself. I find myself crossing a horizon which I long thought behind me. One runs in circles, yet in a straight line, and that's the curious part.

One resolves the conflict of dream and reality by no longer comparing one to the other. Most people abandon dream in favor of reality. But one could easily take it the other way around. This is my new goal, and mission. Yes, I call it a mission. To abandon reality in favor of dream.

To abandon reality in favor of dream requires the opposite steps. The reality people reject dream scenarios, but the dream people reject reality. Dream must be cultivated. Whatever fuels the dream, needs to be nourished and developed, everything else abandoned. Dream is like a beautiful behemoth, that you need to feed all the time.

The dream people choose dream over reality. Reality needs to affirm dream, or cease altogether. When reality collides with dream, reality, not dream, should buckle. Dream should never buckle, it should reign like a tyrant.

Anything that empowers dream is approved. Anything that impoverishes dream is rejected. Dream becomes the sole criterion. The dream people do not care for the reality people, for the reality people are poor in spirit and heart.

In reality, one becomes bland and generic, but never so in dream. One turns into a dreamer, and is there anything better? Once in dream, the world changes in front of your eyes. One never sees things less clearly than in dream. To see things clearly is to not perceive beauty. Beauty is in the seer, not in the seen. I wish I could claim credit for this observation, yet I believe it was Santayana who said it.

One should not see the world for what it is. In that case, there is no point in looking at it. One loses purpose if one rationalizes the world. One should irrationalize it instead.

One should never compare dream to reality. Instead one should focus on dream and remove reality from the equation. Reality has no place in dream, and if you take it there, you spoil them both. You spoil reality, by comparing it to dream, and dream, by comparing it to reality. There is only one way to resolve the conflict. You have to sacrifice one or the other. But which one to sacrifice, this is your choice.

Reality has no place in dream. If one tries to turn dream into reality, one will inevitably fail. Where there is dream, reality cannot be. When reality becomes a necessity, dream needs to be halted for the time being.

There is a reason why they're called the dream people, this term exists for a reason. The reason being, that all dream people, while separate and different, are alike.

It's nice to lose one's pretensions, it makes life easier. A dream. That bears no resemblance to real life. To dream is to seize. And to seize I want. Oh stupid ramblings. Relieve me from my voice, and let me dream again.

When in dream, I am in heaven. It's when I wake up that I despair. Consciousness is a burden. One should never grow conscious to begin with. Life is never lived more blissfully than in the unconscious state. When one exists without being aware of it. Dream is just another word for that state. When in dream, I'm no longer myself, or in dream I finally am. The only thing that makes the dream painful is its lack of reality. Only when you compare it to reality, will the dream turn sour. But the lesson here is not to stop dreaming, but to stop comparing dream to reality. One needs to find a way to live in both dream and reality without making them interfere. For they don't interfere, they only collide.

A dreamer feels all sorts of things, but never hollow. Hollowness is not a feeling, it's the absence of feeling. The hollow feel themselves no more. The cure for this is to re-engage in dream. One needs to bring back dream, and this is done by abandoning reason. Reason is perhaps the most overrated thing in the world. It takes away all the joy. In dream, one finds another world, the world of unreason. One feels as if controlled by a higher power. This is self-abandon, and self-denial, only here life becomes beautiful. This is the spiritual, the subjective component of religion. It's like gently falling down into a cloud, which carries you like the softest cushion. The rational people are often just unhappy people who rationalize their unhappiness.

To create beauty in the world. Only the most delicate souls achieve this. For they materialize something which in itself is not material. To materialize the sentiment into art, one needs to have a strong and immediate connection to dream. One needs to be able to dream intensively, as if on cue, meaning one has to have the capacity to bring oneself into dream.

Dream is considered the realm of the hopeless. Yet the truly hopeless are those who abandon dream. For they no longer have a home in themselves. They seek for dream, but all they find is thought corrupted by reality. Thoughts evolving around things. They are hopeless, not us.

When two people love each other, they make each other dream. Love is one dream in two. When it's a single dream, it's unhappy, but still better than no dream at all. One should always prefer unrequited love to no love. Love is a capacity, and if one has it once, one will have it again. It's a good thing to be unhappy in love, much better than not being in love.

Unrequited love is superior to a love well returned. The latter is good for the heart, but not for the art.

There are those who say you can be a great artist and a great lover, but this is a myth, and a lie, for one can only be one. A great artist can at best be a failed lover, and if he has it in himself, he never becomes a lover to begin with. Only then will he supply his art with maximum potency. A great lover, vice versa, cannot be a great artist, as he prioritizes his love over his art. Love and art are inconsolable. One can either be a lover or an artist, never both.

Now there are those who will disagree with this, and to those needs to be said, that they're just plain wrong, for this is a thing as sure as death in Texas. I believe that's the expression. One cannot be both a lover and an artist. This is why all artists are unhappy. Because they want to be lovers, but they know they can't be, for they would no longer be artists. And there is only one thing an artist wants more than his love, and that is his art. Or her art. If they're a true artist anyway. A true artist will never not choose their art.

One has to choose between art and love. Even if an artist becomes a lover, he'll never truly be a lover. He'll only play the lover while continuing to be an artist. Vice versa, someone who chooses love, is abandoning his art, for he truly has become a lover now. Love needs to be encouraged in an artist, but it needs to be single, not double. The worst thing that could happen is that his love is returned. If this happens, the artist needs to flee at once, and never return, for at this point his art is at risk.

Picture this, your love is returned. She, or he, but I will say she, since I'm a he, she returns your love, picture this, you say, ‚I love you', she says ‚I love you also', you correct her, you say ‚I love you, too', and she looks at you funny for correcting her, see, now everything is ruined, both the love and the art, and that's why love should never be returned.

A true artist can only love one. The girl or the art. But the artist will always choose the art. In fact, if he chooses the girl, he's not an artist. Not anymore, and probably he never was, for his art was only the placeholder for the girl. Hence, and this is a logical conclusion: any artist with a lover is not an artist. This goes for man as well as woman, there's no distinction. It's my conviction, that the artist shall never have a lover, otherwise he or she's not really an artist.

Love, when realized, kills the dream. The only way to protect the dream is to not realize love. One needs to make sure that love stays unrealized. For the feeling that results, one of unhappy love, keeps the love vivid. One must never realize love, one must keep it unrealized. It's the difference between looking at a beautiful orange tree and picking the oranges and squeezing the juice out of them. The juice will be gone, the tree will be bare, and the impression will be lost. One needs to look at the orange tree, lovingly, longingly, yet never touchingly, and instead one needs to capture the impression. This alone is art. And it distinguishes the artist from the lover. A lover touches to feel alive. An artist touches *not* to feel alive. To restrain oneself, to keep the sentiment for oneself, to use it to create, this alone makes the artist.

An artist doesn't engage. For to not engage is to capture the dream, and to remodel reality, to make it more beautiful, and to create within reality a second, more beautiful reality, for others to admire. This and this alone is art.

True art doesn't capture reality, quite the opposite, it refrains from it, and what it captures instead is dream. Art captures the dream which it then turns into a reality. What's the point of capturing the real world anyway? We all see it. We don't need to capture it. Just look out the window. In writing, realism is unreadable. Dickens, Zola, Mann, who wants to read that? Give us the dreamers instead.

I discussed this theory of mine with a man. He disagreed with me and an argument arose. He mentioned a number of great artists who were great lovers. I said this couldn't possibly be the case, for if they were true lovers they couldn't possibly be artists. He didn't follow my logic. I reiterated my point, to which he disagreed, stating that true art doesn't exclude love. This made my world shake a little, for I had strongly built on the hypothesis that true love simply wasn't possible for an artist like I. But I wasn't defeated yet. My argument went as follows. If true love is achieved, then love is the item selected, and art is therefore degraded.

I talked to a girl, who told me she was interested in the arts. I wanted to encourage her, so I decided not to share any of my views, which I know to be extreme and mostly incorrect.

I talked to a guy today, who claimed he ran a successful business. I was impressed with the statement alone, for I really have no business with business. When people talk about business, I don't even have a mental association. He claimed he ran a small financial enterprise, which made me respect him even more, for the word sounded quite fancy. I always respect business people, because in my view it's important to respect them. One should always respect people that use words one cannot make sense of. This is why I respect foreigners more than the people I understand. I always give them the benefit of the doubt. Perhaps, after all, they discuss business, or financial enterprises. In any case, the financial business man told me about his enterprise.

The business people give me a good vibe, and most of all the financial industry. They have this beautiful combination of confidence and authority, and at the same time, they have science and numbers, so I know I can trust them.

I always trust business people. I am a good people reader, and I can tell they're confident, so I know I can trust them.

They wouldn't speak like this if they were not so confident. They would speak differently, and I would pick up on that.

One should always trust business people who have numbers to back up their claims. Otherwise they could make up anything, and they might lie to you. So I feel re-assured when numbers and data are introduced, because then I know I'm on the safe side.

I read about the financial crisis the other day. If I remember correctly, it all started with people losing their faith in the financial industry. I don't understand how this could have happened, for I always trust the financial industry and so should they. It must be a society phenomenon. The term ‚financial crisis' is a bit misleading because it implies that there was something wrong with the financial system itself. It should be coined the „people's crisis in regard to the financial system". This is a better term, albeit a bit long, because it captures the fact, that the crisis was with the people, not the financial markets. It's important to make that distinction in order not to confuse cause and effect. The cause was the people's confusion. The effect was the shaken financial markets. One needs to make sure to prevent a similar crisis in the future. In my view, the financial markets should not be dependent on the people's moods and swings. They should be independent, and the same goes for the financial business people. Back to the topic, or I should say back to history, for this is something I only learned about recently, and I'm excited to write about it. Back then, the people, for some reason, which is not entirely clear, lost their faith in the financial industry. I'm theorizing a connection to the dawn of social media, since this falls into the same period. It must be connected to the internet. During that time, people lost their faith in the institutions, which had a devastating effect on the economy, and namely on the financial system. It was labelled the financial crisis, but again, this is not a good term, for this was, in its root, a society crisis, which only spilled over into the financial markets. There it grew bigger and bigger, but the root of the problem was in society. One bank after another got seriously damaged, some even collapsed, and this shows you what happens, when the crowds are at the helm. They really tear down even the most established financial institutions, which is a pity. The financial markets collapsed, and it had terrible consequences for all of society. We need to trust in the financial industry, and this was a clear example of what happens if you don't. If you stop trusting the institutions, you reap pandemonium. It annoys me that there are so many people in society who think they know better than the institutions. You saw where it led you. I cannot feel pity for these crying citizens losing their houses, for they started the whole thing. When they lost their faith and brought down century-old institutions, they brought it upon themselves. Maybe this is reaching too far, but this has an old testament vibe to it, doesn't it? When the sheep leaves the flock, it shall be punished. Next time, they will know better, by not turning their back on the good old institutions. They will think twice before they revolt, for they saw where it led them, into losing their houses, mortgages, their possessions, and their money. He that will not hear must feel. What are the lessons of the „people's crisis in regard to the financial markets". Firstly and most importantly, we need to protect the financial industry from society. I cannot overstate how important it is, that the people do not have influence over what's going on in the financial markets. The financial market must be independent and autonomous. It's important that society's behavior cannot shake, let alone bring down the financial markets, and that the financial markets should be understood as fully independent of the society's moods and swings. The oscillations of the financial markets are clearly an effect of the oscillations of society, and therefore, logically, one must remove society from the picture, in order to stabilize and protect the financial industry. Secondly, one should do away with the old myth that society knows better, because it doesn't. The financial markets know better, they are full of smart people, who have studied long and hard to get where they are. They know what they're doing. Let them cook. Society needs to back off and let the financial markets take care of themselves. They always do. There is no need for us, as a society, to impose. Society, and that's the link with social media, has developed a tendency to want to control everything, and this has produced negative effects on the whole economy. The financial industry needs to be protected from society, and also from any political influence, since politics are just the extension of society into government. Both politics and society need to stay well away from the financial markets. In my view, the financial system needs to control itself, and all external links need to be severed, and this is for a simple reason. The financial system has in its own interest its growth and money generation, and therefore the more we leave it alone, the more it can grow. Which we all benefit from, because the growth in money, through taxes, and dividends (if this is too technical, I apologize), the growing system will pour out money for all of us. But this only happens if and when we let the financial industry cook. After all they are great cooks. And we are, to employ this picture, the hungry guests, who will greatly benefit from the cooking of the financial industry. Long story short: the financial markets need to be deregulated completely and removed from any political influence, so they can be independent of the moods and swings of society, and instead need to be largely, if not fully isolated. The freedom of the people working in the financial markets needs to be ensured, in fact, it should be limitless, for limitless markets equal limitless growth, and money for all. I don't understand why, as a society, we haven't come to this simple realization, that whenever society interferes in the financial markets, the markets suffer from it and we all do, whereas when society leaves them alone, they flourish, and who knows what happens when we regulate the financial system further, it may in the end be completely regulated by politics and society, and then we might as well just get rid of it.

One never hears one's thoughts while talking. Talk and thought are enemies. Those who think need to make sure to not talk a lot. But the world talks, hence it doesn't think.

Talk and thought should never coalesce. What one says, should not reflect what one thinks. Instead it should reflect nothing. Thought is not to be shared in talk, it needs to remain thought. Thought may become art, and express itself in the written form. The fact that books today reflect talk not thought is the reason why they're unreadable. There is no thought in books anymore. All other art forms are talking, too. One never finds thought in art anymore. Only idle chatter. Thought has all but vanished from art. The world belongs to the talkers now, and unfortunately so does art.

Talk should not express thought, it should only express talk and nothing more. He who says what he thinks is a fool. Only those who say what they don't think have understood the game. What one thinks needs to remain in thought. Silently, and delicately, it should pour itself out. Into deliberate action, and the way of life. Into art and theory. Never into words. Talk is for the mob. Thought is for the mobsters. Whenever you meet someone who says their thoughts, you need to take to your heels. For people who speak their minds, empty it in the process. A mind is not made to be emptied. It's made to be filled and to never say a word.

I believe it was Pessoa who wrote that he always gets mistaken at his workplace and that he takes pride in being understood as a good workman. This is music to my ears. One should do everything in one's power to be seen as the person one is not, while your true self stays hidden in plain sight. This is the way to go, for this ensures that thought and art stay well beneath the surface of idle chatter.

Talk and thought have no business with each other. When talk enters the room, it's each for himself. Talk is like your shoes, while thought is your clean and cozy home. Just like you take off your shoes before entering the house, you take off your talk before entering your thought.

Talk needs to remain outside of thought. And thought outside of talk. The world calls those who talk their thoughts wise. This is a great misconception, for they are not wise, but stupid. One needs to talk the talk, not the thought. The goal is to say one thing and to think another. We should say what we don't think, for this ensures the purity of our thought. Those who talk should never be trusted, bottom line.

Those who say what they don't think, prove their worth, through their capacity to split thought and talk. This is a skill not easily learned, and not accessible to all minds. Most minds simply don't have the capacity to think something different from what they say. Most minds don't have the capacity to think, period. To think one thing while saying another, is a sign of intelligence. For it requires a duplicity of mind which most people struggle with as they barely have one mind, let alone two. A person who has two minds is intelligent, and if history has told us anything, it's that you can't go wrong trusting the intelligent people.

I mean this quite seriously. Whatever you think, you should not say that, and instead say something else. This is a way of controlling both your talk and your thought. There is intellectual beauty in this dichotomy. As well as a level of control over yourself and the others. No one should of course control the others, but if one wanted to, this would be a good way. It is also quite entertaining, for one is so detached from one's own speech, that one can take it to any extreme. It turns the world into a playground, and reality into a simulation of sorts. The situation becomes increasingly absurd, and the whole event is something to witness.

Talk has no place in thought, and thought no place in talk. Those who think the words they speak, are fools, and beyond help. One should never think what one says, for what do you have to fall back on. If your thought turns out to be incorrect, would you want to know? It's better to stay cozy in thought, while the talk can be anything. This allows for maximum flexibility in conversation. One says whatever one has to say in a given situation. Thoughts and morals stand in the way, and the more they can be skipped the better. Picture a world where you can say anything depending on the situation. You could rise up the ranks and slide down the hills, for there is nothing holding you back. At the same time, your values stay intact, for you don't include them in your speech. Morals and convictions have no place in our talk anyway.

The lesson to be learned is to achieve a maximum flexibility and leniency in regard to one's words. Talk should be largely, if not fully devoid of thought. He or she who brings thought into talk, truly brings a gun to a knife fight.

I will give an example, which will illustrate what I mean. The other day there was a guy who told me about a movie. He tried to convince me to give it a watch, when I dead-stopped him mid-sentence. I said: ‚Let me stop you right there, I'm not watching a movie with Meryl Streep, that's where I draw the line'. He was baffled. He couldn't understand why I would think that way. Little did he know that I was barely listening. I had been thinking about something I had read in a Paul Valéry book. I couldn't come up with the exact words and that kept me well occupied. However, this would have been a rather awkward thing to mention at this point of the conversation, since it wasn't at all connected to what he was saying. So I decided to say something else. If I had spoken my thought, I would have ended up talking about Paul Valéry which would have made the situation awkward. So my ability to detach my speech from my thought pre-saved me from this predicament, which would have presumably arisen, had I spoken my thought instead of my talk.

Talk and thought do not mix. This is the piece of wisdom that I want to get across. Those who mix talk and thought, set themselves up for failure. Either their thought becomes corrupted and diluted by talk. Or their talk will express their actual thought, which gives the talk a seriousness that the situation neither deserves nor necessitates. To talk serious is foolish, for talk is in its very nature unserious. The serious needs to remain in thought, while only the unserious should transition into speech. Those who talk seriously, have not understand the concept of talk even remotely. One speaks unseriously and thinks seriously, that's how it works.

One should neither talk the thought nor think the talk. One should talk the talk and think the think. Not think the talk and talk the think. People who speak their thoughts are foolish. They think that anybody cares. It's good to learn this early. Nobody cares what you say, they only care what they say. You should say exactly what they want to hear and think something else in the meantime. This keeps your thought pure and your talk flexible. Thought is a burden when it comes to talk. When thought sneaks into thought, it needs to be told off, like when the dog sneaks into the kitchen.

Talk without thought is the most powerful thing, and it makes you limitless. For example, Albert Camus won a Nobel Prize for mastering this technique. Once you are a master of saying anything in the most beautiful words, it doesn't really matter if it contains any thought. This is the lesson here. Sound as if you think, but never actually think. Those are the real winners, they go places. For in the world it all comes down to not being smart and thoughtful, but to appearing that way. I'm not being a cynic here, I'm quite serious. True thought and wits only hinder you when it comes to dealing with people. You need to appear a thinker, without being one. The real thinkers are fools, for they haven't grasped the simple truth, that not the real thinkers go places, but the apparent thinkers. One needs to appear cultivated, instead of being cultivated. Why be a composer, when you can be a conductor? Just put your face on the record, and nobody will notice the difference. It's easy actually. Life imitates art much more than art imitates life. This feels like an original statement, but I also feel like I've heard it before. Which proves my point. Nobody cares who originally said it. The glory goes to those who can recite it in front of an audience. The whole book market works like this. E.g. it's better to write a book about a writer than actually being one. Nobody needs originals, and for sure nobody needs an original thinker. We want the re-thinkers, and the re-re-thinkers. The world belongs to those who do the talking, not the thinking, and if you follow my advice you will go places.

The more you can avoid thinking, the better. Imagine, for example, you were Robinson Crusoe and you were thinking. You would have gone insane on that island within a month. Yet without thinking, you will survive much longer and settle into the situation. I believe that seals my case.

Don't be smart with me. When you hear this sentence, it's meant as a genuine piece of advice by an older person who advises you not to overthink something. I have heard this sentence many times, and I'm always grateful, for I know they have the best intentions for me. Another common advice is: think before you speak. This is, however, ill-advised, for you should never do that. Instead think about whatever, and say whatever else, as long as the two whatevers are not identical. I can't over-emphasize how important it is that you shall never speak your mind. Instead speak anything, pick random words, honestly, that's how I do it. It's never good to say what you're thinking, for the world hates the thinkers and it loves the speakers. Do you want to be loved? Then speak. Do you wanted to be hated? Then think.

The only thing that matters is that you sound good. If it sounds good, people will like you. If it doesn't, people won't. Appearance is everything, after all. Now I really do start to sound like Mr Wilde, but I can't help it, he was right about these things. Don't try to be thoughtful. The name of the game is appearing thoughtful. To actually be thoughtful is a drag. One must spend a lot of time in thought and that's just time we don't have. Every minute spent thinking is a minute spent not talking, and we cannot have this. This is important, and please underline this twice. Under no circumstances are you to stop talking. You need to accept the world for what it is. Just keep that one thing in mind, only idiots think, and true wisdom is to sacrifice thinking to speaking.

Speech containing meaning is heavy speech, and nobody wants heavy speech. We're all heavy enough. We need light-hearted speech, and more of it. In fact, if the world is in need of one thing, it's more idle speech. Meaningful speech only makes us depressed. All thinkers were depressed, this is a fact as universal as gravity. There are only few such facts in the world. Another one is that girls who like sunsets are boring. Girls who like cats and dogs are also not to be trusted. Girls who like crocodiles, those are the keepers. In any case, nonsense creates much better verse. This is why nobody reads philosophy anymore.

Honestly, who does. Who needs wisdom, when they can have conversation. Poetry should never carry meaning. Only when it expresses nothing beautifully, can it be called poetry. As soon as it carries meaning it becomes boring. I believe that all I'm sharing here, proves my point, for it's clearly a lot of nonsense, yet it sounds compelling. If I had to make sense, how unbearable a read would it be.

One must be unique. If not unique, man and woman become ugly beyond recognition. The imitators are the lowest class of humans. Only the originals live up to their names. One must develop healthy fission between being and appearing. What you are, the world has no control over. It only controls your appearance. Let the world have it! Protect what you are, shrug about your appearance. Au diable everything else, to the devil with it. Appearance is a throw-away thing. Let it play in the background like elevator music.

Am I dark, or am I dumb. I certainly don't feel dark. I think I'm a bright spirit. If only I wasn't trapped in this dark soul of mine. I might be dark then, but at least I'm concealing it.

And yet. I can't help to find some curious inspiration in it. My hopes were never hopes, they were failures in the making.

To set a goal that is completely unrealistic. To nevertheless try to reach it, and to die in the process. This a life well lived. Only the weak reach their goals. The strong fail them. If the world imagined can never be, the goal is proper. Proper to the man or woman aiming for it. It embellishes the soul to desire an unattainable ideal. It shows greatness, as well as a beautiful mind. „Only perfection is sufficient". Simone Weil wrote that. I agree with this statement. We cannot reach perfection. Only God can, or nature, or the universe. We can't in any case. And this is beautifully humbling. We look up to the perfection of the world, and we bow down to it. We cherish and admire, we give ourselves up to it. We become passive, beautifully passive. We forget about ourselves. There is so much beauty in the world. All of it can be appreciated, but only if it's acknowledged. To accept your imperfections is liberating. It's not about reaching perfection, it's about trying to and finding wonderful things on the way.

To feel sufficient makes you vulnerable. To whatever you consider sufficient. If that condition is no longer met, you feel insufficient. It's a way of becoming dependent on your own definitions. Therefore, it's better to feel insufficient. To accept that we are insufficient. This is beautiful. We accept our own insufficiency, and we start focussing on the world around us. As long as we try to be sufficient, we are focussed on ourselves. Once we accept our insufficiency, we can start paying attention to our surroundings. We see the beauty and the fragility of the world. We start noticing the insufficiency of man and woman. We become their friends, and we show them that there is nothing wrong with being insufficient. It's beautiful to offer friendship based on a shared insufficiency.

There is no such thing as human perfection. There is only superhuman perfection. The perfection of nature, God and the universe. But this perfection, we can never reach. Or even penetrate. We can only bow down to it. True perfection is never in us, it's well beyond. And this is a beautiful lesson to learn. You are not perfect nor will you ever be. You are perfectly imperfect. To reach for perfection will only lead to misery. We should be what we are. Imperfect admirers of the perfection that surrounds us.

It's beautiful to understand one's imperfections. It's one of the most liberating experiences everyone should go through. People who continue to believe in their own perfection are insufferable. They have not understood the slightest thing.

He's dark, he'll drag you down. They said that to her. I don't think that's fair, for when I met her, she was at her downest. If anything, I picked her up.

Yet. In a moment, just a glimpse into a stranger's soul, you find that there is something. Deeper. Truer. Prettier. You see it in them, and they return the vision. Or there is something which justifies it all. A short moment of relief. Dare I say. Redemption. A brief moment that fills you with the hope of a misery shared. Shared misery evaporates shared bliss. Its power is enormous, its appeal irresistible.

I would gladly live in an illusion. There is nothing better than a pretty idea that you believe in with all your heart. Life becomes dull once you stop dreaming. The goal is to never stop. To long for something which you cannot have.

Beauty is ephemeral. Beauty comes and beauty goes. But the admiration stays. You admire and you appreciate.

Beauty induces sadness, because we know it will cease. All the things that passed. In a way they never were. All lovers of all times, they loved each other much. And yet it is as though it never happened. Time is cruel. She's always moving on. People look out into space, and they get scared. But I am much more scared of time. It only affirms the present moment. We have minds, so we are aware of its passage. We see a past that no longer exists. The moment is gone. And so are the people. All the young children that saw the world for the first time. They grew up, and they grew down again. We know they existed, but there is no trace of them. They only exist in our memories now. But even that won't last forever. It's for a finite time, in the finite minds that remember them. And then it's back into nothingness. They emerged from it, they returned to it. Yet at the time, they were, like we are today. They saw the world and found it beautiful. But it made them sad too, for they realized that all things disappear.

We're just a fleeting moment. Made to decay. It's life, yes, but what about the ones who have passed? They were us, were they not? They felt the sun on their skin. They had thoughts and afflictions. They were in love, too. It was all very real to them. And now, it's the same world, but they're not in it anymore. Only our memories keep them alive. And just like that, we will be. Alive only in memory. No trace we'll leave behind. What I'm feeling now will be forgotten soon. Even by myself. I appear to myself like an alien memory. I wonder, is myself just a memory of another. Am I reminiscing about a person that no longer exists. I am confused by the distortions of time. Some moments seem so long ago, yet they're vivid to me. Other moments are recent, but they feel like memories of another lifetime. Time forgets immediately. It memorizes nothing. It changes, but not from one state to another. It simply changes. Change is time's permanence. We are born into time, and we are removed from it. One falls out of time, as though time was a surface. It's strange. Time has no memory. Why does she have no memory. Her memory is incorporated in the present. I wonder, hear me out. Is time

God? Should we write her with a capital T? Time is almighty, Time is invisible, Time is everywhere, Time is limitless. Time is not within the universe. The universe is within Time. We are born and we die in time. Time is the soil out of which we blossom. Time is the soil into which we decay. Man and woman create the child into Time. Time is the heaven we return to at last. But heaven is to Time what a haven is to the sea. The sea is still around, we're just not on it anymore. We have reached the haven of Time. What if Time is the message? What if space is but a messenger. What if the meaning of space is Time? To live for Time and Time alone. To dismiss everything else. We are, strictly speaking, a unit of Time. We live for God by using our Time.

The people of the past should not be forgotten. We must imagine them as though they were still around. For they were, and so in a way they still are. What we feel today, is what they felt at the time. It's not that life passes that worries me. It's that things simply disappear. It somehow makes it seem like they never were. This is why I believe in the arts, which at least touch on the eternal. They solidify that which cannot be solidified. Namely the human experience. I believe, unlike others in our day, that religion is important too, and perhaps even necessary. Religion, art, and I would add: thought. Thought is also a great way of being unburdened from the passage of time. Be that as it may, there is a vacuum in the modern soul. We have lost too much and we haven't replaced it with anything. There is a logical chain here, that I would explore further if I had the stamina. Since I don't, I will just briefly touch on it. Because I had this thought the other day: In the Catholic church, the Pope is considered God's deputy on Earth. This is a matter for theology, and my point is another. We used to believe in the soul. It wasn't just a word for us, like it is today. It used to be a real thing, as real as the body. We thought we had a soul in us. And the soul was our connection to God. Our parents gave us the body, but God gave us the soul. In other words, the soul was God's deputy in man. God created our souls, and our souls would return to God eventually. Now it doesn't take a genius to understand how traumatic the loss of God really is. For the loss of God is then equal to the loss of our souls. If God doesn't exist, our souls don't exist either. Meaning what we really lost is our souls. It's not that we physically lost something which we had before. It's that we lost our belief that it ever existed. Man comes to the realization that he has no soul. This is a traumatic moment. For we all feel that we do have a soul, even though we don't know what it is. For all the scientific wisdom around the body and brain, it doesn't reflect the human experience. We don't feel like organic machines. We feel like minds, not brains. The data doesn't match the experience. In any case, it's traumatic to realize that the soul may not exist. When God disappeared from our minds, our souls disappeared from our bodies. The soul is inseparably linked with God. It isn't really, actually, but it is in our Western conceptions. I believe this is why many feel drawn to the Eastern religions and philosophies where other solutions are offered. Including solutions which allow the soul to exist without God, or separately. But this is a religious matter, and science supports no such theory. We have replaced religion with science, and I'm tempted to say that this is a good development. We should not aim to go back to blindly believing in things. Science, once in the room, cannot be expelled from it. She's here to stay. In any case, this is what I thought about. We used to have a word for what we considered ourselves to be. This word was Soul. But when we lost God, we inferred that the soul cannot exist either. The soul is God's creation, it's the divine matter in us. If there is no divinity without, there is no divinity within. God was the center of our minds. Our souls were moving naturally in his environment. But then he disappeared and so did our souls. At once we were alone. This is the reality today. We have lost not a concept, or an idea. We have lost ourselves. Our souls don't exist. At least we judge like this. A part of me wants to dive into this topic and elaborate. Another part of me, and this is the more dominant part, is already getting bored with it. Which is why I'll drop this topic now.

I wonder sometimes. Was it my choices that led me here. Because there is this eery feeling, that I would have ended up here anyway. What felt like free will at the time, turned out to be rather determined from the start. Sometimes it feels like the destination is decided, and it's only our path that we have some control over. Well, I chose the adventurous path. But now I'm closing in on the finish line. I can see the tunnel at the end of the light. Oh if only I could travel to the end of the night. But I can't. Celine is right. All philosophy is self-deception. You only deceive yourself into thinking you're free. While walking the walk in your mind, your feet know the destination already, and they drag you there inevitably.

You should not be an adult as a child. If I had children, I would want them to be children, not adults. I would only talk silly language with them. To a point where they develop a speech disorder. Then I'd send them to a speech therapist. To whom I'd also speak in children's language just so he spares me the weekly updates. I would ask my children elaborate questions about their teddy bear. I would want them to have silly children's thoughts for as long as possible.

A child is so fragile, yet it's protected so little. The world determines the child's fate. And fate determines the child's world. Grown up in a broken world, the child develops with a broken soul. Everything's a little broken.

In order to become somebody in the world one has to be like the others. I cannot share the premise, so I won't share the privilege. That's a ‚fair enough'. I'm imagining the sad people, who are alone, the beautiful souls, who never share their innermost. It's for them that I write.

The world is a stage now. I don't want to be on that stage, and I don't want to play a role. I also don't want to watch the play. Everything about it bores me.

It's superficial to call the world superficial, but it's also true. Picture this, collective silence for a while, just the beautiful sounds of nature. Wouldn't it be incredible?

The world belongs to the loud people. This is why it's going under. I don't care for the loud people, and they don't care about me. To become somebody one needs to be loud. I don't accept the condition. No deal. I want to stay silent.

The loud have never produced a beautiful thought. Let me correct that. The loud have never produced a thought. They don't think. That's the whole problem. Noise drowns thought. One should never engage in conversation for this reason.

I like the silent people. If only all the silent people could be my friends. If they're sad, I want to console them. Not the loud people. They can go to the devil.

Here is a guy who talked to me about online dating. This was mind-blowing to me, so I need to share it. He said. In online dating everyone embellishes their own profile, so they look three levels better than in reality. But since everybody does it, it translates. Meaning, in my words, not his, that two beautiful people online share their ugliness in real life. It works well, because the two of you move down the ladder together. You can do the math, so to speak. When he finished speaking, I looked at him puzzled, because I couldn't quite believe what I was hearing. He said: don't pretend you're not doing it. So I said this in return: please, for the love of God, I never want to hear another thing about online dating in my life again, my brain cells just committed mass suicide in my head, my soul spun around itself tenfold, so now it looks like the headphones in my pocket, my blood cells developed OCD while listening to this, and I truly feel intellectually and psychologically violated by every single thing you just said. It goes without saying that I will never do online dating.

But seriously, how do you react, when you expect to meet mister or misses charming, and you end up meeting a beautiful monster. I shouldn't have used these words. Mister charming, I mean, because it reminds me of poor Sibyl. I always get so sad when I think of her. I'm talking of course about poor Sibyl Vane who falls victim to cruel Dorian Grey. Sibyl calls him her Prince Charming. She is very talented, and gifted indeed. Dorian sees her, and he falls in love. And so does she. She loves her Prince Charming very much. But as a result of this she no longer acts well. Her acting becomes generic, artificial, she doesn't put her heart into it anymore. This is what I was saying before. I may have seemed like I was joking, but I was serious. Love and art are mutually exclusive. Ultimately you have to choose one or the other. Because your heart can only go into either one. Your art or your love. And here it happened, that poor Sibyl no longer put her heart into her art, but her love. She was no longer any good at acting. In fact, she became quite awful at it. Dorian Grey saw this, and he lost interest. He said, you're no longer as beautiful as you were, I don't want you. Poor Sibyl was desperate. She was only 17, a child still, and in love. She said, don't, please, I will change for you. But Dorian Grey left, and poor Sibyl killed herself. My heart sinks for her. I can never think of her, it makes me very sad. By the way, and this might interrupt the sentimental mood a little bit, but Dorian Grey is clearly gay. There is nothing wrong with this, but that's not the point. The point is: Dorian Grey is not supposed to be gay in the story. He is supposed to be straight. And he clearly isn't. In fact, every single guy in this book is gay. Once again, nothing wrong with this. But they're all not supposed to be gay in the story. They're supposedly straight people. I believe the first words that Dorian Grey said about poor Sibyl, after he saw her, was that she has a beauty that „fills your eyes with tears". No guy would ever say this about a girl he likes. And particularly not a 20 year old guy, or however old he was. I actually looked up the verbatim now. Tell me it doesn't sound extremely gay: „She was the loveliest thing I had ever seen in my life. You said to me once that pathos left you unmoved, but that beauty, mere beauty, could fill your eyes with tears. I tell you, Harry, I could hardly see this girl for the mist of tears that came across me". I argue that in the history of men falling in love with women, this sentence has never been felt, thought or conceived. It's simply not what a guy thinks when falling in love with a girl. He doesn't think in those distinct terms. A writer does that, an artist and a gay person (that's a compliment). A straight guy thinks: she is beautiful, and if he becomes particularly infatuated, he may think something like: woooah, she is beauuuutiful. I.e. the amount of affection he feels is embedded in the amount of vowels he uses. Not in the amount of words, and certainly not in the amount of adjectives. But that's not the point. The point is multiple points. First of all, poor Sibyl makes me sad. Secondly, bloody Oscar Wilde, if you had sat down and wrote twenty novels, you would be on one level with Shakespeare.

You should have done less of that „nothing to declare but my genius“ and more of the actual writing. I can't believe he wrote Dorian Grey in six weeks. It's psychological, poetical, original, it has layers, levels, even philosophy, the prose and style are masterful, the dialogue is beautiful, the monologue is brilliant, it makes you feel, it makes you think, everything about it is special. He should have written 20 of those. Instead he only wrote the one novel. And all the plays. Plays are nothing but a writer's aberration. That's why Ibsen is never quoted these days. Even his essays are masterful. He's got the absurdity, the personality, and the style. I'm so sad for both them, Sibyl Vane and Oscar Wilde.

It's always lovely to read from one of those converts on social media: „I recently spent 72 hours without social media, and this is how it changed my life.“ 72 hours? That doesn't change anything. Especially if you return to the same habit afterwards. An alcoholic doesn't skip drinking for 72 hours and then buys a six-pack to celebrate the 72 hours. Well, quite a few do, but they're not supposed to.

As Tolstoy says about the families. Each being happy in a similar way, yet unhappy in their own. He could have left out the family part. He was talking about sadness. When we're happy we're all the same. When we're unhappy we're unique. Tolstoy as a thinker is negligible, but this was a good observation. The happy consume, the sad commiserate.

Reach for the unattainable. Miss it by a mile. Only if you set the goal unreasonably high, will you truly feel your forces.

Sometimes I endeavor, to go into the light. But the light is so bright. This is what bothers me about it. In darkness I prosper. Like a black flower that blossoms when the sun disappears. I flower ever so gently.

Wisdom. Truth. Who cares about these things? I should have never started living. If only I had been more afraid to live. My mind would still be innocent. Now I've seen things, and I've done things. It's my deeds, and my words. It's what I said, it's what I wanted. My desires have led me astray. I look up, and I see the beautiful night. I should've been more like this. Beautiful and silent. Beautifully silent. I should have refrained. Should have stepped back. Live life to its fullest, they said, oh I wish I hadn't. If only I could be afraid again. How I wish I could. Be afraid of the dark woods. But I walk in it without hesitation. If a bear attacked me, I would probably fight him ironically. Everything has become a joke.

I have seen the summer one too many times. The spring only entertains me for the shortest while. I have frozen up in the winter, too many times. And autumn. Actually, autumn gets better as the years pass. I have lost my susceptibility. My sensitivity. Or, I don't even regret. To regret one has to feel still. But I feel still. Still is my thought, still my heart. Everything is slowing down, toward the inevitable end.

My mind is lurking from behind the tree. Is he still there? Yes, the bloody fool is still there. Let's finish him off already. The mind is such a powerful thing. If only it wasn't tied to this useless body of mine. And what about the soul? I sure hope it's not immortal, that would be the worst.

You're a cynic, sir. Oh no, I'm not! I'm too indifferent to be a cynic. I'm a depressed stoic. Or I'm not depressed. I'm just a realist. And that's what a depressed person would say.

Oh how I wish I could've stayed an innocent fool. To live a fool, to die a fool. To be innocent. Forget the fool part, it's the innocence that I miss. I wish I could be innocent still.

When life gives you lemons, yeah yeah, bla bla, go to hell. I never wanted lemonade. I would've been miserable anyway.

I can't even regret. For regret requires a minimal amount of hope which I do not carry in me anymore. Regret is inverted hope. It looks backwards and hopes, yet what it hopes for can never come true, because everything has happened already.

I wish I could lay down with the cobble stones. Would they accept me as one of their own? They must. Or else I will take them. And throw them away. From their cobble stone friends.

I will make them like me. Or I will beg them. I'm sure they will find it in themselves that I can be liked by them.

At anxiety I departed, at agony I arrived. How about that! I went through the maze of my riddles, and when I exited, I had gone all vertigo. When your hand trembles and shakes, not even in fear. One dissolves slowly. To implode or to explode, and perhaps a bit of both.

She said, there's no hope for you. I hung my head in shame. Oh if only the stars were not these eyes looking down on me.

The key is not to fool yourself. Or the key is to fool yourself. It's one of these two. At least I was destined for misery. My mind is drifting, the past, so long behind me, yet so fresh. It's always memory that weighs you down.

I'm never afraid of killing a situation. This reminds me of the time, when an influencer girl showed us around her apartment. When she was finished I asked her: where are your books, with a straight face. That entertained me personally, but it also made the situation awkward.

To go a little further. I can't bring myself to do it. Not because I don't dare. But because I don't care. I've seen it.

There is beauty in misery, and no one convinces me otherwise. Misery gives me hope. Paradoxical, sure, but I can't stand the optimists. I wish they would shut up forever. I want to hear the miserable, les Miserables, but please, for the love of God, no singing. I want to hear them sob.

Misery is a fall that once commenced will never end. It's an eternal fall into the beauties of poverty. The soul wants to be poor. I have no intention of leaving this kingdom of mine.

I saw a boy. No twenty years of age. He was struck down by misery. I wanted to turn him into my brother. But I refrained. I would have a made a bad situation worse. I know that I'm cyanid to people like this. Only the damned hear my prayers.

Everything is a joke these days. But I'm not laughing. I'm still waiting for the punchline. This is life, isn't it. Waiting for the punchline, until you die. What's all the fuss about. One who lives a dying man, will die a living man. To live in vain, to die in pain, to hold your hand against the sun, so you're not blinded. There is something not right about me. I hold my head in shame over the person I've become. But once again, I see nothing but light interrupting my darkness.

There is something tragic, yet comedic, about a clueless person talking with confidence.

It's easy to be liked by a fool, you simply confirm their views, and that's about it.

I never thought about this, said I, having thought about this a hundred times.

Dark, they say. He's dark. Stay away from him. I replied that I was a bright spirit, and that I had simply fallen into a barrel of black. But I'm still bright. Bright and dark at the same time. In any case, people do me no justice by calling me dark. They should call me weird, or strange, or absurd. I take those, any minute any day. To be strange is a great thing.

I don't understand why people are afraid of snakes. You never see a snake. I'm much more afraid of deer. They are so stupid. I'm always afraid that a deer will run into me. They run away in a random direction, to which they are fully committed. If there is an obstacle in their path they run straight into it. I respect that commitment, but I also fear it. Because what if I am in their trajectory? I wonder how they choose the direction. They are like a spider, they always have 360 degrees available to them. But a spider changes direction. A deer never. Once committed, a dear never falters. A deer is brave and cowardly at the same time.

I talked to a Spaniard today. He had a lot to say, and with everything he said he delivered his explanations along with it. The only thing a Spaniard loves more than to share his opinions is to share his explanation for his opinions. I let him talk. He shared his philosophy. Yes, you heard right, his philosophy. It was a lot of nonsense. Spanish philosophy is an insult to any sound mind. To this day, whenever I can't fall asleep, I think back to reading Miguel de Unamuno's Tragic sense of life, and I fall asleep almost instantly. In any case, his philosophy was a lot of mumbo jumbo. It contained love and life, and nature, and the rising sun, and the setting sun. I'm always impressed by a Spaniard's ability to say nothing in beautiful words. I nodded. It's what I do to avoid talking. It's my trick. He liked my nodding, and he felt encouraged to now connect his philosophy to the greater scheme of things. He mentioned the „universe" and that's when he lost me for good. The rest was idle chatter. I only listened half-heartedly, while thinking about my dinner plans. I decided on salmon and beans, as this is seldom a bad choice.

I like to talk to people. But without being serious. It's the only social enjoyment I can feel. To pretend to be socializing instead of socializing. When they ask me a genuine question, I give them a genuine answer — in my disingenuous persona. To give a boring answer to a boring question, and watch both sides pretending it's interesting. One side willingly, the other nillingly, or let me put it this way. Ah, let me not.

To socialize ironically is the only way I socialize. It's their fault, they should've known better than to humanize me. But I love it. Not because of the power, but because of the absurdity. I like to turn a boring situation into a spectacle.

To be bad at living, is to gather knowledge which the smart people don't posses. You have to be stupid to become wise. Paradoxically. One doesn't get wise from being smart, but from being dumb. Nothing has taught me more than my many mishaps. I line them up like dominoes.

Those who were never dumb, seldom become wise. Wisdom seems to be a by-product of a lot of poor decisions. Why is that, I wonder. I guess it's because wisdom is understanding how seemingly smart things can turn out to be stupid. One realizes that the beliefs one held were rather delusions. To understand this is wise, but in order for it to become wisdom, one needs to have made the bad decision in the first place. The smart make good decisions, but wisdom evades them. Wisdom requires stupidity, which is funny when you think about it. The formerly stupid are the latterly wise.

Wisdom is a strange feat. It's like a by-product of a life well lived. Or poorly lived. That's the paradoxical part. That one can become wise by being stupid. Wisdom is perspective. What used to be clear at the time, in hindsight turns out to be far from it. It was a particular perspective one had at a particular time. At the time one was convinced that it was the only possible solution. Later on one realizes that it wasn't. One sees all the other options one had available, and all the things one didn't consider. This allows you to see the matter differently, and it makes you wise. When you talk to someone, you understand their perspective, however, you also consider all other perspectives. You share it with them, and that proves your wisdom. You are wise to consider all options, not just one. If you had never committed that mistake, you wouldn't have acquired that wisdom. You'd still think in terms of right and wrong. You wouldn't have found out that good may turn out to be bad, and vice versa. This is wisdom. To understand that the good may only seem good, while being bad. And the bad may end up being good.

A wise person is one who has gambled high, and in all likelihood lost. The wise understand that reason, too, has her flaws, and that she's far from perfect. One cannot know beforehand what the outcome will be. The outcome is not predetermined, you determine it along the way. Sometimes you reach your goal, just to find yourself more miserable than ever. Other times, you'll miss it by a mile, but you end up in a better place. You never know how you feel once you get there. You're thinking about it from today's perspective, with your present emotion. But once you get there, you will experience it with a future emotion. This second one cannot be predicted, and it mostly develops unpredictably. Life takes you on a different route. It's impossible to predict how you feel at the finish line. Bear that in mind if and when you despair over not being there yet.

When you're young, you put all your energy into your great scheme. You're thinking of yourself reaching the top, being full of energy. This is a good news, bad news situation. The good news is that it's absolutely possible for you to reach the top. The bad news is, it's pretty unlikely that you'll still be full of energy. More often than not, it takes more time and energy than you anticipate. The drive, and the ambition, is your fuel, it powers your journey. Once the journey is complete, those things are gone. That's why it's so important to just go for it. A road is something that needs to be travelled. Otherwise it's not a road, it's just a strip of land.

Wisdom is the product of repeated failure, and consistent stupidity. It seems paradoxical that one can become smart by being stupid, but wisdom is exactly that. The wise people are usually not successes. They are mostly failures. Yet of course, they couldn't be further away from that. The wise have come to realize that success is a fickle thing, which doesn't really relate to how we feel about it. Never forget that the world is full of successful people who feel miserable. Success doesn't make you happy, it only makes you successful. The wise know this. They fell from grace, right into wisdom.

Wisdom is the smartness of the stupid. We are stupid, but we are good at it, in fact, so good, that we have become masters in our own realm. Wisdom laughs in the face of success. For the true failure is obviously to associate success with things.

To become wise is a side effect. No one could aim to become wise. What road will you take to get there? To be wise, one needs to gain perspective. One understands that for every option out there, there are ten others. You reach wisdom by walking a number of paths, and probably by reaching many dead ends. No one wants to hear the tall of a self-made man or woman. Let's hear the tales of the self-destroyers.

To be wise one needs to have lived. To live, and to err, those are the silent creators of wisdom. Wisdom develops slowly, and usually, one didn't ask for it. One wanted success — and got failure and a little wisdom instead. Wisdom is precious. It comes from having perspective. What seemed to be clear-cut, in hindsight turns out to be far from it. This is the essence of wisdom. To understand that there are multiple views on a matter, not just one. When you're young you don't realize that. You see the world in one particular way, thinking it must be either right or wrong (probably right). Later on, you realize that things are seldom right or wrong. They are right under one perspective, wrong under another. It depends on how you look at them. Perspective is one of those precious goods that only life can bless you with. Most people remain stuck in their own, and the successful tend to be the worst victims of this phenomenon. Wisdom is a direct function of failure. This is why one should not turn one's back to failure. Failure must be appreciated, for it paves the way for future success. Many a success would have never been possible without early failure. Those who haven't experienced failure, won't be ready in times of success. For they don't really know how they got there. While the ones, who succeeded after experiencing failure, view the matter differently. They know that whatever happens to them, they'll be fine. Success is a fickle thing, and despite what you think today, you may not feel as a success when the time comes. The history is full of people who, at their greatest peak, felt miserable. The history is also full of people who at their lowest point developed superhuman strength to change the world. Only in failure will our true personality come out shining. One should aim for failure, just for the sake of finding out how it feels.

When you're young, you dread failure, and you dream about success. We all remember this, for we all were young. It's natural to think that way. But a couple of thing should be remarked. First of all, success doesn't mean that you feel successful. This is far from being obvious, so it needs to be emphasized. The fact and the sentiment of success are by no means the same thing. At most they correlate. You can be successful without feeling so, and you can feel successful without being so. Don't expect to obtain the feeling by becoming successful. If you're not feeling it right now, it's very likely that you won't feel it then. The capacity to feel good needs to be developed independently of success and failure. It may also be added that failure is essential for one's personal development. Failure makes you human, and that's good. It might not seem like a lot to you now, but wait until you experience an emotional crisis, and you talk to someone who understands you. You will then see how valuable it really is. Try to be the person you would want to have by your side in times of emotional turmoil.

One memory is bad enough, but I have so many of them. If only I could exchange my memories for smiles. To memorize is to mesmerize. Thyself in eternal shame. If only I could remember my innocence as well as my sins.

My vices fulfill me. They provide me with joys my virtues couldn't think of. It's pathetic to be good. I'd rather lose my ways again. There's nothing better than to be caught talking to yourself by a random passerby. It's so awkward that it becomes extremely funny, and then you laugh, and they laugh, and all you want to do is cry and fall down to their knees, and beg them to finish you like Brutus did Caesar.

If only I could go insane. Finally my relatives could point their finger at why they're ashamed of me. But I would be proud. I'd be a proud madman. I would happily discuss world politics with the man in the mirror. Oh how I would love to befriend the trees in the woods. I want to hug them, and tell them all of my sorrows. I sure think they would be good listeners. If I was a tree, I would hope for thunder. It's the excitement. Any lightning can be thy last.

I'm always interested in interacting with the world in unconventional ways. To take the train until the end of the line. Or to go into a movie that I don't care about. It's always as pointless as it seems. But to embrace the pointless nature of things, is a different kind of liberation. To be pointless is to acknowledge, what life really is — pointless. Imagine I'd be one of those guys talking seriously while nothing matters.

Who wants to befriend ants? They crawl and creep across the forest soil. Immortal, in eternal resemblance to each other. Are they millions or billions, they all do the same. Their eyes focused on the wood in front. Never have I seen an ant look up into the blue sky. Never have I seen it watch the trees above. So I sit here, and I observe them. Whether they know what it is, life and the world around? By all likelihood not. How blissful. One ant made its way onto my arm. Ants are like God. They move in mysterious ways. Once you're around them, they're everywhere. Interact with them you cannot. You're just another piece of wood for them. But this is how they are. Small and simple. They don't look up, and not even ahead. They don't know the sky above, nor the forest around. They simply are, until they are not. Indestructible in their own way. A unit of life, alive in the moment, never to be changed, beautifully stubborn. They know nothing about the greater scheme of things. Their forest is as infinite to them as the universe is to us. There is no purpose, no point to this existence. Life's purpose is life. We all know this, and yet we're not satisfied with this answer. The ants have a wisdom that exceeds ours. The wisdom of frugality. We are the heroes of this planet, but here, around my tree stump, I've entered their empire. They are millions or billions, and I am alone. So I sit here, and I observe them. How they crawl and creep across the forest soil. Who wants to befriend ants? I do.

The forest is beautiful. In my top three ranking of the forest, the mountains and the sea, the forest takes the first two positions, then nothing for a long time, and finally a shared third position for the mountains and the sea. Nothing beats a beautiful forest. The light from above. The beautiful green. The delicate combination of the brown leaves, as well as the trunks, and then the green, which is everywhere, and the pretty orange pouring in from above. It's incredible. Every hour of the day is beautiful, too. The morning, the noon, the afternoon, the evening, the night. The forest is majestic. It's by far the most beautiful thing nature has to offer. I want to go to New England, to these woods in Maine. America is unique when it comes to nature. Europe is a bad excuse in comparison. Once you've seen American nature, you can never go back. I love the forest, and I wish I could spend all my time there. It's the quiet combined with the soothing noises of nature. Birds which I have no idea what sort of birds they are. Everything is quieter, softer in the woods. The wind is gentle, not annoying, like in the lowlands. There it is intrusive, and cold. In the forest it's subtle, it only adds to the musical ensemble. The forest accepts you as you are. Then again there are bears, and this is why I don't go to the forest very often. Bears scare me. They are not supposed to be killers. They are way too cute for that. Not the black bears. They are weirdos. And also polar bears, because their heads are so little. But grizzly bears are cute, there is no denying it. If one attacked me, I would probably be more sad about the rejection than the attack. I wonder. Is it possible to hug a grizzly bear in a way that you don't fall off him. Hear me out. In the moment of the attack you jump him and hug him really hard, so that his movements equal yours. He couldn't attack you now since you would move along with him. As though you were a backpack he was wearing. A frontpack that is. It would be hard for him to attack you, for he cannot move his paw against you. Since you move with his paw. He would basically have to attack himself, in order to attack you, and I don't think a bear is intellectually capable of that. It must go against every animal instinct to attack oneself. It would simply leave him puzzled. He couldn't make sense of what's happening. And if I know anything about animals, it's at that point that an animal decides: abort mission. The animal escapes. As soon as that happens, I would simply drop from him. Once the animal flees, it continues fleeing, that's also classic animal behavior. It's called ‚fight or flight' after all, not ‚fight and flight', or ‚fight by flight', or ‚fight in flight', which is what the Americans do upon entering an airplane. Once the bear escapes, it will not return to attacking you. I'm pretty sure about that. Next time I'm attacked by a grizzly bear, I shall try this method. If you don't hear from me again, then it means that my method has worked and I simply omit it, for a gentleman never hugs and tells.

One day I shall be wise. Until then I shall be stupid. Of all the things I tried to be, this one came most natural to me.

Passivity is beautiful. It makes you receptive toward the world around you. Every impression, every color will be different. It's like inhaling the world. It's beautiful to not react to the world. For reacting includes the word acting, and when you act, you impose. Passivity means, you don't. A passive soul is one which receives everything while giving away nothing. To live like this among people is powerful. In everything that happens, there is an almost divine level of control. Since you don't apply yourself to the situation, you become invisible in plain sight. People, when looking at you, are seeing right through you. They don't see you at all.

The art of being passive includes never touching the world, only being touched by it. Every person becomes a whisperer to your ear. There is so much you can pick up on. You see a detail which no one else has spotted. How her ears move a little when she laughs, or how she lifts herself up, when she wants to say something. You see the beautiful grey in her bluish eyes, and you notice the soft speech defect that makes her extra likable. And if you look a little further, you can almost see her thoughts. It's possible, if you become passive. Passivity means receiving without imposing on the world. It's a beautiful craft that only few ever master.

I love passivity. It's taught me so much. To be still, and receptive. To not impose on the world. There is so much beauty in being receptive. In never actually engaging with the world. For engaging is aging, the word is included in there. To engage means to corrupt, one's innocence that is. It's beautiful to allow the world to act on you without reacting to it. The need to respond burdens the soul. The mind, on the other hand, becomes limitless, when it frees itself from the urge to respond. If the mind is only used for production, it becomes one-dimensional.

To be passive in the face of another is beautiful. One sees them for who they are. Since one does not impose on them, one has nothing to gain from them. This a rare thing, much rarer than is commonly assumed.

The more passive I become, the more beautiful I feel about the world around me. I have never loved it more dearly than in times of passivity. One should barely feel alive, this is the level of passivity that I aim for. No one can resist a passive soul. Those who have abandoned themselves, reach the higher planes. Or the lower. There is no difference here.

I want to remain what I am. Passive, and incapable. They call me strange, and they're right. I am strange. Passivity has become my poison and my medicine at that. ‚Our remedies often in ourselves do lie'. Shakespeare, I believe. It's true. Passivity is the way to go. Those who are passive, find they already have everything they need. You don't need to conquer the world outside, you need to conquer it within.

Acceptance is still a struggle of sorts. Passivity is beautiful indifference. One allows the world to act, one becomes passive in it. Like a pebble stone on the bottom of a lake, or a branchlet in a flowing river. A dreamer is of passive nature. The active people become something else, politicians or media people. We should not follow their example, there are enough loud people in the world. Passivity is the art of silence, and it's us, not them, who rule the world silently.

Passivity is a discipline that consists of being fully inactive, no matter what happens. One speaks, but never the truth. Not untruth either, one says random things. While one speaks, one listens. Thy own speech has to be detached from you. This is beautiful, because one overcomes the idle chatter of the world. One should never say smart things, otherwise one starts to mistake oneself with the person who is talking.

I love a passive soul. When I see one, I want to hear her talk. A passive soul has so much to give. Since she always withholds, you'll find the purest treasures in her.

Passivity is beautiful, it never degrades itself.

The passive are not noticed, and they don't want to be. This is proof of their beautiful character. The silent have a natural aptitude for passivity. This talent includes the ability to not act, when action is required. To not act is a virtue. The world is full of actors, we shall not become another one.

People are no longer capable of this. To wait and see. Reception is the number one duty of a beautiful soul.

He or she who receives without reacting is virtuous. It's beautiful to delay reaction, ideally forever. Those who never act, retain their class. Passivity describes the fluent state of reception, and reception is rare, in a world full of producers.

Dizzy. A little dizzy. Not enough to call it a dream, but enough to remember it. Never was I happier than in my dizzy days. The way I greeted people, clear signs of developing madness. But never did I get along better with people than during these days. If only I hadn't grown up. I hate this.

I love to see it in their eyes. When they don't know if I'm normal or not. I love the unresolved nature of it. There's something they see. They think it character. They don't know it madness. They might suspect it, though. I'd rather be a delusional fool, talking to the trees. Just saying that makes me happy. Perhaps it's true. One should never enter the competition. The one who wins the game is the one who doesn't play. I don't want to be good at anything. I want to be terrible at everything. I am so amused by my own inability.

I'd love to go to a good restaurant. On a Friday night. Where all the handsome people dine. Where everything is perfect. The lighting is perfect. The music is smooth. The women are breathtaking. And so are the men. There I want to go. Among these good people, I want to order the finest dishes. Give me the best of everything, waiter. Ma mom says, I'm her special boy. And special I am. Special interest, special ed. Give me your best steak, and your best knife, give me your finest wine, and spare no expense. Give me one of those towels, so I can dine in style. Give me some of that fine small talk of yours. Thus I dine, and I enjoy myself. A brief chat with my next door neighbors. He is as pretty as she is. They are perfect. Obviously they are. I love being part of this beautiful world. An integral part. I made it! I enjoy the night, until at last I order the bill. But when the waiter comes, I burst out crying. I say that indeed I don't have a single dime, and if only he could sympathize with a poor boy like I. Or was he never a poor boy like I. Oh yes, I would love that. I would ask my neighbors, if I can accompany them home. Weirded out by my question, they would refuse, and I would be sad. But only for a moment. Then I would ask the waiter for a drink on the house. After all, I did order the most expensive steak.

I like it when misery floods me. It's like a tsunami from within. One can drown in one's misery. But to drown is just to drink a lot. Technically, I'm not dying, I'm drinking — I'm just drinking way too much way too fast. A little misery is not bad. It's only that I have so much of it. Sometimes I see a beautiful girl, and when she looks at me, I just want to die.

Go on vacation, they said. Go see the world. I don't know about that.

I want to write a bible of nonsense. It will inspire generations to come. But it will inspire them to nonsense. That's my vision. An empire of inspired idiots, all looking up to me. Like the Jesus statue in Rio, this is how I see myself. In that empire of idiots, though.

Sometimes I think of her, and poetry ceases to be poetry. I'm only a sad boy. But then I laugh again. I point at the stars and laugh about everything. The darkness of the sky makes the lightness of my mind. Or to embrace poverty. To plunge into madness, like a walrus into the sea. To chase after a polar bear, to run away from a penguin, this is my sense of humor. They never meet, the penguins and the polar bears, do they? The penguins don't even know about the polar bears. There is a whole world of threat they don't know about. In the seal world this is referred to as penguin privilege. Imagine you're a north polar seal instead of a south polar seal. How unfortunate. Are there seals on both poles? I could find out, but I'd rather die in ignorance. In any case, the penguins don't need to be scared of the polar bears. Shouldn't they be called north polar bears? Because they're not south polar bears. If I was a country, I would claim Antarctica. With climate change, I'm sure it will be an incredible piece of land in no time. Or Greenland. I want to go to Greenland. And then I want to complain that I'm in Greenland. Or I want to live on the ice, and complain about the temperatures.

I want to be cold, but when I am, I want to be warm. Then I'm warm and I want to be cold again.

My soul has a color, and it changes all the time.

In a daze. Today I'm in a daze.

I wish a daze would be a state one could fall into. What would be the last thing you would think when falling into a daze? I think it would be ‚daze' and nothing more. These days I daze a lot. I daze for days in weaker weeks.

The daze comes as if I lowered my mind down into my soul. As though there was a leak in my consciousness and liquid is pouring in. I like it when I feel my thoughts drifting. Her picture always appears.

She sees in my eyes that I'm not in the world.

I never engage, let alone talk. But when I see — her glancing at me — then I cannot help. She is everything. And I am nothing. I can't resist her beautiful glance.

Yet I never engage, for dreamer I am, and she is not. She don't deserve a wicked mind like I.

When the snow falls, and the wind blows, when the skies are grey, and you dread going out. When thought is refuge, and the soul weeps softly. I find that the soul finds comfort in misery. It's good to accept the hopeless nature of things.

Hope is to dream of a better reality, and that's not the point. One doesn't dream to embellish reality, one dreams to abandon it. So I shall. Dream all the time.

I was walking down the road, when I saw a group of sparrows fighting for bread crumbs. One of them wasn't fighting. He was the biggest one, and that touched my heart. There is nothing cuter than a chubby sparrow. So lazy he was. He figured this fight is not worth fighting. Whereas the others went haywire, he went stoic. I'm sure he was thinking of the bread crumps anyway. One doesn't get chubby by skipping a lot of bread crumps. But he remained where he was, and I wanted to befriend him. Unfortunately, they were language barriers, and when I approached, he flew away.

I saw a place the other day that was selling Asian furniture. Apparently that's a thing. I mean it makes a lot of sense for furniture to exist in Asia as well. I had a look inside the window, and there were all sorts of items. For the life of me, I did not understand what functions they served and where they belonged in the house. The sizes were all odd. Too big to be decor, but certainly too little to be actual furniture.

Life is constant distraction, then five minutes of deep regret, then death.

I don't understand people. Or worse, I do. I just don't like them very much. I took the train the other day, and I was appalled. I was just sitting there, minding my own business. But I was quite exclusive with that. Everybody else had to busy themselves, with an urgency that bordered pathology. The train started rolling, and a bunch of them grabbed their food packages almost instantly. One of them ate a home-made lasagna from a plastic box. One has to be a particular kind of obnoxious to eat a lasagna in a packed train wagon. Others started to play games, even board games. I was amazed to see what people do to avoid inactivity for even a split second. One was on the phone, talking all important, and yes, of course, this was the perfect time to have a loud conversation about business related issues. I also loved the big woman who decided now is the right time to take off her shoes. In her logic it made perfect sense, after all she had finally arrived on the train and was settled. That's what I mean. I don't dislike people per se. I don't dislike people as a concept. I dislike what they choose to be. The way they are. Which led me to a bigger reflection. Because not all of them were like this. There was a couple with their newborn, and they just lovingly looked at their child. There is nothing, I mean it, nothing in the world more beautiful, than a woman and a man united in their newborn child. I saw a young girl, who was studying, and she was as unobtrusive as could be. A couple of men were traveling by themselves, one had his eyes closed and listened to music, another one was looking out the window, he was my favorite. These people exist, and not too few of them. So shouldn't these people be ruling the world? Obviously they don't bother. For who wants to deal with the shoeless woman and the lasagna people?

I was caught up in that dreaming state of mine. Where one doesn't think, but sort of floats. I love floating. It's the most inspired way of living. One should always live floatingly.

I once walked past a little restaurant. In it I saw the chef. He was sitting at a table by himself, looking at his phone. There were no guests in. It made me so sad. I wanted to go in and order the whole menu. I wanted to hug him and never let go. He didn't even look sad. He looked bored, more than anything. All he wanted to do is cook for people, but nobody wanted his cooking. I am so sad just writing this. But what can I do? It's silly to go in there and be so dramatic, when he is probably not. He bothers about paying the bills and his nagging wife. So why make it emotional, when it's not. But for me it is. I wish people wanted his cooking. I would give my life for that. To see people entering. A chef that can cook for people is always so happy, and there is something so sad about an empty restaurant. If only I could erase this memory from my memory. This is why I never look into shops anymore, for I'm always afraid to find them empty.

This reminds me of the time I went to southern France, and there was a store selling coffee accessories. This was cute, as this was the only shop that sold products of this kind. It was also, little surprisingly, the one shop that wasn't frequented by customers. I once made the mistake to look through the window. The worst I could have seen — I seen. The shopman stood at the counter, of that empty shop, and he met my eyes. I wanted to die. He looked so sad. There was no denying that it was absolutely pointless for him to stand there. No one was there. He just stood there, ready to assist the customers he didn't have. I felt shattered. And I really, for a whole minute or so, while walking on, tried to convince myself that this was the right time to buy a glaring red

French press, which I had seen in the window. I had almost convinced myself when I suddenly realized that I didn't actually need a blaring red French press. It wasn't so much the blaring red that I had no use of. It had more to do with the French press. On my way back I did what any sane person would do, I didn't look inside. However, I lost some of my sympathy when I found out about his opening hours. They were closed on two days of the week, and on the other days just opened for 5 or 6 hours. With a place like this I'd be open around the clock and still pray to Jesus every night.

Darkness. All encapsulating darkness. Among me. Along me. Above. And below. Darkness where I stand, darkness where I look. How is it living in darkness? It's dark. Above all.

To see. Like a painter to see. Which seems to me, beautiful.

The picture paints the painter.

My eyes see nothing but a past, long forgotten, long decayed. Once, I will return for once, to earn, to yearn, commiserate.

But all I see is misery, trapped within my memory.

A wordless word, is uttered still. My silent pictures never leave.

An image will forever last, if never you depart from it.

Silent night, my loyal friend, in thee I find my poetry, to be where others don't exist, in silency, in silency.

Silency, is silency, silence and integrity.

Pictures, that I loved so much, pictures, that were real to me, whence cometh thus my misery, from pictures, ah!, from pictures still. Pictures are my everything, everything that left me not, everything I owneth still, pictures, pictures, everywhere.

Every picture that I see, wears her fateful memory. I will believe, in agony, one finds a broken heart can heal. But what if I, and what if I — what if I don't want to heal.

Pictures, I will not depart. Pictures will remain with me. Never trust thy memory. Only trust in pictures still.

I wake to fateful memories, in dreams and silly industry.

I saw in her, a twinkle thing, it threw me back to her. And in my head, the pictures were, resuming, as if paused no more.

In broken moments of despair, in silent nights, on silent days, in silent daze, I find her still, inflicted minds see deeper things.

She saw me thus, I saw her not, she spoke to me, and favorably, I once again was someone else. Someone else entirely. I felt so sorry, yes I did. Why was I not a normal one. I could've been, I could have not. I am at last a silhouette.

Her piercing eye, her tender ways, her beauty and her innocence. Tempted, for a moment there, only for a moment there. Not by her, but by her sister, by the one I never leave. Pictures, pictures, never leave, pictures I am loyal to.

I loved her almost everything. Her pretty eye, she looked at me, without a hint of misery. A daring word, a hintful smile, a gesture in her loving eye. I found in her most everything, but never her, who had me left.

Her pretty hair, her pretty eye, her every word intelligent. She saw what truly I must be, convinced she saw it all. But never did, she never did. Reality just scares me so.

She spoke so true, she looked at me, she liked me, I could tell. I guess it helped her telling me, she said she liked me well. But I departed, sorrily, I couldn't tell her why, I never could've liked her back — I loved her almost everything.

The setting sun was violet, orange was the sky, the landscape was Arabian, almost desert-like. I saw out in the distance, the shadow of a man, 't was I, that I had spotted, myself in early night. And so I rode into the, distance that I saw, I watched the setting sun, dreamingly in awe. As I was riding still, the orange world around, 't was as if on Mars, my eyes were laying down. True it felt to me, this strangest state of I, until it dawned on me, this saddest state of I. The setting sun was orange, violett was the sky, the night came ever-lasting, for you and I alike.

Today, I went to the dentist. Not that I had to go, but I was in the mood for some socializing. Odd as it may seem, the dentist is a great place to socialize, and that's because you don't have to talk. After all, you can't. Whereas the dentist does a lot of socializing on you. I asked for a check up, knowing full well that the problem was less with my teeth, and more with my soul. But I figured, you have to start somewhere, and why not start with the teeth. I let him have a look, at these teeth of mine, and to my surprise, he found no surprises. He gave me tips on how to brush my teeth, and I felt the warmth of having made a new friend. I wondered if this was a good time to ask him if he wanted to hang out. But I thought it might be strange. After all, he was a dentist, and I don't think dentists hang out. I figure that a dentist only has dentist friends. And they meet at dentist places, where they engage in dentist activities. Maybe they look into each others' mouths. I reckon there is a whole world of tooth jokes that we don't know about. So I figured that the dentists are probably a closed circle. It's also that every dentist I've ever met was in a relationship with another dentist. I've never heard of a dentist in a dentist-no-dentist-relationship. Also, I am always skeptical with people that have too good teeth. I find that more often than not, they lack personality. That's why the French have such bad teeth. But above all, I figured that my dentist was somewhat off-putting. I found it odd how he treated our friendship like a professional relationship of sorts. I also didn't like that he spoke in puzzle language to his assistent. It was, I believe, some sort of morse code, as it included letters and numbers, but no words. It sounded like this: M9, A7, B7, B8. I tried to decipher it but I failed. It's possible that it had to do with my teeth, but it's also possible that he was making fun of me. In any case, his morse code did not impress me. The only morse language that impresses me comes from pilots. Charlie, Tango, Alpha, bravo, 35, 9er, ILS, lima, delta, 69, Propellor Airways 123. This impresses me. Whereas the dentist's language didn't impress me at all. Which is why I decided against hanging out. He seemed disappointed. I feel like he may have already considered where to go and what to discuss. I felt bad when I left. But leave I did anyway, fully convinced to not socialize with dentists ever again, as this guy had clearly wasted my time.

I got a letter today. It was, I believe, generic, as it didn't have my name on it. But I figured I wanted to read it as if it was intended for me specifically. It was advertisement. The letter invited me to play a game, that, in the best case scenario, would result in me winning a brand new house. I looked at the house, and I saw that it was a mansion of sorts. For me it was almost too luxurious. So I decided not to play this game, because I wasn't really interested in the price.

My dream is not connected to the real world, which makes it both tempting and dangerous. It's beautiful to forget about reality, especially if that reality is not very beautiful.

Dream doesn't give me clarity. Dream gives me confusion. It's pretty when the world slips through your hands. One finds comfort in one's delusions. People always to try to control their circumstances. But I like to lose that control, and see the world turning into something else.

To be elegant is to not interfere with oneself. This may sound strange, but it's exactly what it means. The soul moves naturally, and the mind can easily counteract. It becomes forceful, vulgar, when it does. The mind needs to minimize its output. Only then will the mind perceive the soul's natural motion. This is the essence of elegance. Elegant motion is natural motion, and when motion is forced, elegance is lost. The mind becomes elegant, not by action, but by inaction.

A mind that only produces is a poor mind. The great thinkers were above all great receivers. They received thoughts and sentiments. Long before they started producing them.

Dream is mocked, and the dreamer belittled. Yet the dreamer is in a state of almost perfect mental reception. It's a misconception that the mind dreams the pictures. The mind only sees the pictures that the soul dreams. That's why we dream so well at night. At night, our mental control is minimized, and our mental output non-existing. Dream is mental reception, and the more passive one becomes, the higher the receptivity. One receives beautiful things from within, if one manages to minimize mental production. This includes not making sense of your state, not trying to interpret it, or to explain it, let alone steer it, or influence it. To allow it to happen, to not interfere in any way. This is mental reception, and it describes the mind being no longer turned outwards, but inwards, toward the soul. The world needs to learn introspection again, it has lost this capacity.

When the soul dreams, the mind must be quiet and receptive. Any interference will disrupt her natural motion. The soul is moving by herself, she doesn't enjoy being moved by somebody else. The mind must not move the soul against her will. It's important that it allows her to move naturally.

A dreamer must be sheltered from the world. The mind will not withdraw, instead it will cultivate the picture. What the soul wants, she shall have. The mind becomes a servant, a disciple. The soul paints a picture, prettier and prettier. The soul dreams for a while, until she retracts. The mind wakes up from dream, and it will be inspired. Mental production is only of value when it's preceded by mental reception. In any other case, it's empty production, not worth receiving.

It's often said that one needs to follow the heart. I did, and it led me astray. Maybe I should have followed my head — but that guy was a goner from the start. I find myself reaching a point that I would have probably reached anyways. This consoles me. Even though, if I was destined to end up here, I should have had more fun on the way. Be that as it may, fun never brought me any fun, and I have found more pleasure in misery. Spiritual pleasure that is. There is a particular beauty in seeing your face in the bathroom mirror, when you feel like your sadness is the final tone of a melody, or you're reading the last page of a book. It's not wise to nap when you're depressed. This is my wisdom. I avoid sleeping now to avoid waking up. I believe I could turn this into therapy which would go like this. Stay awake until you die, so you never have to wake up again. But there is beauty in it. To walk like a shadow, stricken down by your grief.

Sadness is beautiful. Just listen to Chopin's Nocturnes when you're sad. There is nothing quite like it. In deep sadness, when your soul is broken, open all windows, in a cold winter night, turn off the lights, drift in and out of sleep. This is intensity, and it's the most precious thing in the world. If only psychologically, do the paradoxical, love thy depression, for it is yourself that you love in it. Depression cures. To commit to your misery, to not push it away, but to pull it toward you, to hug and caress it. To say: I love that you're here, because you are intensity. To delve in it, indulge in it, to love it, because to love is a capacity, and it doesn't matter what you love, as long as you do. If only psychologically, you should try it out, to love the feeling, to do the absurd. When depression attacks you, you say: ah here you are, my friend, I was waiting for you. Your depression will look at you funny. One should never be played by one's emotion. One should play with it instead, with a smile on one's face. Only those who are fearless in the eyes of their fear can surmount it.

Sadness is beautiful, for it has intensity. Only the faint and the feeble is awful. Sadness preserves, and that's a virtue.

To feel sad is better than feeling nothing. A sad soul has not died within. It has, in a way, died without. It lacks what it needs to be happy. But to lack is not a bad thing, not a bad thing at all. It becomes the driving force. A satisfied artist would be a terrible artist. Only those who long, will sing from the heart, and their voices will sound different.

Sad as you feel now, in hindsight one doesn't feel sad, but almost nostalgic, because one misses the intensity. How wise would we be, if we managed to remember that in times of sadness? If one, instead of fleeing it, greeted it: there you are, my old friend, I missed you. You would find that sadness, instead of torturing you, would welcome your company, and you could love it just as dearly as any other emotion. Sadness is you, 'tis you who is sad, not somebody else, and to love thy sadness is to love thyself. It's good to love thyself, somebody has to after all, and when you start laughing and being sad at the same time, you're on the path of becoming a philosopher.

Memory never fades, when sadness is involved. The saddest memories remain present, they do not disappear in the background like all other memories. One indulges in them, how one walked like a broken soul, and how sad the eye was, how weak the taste, and how limited the interest. But also, strangely personal. As if the world was soft, as if it was made from dough. Every impression is like a bomb thrown into your consciousness. One is engulfed in obliterating sadness. There, and there only, you find a piece of gold, within your frozen soul. But this piece is the stuff of dreams, it's the seed of all art, and it's that which turns man into a human.

Intensity is the most precious thing in the world. More precious than gold still, is precious intensity. To feel intensive is to feel alive, and to think intensively is to think, period. One who doesn't think intensively, doesn't think at all, he just repeats what others have thought before him. If there is no intensity, then life is just a word. Sadness is always true, and that's why it should be welcomed. True emotions are good emotions, whatever they may be. There is nothing better than to feel sad, for it reminds you that you're still alive. If you weren't, you wouldn't feel sad, so to feel sad is the goal of a lifeless experience. If one feels nothing, one's goal is not to feel happy but to feel sad. Sadness is the path, and sadness is the answer. To hide from sadness, is foolish. One cannot hide from it. Sadness is not like a burglar in your home, but rather like the air in your home. You cannot evade it.

Sadness, once identified, should be welcomed in the house. It should be appreciated, like an old friend returning. Sadness is pure, and whoever is sad, has potential to become human. As the world is trying its best to turn us into figures, sadness alone protects us from becoming caricatures.

He who doesn't live intensively, has failed to meet the most basic task, which is to feel alive. To be alive without feeling alive is a human tragedy. To go, not away from sadness, but toward it, is a virtue, and the seed of a future unforeseen.

One should commit to one's misery. Misery is a blessing, happiness a curse. Happiness lulls the soul, it makes the mind weak. One needs to dive head first into sadness. It's virtue to commit to one's misery. One should never reject oneself, let the world do it for you. One should not pretend to be strong, when one is weak. One should try to become even weaker. For in weakness one finds the most precious truths. And everything will gain in intensity.

When one is weak, and without hope, recovery begins. One experiences a beautiful moment and another one. This happens unexpectedly. It happens when you read a line, you pause, and you smile, why did you smile, but you did, didn't you?, and it was love that made you smile. You meet someone, they are kind, and so are you, and what a pretty moment it is. You see a young family, a mother, a father and their child. They are not three, they are one, and they are love. You look around, and you find that the world is quite beautiful now. You like the cold, because as much as it made you sad, it was honest to you. It never spoke a false word. You see the people, and the little things. You are better now, and it was your sadness, that made you that.

Every tear shed is a glorious victory. It's those who despair, that write the hymns of tomorrow. It's always the suffering soul that creates some humanity in the world. Happiness is a curse in disguise, seldom mentioned, but it is true. Happiness is bland. It turns you into a figure.

Sadness is the bud whose blossom is love. Love will arrive eventually. But one doesn't despair in the meantime, one has faith, and one loves the bud as much as the blossom.

Sadness is terrifying when you're in it — but it becomes beautiful later on. If you don't find it beautiful yet, then you haven't crossed it. But the way to cross it is not to flee it. You don't run away from your sadness, you run into it. The task is to find your sadness beautiful. It is hard, but it can be done. To find your sadness beautiful is the way to overcome it. One has to step into sadness as though into a dark forest, or as if one jumped into the deep blue sea. To dress yourself in sadness. To find some beauty in it. To discover a new thought. To pause and to appreciate. To pay attention. To understand the other because you understand yourself. To find truth, and beauty in sadness. To reverse the old pattern, to love it when it's there, to miss it when it's gone. To do the paradoxical and surrender to your sadness, instead of opposing it. To ask for it, when it's not there, to bring it back if needed. To find an active way of engaging your sadness. To find that there is so much to be found in a sadness so pure. To purify it. To isolate the feeling from thought. Or to look for sadness as if it was gold in your soul, the most seldom of substances, hidden beneath your thoughts. To see in others grief and misery, to commiserate. To look into their eye, to make them feel — not alone. To become a precious human.

A lovers' strange reunion, can never be explained.

She alone had shown to me, what years and years had not.

I dream in verses, I prosper in gloom.

Her glance remains my guide. If it's beautiful, I know she would approve. If it's sad, even better. If it's written with love, then I know I've done well. It's her eyes that assess my work, and I find bliss in this beautiful domination of mine.

Her glance, before my mental eye, never fades. It is as if God was a Goddess. When I think of her, I think beautiful.

She is the silent ruler in my kingdom of thought. A kingdom, 'tis not, it's a queendom. She alone rules in this empire of hers. I'm but a suitor in my own fantasy. She became the world to me, and I became a pawn.

Her eye is my silent ruler. Would she approve? If she would, we shall have it. If she wouldn't, discard it. She is my silent judge. I think, would it touch her, would she feel it within? If so, we shall have it. If not, throw it out. Her word, so innocent, so simple, yet so true as if she was truth herself. I think would my word resonate in her thought. If it would, we shall have it. If it wouldn't, leave it out.

She introduced me to concepts so foreign and strange. To love, not to think. To pause and refrain, not to play the silliest games. To not be liked by anyone, only by her. She taught me to see when I look, and to hear when I listen.

She looked at me, and I knew I would love her forever. I had never seen a soul so pure. I cannot describe her without falling in love again. She wasn't weak, her whole demeanor was, but she was above me, and beyond, or she was strong, so strong, that I collapsed under her sight.

I loved her all the way up. That is not healthy, they say, and they're right. It wasn't to last. It was only during her misery that I was enough for her. But her misery is forever within me, and mine, so I hope, within her.

Beauty, sadness and love are like a three-legged chair. Take away any one of them, and it all comes crashing down. Beauty and love without sadness, are melodramatic, they lack depth. Beauty and sadness without love are aesthetic, but they lack volume. Sadness and love have volume but they lack style. There is always something missing when only two of them are present.

She is the one I think of when I write. Would she like it? If so, we shall have it. If not, get rid of it.

I never knew what beauty was, before I saw her. But when I did, I knew right away. At that moment, I had read the whole book of beauty. What was once theoretical, became practical to me. Words that were empty, started to make a sound. Colors were colors no more, they were worlds and visions. My eye became as powerful as my mind. I was no longer in my own sight, I was removed from the picture. So much I enjoyed it, this feeling, of seeing both so subjectively and objectively, or to see into other worlds and souls. When somebody wept, I became their weeping soul, and I wept with them in harmony. It was as if her glance ignited my eye.

She taught me vision. Above all she taught me that. She taught me to see the world, not myself in relation to the world. She taught me to detach. From myself. And attach to other people, and their sentiment.

Before her I saw the world, but I couldn't love it. She taught me to love what I saw. Not to grasp it, but to let it be.

She humbled me, but she didn't humiliate me. She elevated me. She raised me to her heights and by that humbled me. I saw, for the first time, that I had depth, but not height. I had wits but no love. I had a mind, not a heart. In the prettiest way she defeated me, and it was everything.

Once defeated, I discovered a new world, one of silent beauty and eternal affection.

I thought I was grand. Grand I was not, in grand illusion perhaps. Her glance was enough, and my empire fell. My lies were revealed. When her tender word, defeated my pride.

From the highest height to the deepest depth. What height I considered was depth all along. When I fell down, I fell up to her soul. She brought me down, all the way up.

I had always considered truth a thing. How foolish of me. For truth is a feeling, it's to believe what you see. Truth is accordance, of I and I, for these two need fitting.

Her glance was everything, and I knew right away what I wanted to live for. To capture this feeling. There is nothing in the world like the glance of the woman you love. If you learn from her, you become everything. It's when you deny her, that you fall down into misery. To believe in her, is the path. To believe in her alone. One never rises higher.

She raised my mind. For the first time, I was not thinking actively. I was thinking reactively. Man is taught to impose. He ought to be taught to receive. I was thinking just for her. To this day I am. What she likes, I think that. What she imposes, I speak out. I think her thought, and her glance. Her sentiment, and her sadness, forever her sadness.

Her glance. The beginning of the story, and the end — and the whole course of it. Her glance is my word. Her thought my censoring. She taught me to win, is to lose one's obsessions. To lose one's pride is to win after all.

I went to the flea market the other day. I figured it would be interesting to pretend to be normal. Just so I don't forget about it when I should need to appear normal again. It's good to stay in practice, as nothing is easier than to unlearn how to behave around humans. I walked around and I found a great bunch of products. People are always happy when they bargain. It's an almost primitive joy they feel, when exchanging one good for another. I saw a couple of children running around, which made me happy, and a couple of adults, which made me sad. But I was at peace, and that was beautiful. The flea market is an interesting place, for one always discovers things that one didn't know one needed. One never comes home from the flea market with a purchase well anticipated. It's always something arbitrary. That's the beauty of it, but it also adds matter to your apartment, which makes it a more material place. One should aim to keep the place as immaterial as possible. The air-matter-ratio is very important at home. Air needs to be in abundance, matter needs to be reduced to a minimum. Is there anything better than these wide, empty Italian bathrooms, which stem back from ancient Rome. This is how it should be. No things should be in a bathroom. Only the essential. And a large mirror. Not because you need to look at yourself, but because it's aesthetically pleasing. A large mirror embellishes a widely spaced room. I guess I would make an alright interior designer. I would keep the whole apartment empty, put two chairs in it, a table, and that's it. And a dish washer of course. That would be my interior design. Obviously in order to design one needs space, and I don't have any space.

On a flea market one can make the most interesting purchases. For example, I did not expect to come home with a wine red doormat today. I didn't of course, but I didn't expect it either. I looked at it, though, because I was curious. I thought the color was beautiful. I have a thing for particular colors. For example, in America I saw these baby blue police cars. It was the most beautiful blue I've seen. Not too bright, not too dark. I still think of those cars, just because of the color. The wine red similarly did something to me. It was a beautiful color tone. I had to memorize it well, for colors are generally good at producing impression. I asked the man what he wanted for it, and he mentioned a horrendous price. I looked at him in disbelief. I disbelieved he was serious. Let me put it this way. It reached the three digits. He justified himself, explaining the material. Little did he know I only cared about the color. I generally care more about the color of a thing than for the thing itself. I have the same with impressions. One should always try to capture the color of a thing, rather than the thing. I did not care about the carpet rug. I wanted the wine red, and nothing else. As I had now come to the conclusion that I was not to purchase this item, I engaged in product talk, to look at it a little longer. I improvised some technical questions, and that proves my point. Entering the flea market, I had not pictured myself asking technical questions about a carpet rug. I asked how it responded to material, e.g. shoes, and I was quite infatuated with my own question. It seemed particularly clever, given the circumstances. I also chuckled a little bit, because I had actually said „e.g." and it made a ridiculous situation even more ridiculous. He responded, that indeed it reacted quite well to shoes, for the material of the fiber made it easy to clean. I nodded in agreement, indicating that I was satisfied with an answer I couldn't have cared less about. I asked the good man if he thought the mat could hold multiple shoes, and even a whole group of shoes, for I was considering to start a family in the near future. He said that indeed it had served his own family well for many years. When he said that, I suddenly felt bad. That last question had humanized the man for me, and now I felt like I was playing a false game with him. So I did what any sane person would have done, I asked another question to suppress the feeling. I asked him, how many years he believed this door mat would still have in it. He looked at me puzzled. And I rephrased. I said, did he believe that this could be the last door mat I ever bought, for I did not intend to buy another one in this lifetime. He chuckled and asked me how long I planned to live. It was strange hearing that question coming from somebody else. I wondered, I told him, whether the doormat really lived up to the price, for it seemed rather expensive. He said that doormats should not be underestimated, they are an unsung hero of a good household, and without it the house will look like a right mess. I agreed, yet I also thought that it's not implied that one doesn't take off one's shoes just because one doesn't have a doormat. I asked him how he settled the succession, and that clearly he must have a new doormat now. He said that he had installed a new one and that it also served his family well. I looked at him, skeptical, asking what made him decide against the current one if it was so reliable, and that surely there must be something wrong with it. He got all nervous and evasive, saying it was indeed just a change of scenery, and that every once in a while, a change should be welcomed. I said he should change the price of the doormat then. He chuckled. He asked what I could pay. Now I really felt bad, because I really had no intention of buying it. Who has a doormat, let alone buys one. Only crazy people have doormats. So I said that I wanted to think about it, as I believe this is the thing you say, when you decide against purchase. It's easier to say you will think about it and never return, for it's always heartbreaking to say No to somebody's face. One feels like one is letting them down personally, and I believe that's part of their strategy. Anyway, I said I will return, which of course I never did, and this is how the story ends.

There is something so precious about snow. It makes the world silent and soft. It's slippery, but slipping is just another way of walking. Less controlled, but control is overrated anyway. White is such a beautiful color. Yes, it's all colors, I know. But to me white is a color. White is everything. Black is nothing. I like these extremes. Snow shelters the mind. The world cannot interfere now, for it has to clear the snow first, and who ever does that. Snow frees the world from the idle people. Only the forgotten souls walk in the snow.

It's not about realizing the ideal. It's about admiring it and leaving it unrealized. The ideal does not desire to be. It desires to not be and be admired nonetheless.

The ideal doesn't exist, but that doesn't lead you to abandoning it. It's all about how you position yourself toward it. Only he or she who admires the ideal will be accepted by it. You reach the ideal by desiring it.

One should not realize the ideal. One should idealize the real instead.

The ideal can only be lost when it's found. To commit to it, is beauty. To find in oneself the beauty of not having.

To love in a girl not the real. To only admire the ideal in her. Therefore to never engage. To not question whether she is real, because you know that she's not.

To see the ideal, is seldom enough. To perceive it, even more seldom. To admire it, nothing compares.

The affection of a girl is only pretty when it's ideal. She has to love in you what you're not. Just like you love her. So the both of you, love an ideal, and not the real. But that is true love. To love what is not real, and put your heart into it.

The real corrupts. It takes away from the ideal. To love a girl, that doesn't exist, and to love her with all your heart.

It's beautiful to love the girl that doesn't exist. Yet she almost looks like she does.

The ideal is that which is never attained, yet always desired. A dreamer's calling is not to embrace the real, but to eject it.

To idealize the real, it's all about that. He who realizes the ideal, is a fool. The ideal stops being the ideal. It just becomes another real thing, and therefore uninteresting.

If she told you her name, she'd become more real to you, but less perfect. Information limits the ideal. One should therefore limit the amount of information.

It's not about realizing the ideal. It's about keeping it, where it is, without approaching it. And why is it desirable. Because it makes you desire. To desire is to feel alive. Not to refrain from desire, but to engage in it. To love desperately, without saying a word. Then, and only then.

To look at the real, without seeing it. To see the ideal instead. To see a world that doesn't exist. To idealize the real, instead of realizing the ideal. It is the virtue of a most delicate soul.

When the ideal appears in front of you. There is nothing quite like it. To long for the ideal, but not really. Or to want the girl with all your heart, yet if you could have her, you wouldn't want her. Because you want the ideal, not the real. But you cannot have the ideal. Because she doesn't exist.

The ideal is not real. That's why you love it. To become ideal is to leave in plain sight. It's beautiful to see yourself vanish.

To love her ideal as if it was real. To look at her, but only see the ideal. That's virtue. To see not what she is, but what she isn't, but to see it as if it was real. It's the view of an artist. To see the ideal in the real. To mistake them, yet knowingly. To despair over it, and to love the despair. To wish that if only, if only she was. Real. Yet knowing that if she was, you wouldn't admire her anymore. This is the spirit of idealizing.

The true test is, when the real enters the ring. Only the brave will refrain. The weak want to possess it. But they can't. They will be sad, and no longer beautiful. The beautiful is the ideal which one has betrayed in the process. When the real knocks on your door, you have to push it away.

True art can never be imitated. The ideal is the test. Choose it by not choosing the real. Only those who abandon the real have a chance of finding the ideal. But it's an ongoing test. If the girl becomes real, her ideal disappears. Now you're with her, fair enough, but with the real, not the ideal. The real is obviously different. And that's good, for she's not supposed to be your ideal. One should never mix the real with the ideal. Either one chooses the real and loses the ideal, or one chooses the ideal and loses the real. One cannot have both. But here is the catch. The world may tell you that you have to choose the real, but it is not so. You can choose freely.

Nothing is more beautiful than nature. In silence the world is close to perfection. There is something majestic about nature. Nature is not a thing, or even a place. Nature is a feeling. It's hard to grasp what it really is. He or she who describes nature from the outside, doesn't describe it very well.

The true beauty of nature lies in her silence. It's powerful, yet to speak it out is to destroy it. Every word on nature is an attack on her magnificent silence. In silence one is abandoned, or relieved. One no longer lingers in idle thought. Thought and silence, these are the states we should be in. Thought is for the mind, silence for the soul.

Therefore, I believe, I never warmed up to Thoreau. For he describes nature from the outside, yet nature is an inside. This is, to some extent, my reservation toward all American writing, which to me seems to grasp the outside much better than the inside. Nature is an inside, and to grasp it, is to internalize it. One misses the meaning of nature, when one speaks of it. One has to capture it effortlessly. This is a poet's talent, to capture the uncapturable, by letting it flow through your hands. Like stepping into a river, opening your palms, capturing the water, without capturing it.

To become one with nature. To fall head first into beautiful silence.

Describing nature destroys what it tries to create. Nature cannot be created, for nature is the creation. Nature will be beautiful only when one admires it, without describing it. The description of nature is not nature, it's nature lost.

Beauty is that which convinces without speaking.

Beautiful thought, is the privilege of the few. Few enough that think, fewer even who perceive beauty, and those who produce beautiful thought — they're but a handful. Beauty is silence of the soul, and thought is silence of the mind. Only when soul and mind are silent together, may beauty and thought coalesce. Beautiful thought belongs to the beautiful thinkers, and these are a chosen few. However, they choose themselves, and they do so by choosing silence.

I catch myself dreading the return of hope. For I started to like the ideal to which I have relocated in the meantime. Here in the ideal, options are limitless. Thought liberates, and when one feels imprisoned, it's because one has imprisoned one's thoughts. There is so much we could think, if we could un-think more effectively. The world becomes a softer thing, and the mind more capable. This is liberation, when the mind detaches from things, and it starts to revolve around itself. This is why I said one should idealize the real. It sounds scandalizing, but it's tantalizing, for the more one thinks, the more one wants to think. To make the mind detach from things is the first step to liberate thought. It's beautiful when the mind and the soul are two again. It is torture when they fuse in a way that the mind is imprisoned by the soul. The mind needs to rid itself of the world, for it's that which imprisons it and forces it into reaction.

One must detach from the particular thing, and attach to its idea instead. The girl you loved is no longer with you, yet you don't try to love another girl. Instead you detach from the particular girl, and instead attach to her idea. You drive yourself into utter dependence of this idea, yet not the girl.

The idea in you becomes perfection, and you love it dearly. Now it could be said that you are ruined for the real world, for no girl could possibly match this perfection that exists in your head, and this is of course absolutely true. It is a one-way street after all. It doesn't lead to another girl, but to the abandonment of girl altogether. You love not in the flesh, but only in the mind, yet there you love most dearly.

One should not attach to another girl, which is ridiculing the endeavor. It's about detaching from her, and committing to her idea. For the idea, if enriched by sentiment, can produce the most seldom piece of thought. Thought flourishes when love is added, and only then becomes unique.

To detach from things, to attach to the mind, that is the path to beautiful thought. Most people are weak in this regard, they are controlled by emotion. Yet the detached mind controls its emotion. Which doesn't mean that one doesn't feel. This is a misconception. For the detached mind can not just lower emotion, it can also raise it. Such mind can by pure thought fall desperately in love again. It's in that state that he lovingly creates. But this works only if he is in direct connection with the ideal. The weak get their emotion from things. The strong mind, by pure thought, evokes emotions that for others requires the presence of stimulus.

I encountered a similar thought in Kierkegaard. He says this: „What is homesickness? It is something remembered that is recollected. Homesickness is prompted simply by one's being absent. The art would be to be able to feel homesickness even though one is at home. This takes proficiency in illusion. To go on living in an illusion in which there is continual dawning, never daybreak, or to reflect oneself out of all illusion is not as difficult as to reflect oneself into an illusion, plus being able to let it work on oneself with the full force of illusion even though one is fully aware."

Only he who loves the idea of the girl more than the girl, can write love. He who loves the girl more than the idea, can only write love once, and namely in connection with the particular girl. But if the girl is taken out of the equation, if the sentiment is isolated, then he can write it a million times. For he has within what others have without. If he manages, then love is isolated from the beloved, and such a person is forever with love, yet never with lover. The flesh only limits, and particularly a lover does. Romance is for losers. The real winners are the dreamers. Who never realize their dreams. Who never even utter them. Actual love always disappoints. It never holds up to his promises. A happy marriage, lasting over decades — what a nightmare. It's nightmare material to realize the ideal. It's just nice to dream about it.

Love is beautiful, until the first word is spoken. Information takes away the charm of it. Her glance is a piece of beauty floating through the air. The soul needs to capture it, without saying a word. It's important to model yourself in beauty.

To fall in love with the glance of a woman is perfect. To tell her that you love her eyes is despicable. It completely misses the point. You're supposed to capture the impression, not the girl. The girl should never be entangled in this madness of yours. In a dreamer's world one has responsibility for others. One must never introduce another soul into one's ideation.

When she looks at you, with this look, that breaks you from within, like boiling water a thin glas, invading, penetrating, this look. When she looks at you like this, that's already the whole thing. You take that glance, and the impression it leaves on you, and all you do is capture that impression. One needs to indulge in the impression, or one needs to fall head over heels for it. She is the giver of impression, but she is not what you desire, for you desire the impression. You feel most grateful toward her, and you love her very much, yet you love her more for what she has presented you with.

You capture the moment by not ruining it. What you feel should not be verbalized. It's more beautiful to let it linger. Don't speak to her, instead think to her. There is something unresolved, which makes the situation beautiful. It is as if the space between you and her trembled. It's pretty to think to a girl, much prettier than talking to her. For the most beautiful girls think, and you must think to communicate with her. To think to her, is beautiful, to confess, but only in thought. The reality couldn't possibly be as good. She is mundane, and you are a fool. That's why it's important to never engage.

All information is bad, and since words convey information, one should abstain from words. Instead one should rely on glance, for glance communicates in the unlimited fashion. To think to her that you admire her, yet to never say it out loud. To have her look at you, with this look of minor confusion, for she sees in your eyes, that you think to her. But what you think, she couldn't tell, and how could she. This is beautiful, to think to her, and to see her beautiful curiosity.

You attach. Not to the real, but to her ideal. Which confuses her, because she recognizes that you're looking at her, but not really. You are looking at her without seeing her, and that is confusing. She sees your range, something on the spectrum between beauty and madness, and quite possibly an intricate mix of the two. Madness without aggression is poetical, make no mistake. One can be a beautiful madman.

Nothing creates an impression like her glance. Her eyes can move empires. Yet the dreamer wants to capture the impression, not the girl. The girl is the muse, not the art. One needs the impression, in order to impress. One impresses the soul on the canvas. But the impression is lost when encounter occurs. Real encounter needs to be prevented by all means. If she were to approach you to speak a word, you should run away. Actual encounter endangers the endeavor. The impression is drowned out by the sound of her voice.

One needs to capture her essence, and that is done by avoiding encounter. Impressions don't last, they die and decay. As soon as the first word is spoken, the impression is lost. If she creates an impression on you, you need to be egoistical, and get every last bit of it. If she looks at you, with this particular look, you think to her, that she is your impression. This is your message, and she will respond to it. She adds to her glance the slightest curiosity. Her glance becomes one of investigation. This is beautiful, for this is like the music fading in. You think to her your admiration, and she thinks back to you her curiosity. It's not a romantic look, and she sees that. She knows the romantic look, all the stupid boys look at her like this. Your look is different. She can tell that you like her, yet not romantically, and that's the confusing part. She is curious, not in a mundane sense. It's an instinctive curiosity. Like her soul switching on for a second. This situation is not romantic, and this is not a girl meets boy story. It's completely unromantic, yet it's better, so much better. For a split second the world is put on hold, and both consider the idea of going away together. It's a brief moment of eternal affection. She's curious because your look is somewhat personal, yet at the same time it's not inviting.

What she doesn't know is that you're not looking at her. You love not the real, but the ideal. You're reminded of your idea, which is called love. Yet none of it is connected to her as a person. It's a brief moment in time, but this moment contains lasting wisdom. It's not intentional on your end either. All of this happens in the shortest time span. It happens because you're a dreamer who lives for the ideal. Whereas she lives for the real. Yet in this brief moment your worlds intersect. That's why she responds, intuitively, to your look. Because you remind her of the dream. She was immersed in thought, real thoughts on the real world. But you were not, and you are never. A brief moment, more is not needed, your eyes meet and your worlds intersect. It's beautiful. To take her into dream, if only for a split second. And for her to bring you back into reality — if only for a split second.

In darkness vision is impaired. One sees fewer things, and one sees them less clearly. It's beautiful for one has to make up the rest. Pictures should never be complete, they should be incomplete so the mind can do its part.

Darkness is beautiful, when understood properly. No one sees better than the darkest of minds. If the only light is the distant light from the stars above, then the eye can rest. The mind will brighten the dark spots, and the darker it gets, the more the mind is involved. A dark sky is beautiful, especially when dimly lit. The mind compensates, and it paints some extra stars into the night. How beautiful is Van Gogh's „Starry

Night". Not because it displays the night sky, but because it displays the night sky seen through the darkest of minds.

In darkness one is not limited by light. And light is always limiting, because it only shows what exists. What doesn't exist cannot be revealed by light. Only the mind can see invisible things. Therefore, it's important to make the world invisible every once in a while.

People say one should be realistic and see the world for what it is. I think that's terrible advice. There's nothing better than seeing a world that doesn't exist, while forgetting about the real world in the process. The mind is in constant battle with the world. Both want to claim my soul, but only one shall have it. My soul is my empress. I'm so empressed by her. Whenever she speaks, I listen and learn. While my mind sees things that aren't there, and how I enjoy it.

A dark mind is unbeatable for it's beaten already. That's the beauty of defeat. The slightest victory feels like eternal redemption. Whereas an optimist can only be let down. The darkest mind sees its visions into the world. It's reverted seeing. To pour out your vision, to embellish by sight.

I am not in conflict with my mind, for I believe it wants the best for me. However, the best may be illusion.

He who couldn't feel illusion, would have no relationship to beauty. Beauty is seeing the world broken. To see the world plain, is not beauty. It's realism, and realism is boring.

It's beautiful in the dark. Nothing is better than the darkening of mind. Nothing worse than its brightening. One should never cheer up. One should cheer down instead.

The world is and has always been terribly overrated. Who wants to succeed in a world so pathetic? I'd rather let it down. To let down a disappointment is to live up to oneself. Dignity is non-negotiable. He who lives without dignity, is beyond hope. One should always protect one's dignity and fail in style. There is in the world something to be captured, and that's the impression it leaves on us. The world is a thing without soul. Human alone can add soul to the world. Soul to the world, like salt to the soup, it is the privilege of life.

My brightest ideas are my darkest. That's beauty. To find the treasure at the bottom of the abyss. Only those who go down in style, will go down in history.

It's impossible to be both happy and an artist. Those who are serious enough about their art, will sacrifice their happiness. But to sacrifice happiness is where art begins.

To only see what exists is pathetic. It proves the limitation of the mind. A powerful mind sees so much more, and mostly the non-existing things.

A group of people were chatting. Somehow I found myself in the midst of this conversation. I couldn't escape, for I would have had to actively announce departure. I was not willing to draw attention to me in this manner. So I stayed and listened. And boy, did I regret not having actively announced departure. It was a non-conversation essentially.

To be human is pathetic. One should be mind instead.

Tragic failure is comic success. The goal is to be as absurd as possible. For example it was absurd for Magellan to try and circumnavigate the world, and yet he did. Well, technically he didn't. I believe he died on the way. Yet dying on the way proves my point. First of all, it's funny. Secondly, I don't know. Anyway. I believe one should always say what one doesn't believe just to see how people react. When you hear a person in a social setting talking seriously, you should immediately drop them from your life, for it's unbearable to surround yourself with people like this. Serious people have a terrible influence on our personality. Whatever can be questioned, should not be questioned, and instead you should question everything else. If something is considered fact, you should call it a myth, just to see how people respond. There is nothing like wholeheartedly believing in a falsity and going under while fighting for it.

Social settings are the worst settings. One must do everything to avoid them. If you get trapped in one, it's all about game management. Seriousness is poison for the soul. There is nothing worse than discussing idle topics in serious fashion. One might say that it's better to discuss serious topics in idle fashion. But that's not true either. One should avoid discussion altogether. If you're trapped in a group of multiple humans and you have to endure conversation, you should steer it in a completely different direction. It's always good to question the consensus of the group. Not to challenge it, or to encourage free thinking, no, that's not the point. You should do it because it makes the situation awkward and that's where the fun sets in. For you control the awkwardness. Controlled awkwardness is great entertainment, yet it almost hurts the others physically. It's great to see them trying to save the situation. It's like a beetle lying on its back.

One should never agree with a group of people, it doesn't matter what on. If they claim the sun sets in the west, then it must mean that it sets in the east.

When in a group discussion, one finds oneself discussing the idle in serious fashion, one's first responsibly it to mask one's despair, and that's hard enough. For some reason, existential dread is always spotted by even the weakest of souls.

But there is always existential dread involved. One hears the clocks in hell ticking, and they're ticking slowly. Words are not words, they are needles on my skin.

There is beauty in darkness, namely the beauty one imagines. For example, it's obviously more beautiful to imagine being in love than actually being in love. To be in love comes with many disadvantages. None of which exist in imagination. It's beautiful to not be limited by fact. Fact is drawn from reality, and one should always draw from fantasy. Those who paint the world real are nothing compared to those who paint it unreal. One needs to abandon fact in order to overcome limitation. The actual girl limits you much more than the idea of her. Therefore, it's better to stick with the idea. One should never talk to the girl one admires. One should only talk to the girl one doesn't care about. Only then speech is appropriate. In the realm of divinity, every word is one too many. The worthy soul never speaks, and it suffers in silence.

Speech is limitation, and a sentiment expressed degrades the heart. One should remain in the unlimited, which only the mind can conquer. Speech is choice, and choice is to be avoided. The same in love, where it's never good to love anyone in particular. It's possible to conserve a feeling, but it requires practice. A bottled feeling is not bottled up, if you don't put a lid on it. In that case it becomes a drug. Like a quantity of opium, one can conserve a quantity of devotion, which can be expensed toward every particular. To keep that impression, to carry it around, one lives as if in dream. To common man, and woman, this would not make any sense, and indeed sound like self-torture. But common men, and women, we are not, and we thrive on the extreme.

Picture this. Every particular is one that you love with all your heart. How beautiful the world appears to you. Through your eyes, everything is love. You simply have to overcome the urge to possess it. But to love without having to own what you love is a beautiful thing to learn in any case. If you have to own what you love, it turns love into a possession. Which devalues both the sentiment and the receiver. And yourself. You should not convert sentiment into a thing. If you do, you have the thing, but no longer the sentiment. By transfering love into the object of your love, you subordinate your sentiment to it, and from that point on you depend on the object. It should be the other way around, you should subordinate the object to your sentiment. Meaning, the object can leave, but the sentiment stays. The fact that this seems absurd to most people, just shows how immature their minds are. A beautiful mind can love without object.

If love depends on the object, it's weak anyway. No sentiment should be degraded like this. Sentiment is above object, not below. He or she who degrades sentiment proves they don't deserve it. Only those who keep the sentiment innocent are worthy of it. Objects come and go, but the sentiment stays.

Sentiment is the feeling minus the object, that produced the feeling. Human is weak, so human needs the object to feel. But human can be stronger, and namely when human conserves the sentiment. It's an inner relationship one has to oneself, or more dramatically put, the relationship of one's mind to one's soul. Like a flame that doesn't die down, the sentiment is alive, as long as the mind stays faithful. It's possible to love someone in their absence. One simply needs to commit to the sentiment, while renouncing the object which produced it. To love the sentiment, instead of the thing, is healthy, for it detaches sentiment from thing, and love from the beloved. That way, one can love without possessing. Loving in the absence of the beloved, is not sad, it's beautiful. The sentiment remains vivid. It's pure love, uncorrupted by the world, and in particular by the particular, who couldn't possibly be as perfect as the idealizing mind makes her out to be. But the lesson here is not to idealize less and become realistic, but to abandon realism altogether. To become realistic is to become like everybody else. And like everybody else we'll be soon enough, when we're dead.

Love cannot be simulated. Therefore it's important to protect the sentiment once found, and to detach it from the loved object, which may vanish. Ideally one is so deeply in love that one forgets whom with. That's the ideal state one should aim for. The object of love should not be pursued. One needs to love from a distance. To approach the loved object, is to reproach love itself, for the action proves that one desires the object more than the sentiment. This is proof that you are not worthy of it, and the consequence will be the eventual loss of the sentiment. The only way to keep the sentiment, is to approach the sentiment instead, and to reproach the loved object. One should not desire what one loves. One should love what one desires. The stoics said this, but they meant it in a different way. They meant one should be happy with what one has. I disagree with that. One should be happy with what one wants. That's better. Only he or she who is drawn, can draw. An empty heart produces nothing. Therefore it's important to love, unrelated to the beloved, who changes all the time anyway. One should love every particular with all one's heart, yet none of them with body and mind.

Only a beautiful mind can do this, a generic mind could never. It would constantly lose its heart to the particulars. One should never attach to a particular. The particulars are just the objects flooded with love, yet love stays within. It's exciting to fall in love every day. It's even more exciting to never say a word. One should not own the object of one's love, but instead own one's love like an object. Only the most powerful can control their love, most people are controlled by it. To keep it within, and to use it as a way of seeing, this is the ultimate path to beauty. Every particular becomes the expressed object of your love, but only for a moment. The moment passes, but the sentiment stays. The particulars are not objects, they are people, and that is important to keep in mind. Sentiment is divine, not many people have a direct connection to it. To love independently is the rarest thing in the world, for most everybody's love depends on the loved object. But this is not a law, it's a circumstance, created in a weak mind. One needs to detach thought from the world, and the sentiment from the thing. To love, wherever you go, and to love every particular, makes you beautiful. One should love the love, not the beloved. By that, one sets the beloved free. And to set the beloved free is noble. One can keep the love, without the beloved, both sides effectively detached.

Some days, I'm intrigued to go further. Other days I revert to a more original state. It's always an interesting question, whether one should adapt or not. It helps to move on. Yet to move on is often equivalent to moving away.

It's a human responsibility to not let anyone grieve alone. Unless they want to of course. But help has to be offered, otherwise it amplifies the misery. To withdraw sympathy from a suffering mind is a crime to one's humanity.

Those who don't console have failed their humanity. Humanity lives off humans being humans, not puppets. A puppet is a human that doesn't commiserate.

Misery can be distributed onto different shoulders. To alleviate the misery of another, is necessary, and those who walk by a suffering soul, have failed in this regard.

Misery is a burden that becomes lighter, when one offers one's shoulder. One needs to abandon oneself and dissipate in the moment. One should dissolve in the impression. Only then you will start to feel from their perspective. It's easy to become another, one simply needs to stop being oneself.

To take somebody else's misery upon oneself alleviates their misery. The sad do not require another miserable soul. What they need is a beautiful soul, that sacrifices for them. A beautiful soul brings beauty into the suffering soul. She recognizes, for the first time, that she is not alone.

If the miserable are abandoned, humanity has failed, and every human not commiserating is part of that failure.

The sad are not alone, as much as it may seem that way. There are many who think of them. They want to console them, but it's difficult, for both the sad and the consoler are part of the silent people. And the silent people never find each other. It's one of the tragic circumstances of the world.

To console a sad soul is a human duty. When someone is sad, they need to be consoled. And how? They determine. One has to adopt their misery and find out how to alleviate it.

A sad person feels that no one understands her. But it's not true, for there are people like her, and if they could, they would console her. It's the loud who don't see her. But the loud are useless anyway. One should never care about them. Consolation comes from the silent people.

She'll be fine. She needs not to worry. It's a privilege to be sad. One is never truly beautiful without being a little sad.

A sad soul needs not to worry. She is not alone in affliction. If she wants a consoling word, she shall have a dictionary. When she feels alone, she must know that this is not the case. The tear in her eye is a tear in his. The love that she's capable of will soon shine again. Her sadness will pass, it is fact, not theory. She will rise again, and she'll be beautiful.

To see a sad person, there is only one proper reaction: to share her sadness. Consolation is not possible without commiseration. Sadness is like a weight, that one helps another to carry.

The world is full of good people who wish they could console her. They would tell her that she'll be alright, because she will be. She will rise from this, and soon enough. What today is her sadness, will tomorrow be love. Her tears will have dried, and her smile will return. She will be happy again. The sad never think their sadness will pass, yet almost always it does. Sadness will fade eventually, but it requires the sentiment shared. Therefore, consolation is human duty.

She needs not to worry that she is alone. For she is not. Let the word console her. What he writes, he has thought, and what he thought, he has felt. He felt her sadness, and he feels it still. He feels it whenever he considers her still. And he does, all the time, consider her still.

She needs to understand that her sadness is not permanent. All sad people think they will be sad forever. But they're not. Sad they are now, but not later.

A sad soul is not alone, and she needs to know. She is seen by people who love her very much. If they could be with her, they would be with her. Before she knows it she would smile again. The world would open up in her. Like the sun rising into the morning sky, so would love emerge again. The warm feeling of a beautiful thought. Or a smile which she didn't see coming. Her sadness would no longer make her afraid. She would recognize the beautiful in it. She would feel that her lonely days are over. Where sadness was, love reappears. Beautiful, and never not, her sentiment is well intact.

While the sentiment is sadness, it's still sentiment. Her misery, so beautiful, yet she feels it departing from her. Her sad thought has quieted. And she feels now, strangely, how close it all was to love and happiness. It only needed a small push. Her thoughts are not confused anymore. They feel almost structured now. She navigates most beautifully in this sadness of hers. She feels as if the night is coming to an end. She can sense it now, a new dawn. She feels that happiness, after all, is possible. Love is growing in her, and it becomes all dominant. Love is what the consoler has given her, love is what she receives. This is the key to consolation. The consoler needs to have the capacity to love. Love is to the soul what warmth is to the body. It's vital. And just like that it grows from inside. It's a seed first, but then it blossoms. It grows stronger, and cures her from grief. It's love that she feels, as her sadness departs. Her sadness, which had always been her potential for love — finally realizes its potential.

Change should be appreciated, for it brings out the unchanging in us. By means of contrast, one separates the true and the untrue. Everything that can change will change, except for that which cannot change. Meaning by way of contrast, one recognizes who one truly is. But those who never change, will not be able to tell the two apart.

Two souls are not to fuse, they need to remain distinct. For every soul is a divine matter, and to dilute it is to abuse it.

Healthy love, opposite to what the world says, is not one where two souls fuse into one. Instead the two remain two, and what unites them is the sentiment shared. Symbiotic love is unhealthy love. Two lovers should never become one. They should remain two, and as two they should love.

The lover has responsibility for the beloved. The beloved is not the carrier of the lover's self. The beloved is independent and needs to remain that. If one fragile part carries the other, it doesn't make the construct more stable. It makes it more fragile. Fragility should not be introduced into another, this is a terrible imposition. It's not loving, it's damaging the other.

When love comes with conditions, it's just a service contract between two. It reduces the beloved to a function. When the lover feels no longer carried by the beloved, they move on. The beloved will sacrifice to continue supporting the lover's self. Yet this is unhealthy, and not good for the beloved.

Man and woman should be free. Love that consists of one carrying the other, often proclaimed as romantic, is damaged. Even though damaged love, technically, can be beautiful, too.

Which leads us to the question if perhaps healthy love is overrated. There is some beauty in unhealthy love, it cannot be denied. A love unrequited is artistically speaking of higher worth than a shared love. Because the latter quickly becomes ordinary. Whereas the other keeps the sentiment alive. Unhealthy love is not balanced, and while in real life it's pretty awful and not recommended, in the poetic realm it's quite beautiful. Unhealthy love liberates a beautiful despair, and a pretty soul could hardly abstain.

This is an artist's fate perhaps. To never be able to love anyone but himself. For he cannot get over the image he sees. Only when he never engages, it's acceptable. He must not involve her in this wicked scheme of his. For he knows, through reflection, that it's not her that he sees. And for that reason he abstains. He doesn't engage, yet he looks at her in admiration. She sees in his eyes that he likes her. Yet he doesn't, and he knows it. That's the difficult part. He looks at her as if in love, and in love he is, but not with her. What she thinks is affection with her — is affection with him.

Today I broke the shrimp-rice-continuum. This needs explaining but I don't think I could possibly explain it very well. It's a thing, though, it's not just a sentence. It has to do with adding too much shrimp for too little rice. Now I feel like I've both overexplained it and underexplained it.

A little less honesty goes a long way. Too much honesty is not good. I wish we were all a little less honest.

Consciousness my malady, dream is now my remedy.

In dream, is no duality, of her and I, and us.

My heart has never left her yet, I did not choose it so, and if I could, I would move on, my heart won't let me go.

Silly, yes, so silly. My every word so silly.

In a situation of two, loneliness is always the elephant in the room. A wrong glance or word is enough. I don't want them to suffer, due to my presence. Yet I couldn't help but pity them. It's easy to be objective, when you're subjectively not affected. It becomes harder, if and when you are. And that's the situation with them. I see their loneliness, but I cannot mention it. On top of being lonely, it would make them sad. So it must be, unfortunately, rather omitted. It must be cured by positive conversation and true connection. Yet it's their loneliness that makes me warm up to them. And in a way, I wish I could make that our connection.

You see in their eyes a sadness so deep. Their eyes are as if, ready to cry, and maybe they do, once they're alone. Which means that I am their relief. So I cannot acknowledge their loneliness, for it would remind them of it. And then, it would be twice as hard for them. When a lonely soul feels caught, her loneliness doesn't fade, it increases tenfold. A lonely soul, in such moments, becomes almost desperate.

I see it in their eyes. They smile and engage. Yet I realize exactly what's going on. They smile because for a moment they're not lonely anymore. And shouldn't this make me happy? Well, it doesn't. I see how they truly feel, or how they will feel, as soon as I leave. There is only one way to relieve someone from their loneliness. It's to truly be their friend. But their friendship rests in the casual and worldly things. While mine rests in sadness and pity.

I have to suspend my heart for a change. And that is good, it's a great exercise. To serve the lonely soul, to relieve her for a while. Until I spot it again. It's something that a lonely person says, just a minor thing, or maybe a moment of reflection. Loneliness is like depression, it resurfaces in every moment of silence. Not spoken silence, but thought silence. As soon as one doesn't think or listen, it's back. A lonely person, like a depressed, will therefore try to avoid the silent moment. But that is a torturous existence, for there are many more silent moments than unsilent ones. What a lonely soul wants is distraction. I'm here to distract. Yet all I see is her loneliness, and it makes it hard for me to see anything else.

Truth is, I cannot do a lot for their loneliness, for I would have to be a true friend, and that is impossible. A naturally lonely soul cannot befriend a naturally social soul. There is something that keeps them apart, and namely it's the fact that each finds bliss in the other's worst nightmare.

To see a lonely soul, knowing what would bring her relief, is natural friendship between her and me. Yet the only bond we have, is her sadness. Without it, there is no bond, for she is a social soul, and I'm not. Our relationship ends with the feeling, but the feeling in this case is her sadness. This makes it a difficult set of circumstances, for the loneliness she wants to get rid of, is our only bond. If she was happy, I would no longer care about her. Not in a mean way, but I would know that she is fine, and I can move on. I only want her to be fine, and I'm sad when I feel that she's not.

I don't want to cure her from her loneliness. I don't have helper's syndrome. This would be an unfortunate syndrome for me to have considering my aversion to social settings. All I want for her is to be fine. Ideally without me setting foot into her life. I want her to be fine in my absence. But when she's not fine, I feel obligated. No, that's the wrong word. I feel devastated. That's the better word. I get so sad, when I feel that a person is not fine. I can't bear it.

I see it instantly that they're lonely. I want to help them, and I know how. By being a friend. And yet, this is the one thing I cannot be. I should paraphrase. It's the one thing I don't want to be. I just want them to be fine. They don't want me to pity them without being a friend. They want me to be a friend without pitying them. But I can do neither one. I can neither be a friend to them, nor can I not pity them.

We are what we are. I don't like happy conversation. It bores me into another dimension, this is how much it bores me. It bores me to death, and then it makes me resurrect, like Jesus Christ, for even in death it would continue to bore me.

A lonely soul wants friendship. But that's not what I want. If I could speak openly, I would say that I see her loneliness, and it makes me sad to see her this way. Words do not express her sentiment, and somehow she can't escape it.

But the world doesn't operate that way. For a number of reasons I can't say this. For starters, it wouldn't bring her relief. It would make her sadness erupt. It would intensify and increase it. A madman like I aims for this, but normal people don't. I would not make her better, but worse. Also, I cannot say this because it would make her dependent on me. The moment I leave her, her loneliness would not just return, it would now be like a gaping hole into which she would fall. Her loneliness would be tangible, as she now has something to be lonely about, and that is me. It would lay terrible burden on myself. If once spoken this way, you essentially have a lifelong responsibility for their wellbeing, since you have opened up something, which remains in the open and needs to be managed. Also, none of this is what she wanted. She wanted relief, happiness, friendship. She wanted, in other words, abandonment of loneliness, not appreciation and aggravation of it. She wanted to escape it, not enter it fully. She wanted distraction, not destruction. And now you have to pick up the pieces, you have to manage the damage, and this is asking a lot, from yourself, too. Also, one cannot live out life like a Russian novel. Real life is different. She would not cry and confess. She would cramp up and look at you confused. She would find you strange, and not without reason, for indeed it would be strange to talk to a stranger like this. She would not become your friend, instead become ever stranger to you. Your ways would part, and she would, again, be lonely and sad. The situation would have ended in utter failure. It could have been beautiful, yet it never would have been. This is the difference between fantasy and reality. It's still good to live in imagination. One simply, at times, needs to make sure that one doesn't act it out. One needs to commiserate in thought, but befriend more casually in reality.

And this is why, one doesn't lead the conversation like that. Instead when one sees a lonely soul, one engages in friendly conversation. This is called „taking one for the team“. For if you're anything like me, it will be a nightmare of a conversation. You see her loneliness, but you don't respond to it. Instead you pretend to care for them — well, this didn't come out right. What I mean is, you are nice to them, and accommodating. You ask about them, and you listen to them. You build rapport, and you connect with them socially. This creates in them warmth and optimism. They like you, and they like the fact that you like them. They sense friendship, which is of course exactly the remedy they need to cure their loneliness. The conversation has to be continued in this exact manner, in order to increase their wellbeing. No matter how hard this conversation might be to handle, for it might include stories of their upbringing in the countryside, or planned vacation trips that make them optimistic. Again, you're doing this for them. The aim is to relieve them for their loneliness. You see them getting happier by the minute, while of course you're getting more miserable by the minute. But that is the price you're willing to pay. When the conversation finally ends, you are released into freedom, but they are happier than before. They feel less lonely, as they made a new friend. It's not that you dislike them. It's just that you don't really care a lot for conversation. So you let them go, a little happier indeed. In all of this it has to be said, that they probably wouldn't like to be treated like a three-legged donkey that needs special care from you. But that's the thing, they kind of do. It's still important that they never learn about your pity strategy, or your self-sacrifice during this train wreck of a conversation. One needs to play a somewhat false game with them. But it wasn't your fault really. It's social conventions. You would have loved to hug them and to cry with them. Then again, you still would have left soon afterwards and left them behind in this state. So I guess you may just not be a very good guy after all.

I have long stopped to ask whether I am happy or not. For I am definitely not happy. But I'm not unhappy either. I have somehow fallen into the chasm between the two states.

When I think back, it's not the loss of love, that I mourn, but the loss of intensity. Then again, and this is uplifting, a love realized burns through the intensity fast. Becoming happy is like slashing the tires of a well oiled machine. One loses the intensity rather quickly.

One should either live intensively or not at all. Even without doing anything, one can live intensively. Vice versa, one can live a life full of action, yet without any intensity. If dream is absent, consciousness becomes a void. Consciousness should never become a void. It must retain its volume. Picture it like this. Consciousness has three dimensions. One dimension, let's call it width, is the object. The object of thought determines the width of consciousness. This object can be anything. If one could make the universe the object of one's thought one would have the entire width of the world in one's consciousness. And everything in the universe, down to the atom. Which leads us straight to the second dimension, and that is height. The height is the subject of thought, or the thinker. The greater the thinker, the higher the consciousness will reach. Every consciousness is comprised of these two dimensions, like a y-axis and an x-axis, and within them are contained idea and thought. The thinker moves along the y-axis, up and down the heights of thought. The object of thought moves along the x-axis, back and forth in the width of thought. But there is a third dimension. And that is depth. Depth is the z-axis, and it's the volume of consciousness. One can think of the depth as the sentiment that is present in a given thought. For example, if one thinks about the state of the world and gets angry about it: The state of the world is the width and object of consciousness. Your thinking about it, is the height, and subject of consciousness. And the anger which accompanies your ideation, i.e. the anger which is now present in your consciousness, like a substance released into the air of thought, this is the depth, and the sentiment present in consciousness. The sentiment is distinct from the actual ideation, for the idea is the two-dimensional product of thought and thinker. But every idea, as the synthesis of thinker and thought, is accompanied by sentiment, which turns the x-y-plane into x-y-z space. Now add to it a fourth dimension which includes the passage of time, and you have the dynamics added to this x-y-z space. You now have a moving inner space, or consciousness in motion. There is more exploring to do, but I'll be honest with you, I'm getting a little bored by the abstract here, so I will stop now.

Now I remembered my point. I completely missed it. My point was this. Modern consciousness is devoid of depth. It lacks the sentiment, and it's reduced itself to the two dimensions of thinker and thought. This is not good, for such thought is plain (no pun intended). Thought should never be plain, it should be deep. If thought is not deep, it becomes generic, and abstract, and everyone knows that abstract thought is never a good idea. This is why one should never listen to the mathematicians. For they have betrayed the concrete for the abstract, and this is unforgivable. But in modern thought, depth has all but vanished, and instead one thinks and lives on two dimensions. We all feel this lack of depth, but we often place it in the world, when self-analysis shows that this lack of depth is really happening in us. It's us who have lost depth, not the world. And this is because we have reduced consciousness to the two dimensions of thinker and thought. To height and width. Indeed, never has human thought gone higher and wider. Yet at the same time it's fundamentally stripped of its depth. This is a curious fact, and artifact, of our time, that thought is both subjectively high and objectively wide, yet sentimentally flat. I believe this is a good description of human thought in the 21st century. It's high, wide and flat. Which is strange. In other times the continuum looked different. For example, in the Renaissance. Back then, the y-axis of the subjective thinker was shooting up like a rocket, and the depth was immense for it was a time of deep sentiment. Yet here it was the width that was lagging behind. It's a characteristic feature of the Renaissance that it didn't produce any great theoretical ideas. The explorings of the navigators were actions, not ideas. While physical science progressed, theoretical, ideational science did not. The Renaissance was intellectually a time with tremendous height and depth, but surprisingly little width. During that time, mankind existed almost on a y-z-plane, which is interesting. It was lacking width of thought, but it was very good at producing deeply subjective ideation. Just take the Dutch painters. Why are we fascinated with Vermeer? His pictures are almost exact replicas of reality.

There is no width in them, no creativity, no ideation, no idea really, and yet his paintings are among the most beautiful ever created. He didn't produce sentiment, he captured it, and he did this with a mastery unmatched. To capture the world's sentiment is even harder than to create it, for the sentiment is only scarcely in the world itself, it's mostly in the observer. To capture beauty in a way that anyone looking at it, will re-feel the moment, is above genius, it's almost divine. While I generally agree with Oscar Wilde that realism as a method is complete failure, I wonder what he would say about Vermeer. Because Vermeer has never created beauty, he truly did not add anything to the picture he saw. He all but captured it, and he reached perfection doing it. And that is pure realism, yet it's without a doubt, among the finest art that has been produced. It cannot be denied that at least in this particular case, Vermeer's realism wasn't failure, but mastery, and any creative touch or addition would have taken away from this mastery.

I drifted again. That was not at all what I wanted to say. I wanted to talk about modernity. Modern consciousness exists on the x-y-plane. I'm going to call it that, for it sounds scientific, and if it sounds scientific, chances are that it is. The x-y-plane of consciousness encompasses the height and width of thought, yet it lacks sentiment, and therefore depth. Volume is essential to thought, and without it, thought stays in the abstract. Modern thought allows for subjective height, and for objective width, yet its sentimental depth is low and often non-existent. This characterizes man's thought in the 21st century. Man thinks, he thinks about things, but he doesn't feel the things he thinks about. I believe this is a quasi-scientific description of the problem. In our day, the thinker can reach tremendous height on the y-axis, celling and excelling, the greatest heights of human thought. In this regard human thought is not limited. Equally, thought can reach tremendous width on the x-axis, crossing the horizon of concept, venturing into the realm of even the remotest areas of thought. In this second regard human thought is not limited either. The subjective thinker is as unlimited as objective thought. No limitations are set, and if they are, they are quickly overcome. However, there is a third dimension, which includes sentimental or emotional depth. In simple terms we can say: what you feel while you're thinking, assigns your thought its depth. If sentiment is absent in your thought, consciousness becomes two-dimensional, and so does the character attached to it. 21st century man is therefore best described as a two-dimensional man living in a three-dimensional world. Our thought is no longer three-dimensional, encompassing subjective thinking, objective thought and sentimental value. It has lost the latter, and is stuck with the two former. But sentiment must not be removed from consciousness. Consciousness without volume strips the thinker of meaning. For meaning, value, and truth, are all scooped from depth. Where depth is suspended, all meaning is lost. It's not good to think on two dimensions, one must by all means think on three.

21st century man thinks on two dimensions, and this is his predicament. He has within himself an x-y-z-space to freely navigate in, and yet he behaves as if the z-axis didn't exist, and he's now limited to the x-y-plane. This is the plane of thinker and thought, which doesn't include sentiment, for sentiment originates from the z-axis. The x-y-z-space still exists within the thinker, but it's almost as if he no longer knew how to navigate the depth. One feels reminded of the silly flatlanders. Modern man doesn't seem to know that there is a third dimension, and when he moves, then along the x- and y-axis, never along the z-axis. This explains his troubled mind, for he feels within himself something more, which he has no access to. This is, however, not his soul, it's not the Freudian Id either, it's instead the sentiment which exists along the z-axis. Man, now reduced to the x-y-plane feels as if he's pulled down into an abyss of sentiment. Yet as he's directed outwards, or upwards, he only ever sees his further distancing from conscious thought, or his backwards fall into unconscious terrain. The z-axis is no longer something he conceives of as belonging to him. As he falls from consciousness he's scared, for he doesn't understand the sentiment as something belonging to him. This is what psychoanalysis calls fission, for here the z-axis has been severed from the x-y-plane, and this is to say the conscious has split from the unconscious, as thought has severed sentiment. Now modern man feels and thinks himself as two, not one, and this is his predicament. All of this is due to the separation of the z-axis from the x-y-plane, which of course is not an x-y-plane, but an x-y-z-space, in which the x-y-plane no longer associates with the z-axis. To fix this situation, one has to re-integrate the z-axis into the x-y-plane and this is done by cultivating sentiment. And this is why my ramblings are perhaps not so much ramblings, but therapeutic indeed. For it's in dream that we rediscover our sentiment. To explore depth, is not an active process, it's passive, and one needs to allow dream to flourish. Only if and when dream takes over, will depth be explored, which leads to the reconnection between the z-axis and the x-y-plane. By that the thinker will rediscover his own sentiment, the consciousness will heal, and finally he or she re-appears in the world reintegrated.

Back to analysis. For this is indeed analysis, more or less on one level with mathematical analysis. Modern consciousness is stripped of its depth, and therefore exists on two dimensions, yet within three, and that's the strange part. It's essentially like a cube mistaking itself for a square. Within this square of thinker and thought man looks for meaning. Yet meaning is found in the depths, which the square doesn't realize he possesses, as he no longer identifies as a cube. Purpose and meaning are drawn from depth, and they're not explicit things to be found in either thought or thinker. Instead they're in the volume of thought, i.e in the volume of consciousness. There is an easy way to explain this rather intuitive visual model and I will share it with you unautistic earthlings. Any given thought that exists as a point in the width of consciousness, i.e. as a coordinate on the x-axis, is always grasped by a particular mind, assigning it a second coordinate on the y-axis. The particular object defines the horizontal location in the world of thought, whereas the particular subject defines the vertical location in the world of the thinker. Loosely put, the higher up the coordinate is on the y-axis, the smarter the thinker is. People who believe in astrology for example always make sure to stay in the immediate vicinity of the x-axis. Smart thinkers will reach similar heights on the y-axis, and if they investigate a similar topic they conglomerate. If a dumb thinker joins the group, he will not reach the same height on the y-axis. Many people gather in different areas on the x-y-plane. Every point on the x-y-plane expresses the unique meeting point of thinker and thought. But each and every one of those points has a depth. This depth is sentiment, or it's the volume of consciousness in this particular point. A given thought (on the x-axis) can have different depths, depending on the thinker (on the y-axis) who thinks the thought. Similarly, and vice versa, a thinker produces different depths with different thoughts. E.g. I get excited thinking about the financial system, yet horribly bored by conversation. In this case the financial system is a point with great depth on the z-axis, for it's in my case accompanied by sentiment. Another one might be bored by it, in which case the point has no particular depth. Any point on the x-y-plane comes with depth, which expresses the sentimental value of thought as well as the depth of consciousness at this particular moment in time.

In modern thought depth is largely missing. The points on the x-y-plane have been stripped of their depth. Therefore, our thought has become two-dimensional. It lacks meaning and significance. We long for depth in our thinking, and yet we never find it. We are stuck on the x-y-plane (that's a new sentence!). Modern thought is poor in depth, and every thinker shares the predicament. We long to return to the third dimension, but it seems to be blocked from view. So we make do with the two dimensions we have available. But two-dimensional thought creates two-dimensional people. Two dimensions cannot create three-dimensional people, and I believe the third dimension is a particular fortay of my writing. I believe it's written „forte" but this bothers me, for the „e" is emphasized, so it should be fortay. In any case, I have rediscovered the third dimension. Modern thought is largely devoid of volume, and it operates on the x-z-plane. That's why we're all miserable. Basically, that's what I'm trying to say. Because our thinking takes place on the x-y-plane but the points no longer have any depth. This is why I advocate for rediscovering dream as the third dimension which leads thought and thinker back into depth. In dream one no longer moves in the x-y-plane, but on the z-axis, and therefore in x-y-z-space. Depth is now rediscovered, it re-enters thought, and consciousness develops volume. I have no idea how this all started, let alone where it came from, but I like the model and that's good enough for me.

He or she who wants to produce should be careful not to become too happy. It's the gap between the happy state envisioned and the unhappy state experienced, in which creative production occurs. One releases the frustrations of unhappiness into beautiful form. Or one envisions a reality more beautiful, and one creates it artistically. If there is no unhappiness, reality can no longer be embellished. Then, at most, the beauty of the world can be captured. However, the true value of art lies in the creation of beauty, not in its capturing. If one captures beauty, then truly it was nature that created it. A true artist is able to create beauty, and he creates it from the discrepancy between unbeautiful reality and beautiful vision. This is why it's so important for an artist not to achieve happiness, and instead only yearn for it. One should cultivate the yearning for happiness, while at the same time — and this is just as important — ensuring that one doesn't actually achieve it. Picture the place you love most desperately. Now position yourself in relative distance to that place, in a way that you can see it well, yet without being there. Fixate your eye and heart on it, and engage in yearning. Yet without moving toward this place, staying right where you are. Now this will put your heart into utter despair, but at the same it will fuel your vision, for you can now envision the beauty and the happiness of a place so near to your eye. This is the state, in which the world is yours, and you can create beauty as well as misery. As I've said before, beauty and misery are just two sides of the same coin. Those who can create misery, can create beauty and vice versa. They only need to destroy the beauty to create misery, or to resolve the misery to create beauty. But as soon as one sets foot into the place, all vision is gone, for the ideal has now been realized, and the capacity to create beauty has been rescinded. This capacity must never die, or the artist dies. Those who can't create beauty in an empty room are no artists to begin with. The receivers of beauty don't compare to the producers of beauty who stand in a class of their own.

Never trust a word I say. It's a lot of untruth, with the occasional truth mixed in. What seems true is mostly untrue, whereas some of the absurd statements are genuine. That's the beauty of it. One can share everything without sharing anything. Similar to what in poker is called „loose" play. One plays the good hands like the bad hands. Simply put. One plays the same way, whether one has aces or the infamous 2-7-hand. Then again, I like the 2-7-hand. It seems a natural fit with my 2-7-personality. One should do similar in life, and live „loose". One should talk „loose" and decide „loose", engage „loose" and disengage „loose". It's beautiful for one can at the same time share everything and nothing. You can share your deepest afflictions, yet if you do so ironically, people think you're joking. You can make up sad back stories that never happened. It becomes impossible to tell the true from the untrue. This is where good writing sets in. When plot feels real, it's not interesting. When it feels unreal, it's simply poor writing. But when it feels somewhat real and unreal at the same time, the craft has been mastered. It's here that a new world opens up. One needs to walk the line between truth and untruth. A good sentence is that which contains both true and untrue elements. One should not have true sentences and untrue sentences, for this shows the craft has not been mastered. Only when truth and untruth mingle within a sentence, is the merger complete. It's then, that the writer disappears in plain sight. Now everything is right and everything is wrong, and the writer has found the right tone. Because it's not a writer's job to tell truth, that would make him a reporter. It's a writer's job to tell whatever, a little truth and a little untruth, fused into plot and protagonists.

To speak truth is not difficult, to speak untruth a lot more so, because the untruth always sounds untrue, as long as the craft has not been mastered. But to make the untruth sound like the truth, is masterful, for one who talks like this, is limitless in plot and expression. One can create a whole world from within. The truth is boring anyway, and it doesn't compare to the excitement of untruth. That's why people fall in love. They don't fall in love with the truth, but with the untruth. Once truth has been uncovered, love fades, and so does the excitement. Therefore it's best to never get behind the untruth of things, and remain in the realm of illusion.

One needs to blend truth and untruth, to create a third reality, which contains the two. Truth is reality and untruth is fantasy, but once blended, they become something different. It's beautiful to believe in the untruth. And disappointing to find out the truth. The truth is a dead stop. The element of untruth is equally the element of fantasy in reality. The untruth needs protecting from the truth. The truth shatters our dreams, and dreams should flatter, not shatter.

One has to mix truth and untruth in a way that it becomes impossible to tell them apart. When the true sounds untrue, and the untrue sounds true, the craft has been mastered. It's beautiful to sell untrue things as true, and to tear down truth into untruth. We all want to see our heroes fall, it's hidden in our souls somewhere. The way to go is to sabotage the truth. One needs to join forces with the untrue, or one needs to side with untruth, and bring it silently into the realm of truth. Step by step, one sabotages truth with clever untruth. Before you know it, truth and untruth become interchangeable.

This craft needs to be mastered, in order to become a beautiful illusionist. One needs to tell the truth like it's untruth, and the untruth like it's truth. Yet not throughout, otherwise it becomes a recognizable pattern. You also have to tell the truth truthfully at times, and the untruth untruthfully. If you add a bit of seriousness, everything else will appear more serious. If you add an obviously absurd statement, it will make it seem like all absurdity is untruth. Yet the absurdity is often a truth, which is not recognized as such. While the seriousness remains untruth, only sold as truth. A serious statement can end up being either true or untrue, and it's impossible to tell from the outside. Only from the inside this can be determined. Meaning the reader is the judging party. It's here that the reader becomes more than just a reader. The reader becomes the writer, as he or she starts to think with the writer. And if it's plot, he or she thinks with the protagonists. The writing comes alive, and the book becomes a world. This is why the craft of telling untruth needs to be mastered by every writer. A writer that cannot tell untruth is a poor writer. Just like happy artists are bad artists, truthful writers are poor writers. Nobody cares about your truths. It's your untruth that we care about. A writer should never speak truth, only untruth. When speaking truth, he needs to check himself, and then correct. For truth has no place in writing. It simply doesn't belong there. Writing needs to be untrue, it needs to be a lie in truth's clothing. Whether I really mean it? Well, that's the whole point.

Never trust a word I say, for I blend truth and untruth like others blend letters into words and sentences. What seems likely to have happened, most likely did not. What seems unlikely to have happened, there is a good chance that it did. For I am a most absurd character. In fact, it's the reasonable me you should distrust the most. Then again, the truly absurd do not reflect upon themselves in this way, meaning there has to be some normality in me. And that would make it more likely that the absurd is just an act and the normal statements reflect myself. The point is you must think. If others do the thinking for you, you will think their thoughts, not yours. That's why you should never trust a word I say.

My words are spoken randomly. I enjoy saying things that do not express my thought at all. This excites me, and I don't feel obligated to the truth. I don't owe the truth to people. It's their imposition to impose on me. Yet this is called etiquette, and I don't want to be rude to people either. I'd rather be kind to them. Telling a beautiful untruth is the best I can do. One should not burden oneself with the truth. The truth is just glorified boredom. There is a longing by the people for the untruth. Tell the people a beautiful untruth, and they will follow you blind. On the other hand, being truthful never gets you to a place that other people haven't been to. Untruth is a solitary path, truth walks with the common man. And you should never walk with the common man. When you see him, turn around and run away.

It's beautiful to be a writer, for one can say whatever, and it all means nothing, yet it all means everything. One lives so beautifully beneath the verse. One can share one's deepest griefs, yet never quite commit to it. One can make up a whole bunch of nonsense and sell it as truth. Truth and untruth blend, until they can't possibly be told apart. But this is beautiful, this is how it's supposed to be. Untruth should collapse into truth, and truth emerge from untruth. Only when truth and untruth reunite, one touches upon the divine. For in the heavens, this distinction no longer exists.

It's beautiful to live on paper. One should never start an actual life. The highest discipline would be to spend a lifetime in thought and imagination. This is a life well lived. The idle don't understand this, as they lack the mind for it. To think, and to imagine, this is the purpose of life.

To think and to imagine, life is all about that. To become something in the world, to buy a house, to start a family, I call that utter confusion. One should only imagine these things, and decide against them. The untruth is beautiful, one needs to stay faithful to it. Once the truth has consumed you, the dream is over. Death has begun silently. One should not die prematurely. And to buy a house, to start a family, is dying prematurely. The real winners imagine buying a house while living in a broken flat.

It's beautiful to amount to nothing. This is winning at life, for those who amount to nothing, realize that meaning cannot be found in things. Possession burdens. All matter is weight. One has to be weightless. The less matter we bring upon us, the less grief. One should lose it all, to have nothing to lose. This is privilege, to be light, to be weightless.

Life's value is not in the things, but in the appreciation of things. Our appreciation should be independent of things. The loss of matter is our exit exam.

I want to amount to nothing. It's my new goal in life. I'm close to reaching it. I am still something, but not for long.

I love the 2-7 hand. It's a good hand. It's said that poker is a game of skill, but this only applies when you play with skillful players. Chance is much more involved in a typical poker game. In this case one should play like someone who is no longer employing sane thought. This is a good technique, for it will get you in the head of the others. For example a 5-5 combo should be played like a 6-6 combo. This is an unpredictable move and it beats the odds of the game. In a game of Texas Hold'em, you should never „hold 'em", for this is what the game wants you to do. Remember, the casino always wins. Therefore, by reverse engineering, you should fold every single hand. Until the 19th hand. Alright, you with me? The 14th hand, you go all in. And you either win it all, or you lose it all. Meaning you have a 50/50 chance of winning the entire pot. This is a random strategy, but don't forget that you're not playing the game, you're playing the players, and they will be freaked out by your game play. In case they all fold, you must cause a scene, cash out and leave. This way, they think you're an unpredictable genius which will solidify your reputation. Next time you join, you play the 14th hand, and once again you have a 50/50 chance of winning the entire pot. There are some exceptions to the rule, and I will let you in on them. For example, diamonds should be played like hearts. However, spades and clubs should be played like spades and clubs.

How to play poker. Here are a set of insights, that will improve your game greatly. When someone bets a high sum, it's very likely that they have a good hand and you should always do as I do and fold. While it's possible that they're bluffing, at least in my experience they always take the pot. When someone bets a smaller sum, they are insecure about their cards and you should play. It's likely that you have better cards. If your hand contains a 2, a 4, or a jack, you should go all in. If it includes an 8 or a 9 you should fold. This introduces an element of chance that nobody could anticipate. When you have a pair, you should throw away your cards, for a pair is never the winning hand and it usually costs us money. When you play poker, make sure to add a telling sign. The other players will pick up on that and realize you're bluffing. Catch 22 is that you're not really bluffing, because you don't really know what you're doing. As they say, play the player, not the game. Don't try to think, this is perhaps the most important rule of poker. Instinct goes a long way in poker. One should never try to calculate the game. This is similar to what the chess masters say, for chess is similarly a game of instinct. The best poker players are those, who build a personal relationship with their cards. It must be emotionally tough for you to throw away your hand, for only then you will commit to it. And you must commit to your hand always, even in times of trouble. When the cards look no good, you must portray strength. Poker is like tennis, above all a psychological game. Believing is everything in poker, and the odds are constantly changing anyway.

Some days I can love another, but I don't want to. Other days I want to love another, but I can't. Unfortunately those days alternate. The bottom line is: I don't love another. When I want to, I can't. When I can, I don't want to. I saw a girl the other day, who looked a lot like her. She did not speak, she only looked at me briefly. She looked at me in this peculiar way. Like she felt for me. Not with pity per se. More like human. She picked up on me.

She looked at me, and she was just like her. She had the same look in her eyes. She had her ways. How else can I put it. I was thrown back. It was as if a substance filled a room, or a fog entered into the clear sky of my mind. My soul was oscillating, like a skyscraper in a strong wind. My thoughts were plunging. I believe she saw my sadness.

I always get sad when I see a girl that resembles her. So I get sad a lot. But at the same time a little happy. For they remind me of her. And that's also a beautiful thing.

It's sad when you still love, but you're not allowed to. What do you do with the sentiment? Do you dispose of it? You're obligated to. But how do you feel about her? Do you deny her existence? I know how other people do it. They trash the other. They tear down the statue. I don't want to do this. I don't want to save myself at her expense. I'd rather not save myself. I want to protect her from this natural development.

I see her a lot these days. Well, never her. I see her in every other. One walked like her, and it was her. Another one spoke like her, and it was her. It's never her of course. That's how it is, I guess. Resemblance is strange. It's so subjective.

It's love that makes me doubt most that the body is all there is. Love is such an illogical state for the body to be in. Also it's such an unphysical state. It doesn't push you into the body, it sort of pulls you out of it. And this applies to all sentiments. It's the same with sadness, happiness, anger. If these were body states, like science says, then should we not feel particularly physical or „bodily" in those states? Yet we feel the opposite. As if we are without flesh. We feel light, almost immaterial. Like the immaterial soul. But the body is material. If love and joy are body states, should they not feel more „material". Yet they don't. Nothing about love is material. One cannot touch it, see it, or feel it in the body at all. One cannot influence it or affect it physically, or physiologically, in fact one can do nothing about it. It comes and goes like a shadow, immaterially. So how is it a physical state? If sentiment is a material state, why does it feel so immaterial? And a fever doesn't feel immaterial. Sweat, headache, tiredness, this is all related to the body. Love is not like that, nor is any other sentiment, if you think about it.

If only I could love another. But if I could, I wouldn't want to. I only want to love another when I can't. If I could, I wouldn't want to. Does that make sense? The point is: I don't want to love another. I'm not going to love her forever. I hope I will still love her somehow. This is why I protect her image. I think it would be beautiful. To be able to love her anytime. This may seem like a strange goal to pursue, but I am a strange guy indeed. I enjoy it, though. I think it's beautiful to be strange. I want to keep her image. For I admit that her image is the most powerful thing that my imagination knows. She is a goddess in my mind. Before her, my mind was sharp, but never beautiful. She added light and color to this inner world of mine. She had a beautiful impact on my thought. Before her I was a thinker, now I am a dreamer. My mind is such a beautiful place now. Sad, yes, but beautiful.

I look at her in thought, and I see where I am. She positions me within my own mind. She is my horizon. She protects me from reality. I forget the world, when I see her image. I am no longer susceptible to the world's distractions. The world distracts me no more. How beautiful. I see my own world now. I call it dream. Within dream one can understand the world in a different sense. You see the world quite beautifully. But to see the world beautifully, requires the sentiment. To love is to see the world beautifully.

Can it be understood? What appears an obsession, is really a protection, of this beautiful vision of mine. I don't want to be objective anymore. I want to be subjective. I want the world to have a meaning for me. To see beauty where beauty is not. To create beauty with my eye. She is a requirement for this capacity. Without her, I don't see the world like that.

Why is it glorified to see the world objectively? Let the world be objective, why do I have to see it that way? I don't want to see the world for what it is. It's much more beautiful to see it for what it isn't. The difference that we see, expresses our soul. It materializes our sentiment into space. Your soul takes the world as its material, but it creates something else from it. The soul wants to appear in the world, not disappear in it.

Whoever thinks I'm not coping thinks incorrectly. I'm coping every day. And I feel vindicated. I notice how I lose her without losing her. This was my goal all along. To let her go, yet to keep her image. To not love her anymore, but to be able to. Yet this time, the feeling fades, and my life goes on.

People don't understand this, for they don't use their minds. To keep love, like a flame that always burns, yet never burns down, that is mastering the sentiment. One has to be a skilled master to love like this. To control love is to control the fire. The power of mind becomes incredible. It goes beyond everything the common mind can conceive. You have to control the sentiment, not to bottle it up, but to release it from the bottle, like the most delicate perfume.

They don't understand this, because their minds are weak. They think like pigeons eat, they think „whatever they can find". Sometimes the world throws them a handful of bread crumbs, and that's what makes them think. We don't think that way. People like I. One needs to master the sentiment, in order to feel it anytime. But to feel a sentiment at the press of a button, takes the most powerful mind. Only few can do this, for only few are willing to pay the price. The price is walking on the edge of madness. But it's beautiful. Picture this. On the edge of the world, there is reality on one side, and the abyss on the other. How beautiful would the world be, how terrifying the abyss, and how powerful would you feel walking between the two. As the creator of your own fate. You can decide, and this is beautiful.

When I'm with people, I hear their thoughts instead of mine. In theory that's a good thing. But in practice their thoughts are so boring. If only they had interesting thoughts. Maybe it comes down to that. Conversation being not interesting. But I'm never interested in conversation, so it might be me. I don't understand why people say obvious things. People like to state things, that could easily be omitted. For example the sky is blue, the trees are green, the sea is nice, and the night is cold. This is how they talk, just a bit more elaborate. When people discuss culture, I want to die. When people discuss languages, even more so. When people discuss preferences, I have an out-of-body experience. I hate when I get trapped in conversation. I always do. Every conversation I have is a conversation I got trapped in. My family says, go out, meet people, you never know what you might find. Oh but I do, and that's the problem. I'm never surprised by what I find.

I am of course just another failed existence. I'm perfectly fine with that. In fact I'm almost proud of it. I would have been ashamed to amount to something. For the world would have won. To please the world, is to disappoint yourself. And all the things you could have not been. It's good to stay a failure, for one can look at things differently. To go for something big and not even get close to it. That's perfect. Not to almost reach it, for this makes you miserable, but to really not get it at all. To want to become the greatest painter of all time, yet you can barely sketch a stickman. Or to want to conquer the world, and fail the task miserably. For example Magellan trying to prove that the world is round by circumnavigating it and dying on the way by falling from the edge of the Earth disk, was very funny. I wish I could lose myself in a crazy thought. That would be amazing. To sacrifice myself for a truth that ends up being complete nonsense. In fact, my whole writing pursues this path. I want to be a writer who writes a lot of nonsense that is never read by anyone. After all, if you can't succeed the second best option is to fail completely. And who really succeeds anyway? Even the successful are miserable. So maybe failure is the best option.

This would be lovely, to fail completely. But to continue believing in it. Like someone who fully believes his day will come, yet this day never arrives. This is to me, for some reason, very amusing, and I would love to be that person. As silly as that sounds, I'm sort of serious about this. I just don't see the point of doing what everybody else does. Many others have done it, why should I repeat it?

I am tempted to make this my life's mission. To become a complete failure in all regards. I'm on a good path. It seems I might be able to reach my goal. Doesn't it make me a winner? A success even? For the successful people reach their goals. So it depends on how you set your goals. The lower the goals, the higher the chances of success. My new goal is to write bad text that nobody wants to read. Then I want to try an enterprise which is doomed to fail from the start. I also want to fall in love and never be loved back. That's another goal of mine. I want to be broke and live off nothing.

Of course, I am a failed existence. Yes. I know. I should feel miserable about it, but I don't. It's almost a relief to fail. Ambition, similar to hope, is a burden. It never makes you happy anyway. When ambition is realized, it's just replaced by another ambition. Like hope. One needs to get rid of those things altogether. Not to become a cynic, or depressed, but to take things as they come. I can't believe I'm saying this. When I was young, all the elder said this, and I called it nonsense. Now I'm older and I'm saying the same thing. But that's fine, see, it's failure. My young self has failed. Maybe my old self can succeed. For wisdom is built on a thousand failures. And as much as I keep failing, I am getting wiser.

And not even older. For the ones that were never young, don't grow old. We stay in the limbo. We are wise and innocent. That's a pretty word combination. I wish I could be wise and innocent. To feel like a small boy, to think like an old man. This is beauty realized in a humble soul. But on the outside it's failure, and I appreciate that.

I want to be wise and innocent. A failure in the eyes of the world. My goal is to never sell a single copy of my verse. It's going well in this regard. I want to keep falling for the unattainable girl. By now I am a master at this. If loving the unattainable girl would be a sport, I'd win Olympic gold. For I always love all the parts in a girl that are not really there. I just make them up. She would look at me, and say: what are you talking about? And I would say: I have no idea.

I can't see the world the way it is. I always see it the way I am. I am flawed, and sometimes I just want to die. But if I manage to aim at failure, then I might become a success after all. I want to be weak and poor. I hate being smart, I wish I was dumb. I hate my thoughts.

I'm a flawed soul, but I'm not unhappy about it. It's my virtues that I feel nothing but contempt for. My wish is to be friends with the weak people, for they are much more lovable. They are quiet, deliberate, inconspicuous. The world belongs to the other kind. I don't like the other kind. And I don't want to be a success in their world.

I don't want to win their games, because I don't want to play their games. Their games are not beautiful, they are ugly. There is no class, and no grace in their games. It really is a graceless game this world we live in. I do not aim to be anything in their world. I'd rather be a miserable failure. I don't want to compete. That's where it starts. I don't want attention. I don't want to be seen. I don't want my name to be known, or my face to be shown. I don't want to market myself. This is such a horrible fact of our time, that we all need to do this. I don't want to convince people, persuade them, win them over. I don't want to be admired, or desired, or praised, I want none of that. I just want to fail miserably, until the end, and then be forgotten forever. How beautiful.

It's not just about whether one wins or loses. One needs to evaluate if the game is worth playing, or if it should be skipped. And society is a game that should be skipped. I don't want to win at this game. I just want to be. I want to hear the winds in the trees. Or the rain drumming down on my attic window. I want to tiptoe in a winter landscape, all noise drowned out by the snow. I want to sit in the late autumn sun. I want to walk in the woods, in their pretty dark green. I want to hear some music, distant to my ear.

My silence is so dear to me, and my solitude. I don't want to be with these people. I want to be well hidden and stashed away. I don't want to play this game. I'll happily be a miserable fool, and a failure. I like it very much.

Success is a calamity. Failure is better. No one reads your verse, yet you love it very much. Picture this, the world loves your style. You'll become a slave to it. Only the failures are truly free. As they only work for themselves.

I had to go to a restaurant last night. I was invited. I was not asked. If I had been asked, I would have un-invited myself. Unfortunately, I didn't get the opportunity. Everyone was overwhelmed by the occasion. I was underwhelmed by the occasion. In fact, I wasn't whelmed by the occasion at all. I was a bit cranky about it. I went through the routines, small talk, you know the drill. I had to pretend I was interested in the recent developments in the workplace of a guy. I know that this is how it works. I just don't understand why. People say things, because they want to fill the silence and they don't know what to talk about. But that's my point. If you don't know what to talk about, don't talk. It's very simple actually. It's not awkward at all. If a stranger was able to be quiet with me, in no time, I would look at him, with a friendly smile, and say: that's nice, isn't it? And he would say, ‚yes, I second that notion', though I'm not sure he would use those words. Then I would say, look at the waiter, what is he wearing. And the guy would say, yeah, what is that, we would laugh, and fall silent again. Until I would look him deep in the eyes, hold my hand toward him, and say: Brothers for life? That's how it would go. But instead he talks about accounting. What's wrong with this guy? Accounting people in particular should never talk about their job.

So I was seated next to a guy that I didn't know. This in itself is bad enough, but he was one of them talkers. I wish I had been dealt a different hand. One of those socially awkward people. I love them, because they are fun to tease. I'm not malicious with them. Probably not exactly good either. It's something in between the two. I like to leverage their social awkwardness. I don't dissipate it. I evoke it. Now this may not paint a very good picture of my character, but in my defense, I never said I had a good character. I enjoy witnessing their life-and-death-struggle in conversation. I usually say nothing intentionally, just so we can have this extended silence that I know they dread so much. I can see their minds racing, what can I say? I love this. Does this make me a sadist? In this case, yes. I'm not generally into this sort of behavior, but when I see a socially awkward person, I enjoy doubling down. For my own amusement of course, that's what it's all about. I like having these long spells of silence with them, just to see how much it tortures them. I could easily alleviate the situation, but I won't. I want to see what they do next. But I'm not cruel. Okay, I guess, this is not very convincing after what I just said, but I don't do this for long. Often the conversation continues quickly, they are happy and I am miserable again. After all, their misery is only my happiness because their happiness is my misery. One should not mistake cause and effect.

I was, however, seated next to one of those social people, and I couldn't have been more miserable. He never stopped talking. He never even paused. He thought he was engaging, but he was only enraging. Yours truly that is. For what he was saying wasn't even close to interesting. It was words. That's all I can say. Words were spoken. And I was there to witness it. I wish I hadn't been invited. I was going through the motions, nodding here and there, adding the occasional ‚yes‘ and ‚I agree‘. He didn't stop talking. I only had one question in my head. Why? Why is this happening? Why is it happening to me? Why can I not be not here? Why can I not be anywhere else? There are 8 billion people on the planet, why am I on the receiving end of this speech. Why does he think it's appropriate to tell a stranger about every little detail of your life? I will never understand social media. But I had enough of the guy. I had to end it at some point, and he had pushed his luck. He was talking about a movie he had seen, when I dead-stopped him mid-sentence. I said: ‚Let me stop you right there, I'm not watching a movie with Meryl Streep, that's where I draw the line‘. He looked at me puzzled. I was thinking, howdyhow cowboy, I'm taking over this conversation and there's nothing you can do about it. He said: 'It's a great movie'. I had barely listened at that point, I was just doing what he was doing, saying random words in random order. But now I was hooked, and I knew him and I were in for a ride. I said a long and extended: ‚Noooo' and then an additional, short ‚No‘, while shaking my head. He said: you don't like these sort of movies? I said: It's not my style. He said: what is your style? I said, I like Belgian and Dutch arthouse movies. He said: Belgian and Dutch arthouse movies? I said: Vinkelhuijz, Kremer, Gadwijk, these guys. He said: never heard. I was surprised that I could improvise names likes that. I was particularly proud of doing the horrible gorge sounding G that the Dutch do. I thought it was a good start and that motivated me extra. I said: you should check these guys out, should I write these names down for you, and also some movies? I said this very affirmatively to encourage him, and before he could answer I wrote them down. Then I started explaining every single one of them. In my defense, this has to be added here, he had talked for a good 15 minutes before that. I pointed to the names saying, Vinkelhuijz, he is a genius, he was born in poverty in the Dutch midland, in a small town, where he grew up around farmers, and their poverty, in the long and cold winters after the war, and this serves as his greatest inspiration until today, and this movie is called The Peasant Revolution, it describes the war stricken poverty of post-war „Holland“, and indeed portrays the uplifting spirit of the simple people, yet the arthouse aspect of it makes it a true masterpiece, because it's all shot in black and white, with a sepia yellow tone, from one particular angle, not horizontally, but from slightly further up in order to show the soil only, never the sky, and this is a metaphor, illustrating the proximity of the simpler people to the ground, and to the soil, and even Earth, and this movie does it masterfully, it won a Gouchin Award at the Bordeaux Film Festival, as well as a the Bruges Brooch which is a brooch given out in Bruges to innovative film directors, and it also excelled in the movie festival Van der Gingelen (Ch-ingelen) which takes place in Groningen (Ch-roningen) every second winter. I was impressed by my own improv ability. Then again, it's easy to improvise if you don't have to stick to any facts. Anyway, he got more tired by the minute, and I saw the life draining out of him. It gave me maximum pleasure to see him suffer like I did. He asked an occasional question, which I answered earnestly. He obviously wasn't interested in the answer, but I pretended that I thought he was. I played it like I thought I had him hooked. It was really meta at that point. It's good to have experience with psychological fission. It helps with conversational fission. I figured I really taught him a lesson. To not be like this. Because it would have been so nice, if we had just been normal people. One needs to be silent at times, I'm convinced of this. Those who can't be silent will never have anything to say. People are no longer able to sustain silence, and it kills substantial thought. It was his fault to bore me into anger. The audacity to speak so much while having nothing to say.

If one can't be silent, one needs to learn it. This is important, because the best thoughts emerge in silence. Only in silence can good thinking occur. In loudness it's impossible. One doesn't think the best thing, but the next best thing. The conversation with my new friend faded out. He was visibly worn out. As was I. The only difference being, I had arrived here in this state. Yet now we shared our fatigue in brotherly fashion. I was tired of his nonsense, and he was tired of mine. At least I wasn't suffering alone anymore. I had made a friend tonight. And so had he. Not in me of course, but in another guy, who he started talking to shortly after.

A good speaker is one who knows how to be silent. A bad speaker doesn't possess that ability. If people don't manage to be silent, I lack pity for them.

Why not be silent together? Silence should be the entry point of a conversation. Only then, slowly and maturely, real speech will develop. Hesitation is good. It means that you're thinking. To be a fluent speaker doesn't mean anything. It just means that you talk a lot. One should aim to be a bad speaker. Or even better, one should not be a speaker at all. In most cases, speech is unnecessary. It's beautiful to remain silent, and let the impression do the talking. Stillness is an underrated virtue. To be still, nobody will give you a price for this. But the reward is vision and thought.

Those who can't be silent, don't deserve our pity. We should drown them in silence. Silence needs to hold up the mirror to idle chatter. When chatter idles, we make it idler. They need to realize that chatter is a bad habit. To chatter is to shatter, my soul that is. It's a bad habit to talk, when talk should be omitted. Those who have no relationship with stillness, are limited, and we don't deal with the limited.

Speech is the commonest thing in the world, yet good speech the most seldom. All speech is idle these days. But this could be a trend returned, if only speech could plunge into silence again. Silence needs to drown speech, in order for speech to become substantial. Speech never allows silence anymore.

What we need is a time of quiet. We need the great stillness. For then we will finally get ahold of substantial thought. We have lost all meaning in the endless chatter of the world.

It's curious. When you're young, you think life is all about reaching your goals. Then you arrive just to realize how many things were missing in your mental scenario. You go: ‚Oh I didn't think it was going to be like that'. Keep that in mind when you regret your dreams not coming true. They wouldn't have been the way you imagined them. The boy you loved would have bored you to death. The girl who seemed perfect would have turned out to be of rather average character. The job you wanted would have killed your soul. The thing you wanted to purchase would have lost its charm almost instantly. Dreams are only beautiful as long as they're dreams. You want something, with all your heart. Then you get it, and you're miserable. Keep this in mind when you're sad that your dreams didn't materialize.

Dreaming is the process of idealizing the world. These days, the ability to idealize is underrated, and it's certainly underdeveloped. Our times are not suffering from an excess of imagination, but from a shortage. To idealize the world has a bad reputation, but this is because the world has lost itself in the mundane. When dream is lost, reality becomes dull. One has to dream, in order to embellish reality.

Dream is as necessary to the soul, as oxygen is to the body. It's the rationalist's fallacy to assume one needs to adhere to reality. It's the opposite actually. One needs to follow dream, and act back on reality. The world is first envisioned, then embellished. Dreaming is an important aspect of progress. You cannot skip the dream part and go straight to progress. That's like skipping sleep and going straight to waking up. The point of sleeping is to sleep. It cannot be skipped while getting the same results of rest. Similar with dream. Dream is necessary to envision a different reality. Without dream, the vision is poor, and the improvement is limited.

The world has lost its relationship to dream. It's painfully awake all the time. This century is best described as the awake century. We're all awake and never asleep anymore. Without dream, the world is doomed to stay the way it is. True change is only possible, if it's preceded by dream.

We talk about dreams, but we don't actually dream. We daydream, but that's not dreaming. That's just being awake and a little off. To dream is to let go of reality. To let it slip through your hands. To allow it to change before your eyes. It's about a loss of control. The dreamer is controlled, not controlling. This capacity has been lost. Nobody can evade reality anymore. We long for the dreams we had.

Dream creates vision, not vision dream. This is another popular misconception. The assumption that one has to have vision in order to dream. It's quite the opposite actually. One has to nurture the capacity to dream, because only in dream you develop vision. You see the world differently, or you see the difference between actual and potential reality. Vision focusses on potential reality, which only occurs when the world is idealized. Dream is the state, which allows vision to happen. It's not vision that makes you a dreamer. It's dream that makes you a visionary. One should not focus on vision, for this is something that cannot actively be controlled. It's a side product of a state we are in. And this state is called dream. It includes seeing the world not through one's real eyes, but through the dreaming eyes of idealization. Only when the seer becomes a dreamer, will he or she become a visionary. Those who claim to go straight from seeing to vision, are not visionaries. It's just words for the ever same thing. To become a true visionary, one needs to drop out of reality, instead of penetrating it. Dream is a loss of control, and the dreamer is one who loses control over himself. There is no such thing as a controlled dream. If the dream is controlled, it's not a dream, and the dreamer is awake. True vision results from a loss of control. One needs to lose the world in order to win it. This is the capacity that we need to nurture in our minds. The capacity to lose control of our thoughts. As long as the dream is controlled, one is awake. One either rationalizes or irrationalizes, wakes or dreams. Vision is the direct result of a dream well dreamt. Those who lack the capacity to dream, won't develop vision. One should not teach vision, because it cannot be taught. A common vision is not a vision at all, it's just a common idea. Vision is the ideation of the soul, and every soul is unique. In order to nurture vision, one needs to nurture the capacity to dream.

Seclusion is an inner focus, yet without object. One focuses on nothing, but one does so in a focused fashion.

The soul's afflictions accumulate. The soul has photographic memory. It remembers everything most vividly. History determines culture, and memory is but the culture of one.

I had this idea, and I stick to it, that I wanted to love her in this pure and uncorrupted way. I wanted to never introduce a mundane element into it. I know it makes me a villain, not a hero. When I say that I did not want to learn about her morning routine. I was more interested in her mourning routine. I did not want to have idle conversation with her. I felt the love draining from us. Slowly, but surely. We became real. I never had any intention of becoming real with her.

What she wanted wasn't what I wanted. This was a difficult starting point. She wanted a normal life. I dreaded it.

We became imperfect, as we grew into reality. I realized I was in love with her image. It's my limitation. My mind never loves real things. It's always disappointed by them.

I was good enough for her, when she was sad. I wasn't, when she wasn't.

When she was sad, she was beautiful, and I loved her. But I loved her always. What I was, she stayed oblivious to. I don't blame her. After all, to understand me is a clear sign of clinical depression. I'm well aware of that, so it's probably good that she didn't understand me.

She was always beautiful. When we went out together, she was my world.

She was real, and she was different. But what she was to me, that was real, too. Her image is what I truly loved.

I saw a guy the other day who had an existential crisis over how many spiders he had killed in his life. I think it's safe to say that he had the existential crisis before and the spiders just tipped him over the edge.

A dreamer always lies about reality. That's the essence of dreaming. But a dreamer is happy, his happiness cannot be denied, and this makes it all worth it.

I only saw a particular quality of hers. I was not seeing her for what she really was. Happy in spirit, only brought down for a time, by a terrible affliction. I saw straight past her beautiful personality, and all I saw was her sadness.

She was playing on me like a harp. Even if I didn't see her for who she really was. I was in love with her, but mostly with that broken side of hers. I realize now, that there was no future for us. She had me figured out. I'm careful now about what I do and who I talk to. I know my personality, despite being weak, is strong. I can make people think what I think. I don't want to abuse that capacity. In fact, I don't even want to use it. I'm happy that she too had a strong personality. I picture her happy now, and that makes me happy, too. All I want is for her to be fine. Some things break and they can be repaired. Other things break and they can't be repaired. We were the latter. I don't blame her for leaving. I applaud her.

I wish I could have stayed in that dream with her. Our dream didn't last very long. It's the healthy way of dreaming. Only I dream all the time. Dream designs a different reality. One which is boundless and free. My mind and soul are friends in dream, and this can hardly be said about reality. I want to continue dreaming, until dream has all but absorbed me.

We were beautiful together. I remember it now. We went outside, in the cold, and we would talk, whisper really, very quietly. The skies were grey, it was cold, not many people around, we were alone, only the two of us, she was shy, and so was I, and it was beautiful. She had a way about her that I adored. She was so beautifully normal. It was with her that I felt we needed nothing. For we had everything already.

I will not forget the walks with her. We had the strangest intimacy. It was like loving her soul. We were always quiet. She had a quality, which I cannot describe. She was broken and sad. But at the same time so innocent, so pure.

She was innocent, yet damaged from the start. I loved her right away. Over time she developed out of it, and I didn't. I stayed at the place that she wanted to leave. She asked me to come with her. But I couldn't. She really thought she could change me. She asked me once: Why don't you want to be happy? I said, I don't know. It's eery. But it's true. Why do I not want to be happy? I don't know. I just don't feel myself when I am. Happiness for me is not to be realized in the world, but in dream. She wanted to sacrifice the dream for a reality together. That was different from what I wanted. So ultimately we just wanted different things.

When I saw her, the world around her disappeared. She was the sole item of my eyes. She was the soul item of my eyes. She was divine, and I was nothing.

When I see her, I don't conquer. When I see her, I vanish. I cannot rid myself of her impression. I'd rather lay my eyes on her and never lay them off. For she is the most beautiful I've seen. Words don't do her justice. She is an artist, in her way. Not a muse. If anything, I am hers. I muse around her. The art she's working on is her beautiful soul. If you imagine something vividly, every mirage eventually becomes an oasis.

I don't cry. For I have solid sadness, and tears are fluid. One has to have fluid sadness in order to cry.

You're telling yourself it's fine. You know it's not. Yet to admit it would make it so much sadder. I saw myself in an elevator mirror today. I couldn't believe my eyes. I saw the saddest person I had ever seen. I don't know what prompted me, but probably I wanted to distract myself from the sight, so I smiled a little. And then I saw the ugliest person I had ever seen. I stopped smiling and was almost glad to be sad again.

My sadness is like a fog which fills me from within. The world around me used to be sharp, an object which I could touch and interact with. No more so, because now the world is full of this fog. It's a foggy world, viewed from within, and there is no distinction or separation between it and me. We are one, the world and I, it's a foggy environment, which has blended with my consciousness. It's beautiful. I sit on the terrace, of a coffee place, it's rather cold, so nobody sits there, except for myself. It's good to be dead inside, for you don't mind the cold anymore.

It's easy to be distracted, and much harder to be focussed. That doesn't seem fair. It should be of equal difficulty. Unfortunately, this is not the case. To focus is hard, and to be distracted is simple. That's why it takes a lot of practice to not get distracted. Luckily, focus can be practiced. I practice it all the time. By focussing on irrelevant topics. I consider this a good way of practicing focus. If you can focus on a silly issue, for example the absolute lack of a topic, it will improve your ability to focus altogether. I think that's what people got wrong about focus. They try to focus on a meaningful topic, and fail the attempt. But that's like playing the championship as an amateur. One needs to start on the amateur level. The amateur level is the immature level after all. When focus is immature, we are still easily overwhelmed by distraction. Distraction is not to be ignored or eliminated. Distraction is to be had, and focus should be achieved nonetheless. The way to reach higher focus, is not to eliminate distraction, but to focus despite the distraction. In fact, one should embrace the distraction, for only when focus pierces through it, true focus has been obtained. Focus is that which governs despite the distraction, not in its absence. After all, if the distraction is absent, it's not very hard to be focused.

Focus is that which pierces through the distraction. The true master of focus, is one who can work and think in the midst of all the action. In the eye of the storm, in a packed train, in the lobby of a hotel, wherever. To focus in the absence of distraction is a children's game. Most people aren't even capable of that, and that says a lot about our times. He or she who wants to learn focus, should focus less on the distractions, for they always exist, and more on focus itself. One does that best, not by focussing on an actual topic, let alone a demanding one. One does it by focussing on a non-topic first. You have to focus on a minor topic, and treat it as if it deserved all your attention. Distraction is not overcome by eliminating it, but by no longer being distracted by it. Meaning the distraction continues, but it no longer distracts you. This happens not by dealing with the distraction, but by stopping to deal with it. Distraction is that which takes away your attention, whereas focus is you taking control of your attention and directing it to whatever you want to focus on. This might seem obvious, but most people have a hard time understanding this. They think you need to eliminate the distraction. But that doesn't change the underlying issue, that you're not in control of your attention. You need to be in control of it. But one should direct it first at simple things, for example writing a whole paragraph on controlling one's attention. This is already a controlled effort to direct one's attention. In the process, one forgets about the distraction, which existed, annoyingly, when the paragraph was first begun. The distraction is still there, but it's no longer distracting. One focuses on something, and by that the distraction stops being a distraction. In fact, the amount of distraction one still feels, is simply the lack of focus one manages to exert. One should always think about it this way. When one is distracted, one is not focused enough. One fixes that by focussing. Because contrary to common belief, focus is not first, but last in the chain. One focusses on something, and only gradually, focus is attained.

But what if one doesn't manage to focus. In that case, one should simply pretend to focus. In no time, one will attain some real focus. Focus is not abrupt in nature. It increases in the background. Those who can't focus, need to behave as if they're focussing for a while. It already helps a lot. If you can't focus on reading, read anyway, pretend you're reading line by line. After one page it will go better, after two pages even better. Focus is hard work. It's an action, not a state. One focusses on something, and the focus one obtains in the process determines the success of the endeavor. In our day, focus is often treated like a talent or a trait of sorts. This is lazy, and it's not at all what focus is about. Focus is a skill, not a talent. It's the result of will and decision. One decides to focus, one isn't blessed by it. Distraction is not to be eliminated. The point of focus is to be focussed despite the distractions, or to no longer being distracted by them. A distraction is only a distraction as long as it distracts. When it stops distracting you, it has stopped being a distraction. A baby screaming in a crowded train should not be your focus.

Your focus should be on your thought. If you manage to focus on it, the baby's screams will disappear in the background. It's all down to your way of focussing. He or she who can't focus needs to learn it by exerting focus, every day a little bit.

Focus is not something that you wait for. You don't sit amidst the distractions and wait for God to bless you with a little focus. That implies that focus is in any way passive, like a state or mood you are in. Nothing could be further from the truth. Focus is something you do. It's an action. When you sit amidst the distractions, and you can't focus, remember that.

I like it when things make no sense at first glance, and at second glance neither. I like the nonsensical. One should never defend oneself. One should simply admit defeat. There is no point in fighting. To win at the expense of one's principles is not worth it. No one told us that when we were young. How much of a burden victory really is. One is burdened by success and recognition. Defeat is good, it is kind. It's beautiful to be a defeated stranger.

Failure is a relative thing, and so is success. It's expectation that is fulfilled in success. If one has false expectations, one should hope they never come true. One is always aiming for something, never questioning if it's the right thing.

Who likes people that haven't experienced defeat? They have nothing to teach us. I love defeat. In fact, I've developed an almost strange relationship to it. Some days, I cannot even imagine myself winning again. I never wanted to be a winner. They say I'm strange, but where is the insult.

Those who are different have a desire to live differently. You only have one shot at life, and do you really want to gamble that shot? I do. Where the road leads? Probably nowhere. But I took the gamble, and I'm proud of it. Here I am, with nothing to show for, not a thing, not a dime. It's courage to live in this state. To not back out and go for the easy win.

Defeat is beautiful. It makes the soul humble and the mind receptive. The world has lost its ability to feel defeated.

Everyone is a winner these days. But I'm not and I don't want to be. Nothing humbles you more than feeling defeated.

Life is forgotten so quickly. Sadness never is. I remember everything about it. I remember the sound of the rain, and the taste of it. I remember the air on my skin, and the ground under my feet. I remember the places I went to, a particular person looking at me as if they understood. I remember the morning sky, and the afternoon sky, and when it got dark, and I remember the night. I was defeated, and poor, and people liked me for it. Finally, they thought, not another winner. We can't deal with the winners anymore. And I can't either. Show me a beautiful loser, and I shall be his friend.

To keep her at a certain distance. Not in plain sight, but still visible in memory. To not let her go completely, for she's still important to me. If I lose her fully, I may lose the feeling. My sense of beauty may not stick with me. Or maybe it will.

Broken I was. As if my soul was in pieces. I slept with all windows open in the middle of the winter. This was the degree of my sadness. I didn't even notice. I remember myself walking like I was barely there. I was desperate at the time. But in hindsight it was beautiful.

I always feel like my sadness belongs to me in a much more personal sense. To a point where I almost miss it, when it's gone. Sadness has the most beautiful colors. It puts the world into a beautiful blue. My loving relationship with sadness makes me appreciate it in others. When I see somebody's sadness, I see their heart, and that's never wrong.

Only when sadness disappears by itself has it served its purpose. Sadness cannot be pushed away, for it will return, and more violently so. Sadness needs to be had, this is the rule of sadness. Those who try to escape it, are foolish, for they're only delaying it. Sadness must be felt, intensively and intimately. But a sad soul is capable of anything. No great artist without some sadness in their soul.

I always think of her when I dream. It's when I don't dream, that I don't think of her. This presents me with the choice between two most unfortunate realities. The inner with her, and the outer without her. I don't dream to get back to her. I just do, and she is there. She is not my intention, she is more of a collateral. She lives in my dream.

After her, my dream was broken, but it didn't end. It almost intensified. I now had the dream, but without her, and that was my sadness. I had lost the last thing connecting my state to reality. She had been my anchor. It was sad, yet beautiful. Have you seen the world as if through a mist? That was me. Every girl I saw was her. I was sad and ashamed, so I looked away. I accepted it, and I continued to be sad.

I was walking in dream. And yet it was the world, I was walking in. I remember a waitress. She approached my table. At first she was indifferent. But then she saw me, and her demeanor changed. She saw that I was broken. I felt sorry that she did. She just wanted to do her job. It felt indiscreet somehow. I pulled it together, I even made myself smile. I guess she was probably scared, for it must have looked like the devil's grin. In any case, she saw that, too, and it made her even sorrier. I was so pathetic, trying not to be, which of course made me more pathetic. She returned a couple of times, and every time I felt like she couldn't bear my sight. I thought I was such a burden to her. She shouldn't have had to deal with me. I left abruptly, for I couldn't manage any longer. Outside it was dark. I cried, all the way home. I was in shambles, held together only by a margin.

I shouldn't have seen them as sisters, but I did. They all reminded me of her. It's difficult, when you lose yourself in this sort of ideation. It's hard to stop, especially if you cultivate it. Which, in fairness, is what I did. It's one thing not to indulge in imagination, it's another thing to intensify it. I was good at it, too. Whenever I saw one that reminded me of her, I cultivated the picture. I wouldn't tell myself things like: It's not her, stop with these thoughts. I would do the opposite. I would think: she really does move a lot like her, the way she picked up the fork, that's exactly how she used to do it. And then I would obviously fall head over heels for this beautiful stranger, and become miserable about it. Yet there was something beautiful about it, too. It was still better than losing her even in thought. Perhaps it was a way to make her come back to me for a moment. When I paid attention to this beautiful stranger, and to the way she picked up the fork, she was once again with me. If all of this sounds obsessive, then it must be said, that it was. Yet it was beautiful, too. I never engaged with any of them, and I didn't approach them. But there was some quality in that way of observing which added to my vision. I started to pick up on details which I would have never spotted if they hadn't been connected to her. I would have never paid attention to how a girl picks up a fork. And of course you can say, it's better so, but I'm not sure. Details are beautiful, and to see details is a gift. Art is ensembled by many small details. All of which need to be spotted and sensed. One trains the eye by seeing things and by matching them with sentiment. It's easy to say, you're a fool and a dreamer, stop looking at girls picking up forks. And that's fair enough from a mundane perspective. But from an artistic point of view, it's where it all begins.

I don't know if I manage to describe it well. When I saw her picking up that fork, she was back with me. My soul was lifting, my mind was plunging. She picked up the fork, in a motion that resembled hers very much. She was perfection, at that moment. I had perfection in front of me. The world made sense again. I was engulfed in this impression of hers. In that moment I could have written a novel of a thousand pages about her, and it would have been a fine one. The way I saw with my eyes, my mind was thinking all by itself, my soul was in love, my body was in ecstasy, my thoughts were all hers, my words turned into verse, and sentiment became like the skies above my head, I was living in sentiment now. It was like seeing God, or heaven for the first time. It wasn't about this beautiful stranger, of course I left her alone. It wasn't anything ordinary. People don't understand this. It was about the impression. The impression is the most important thing for the artist. Once spotted, it needs to be captured. And captured it can be, for the loving mind sees eternity.

She was doing everything beautifully. I loved her at once. I saw her nod, and I thought how can you nod so beautifully. She sat down, and she did the most incredible things. She didn't rearrange the table, she arranged herself around it. She made herself fit the situation, how very beautiful. She seemed in thought, and that, too, was beautiful. But then she picked up the fork, and it was in that moment, that I loved her the most. She did this like no other.

But then I left, and of course I did. I know she wasn't real. I'm not even sad about it. Maybe a little. But one has to be careful. It's a dangerous game to indulge in fantasy. It quickly becomes overwhelming. Only the strongest mind can control it. Even then, fantasy is not something you should control. That makes it dull and disposable.

He had called me an autist. I debated him long and hard, so he took it back. He even apologized saying he didn't mean to insult me. This was strange since now for the first time I considered that I had been insulted.

Thought should wander naturally. Only when there is no aim, thought becomes original. It's a delicate procedure to think unintentionally, yet intentionally so. One has to focus on not focussing. It's how they say you fall asleep best, by actively not thinking. Yet this is something that you have to think of, otherwise you'll start thinking again. Which is strange. To think of not thinking, in order not to think. It's like killing yourself with the weapon that was supposed to defend you. With creative thought, I figure it's similar. People are scared of a white canvas, but they shouldn't be. It's beautiful, the options are limitless. It's when you start writing that the depression kicks in. So many words you have to shut the door on. I wonder, could I sell a book of empty white pages and call it my work? It's a choice to not write anything down. Almost an artistic choice. The literal content would still be higher than most books printed these days. I get bored by reading contemporary literature.

If you intentionally think about something, you need to know what it is that you're thinking about. Yet the true power of thought lies in thinking about what you don't yet know. This sort of thinking is unintentional. But you have to do this intentionally. One has to intentionally think unintentionally, without unintentionally thinking intentionally. Intentional thought kills literary production. It should never enter the picture. I dream of a state where I learn about my thoughts only when I see them written down in front of me. It's all beautiful nonsense, of course, but it's beautiful and that's the point. People who speak truth might be right, but they're also boring. It comes down to style. If the style is good, the message is right. Contents should not interfere with style. Words don't matter, everyone knows that. If untrue words sound good, they must be selected. Style is a writer's truth, and only a writer with style is worth reading. Most writers have terrible prose, and even worse style. I hate when people say they're writers, I would never call myself that. I don't want to be mistaken with these online people.

I saw a man today with his son. He was explaining things to him, about how stuff works. We were near a construction site. The little one was in awe with the cranes and that touched my heart. More importantly, I was interested in the lesson. The bigger one seemed to possess inside knowledge about the proceedings of a construction site. I liked the fact that he explained it in plane English. It was easy to follow. This might have been connected to this little recipient of his, or perhaps he himself was rather limited in the head. He explained what the cranes do, and I was surprised to learn that they serve an actual function. I always thought they were like flags, basically indicating: this is a construction site. But apparently they lift and move things around. He talked about the guy in the crane. I wonder how it feels to have this amount of power over a crane. I would definitely abuse my power if I was in that position. He also mentioned that a construction site brings together different people from different cultures, and it's all about teamwork. I thought this motivational bit was unnecessary for I assume the little one barely knew how to spell his own name. But it's true, many people work on a construction site. I was still waiting for some additional information, e.g. why construction people feel the urge to start working at 5 in the morning. Just give it a good night sleep, and get there at 11:30.

There is something so wonderful about a young couple and their first child. The way they are united in the child. How mom is always exhausted and can barely keep afloat. Mother love is incredible. It's one of the most precious things in the world. And dad is so fascinated with this young being they created. For a man, it's almost a spiritual experience. A woman is more selfless by nature. I don't know why, but she is. A man, on the other hand, never loves selflessly, until his child. It's like a new chapter to his soul. I watched a couple with their son in the train. She was napping, while he was walking around with the little one. It was beautiful. I wish the whole world could just be nice, and we could be friendly with each other. There is no need for all this commotion.

As the man was talking about the construction site, the little one listened carefully. The boy was in this undefinable age range. So something between 2 and 8. I could describe, if he was walking yet, but it was a mix of different motion types. He moved by intermittent means. The little one was asking a question, which was barely intelligible, but somehow the big one understood. He explained in adult language which allowed me to understand his answer. It was about cranes. I got hooked on the conversation. There is something so cute about a little toddler boy looking at cranes and trains, and you name it. What is it that they like so much about them? I'm an adult now, and I'm not very interested in cranes. Then again, I've seen them. I'm trying to think of them without the corrupted mind of an adult. And you know what. I kinda get it. They're pretty cool when you think about them. They go aaaaaall the way up and then aaaaaall the way to the side. I'm not sure if it's the geometry that the little ones are fascinated with. By that logic, they should be quite fascinated with gallows and the letter L. But cranes are cool, I agree. Perhaps it's also that a child thinks that cranes are powerful. When you grow up, you realize they barely move, and the guy inside hasn't spoken to his son in three years. As a child you consider them the heroes of our society. They're not, but that's fine. They're still heroes in our childish hearts. I call them the crane people. The crane people are admired by children and ignored by adults. Cranes are cool. And how about trains? They're also cool. They move on rails. I would love to move on rails, e.g. to the supermarket. And how about the ambulance? They got the sirens, and the flashy colors. The uniforms are a negative point, though.

It's all a bit absurd, but what's the point. In a world that values conformity, under the disguise of diversity, it's good to be a little contrarian. The absurd is enjoyable. I don't think its value is properly understood. To be absurd is to be different, and that makes it all worth it.

I talked to a kid today. This is a promising start but it gets better. The little one, who I reckoned was closing in on the two digits age-wise, asked me to buy apple juice he himself had made. I should probably add that he had a little stand next to the road. He didn't approach me in the middle of a train station or so. I was interested to learn about the process, so I asked him how he made the apple juice. He explained it to me, and I'm not proud to admit that it went right over my head. It's a pretty humiliating experience to be intellectually outmatched by a 9 year old. He clearly knew what he was talking about and I had not expected that. I expected a child's answer, not a freaking manual. But I paid the price for my arrogance. I thought, look at this mini person and his apple juice, how cute. And then he dropped an Oppenheimer on me. I didn't believe you could know your stuff so well at this age. I barely understood what he was talking about. I couldn't deal with the humiliation so I needed to double down. I had to ask him something which by no means he could have an answer to. I asked about the vitamins in an apple, and what physiological reaction they induce in the body. He said nothing, and just looked at me clueless. I felt vindicated. I had done to him what he had done to me. I was victorious, and celebrating inside. But then I felt bad, for I thought it was unnecessary that I turned this into a competition. After all, he was just a kid, and it wasn't his fault, that I thought he was going to struggle with basic speech. I think 9 is a strange age. They know things. At 9. It's so weird. I don't even have memory from being 9. And yet, these kids, at 9 years old, already know things. I wonder where is the line of what they know and understand. What could you explain to a 9 year old? Could they understand everything? Or maybe they do, and they just don't tell us. I'm always afraid of children for this reason. You never know their intellectual capacity. In some ways they understand things so well. In other ways, they don't. But which ways are which? I think one day children will take over the world, and we won't even recognize them, because they will appear in the form of adults. Then again, I'm not any better. On the one hand, I'm smart. On the other hand, I'm stupid. It's very hard to say which one I am. So I respect that in a child. I still can't believe he knew the world „apple corer".

I love talking to animals. It's funny, because they realize you're talking to them, but they don't know what you're saying. They are trying, though, and that's the funny part. Also the cute part. They really make an effort to understand you. I love talking to cows for example. They listen so well. I think we should all talk to cows more often. Sometimes all it takes is someone who listens. A cow is always interested in you. Isn't that cute? They are fascinated with you. Animals always try to understand you, which distinguishes them from humans. Human is the animal that doesn't try to understand you. I prefer talking to animals. For they always have my back. I wish they could talk to me, too. I would love to know their animal thoughts. Wittgenstein said that we wouldn't understand a lion even if it spoke our language, and that's an interesting thought. I wonder, though, what parts would we understand? For example, if a cow told me about its day, could I not understand this? I also thought about this: there are clearly differences between different specimen of a species. So in animals there must exist an equivalent to intellectuals and even geniuses. I wonder who is the Isaac Newton in the cow world? And how does it manifest itself. Imagine you're Isaac Newton, but in animal form. It must be a shattering realization. I could discover gravity, if I wasn't a cow. There must be an equivalent. There must be peaks and heights to cow intelligence. I wonder what they are. They don't have abstract thought, do they? But could they intuit it? It must be a different sort of intelligence. How does the intelligence of the smartest cows show? I wonder if they have theories on the sky and the soil. Is there a cow religion in the cow species? Cow intelligence must be limited to the cow world. What is a smart thing in the cow world? Is it all practical intelligence? I don't want to believe that. There must be more. I wonder: do cows have political thinkers. Yes, I think it must be in that direction. The greatest minds of the cow species must be those, who think of the species as a whole. Cow politics, and cow philosophy. What is cow philosophy? Milk is the essence of life. Milk is God. Milk the day. Is there a Shakespeare in the cow world? I think Wittgenstein is right. I can't even imagine any of this, but that doesn't mean cow intelligence isn't a thing. I'm just too human to understand it. Now apply this to humans and the universe, and I think it's a quite profound thought.

It's good to talk to animals, I think it's therapeutic. I'm not sure how the animals feel about it. I'm always sorry for them for they make the conscious effort to understand you. Which is cute, when you know how hopeless the endeavor is. Yet they try their very best. I wonder how human speech sounds and seems from their perspective. It must be like listening to noise from under water. Drowned out noise, and a mouth moving. And you see this through your animal eyes. It must be quite the experience. You look at this human. He's not moving, he's only talking, so you pay attention. If he was to move toward you, you'd react in one way or another. You see them through your animal vision, which is different from ours, but close enough. You see their mouth moving, which corresponds with the drowned out noise. Your animal intelligence is probably good enough to match the perceived sound with the observed motion. You also realize that their speech is directed toward you. I believe the eyes would give it away. The eyes go interspecies, two sets of eyes recognize each other. Even though that's interesting, too, because at what point do they stop doing that? For example, it's very difficult to have intensive eye contact with a spider. There has to be a cutoff somewhere. In any case, a normal mammal, let's say a cow, will have eye contact with you. Back to our animal perspective. You see the human looking at you. You hear their speech, corresponding with the motion of their mouth. You see gestures and mimic, which I'm pretty sure you can't interpret at all. I think you base it mostly on direct physical motion on their end. If motion is abrupt, it's considered a potential threat. If motion is fluent and controlled, you are more at ease. And then you try to understand what they're communicating, but it's impossible. I don't know where any of this is going. But I find it interesting to consider this, how communication appears to an animal. I love talking to animals, it's good for the soul. One should always be kind to animals, because they're so kind to us.

It's important to keep one's grace. Grace has to do with dignity, as well as beauty. Grace is beauty in action, or dignity in motion. When I see it, I stand still, and I watch it with all my soul. A graceful being holds power over us. Grace is to be beautiful without thinking about it. One should always aim to live gracefully. One can be invisible and oblivious, even ignorant. As long as one has grace, we're in the clear. Grace is the ability to live beautifully which is a rare quality. This is not a world that inhabits many graceful beings. To be graceful is not the same as being grateful. In order to be grateful one needs to reflect, and this is what grace never does. Grace is innocent, it comes down to that.

Grace is a quality, almost a trait. It's to be beautiful in the eyes of misery. Or to face misery beautifully. This is grace. To stay beautiful and intact, while the world continues to break you. To stay innocent, despite the odds. Grace is original, it can never be copied. No two graceful beings are ever alike. I cannot describe what grace really is. You see it, and you know it, but you can never quite capture it. You can describe a graceful being. The way she picks up the fork, or how she eats as if ashamed of it. Graceful. She cannot stand herself as human, and who can? To be human makes one ashamed, of the body, and the figure, everything is so ugly about it. Only the graceful understand that. One wants to forget one's human form. One wants to be soul and mind instead.

Grace is rare. The impression requires both the graceful creature and the graceful observer. It's seldom enough in either one. To find two who share grace, only happens every second century. It's the most rarest thing of all. What does it mean to be graceful? It means to not be corrupted by the world, and by experience. Experience makes people ugly, and wise, yes, but ugly, too. To become wise without becoming ugly. To stay beautiful despite the hardships, this is grace.

To be graceful, means to stay in one piece, against the overwhelming odds, to not shatter, to stay afloat, yet to speak never, to not say a word, to be silent, to be pretty. To show what man and woman could be, if only they succeeded at being quieter still. Grace is always quiet, and never loud. Grace belongs to the quiet souls.

Once you see a graceful creature, you may never mention to her that she's graceful. Thought is poison to grace. Grace is immediacy, it exists unconsciously. A graceful creature must be protected from her own thoughts. Her mind must never tamper with her grace. Grace is not part of the physical world. It gives us a taste of the life beyond.

Grace is not for everyone. Grace is for the few. The quiet souls, that never speak. Grace must not be spoiled, by thought or chatter. Those who mention it, in the face of grace, have contributed to its destruction. Grace is protected by protecting the graceful creature. You don't protect her grace, but herself, and along with herself, her beautiful grace. Grace is very rare, especially in men. There are many more graceful women than men in the world. There is so much to learn from women, especially their ability to be graceful.

One cannot imitate grace. Grace manifests itself through behavior and motion, but never is it grace itself that can be captured. Grace remains elusive. A graceful being does things gracefully, that's the best definition one can give. Grace is connected to the mind obeying the soul, and the soul being beautiful.

Only a beautiful soul can be graceful. She can be broken and torn, sad and forlorn, yet none of that stops her from being beautiful. Grace is never reflected, this is the important part. When grace becomes aware of itself, it stops being grace. It becomes profanity or pleasure, nothing worth protecting. Grace must never self-reflect, it needs to be unaware of itself. When grace becomes an idea, the feeling has vanished. Grace is home in the soul, and to bring her into thought, is to take her away, from her natural place. Grace is a soul in the world of bodies, and the graceful are souls among bodies.

A young boy and a young girl, both in possession of a soul, should protect their innocence well. A graceful youth is the most precious thing in the world. It gives us hope for the species. If only man and woman could be more graceful. To live gracefully, one must resist temptation, to become another one of those people, that the world already has too many of. It's important to stay distant from all of this.

Grace cannot be taught. It's the presence of soul, and the submission of the body under the soul. The graceful are those who live with soul and mind first. Or those who have a soul, and decide to listen to it. Grace is to live beautifully. To be silent, even in thought. It comes down to that. To think little, to feel more. Not to feel loudly, but quietly. To feel the beautiful feelings, not the ugly ones.

I want to describe what I find graceful. I saw a girl the other day. She was seated at a table. While in thought, she felt unobserved. On the table there was some chocolate, broken in pieces. I could tell she was debating herself on whether to get a piece. She was one of these girls who didn't allow herself, for some sort of inner restriction. No one would have minded, but she did. She wanted a piece, but she didn't give herself permission. She was unsure, clearly. And then she did this. In a very smooth and beautiful motion, she took the little knife nearby, she cut the piece in half, and she ate half a piece. The whole scene for me was very beautiful. If she had taken the piece, she would have been uninteresting. If she hadn't, one would have told her to get a piece already, it's just a piece of chocolate. But the fact that she resolved the issue like this was beautiful. It was a beautiful compromise between necessity and possibility, desire and discipline. I liked her very much, and I can only imagine how beautiful the things are that she does every day.

There is nothing like a graceful woman. She is to me, a goddess. I would be a servant and a fool for her. If I see her cut the chocolate like this, I will love her forever. That's the beautiful thing about grace. It doesn't age. I have seen incredibly graceful women of all ages. If I see a graceful 60-year old woman, I love her just as much. I don't love her jokingly or anything. I mean no offense. It probably sounds a bit offensive. Not that she would like me back. I'm just a foolish boy. Anyway, how did we get here? My point is. Grace doesn't age, and that's incredible. Man and woman who have grace, will never age. They will always be beautiful. Isn't that great news? I think that's amazing news. I want to whisper this into the ears of all graceful boys and girls out there. You will always be beautiful, if you don't mess with the formula. But what the formula is, I cannot tell you. You just have to be beautiful inside. Well, that was pretty simple. I think it comes down to that. To be beautiful inside. This aspect of beauty is often misunderstood. Beauty grows from within. The other sort of beauty, the one that the world knows about, goes by fast. When it passes, you're only a memory of a beauty that used to be. This is not the good beauty. This is the bad beauty. The good beauty is the one that stems from inside. The one that never fades, and never dies.

The reason why I'm so good at falling in love with women that I don't know is of course that I don't know them. This is both a sad and a healthy realization. I just like the possibility I guess. This is silly of course, so I keep to myself. But I also don't want to let go of the capacity. I think it's beautiful to fall in love all the time. Just a little bit. Or less neurotically put: I find something beautiful and good in every girl I see. I don't pay attention to the bad things. However, they exist in abundance, and reality reveals them rather quickly. But as long as reality doesn't enter the picture, they can be left out. I think it's better to see the good in people, rather than the bad. Does it make me a saint? I don't know. Maybe. Time will tell. I fall in love all the time, but never seriously. With her it was different of course. For once possibility and reality matched. This doesn't happen a lot in my life. Yet I also understand that in the end they didn't really match. I still don't want to lose the capacity to feel this way. The world tells me to, but I don't want to. I love paying attention to the small things. I always discover so much. For example grace. I would have never thought about it, let alone muse on it. Grace would have never entered my life, it had barely entered my vocabulary. Now it's different, it's very real to me. I think of the graceful girl cutting the chocolate, and she makes my world beautiful. I thank her for being so beautiful, yet did I ever say a word? Of course not. Did I go to her? No. I let her be. So I don't hurt anybody with my thoughts.

Habits are formed, they don't form themselves. For example in order to read, one has to read. This seems like a truism, but it isn't. People think they want to read, and that makes them read. The reality is often reversed. People read, and that makes them want to read. Don't wait until you want to read. Reading is work, before it's fun.

People are lazy, they don't read. They try, but they're absent-minded. They have to re-read the same paragraph multiple times. This is connected with the mind being too active. The mind is like a vehicle out of control, it never stays fixated on anything. Yet reading demands that. This is why reading is beautiful. People think it's about information and education. This couldn't be further from the truth. Reading is spiritual. It has more to do with prayer than entertainment. When one reads, the mind, ever so active, stops wandering, and it focuses on a single point in front of its eyes. The single point is the written word and it's a point in motion, for the word changes all the time. One moves through the words, which are connected in a line. These lines are called sentences. One line ends, the next one begins, and one finishes a succession of lines. A succession of lines is called a paragraph, and the multitude of such paragraphs form a chapter. The mind in this process becomes beautifully passive and receptive. It fixates the mind, it brushes off the excitement and the disquiet of everyday life. Reading soothes the mind. The mind is slowed down, and thought is freed from outside disturbances. While reading, one is passive and receptive, toward the contents of the written word. Reading teaches us to be receptive, and to forget about ourselves for a while. This is a skill that the world seems to forget about. The ability to understand the perspective of another, without commenting on it. To be absent from the picture, to immerse into a different mind. People who don't read, often lack this simplest capacity of grasping that there are more minds than their own. One needs to develop the capacity to not know, to be oblivious, for you never know what you may find, when getting rid of your own prejudice. Reading makes the soul beautiful, and that's why it needs to be cultivated.

The capacity to focus, needs to be nurtured. If this capacity is lost, it needs to be regained. To say, I didn't read because I couldn't focus, is a coward's statement. It doesn't even begin to present an excuse. It honestly makes it even worse. To be so weak, that one cannot read, is pathetic, and out of pride alone, one should continue reading in that case.

Reading is not about absorbing information. If it was, you wouldn't have to read, you could just go on the internet or watch a documentary. Reading is something you do for your mind and soul. It belongs in the category of prayer and meditation. Its aim is to reduce distraction as well as expelling external thought from your mind. Reading allows for a healthy forgetting, about your day and your everyday annoyances. It's about focussing the mind, and relaxing the soul. Being receptive, instead of productive. Reading is about rhythm. In a world that breaks the rhythm constantly, like a rollercoaster ride, reading is smooth, consistent motion. The motion itself soothes the mind, and it relaxes the soul like a lullaby. The words of another become the thoughts of your own. Your own thoughts are forgotten for a while. You read a page, or two, and you start to understand the perspective of another. What they say, becomes vivid in you. Here is a person you don't even know, yet you understand them. Reading can turn you into a saint, if you understand the other well enough. Their thoughts and sentiments, their hopes and dreams become yours. You start to live their life, and to see the world through their eyes. Your own mind, in all of this, becomes beautifully passive. That is, it doesn't produce, and instead receives. Like the body needs sleep, to recover, the mind needs to read in order to pause for a while, to discontinue the productivity, which in excess drives the soul into vertigo. The soul herself will decelerate her motion, she will slowly untangle. Vertigo ceases, the mind receives, and reading is the patron of this inner homecoming of yours. You build a true connection. The mind of another has been adopted by you. Reading connects people like nothing else. Remember this beautiful fact: Reading only ever includes two people. The writer and the reader. They are two. The writer writes alone, and he speaks to one alone. He doesn't speak to many. He speaks to one. He speaks to you. And he or she is also one, never many, in the moment of reading. It's two people, who connect through the written word. Isn't it beautiful? That there are people who have been dead for hundreds of years, yet when you read them they're well and alive. No other art form does this better than writing. Music is eternal, and beautiful, but it's less personal. It captures the sentiment, yet the human side disappears behind it. Painting is equally eternal, yet much more indirect, and open to interpretation. Different people feel the same painting in different ways, and the painter probably felt it in a different way altogether. Reading, on the other hand, builds a personal connection, and always between two humans. One human reads what another one wrote. In the moment of reading they're connected. There is, of course, temporal asymmetry, for the writer has written in the past, what the reader is reading in the present. But that makes it almost more poetical, for it shows how we need not to worry about time. Sentiment is eternal, and since it doesn't exist in the physical world, it can not decay in it. It reconciles one with the world's evanescence. Reading makes a person beautiful. To read is an investment in one's soul. Everyone should read, for it teaches us to connect to others. A writer who doesn't read can only be a terrible writer, and nothing convinces me otherwise. The world is full of people who read poorly and write even worse. Don't call yourself a writer. Call yourself a reader instead. I personally cannot imagine a beautiful soul which isn't well-read. Reading almost distinguishes the good people from the annoying. I didn't say bad, I said ‚annoying'. Which is worse, for the bad people are at least interesting.

In the beginning she was always afraid. She was anxious by nature. I told her it's okay that she was. She said, no one has said this to me. I asked her what she meant. She said, people always tell me not to be anxious, no one has told me that it's fine that I am. And she smiled a little, just for me.

It was like her soul was trembling. Everything alarmed her. There was an element of disquiet in her. Initially it was hard to console her. I talked to her, or I let her talk, whatever helped her settle down. She was always trembling, only that she wasn't. She seemed to be trembling inside. As though she was tormented by her own thoughts. She didn't find any relief. In the beginning she barely talked. Our relationship began in the quiet. My presence seemed to calm her down. She wanted me to stay, and so I did. I was silent, but when she wept, I, too, wanted to weep. She moved me somehow. I don't know how she did it, for she didn't do anything. She was broken, yet so innocent. She was of course complicated. She's the most complicated person I've known. The longer I knew her, the less I understood her. At no point did she make any sense to me. But I loved her anyways. Slowly her beautiful, positive sides would show. She would smile, and I remember when she truly smiled for the first time. She had her tender ways, yet she was determined, too. She had the most confusing personality. I thought she was overwhelmed with herself. Over time she spoke more. She was still sad, but her anxiety passed. She was soft spoken, but she had her beautiful ways. I could feel she was recovering her strength. And that's when she slowly overcame her sadness.

If I ever get out of here, I may just leave everything behind. This is my vision. To leave, without taking a single thing. To leave behind my few possessions, even my books and notes. To go away. As a way of securing my freedom. I think this would be powerful. Where'd I go? I don't know. That's not the point. It's not about where you go. It's the simple of choice of going, that gives you freedom. To depart, that's the decision. It's not about arriving somewhere else.

I once got into a heated discussion with a postman. How did you manage that, you may ask, and I'm happy to elaborate. He had a lot of letters, and I asked him, who are all these people and who is sending them letters? I was surprised, when he said that all people get letters. All except me was what he said, or what I heard anyway. I said, in angered fashion, perhaps overreactingly, how dared he say that I had no friends. He looked at me surprised, and stated that he didn't say that. Technically not, but I can read between the lines. I told him that this was an unnecessary insult, which I didn't see coming. He didn't either, which was proof that he was not in control of his tongue anymore. I said, this is uncalled for, I was only curious about people getting letters, I didn't come here for a moral lesson. He said, he wasn't there to deliver one. I said, he was there to deliver letters. He smiled, and so did I. We were friends again. I asked if, now with our rejuvenated friendship, we should open a random letter. I saw he was intrigued. Here was someone who didn't care about their job, and I always get along great with those people. I said: it's just a letter, come on. He said, alright, one letter. I got all cheered up. We picked a letter, and opened it. And boy was it awkward what we found. It was an eviction notice. We looked at each other in despair. This was not the sort of letter that could have „gotten lost". This letter required delivery. After all poor Mr. Trzeptczyzkski deserved to learn about his fate. Now the both of us felt bad. We didn't expect this. In fact, it showed how naive we were. We expected a normal letter, like „Hey Brother, we have arrived on the Philippines, the smells here are something else." We did not expect: „Your tenancy is hereby terminated as of September 30th". So we had navigated ourselves into quite the situation. But then I had a brilliant idea. We simply bought a new letter envelope. Actually we bought 500, since for some reason supermarkets only sell them in superpacks. We repackaged the eviction notice, and put it in the letter box. I guess the postman was fired anyway for being off duty in the middle of the day. Be that as it may, we learned our lesson that day. Before you open random letters, check the sender address, so you don't end up opening eviction notices.

I thought about mathematicians today. To be a brillant mathematician is kind of a waste. It's great of course, but no one will ever know how brilliant you are. It's not about that, I know, but still. In almost every other area the best and most brilliant minds are well known. We know the brilliant entrepreneurs and politicians, artists and scientists, mostly at least. In mathematics, we don't. Name three mathematicians alive today. How many do you have? I'm stuck at zero. Which is crazy, because they're probably among the most gifted people alive today. Yet we have no idea. We don't even understand them. I know they do it for other reasons, the noble reasons, even though their noble reasons aren't prized. Maths is fun, and aesthetically pleasing. I love maths, always have. I think maths is the ultimate discipline. If I had a whole life to waste, I'd waste it on maths. Maths is not a waste of course, it just sort of feels that way. It's the purely abstract, which makes it very cool, and impressive, but also you can't really show off with it. It's not the point, I know, but what is the point? Maths is of course superior. Whoever deals with maths quickly develops the idea of never talking to people again. Numbers after all are the better people. I'd rather live among numbers than people. Maths is truly as beautiful as it gets. The whole elegance of it, is quite incredible. It's superior, no doubt. But then again, you could be the single most brilliant mathematician in the world, and nobody would know. Even if you tell them. You have completely left the realm of the concrete, tangible world which most people inhabit. And these people could never tell that you are brilliant. It's kind of a bitter pill. Everyone admires a great business person, or a scientist, or an artist, for they can communicate in one way or another. Mathematicians can't. They have completely detached from the common man, whose language they don't speak anymore. To a point where in the common language they seem almost dumb. Imagine you're a brilliant maths guy and you can't say a simple sentence to a woman. So imagine you're a brilliant maths guy. It's crazy, when you think about it. How do you flex? Seriously? I mean your higher maths sounds like gibberish to everyone else. It doesn't sound brilliant at all. For normal people it seems like you're part of a species from a different planet. Basically the situation you are in. A human woman, and you, the alien mathematician, lost in the abstract. Who's to blame here? Clearly the mathematician. For he has learned a language that nobody speaks. Yet he's obviously superior. The language of maths is superior to human language. It's a superhuman language. In fact, if we ever meet aliens, we should probably speak math to them, for this is most likely to be understood by them. But this in itself, is a rather abstract thought, and an idiot wouldn't really grasp it. They couldn't understand the idea that an alien would make zero sense of our human languages, but could well understand patterns and relationships in mathematical equations, which, if they were sophisticated, they could match to their own patterns, whatever they may be. But this is an abstract thought, and you couldn't debate this with the common man. For he would not really imagine the aliens as aliens, but as different humans. This is silly, because if we ever meet aliens, they will be so different from us, and probably neither hostile nor friendly, but just weird as hell. Anyway, where was I. The mathematicians are absolutely brilliant, but their brilliance is imprisoned in this superior language of theirs that the common man and woman don't speak. Meanwhile, his or her common language has degraded significantly, to a point where normal social cues have become higher mathematics to him. Basically he's turned the world upside down, turning language into mathematics, and mathematics into language. Now he's all alone with his fellow genius friends, seemingly a fool in the world, and laughed at by even the simplest of minds. Now that's a bitter pill. They would never understand his intelligence. He could tell them the most sophisticated mathematical wisdom, yet it would not resonate with them at all. Zero percent. And this is the point here. Any other discipline connected to maths has concrete applicability. The world admires a great chess player, a genius programmer, a NASA astrophysicist, or a financial analyst. But the pure mathematician, brilliant as he or she is, seems completely idiotic to the common man. And even worse, as his language degrades through his improvement at mathematics, he not only doesn't make sense in this brilliant language of his, he also stops making sense in this unbrilliant language of ours. So we start to think of him as an actual idiot. Now picture this guy in a bar, brilliant as he is, absolutely gifted, a mastermind, yet purely mathematical, approaching the object of his interest. It will be most tragical. For he no longer speaks the language of the other. It's almost like dementia. The more one deals with mathematics, the more one loses one's ability to speak human. Their counterpart will think, look at this fool, barely able to talk. But here is an absolute genius. Let this genius speak what's on his mind, and it's the purest, most brilliant stuff you can imagine, yet it would make the impression even worse. The common man would say: what a loser. And it doesn't stop there. Think about this. The world is full of fakers and fraudsters, who pretend to be brilliant. But since they only pretend, they are oriented toward the common man or woman, whose language they speak a lot better. Meaning they get all the credit for their fake brilliance, without actually being brilliant, because they can talk brilliantly to normal people. And these people are now hailed as geniuses while being absolute tools. Whereas the geniuses are hailed as tools. This is a bitter pill indeed. So what's the takeaway here? The takeaway is, it's better to pretend to be a mathematician than actually being one. In theory it should be possible. You simply need to learn to sound brilliant, without losing touch to the common man. This way you will be hailed as brilliant, plus you don't even have to deal with the real mathematics. It's a win-win. Just make sure to avoid the real mathematicians.

This is tough, though. You are an extraordinary mind, but to the common man or woman, you don't even seem of average intelligence. They look down on you. Dwell on that. The common man or woman, who's never produced a single original thought, looks down on you in contempt. What do you do, warrior? You're gonna hit them with them formulas? You can do nothing about it. Either you respond in your brilliant language, which sounds like mumble jumble to them, and it doesn't help your case. Or, even worse, you fight them with their human language, and let's face it, in this regard you've become pathetic. Which is not a big deal, it almost qualifies someone to not deal with people too often. But you will not be good at their game. So you can either avoid the situation altogether, or, what I suggest, you insult them for their stupidity. This is satisfying, albeit a bit dangerous, so always make sure they're not threatening.

It's brutal when you think about it. These are the finest minds in the world. If we had to choose a representative of the human species, it would probably be a mathematician. To be a master at mathematics, is something one should be proud of. But the world is idiotic, we all know that, so you never get the credit. You can never communicate your brilliance to the people. And bear in mind that this is how it generally works. In our time, we hail not the ones with the brilliant ideas, but the ones who explain those ideas to the masses. These are hailed as heroes. When some dude writes a book about mathematics they call him brilliant and gifted. Yet what has he done for maths? Some guy playing Chopin in front of ten thousand people. Good for him, but what has he done for music? I will never understand interpreters putting their face on a CD cover. Write your own music. But this is how the world works. The greatest business people are not the ones who pioneer. It's the ones who find a way to monetize. The politicians are hailed for saying what everybody thinks, they're not unique figures anymore. The artists of today are just common people with colored hair and eccentric names. Mathematicians bring this into formula. They are ultimately these brillant minds who never get recognition. I wonder why a society cannot praise the right people. This happens by choice. A society chooses its heroes. And the heroes it chooses, reflects the state of society. It's quite pathetic actually. We should hail the mathematicians. We should try to understand them, and if we don't, we should try harder. I have read about Noether's Theorem many times. I still don't understand it, but I continue to try my best. It's a strange world, where not the great minds are hailed, but the mediocre minds that appear as great minds to the mediocre minds. It's called democracy, I guess. I for once think that the mathematicians are the true heroes of our society. We should all aim to be more like them. I think there are few things more pathetic than the pride people take in being bad at maths. That just means one is bad at thinking. I admire the mathematicians. Of course I don't understand them either, and if I saw one I'd probably mistake him for a fool. On that note, I also suffer from this phenomenon, because everything I write is brilliant, but one has to be brilliant in order to understand that. To the unbrilliant people, it must seem like a lot of nonsense, but that is because it's read by an unbrilliant person. Now of course I would also say this if I was an unbrilliant person only claiming to be brilliant. So it comes down to the reader to assess if this is unbrilliant writing pretending to be brilliant or brilliant writing misunderstood as unbrilliant. Most people are unbrilliant, meaning their unbrilliant judgement will mistake the unbrilliant for brilliant, while calling the brilliant unbrilliant. Which leads to a cultural shift, in which society develops a tendency to produce unbrilliant work, which then reproduces and multiplies. In the meantime, the brilliant work silently slips and sleeps away, and it stops being produced. Then again, this is what an unbrilliant person would say, who's only claiming to be brilliant. Once again, only judgement will tell if this is brilliant work mistaken as unbrilliant, or unbrilliant work claiming to be brilliant. It's an eternal loop. Bottom line is this, you better call my work brilliant, otherwise I will call you dumb. How did we get here?

The simple minded have no relationship to the abstract, so they end up dismissing it. Bear in mind that Schelling, who was unbearably shallow and empty in philosophical contents, called Spinoza „too abstract". This is what happens when you let the fools judge the geniuses. You get foolish judgement.

I always felt like making it all about money is failing at life on a different level. What's the point? You can't bring it with you to the next life. Even though technically we don't know that. Maybe there is a point system of sorts. And your wealth determines where you're seated in heaven. If that's the case, heaven would be the reward, and the poor would go to hell. Which means that money is good. I love money. My new goal is to make a lot of money to secure a good place in heaven.

One should remain individual, by all means. To seek comfort in the many, is a sign of cowardice. One must shoulder individuality, and some days one must carry it like a weight. It's not easy to be an individual, but it's necessary. The pressures of society are intense, and constant. It's easy to get overwhelmed. One must fight the urge to become generic.

There is a time to reflect. The time of anxiety isn't one of them. The mind is anxious, because the soul is in vertigo. She spins around her own axis at high speed. Since the soul is not physical, she cannot be affected physically. Vertigo is a motion, which ends by itself, but only after some time. It can be compared to being drunk. Picture this, you are drunk, and you feel sick about it. You cannot stop being drunk now. You brought it upon yourself, only time and rest will make it pass. If you continue drinking, it will get worse. If you stop, it will still be bad for a while. Now apply this to your anxiety. Anxiety is brought upon you by yourself, essentially by over-exposing your soul to the world. Like a baby that starts crying because its senses are over-stimulated, the soul starts spinning when you keep her in motion all the time. The soul's motion is an angular momentum, everybody knows that, and since angular momentum is conserved, it doesn't just stop. This motion can not be impacted, only the friction of time will slow it down. Anxiety is a synonym for the soul's vertigo, and it cannot be influenced directly. One must wait until the soul calms down again. As you stop thinking, you still have to suffer the terrible vertigo for a while. One way to stop thinking is to do something, anything, in order to distract the mind. Or in order to distract yourself from your mind, that's the better way of putting it. If you continue thinking, your anxiety will increase, which will spur the soul's vertigo even further. Don't let that scare you, for I know what you're thinking. Once you panic, you can't stop reflecting, and now I'm telling you this makes it worse? No, I'm not. We must distinguish. You will think your anxiety one way or another, this is unavoidable when anxiety has broken out. It's like being drunk, at this moment it's a fact, there is no denying this fact, and no fixing it in the moment. But the question is will you keep thinking and make it worse, or will you allow time to discontinue the soul's vertigo.

We must be individuals, it's very important. Life is to be understood as time. Even if you're religious, you will agree with this. You only have one life means you only have one time. What do you want to do with your time? Nothing is remembered, remember that. It's good to try hard and fail harder, for to try means one has not settled like the others. One should always attempt fate. Not all the brave are fortunate. Not all the fortunate are brave. But many are. By being brave one increases the chances of being fortunate. By being hesitant one diminishes them. Being brave is not about reaching or not reaching the goal. It's about investing in yourself. Once you close in on the goal, you're not even interested in reaching it anymore. For you have found on your path, different things, and different people. The path should not be walked to finish it, but to find the branches and junctions along the way. You change direction, again and again. You develop the capacity to navigate. This is what life comes down to. Deciding, not for the sake of decision, but for the sake of deciding. Learning to think on one's feet.

She was beautiful when she said my name. It was my favorite word out of her mouth. She spoke soft, yet distinct. It always felt like she was whispering into my ear. Her voice was never shaking, and never indecisive. She was one of these beautiful silent people. I feel like I remember every single sentence she ever said to me. Her intonation, and her choice of words. I remember how she looked at me, while speaking, with her beautiful daze, so eerily focused on me, yet somehow distant. When she said a thing, she silenced herself, and waited for me to respond. I looked at her, like a right fool, so very much in love. She was silent, for a while, but then she spoke again. When she did, I held my breath. I could have listened to her forever. I would have asked her to read me a lullaby at night, if it hadn't been so silly. I cannot describe how beautiful her voice sounded to my ear. She never hesitated when she spoke. It was before she spoke that she hesitated. She said everything beautifully, then stopped and looked at me in anticipation. I almost had to remind myself to speak. Sometimes she laughed at little, for at times I really did forget to speak. She spoke little, I spoke less. It gave us beautiful intimacy. We never spoke in vain. We were protective over our speech, as if it was our last provisions.

She was anxious, and always so. She didn't speak, and she didn't want to go out. It may be hard to believe from the outside, but I was the normal one. I went to her as though she was on her dying bed. She was sad, and wanted me to take care of her. I did, and she got better. She spoke more, and she smiled again. She was still complicated, she was never not. In fact, she was almost more complicated when she got better. We went out sometimes, and she even spoke to people in public. She was beautiful during that time. Mostly her ways and manners. She was soft spoken, and gentle, and always discreet. People noticed her never, until they did. But when they did, they loved her instantly. I let her speak when she wanted to, and when she didn't, I would speak for her. I would always allow her to decide for the both of us. During these months, we were near perfect. Not a word of conflict was exchanged. She was passive, and I was cautious. We had a beautiful way of making it work. She wasn't self-centered. After she improved, she was devoted to me. She said I had saved her. I said it's not true, she only needed time. She said, no, it was you. I wonder if she forgot this later on. In any case, it was her. She got better by herself. I was present, and perhaps that helped a little. She overcame her anxiety. She was no longer afraid of everything. She felt she could rely on herself. Somewhere along the way she had lost that feeling. I'm sure she had always been a little broken. I'm saying I am sure for she never shared anything. As little as I share, she shared even less. Sometimes she did. But it would make her sad and agitated, so I had her stop. Then we went back to being quiet. She was beautiful, and I asked her if I could do anything for her. She said No, but she smiled a little. We went back to normal, and normal requires a loose definition of what we had. We were not normal, yet happy somehow. I know there was trauma in her life. People don't just become like this. There are reasons, but she didn't share them. Sometimes she tried, and all times she failed. She couldn't touch on these things. I didn't want to make it difficult for her so I let it go. I didn't need to know, if she didn't want to share. I wanted her to be happy. With or without secrecy. It's beautiful to know more than one says. It's also beautiful to love without having to say it all the time. Love should be essentially mute. When love is verbalized, some of it gets lost in the words. It's courage to keep one's love protected by not mentioning it too often. Her and I, we were alike in this way. If anything, our love was too intensive. Perhaps it was that which broke it. One should love more slowly. A bond must forge over time. If a bond is immediately there, chances are it may snap in an instant. The strongest bonds are slowly formed. We, on the other hand, never formed slowly. She was dependent on me from the start. And I would have given my life for her, after a day or two. It was not healthy, I see that now, and even then I was aware of it. I didn't mind, nor would I ever have. She did, and I think it may have overwhelmed her in the end. Or I don't know what to think, her behavior made little sense to me. I accept the fact that I simply didn't understand her.

Prayer is the condition, as part of which we discontinue mental production, and replace it with mental reception. It can be compared to other spiritual activities, for example meditation, reading, musing, observing. Ultimately it comes down to receiving, as opposed to producing. This is a lesson which cannot be overstated, in a time that has a pathological relationship to the spirit. This time always produces, never receives, and through that has become spiritually restless.

Prayer is not what the atheists say, believing in a big man with a white beard and hoping he'll fix our problems. This is a very superficial understanding of faith. Prayer is much more. A means of re-focussing the mind on what's essential, and a way to make the mind find the soul. Because the mind easily loses sight of the soul, and it's important that the connection is intact. Faith and prayer restore it. The mind, in constant production, loses its ability to receive, for even in quiet moments it cannot stop producing thought. The mind becomes a machine out of control, it's running late at night, when the factory should be shut down. But this is the modern mind, constantly running and producing. Mental production is like a shop that should be open only during weekdays, and is now open 24/7. We are not supposed to live like this. Mental production and mental reception need to balance each other. They don't, in our times.

My thoughts became dreams when she was involved. It was as though I wasn't thinking straight. I looked at her, and I was stunned. I never started dreaming. I only had to think of her. And this is how my dream will end. By slowly forgetting about her. The dream will fade and so will her memory. I only see the past now. Yet as vivid as the present. She'll leave me one more time. This time it will be in my thoughts.

She has taught me three things fundamentally. Sadness, beauty, and love. I loved before, but always unhappily. Only with her I realized what love could be. When it substantiates, when it becomes mutual. I was a master at one-sided love. Even today, it remains my major skill. So she taught me that. Secondly, sadness. I knew sadness, but it was, dare I say, a rather masculine sadness. The ugly sadness, I want to call it. A woman's sadness is a lot more beautiful, and she taught me that. She didn't make me a man, she made me a woman. And to any man mocking me, saying „what a wuss", I will say this: How dare you talk to a woman like this?! In any case, she showed me the other side. The woman's side of sadness, and it's incredible. What I mean by that is a man's sadness and a woman's sadness are distinct in multiple ways. A man's sadness has ugly adjectives. It's typically: bitter, grumpy, self-pitying, wallowing, grave, as in heavy, not at all poetical, and ugly, because ugly is also an ugly adjective. A woman's sadness, on the other hand, has beautiful adjectives. It's melodic, melancholic, tender, quiet, light, it's beautifully light, despite being deep, it's never heavy, it's not self-pitying, that's one of the things I admire about women, a woman doesn't pity herself, a woman *blames* herself, how beautiful, while a man blames everybody else, how ugly. What else? A woman's sadness is not verbal, if it is, it becomes a drain, it stops being beautiful, more often than not, it's quiet, reflective, introspective, it's not angry, or aggressive, there's nothing threatening about it. A woman's sadness is different from a man's sadness. And I learned that from her, how beautiful it is to have a woman's sadness. To not fight the world, but to accept it. To be passive in the eyes of it. I know, I know, it's not all good, and many women suffer from the fact that they cannot be more active and self-destined about it, I understand that, but in terms of beauty it's incredible, in men as well as in women. I've seen a few boys and men who are like this, and I love them equally. I want to make this clear, that it is the type of sadness I find beautiful, not the gender. There are boys who have this sort of sadness, and I love them very much. They become my brothers instantly, and it's on them I think as much as I think about a sad girl. Now for those who were to oppose this point, saying you're just describing the difference between introverted sadness and extroverted sadness, that proves my point. Yes, I am. The world belongs to the loud men, not the quieter women, and that's a pity. It's a pity, too, that we seem to tell women, either subconsciously or even actively, that they need to become more like men to become equally respected. Which is stupid for a number of reasons. First of all, men are annoying, let's face it, and the last thing we need is more of them. We should have men learn from women, not the other way around. Second, it serves as a strange incentive to women, telling them they should become loud, aggressive, and dominant like men. That's not what they should become. It's the completely wrong message. Women are perfectly fine, the bigger problem is with men. It should be men becoming more like women. But the result of this is, that the most successful women often seem to be the ones equally loud, dominant and vulgar as men. That's annoying. These women are as annoying as men, so once again no discrimination. They're all annoying. Third, the lesson is not that women should behave like men, the lesson is that they should behave as they please and they should be allowed to. Men who behave vulgarly, should not present the norm, and if they do, this norm needs to be opposed. It's troubling, that this is our way of dealing with gender equality, to tell women to become like men to prove their worth. I don't understand, why we keep saying women can do anything that men can do. This is not in question. Only idiots question that. Be that as it may, the last thing we need is more vulgar people who take it all out on the world. We need more grace, and beauty. We escalated this topic into a discussion of equality, that was not the point. I wanted to describe the different sadnesses. A stereotypical man in sadness is ugly, not pretty. He blames the world, he doesn't speak, he becomes bitter, he's not to be helped, he doesn't talk, and when he does, he just depresses us all into his depression as if it was the influenza, and all in all, it's just not a pretty sight. On the other hand, a stereotypical woman in sadness is pretty, not ugly. She blames herself, not the world, she doesn't speak up, yet she reflects a lot, how beautiful, sometimes she looks up and wants to say something, but she doesn't, she should of course speak, but her speech would kind of take away from her grace, so there is some beauty in her not speaking up. She doesn't think that the world is wrong, like man does, she thinks herself is wrong, and that's very touching, one wants to tell her: no, you're alright, it's just not a world for us. But she is touching in her sadness, as opposed to man, this silly dumb creature can only help himself, whereas woman allows help from outside, not because she's weak, but because she actually connects with people, she builds rapport, while she speaks and listens. When you are sad, you don't want to talk to a man, unless he has a woman's qualities of being a person that understands. Most men are too focused on themselves, and they don't help you. A woman does. She forgets about herself, that's her advantage over man, for she has this capacity that man simply doesn't have: she is selfless. Why that is? Perhaps sociological, or even biological, for she gives life, and to give life, one must be selfless, she must forget her own self, to create another. Man doesn't do this, he fails at the simple task. He is inherently selfish, he doesn't even mean to be. I'm sad about it, because man could be as beautiful as woman, if he managed to be selfless.

A woman's sadness can also be loud and dramatic. Then, of course, it's very ugly, arguably even uglier than a regular man's sadness. See, I'm not a wuss. I'm an aesthete. This may seem like the same thing for you, but it isn't. An aesthete likes the beautiful, and this just happens to be more often connected to women than men. But not always. Picture a woman crying loudly, making bitter accusations, screaming, and moaning. It doesn't get much uglier than that. It really hurts my soul just thinking of it. All is lost with a woman like this. On the other hand, picture a man, almost a boy still, and he's silently accepting his sadness, while making a good-hearted effort to be better again, trying his luck at a smile, but not convincing anyone, hanging his head again, for his sadness doesn't leave, yet what can he do? Give me this boy, and I shall be his brother. I shall love him like family, and give him all my wisdom, and talk to him, and find him one of those beautifully sad girls, who exist in abundance. See. I don't discriminate, in this particular case, I love the man more than the woman. Yet, this is the exception. More often than not, a woman is beautifully sad, and a man is ugly.

It's the type of sadness that I like. Whether that's strange? That's an „affirm". Does the strange become a little less strange when you acknowledge it? I would say so. The quiet sadness is a lot more beautiful. Sadness must be felt, and reflected on, yet never be shared publicly. I believe in the importance of that. You find this absurd? Well, you're not a dreamer then. A dreamer cherishes his sadness. He protects it in fact, for sadness is an inner condition which is second to none. No other emotion, perhaps love, is more stimulant, no other better at producing art. In fact, if I could choose two emotions to always carry with me, it would be sadness and love. She gave me both, and I'm thankful for that.

The feeling of sadness adds a beautiful touch, which can not be simulated, or imitated, without the sentiment present. One needs to be sad, to write sad, there is no way around it. But he or she who is sad, can become a saint, for nothing connects people stronger than their sadness. In love, we might be connected, but mostly through our shared feeling. With sadness it's different. There it feels like our souls leave our bodies, they approach each other, and they fuse into a shared soul. Sadness transcends the individual.

Sadness has a bad reputation in our day. Everyone runs from it. We should run toward it instead. You know the feeling, when someone shares a sad story. Does it not warm you from within? Not because of their misery, but because it loosens you up. How close you are now to calling this one your brother or sister. You tell them, it'll be fine, and they smile. This is beautiful. And not sad at all. Sad times sad equals beautiful. It works like that. You hear someone tell their sad tale, and is it not the most beautiful thing you've heard. Do you not feel like telling them about your own sadness, returning the favor. And this is not egoistical anymore. We listen differently, when sadness is involved. We feel a strange bliss in that moment. It's beautiful to see another be not another anymore, but an extension of self. At that moment one forgets all the redundant elements of everyday life.

You feel no longer competing with the other. This is one of the worst afflictions of modern man, that we constantly compete. Capitalism has destroyed our souls, we all know that. But in sadness, we become human again. One is only truly strong, when one is strong despite the sadness. Strength without sadness is fickle and easily brought down. Only when sadness is present, strength becomes spiritual.

Sadness must be experienced. Those who have never been sad are limited in spiritual terms. They can only give fortune cookie advice. The sad soul, on the other hand, is a spiritual guide, quite irresistible. One has to remember that sadness is not the worst thing. Numbness is. And numbness is the incapacity to be sad. That's why depression is numbness rather than sadness. The depressed are those, who have lost the capacity to be sad. When sadness becomes so solid, that it's no longer experienced as such, depression sets in.

Depression is often called sadness, and this is simply not true. Depression is a particular evolution of sadness, one in which sadness is replaced by numbness. Sadness is no longer so experienced. The amount of „no longer so experienced", is the amount of depression blending into sadness. Depression replaces sadness, it's not the same thing at all. Numbness means not being sad, but not because one isn't sad, but because one doesn't experience sadness anymore. Sadness, objectively present, becomes subjectively absent. One doesn't even feel sad anymore. One feels numb. Depression is the inability to experience one's sadness as sadness. Which shows that sadness is present, but no longer experienced as such. „Experienced" is the word, not „reflected", for this is not a mental or intellectual process, but a sentimental or emotional one. One no longer feels the sadness, despite its presence and dominance. It's almost like being blind-sided by something, like a whiteout in the glaring snow. It's the inability to experience sentiment emotionally. One only somewhat experiences it mentally, which creates this strange out-of-body experience of depression. One „thinks" one's emotion, instead of „feeling" it. Very confusing, and disconcerting, yet even this disconcertment is not felt anymore.

The depressed are not sad people to be cheered up. This is a common misconception. In fact, it's almost the opposite. The depressed are numb people that need to be made sad. This seems paradoxical at first, because we consider the depressed to be sad already. But they're not. They are numb. They should be made sad, yet in controlled conditions and under special care. This cannot be done light-heartedly, and they should not be alone. But sadness is like a fever that needs to break out or else it will never pass. When it's there, we need to bleed it out, not by pushing it away, but by pushing into it, by diving head first into sadness. When sadness, for too long, is repressed, it becomes numbness, and accordingly depression. Therefore depression is often a sadness too long suppressed. The first step of fixing it, is to no longer suppress the sadness, to allow it back in. When one suppresses sadness for long enough, it becomes a hidden sadness, which is the most dangerous kind. A hidden sadness is not recognized as such, and therefore cannot be cured. Depression is, on the most fundamental level, suppressed sadness. Sadness is no longer experienced as sadness. It is still reflected as sadness, meaning mentally one is well aware of it. But emotionally one no longer experiences it as sadness. The feeling itself, that is the „feeling sad" is suppressed and replaced by the numbness of not feeling anything at all. This numbness is depression. One could say depression plus sadness equals the emotional state, and one diminishes depression by increasing one's sadness. Not by decreasing it, for this is further suppression, and it keeps the depression not just alive, it makes it stronger actually. It's the process of suppressing sadness which becomes the vivid quality of depression, and it's the suppression, not the sadness that needs to be fought.

It's important to make this distinction, and explain the dichotomy of feeling and thinking in depression. The sadness is understood by the mind, so a depressed mind is still a sad mind. However, the feeling has ceased to be sadness, it's replaced by numbness, which makes it an odd condition. One *thinks* a sadness, that one doesn't feel anymore. We advice the depressed to no longer think of their sadness, but that's the wrong path. Instead they must not just think the sadness, they must regain the ability to feel it. In simple terms, a depressed person is one who's no longer able to cry and needs to re-learn it. When the depressed start to cry, they're well on their way, and while they may think of it as a new low, it's actually a new high. „It gets worse before it gets better" is almost a natural law when it comes to depression. When the depressed become utterly sad, they're finally suppressing the suppression, and they become human again.

To feel sad is healthy, and there is no problem with it. To instead feel this: ‚I don't know, every day is sort of the same, but it is what it is' — this is the real enemy. The goal is to create stable conditions, in which we may rediscover the feeling of sadness, that is clearly present. Of course the depressed are sad, but in their condition they no longer experience it as sadness, rather as a grey dull mix of nothingness. This is numbness, and the mind is not to blame for this. Don't let anyone tell you, that your mind makes your depression, for depression is an affliction of the soul, not the mind. This is one of the greatest misconceptions about depression. People think it's their thoughts and reflections that make their depression. But this is just you commenting on a condition, which exists in your soul. Depression is the numbness of soul, it's not the numbness of mind. The mind is not numb, it just improvises over the numbness within.

Depression is not a mental state. The only people who say that are people who have never experienced it. The reason why it's not associated as an emotional state is because of its particular phenomenology. Depression is the feeling of not feeling, which is why it's easily mistaken as „not a feeling". But it is a feeling, it is the inability to feel, or the emotional numbness. It takes place in the soul, and all the skeptics not liking the word soul, call it the brain then, or the body, even though this is very much open for debate. In any case, it's not what we commonly associate with the mind, that is with thinking and thought. It's an affliction of emotion, feeling, experiencing. And therefore it's silly to approach it, as if one simply has to think differently, in order for depression to resolve itself. Thinking doesn't affect the depression, the depression is there anyway. That's why it always returns. This is one of the worst aspects of depression. That every day you experience a hundred setbacks. Depression always sets you back to the depressed state immediately. Any happiness lasts only for as long as it does. As soon as it's over you're back to the depressed state. Now to think to yourself, I myself am producing this state with my thoughts, puts extra pressure on you, and wrong pressure, too. For whatever the world says, they're wrong, depression is a real condition. Like cancer in your body, depression in your soul. It's not in your thought process, or in your way of thinking, it is a thing, within you, but spiritually, emotionally. You're thinking about this thing, yet your thinking doesn't cause it, and it doesn't cure it

You cannot cure the emotional intellectually. You need to cure it emotionally. Which means you cannot think yourself through a depression. That's why so many people remain in it forever. They assume that by thinking, and understanding it, it can be cured. Don't get me wrong, this can help, but only indirectly, as it basically helps the individual to allow the feeling to resurface. By conceiving it, one creates an inner safe space for the soul, which is then allowed to be sad again, experiencing the feeling which the mind suppressed. So the mental aspect facilitates the cure, but the real cure takes place when the soul can breathe again, as its sadness is no longer suppressed by the mind. Sadness needs to blossom like a flower, else you'll never overcome your depression. As long as sadness is suppressed, depression persists.

In depression, one may think and reflect and talk and understand, that is the mind may play its part in it. But the most important thing that the mind has to do is stand back. To allow the depression. It seems counterintuitive, but it's crucial. For this is the early phase of what will later on be the mind allowing the soul to be sad. Yet the sadness has been suppressed by the mind, and this is the traumatic process. On the one hand, the mind needs to learn to no longer suppress the soul. On the other hand, the soul needs to shake off its numbness, and this takes time. The soul will not instantly become sad again, it will remain numb, and the mind needs to support that. It will be a time where the soul is still numb, and the mind has to sustain the vacuum. It's a difficult stage of depression, one which most people try to escape from. But the escape from the void is the reason why the condition persists. The soul remains numb and suppressed, by a mind that constantly escapes the feeling. The mind should never turn its back on the depression, instead face it and embrace it. Depression must be felt, it really truly must be felt, or it cannot be resolved. It's impossible to get away from it, depression always catches up. And it's a cumulative force, this has to be said, so it gets worse, the longer one evades it. When depression hits, the mind is not to deny it, or to rationalize it, or to belittle it, that is to fight back. When depression hits, the mind must capitulate to it. Depression is not like anxiety. Anxiety is an emotion in which the shaky, volatile elements need to be controlled, by calm and collected reason. In depression it's different, one cannot fight depression like this, for this supports the suppression of sadness, and therefore increases depression. Depression is the indication that a sadness present is no longer experienced as such. The cure for it, is to experience it again.

Depression is sadness objectively, but numbness subjectively. The mind only plays the role of a reporter. It's silly to think that the mind can cure the depression, for depression is an affliction of the soul. However, the soul, like the body, is good at curing itself. That's the good news. The reason why the soul so often doesn't manage to, is because the mind doesn't allow it. Our soul is suffocated by our mind. This is unfortunately a modern condition, and it's cured by teaching the mind to withhold. The soul, in depression, must be allowed to be depressed, and the mind must facilitate this process. Eventually, the depression will convert into sadness again, but this only happens after a while. One must ease into one's depression, and allow it to unfold. Again, this may seem counterintuitive, and probably scary, when experienced, but depression cannot be overcome without being felt. The feeling of depression is almost the entire path of it.

You cannot think yourself through a depression. You must feel yourself through it. A depression must be felt, otherwise it cannot be cured. For this is just a way of saying: The soul must be felt, or she cannot be cured. Depression is the numbness of the soul, and when she feels numb, so do you. It's like the soul freezing into ice. But the soul, as you know, is a liquid, and it must flow and move within you. When the soul freezes, it feels itself no more, and the resulting numbness is depression. The soul will only heal, once the ice thaws. The ice, in this analogy, is your depression. Like ice thaws, the soul must feel again. You must feel. By feeling the depression you feel your frozen soul. Over time, the soul will thaw, and depression will liquidize into sadness. The numbness gets enriched by sadness, and you may feel even worse. But don't withhold, and don't refrain, for this is the natural course out of a depression. This path leads through a valley. But a valley is not an abyss, it only appears to you so, because you don't see the ground. The ground is hidden in the future, and you haven't reached it yet. You're still descending. Not forever, only for now. Your task is to go down this valley. You don't see what's ahead of you, you only see it's going down. You don't see it actually, you feel it. See. You already feel a depression that you used to suppress. This is good, it's the slow path of recovery. Stick to the path, and trust that there is a plateau. The plateau is waiting for you, further below. You need to venture down, and trust you'll be alright. A valley goes down before it goes up. Feelings await at the nadir. You go toward it, to feel it, to immerse in it. When depression is not felt, it's never resolved, and it lives on within you. Don't run away, for you'll lead a live on the run. Instead halt, and let it catch up to you. Put your faith in the hands of fate, or God, whatever gives you strength. Allow it, for depression needs to be allowed. When the mind doesn't allow the depression, it depresses the soul further.

It may seem like an abyss, but it's a valley. There is a plateau. However, it might be deeper down than you think. It's scary to allow sadness to unfold, especially when you're used to suppressing it. But this is the cause for your predicament, suppression of sadness, and unfortunately the only remedy is to undo this process. One must un-suppress the sadness. Depression is like the final message sent by the soul to the mind, like a dying whisper. The soul is whispering: I've been sad for so long, I will freeze now, I will return, if and when you return to me. The mind must return to the soul, but the soul is in the valley. She waits, down there, at the bottom, and you must come to rescue her. The soul is frozen, it's her way of protesting the life you lead. She wants it no more, she's tired of it. The mind has starved the soul for too long, the soul has lost her nourishment. Like a car running out of gas, the soul is stopping, just like that.

What the clinics do, doesn't fix your depression. It just sends it back into oblivion. Medication may help for the moment, but it doesn't cure you. You must tackle the root of the problem. Depression should not be fought by suppressing it. Instead, one should attend to it. Depression is the numb state of the soul, and the soul has become numb, because she wasn't participating in this life of yours. When the mind detaches from the soul, when it flies to a different planet and leads a different live there, then the soul starves back home, and she will eventually shut down. But you are your soul as much as your mind. Don't divide yourself into two. Depression is the signal, that one's soul has shut down. That's why there is no feeling anymore. The soul has lost its ability to feel. This is fixed by feeling again. Which is easier said than done. The way to do this is to feel one's depression. To feel it, to give it space, despite its heavy weight. For this state is not meant to last forever. It only does that, if you keep suppressing it. Depression never leaves by itself, it's the one thing depression never does. Depression is supposed to be a temporary state. It's you who turns it into a permanent state. By keeping it alive, and how? By fighting it. You're not supposed to fight your depression. Depression is not your enemy. Depression is your soul, frozen to ice. He or she who fights their depression, fights their own soul. This is absolute confusion, and total chaos. Your mind must never fight your soul. Your mind must love your soul. Your mind must see your soul. Your mind must feel your soul. And now replace „soul“ with „depression“. You must enter depression, not push it away. Depression is your friend, think of it this way.

Depression doesn't go away by itself. Because depression is an affliction of your soul, and your soul never goes away. In depression she doesn't feel anymore. Of course you can get used to the feeling of not feeling anymore. But this is the path of nihilism and it silently destroys the world today. Depression is not a sickness of the body. Yes, I know what the world says, and the medics, and the scientists, so let them have the truth. For we speak spiritually and personally. And in this sense, depression is an affliction of the soul. Whatever or wherever it may be, and let it be the body, it's still is a sickness of the soul. And therefore, one must treat the soul in this case. Not the mind. It's not the same thing. The mind is almost the medic in it, the patient is the soul. Yet you are both, and now you see why it's important to attend to yourself. Your soul is sick. You alone can help her heal, for you alone have access to her. Let the medics be your guides, if medicine is needed, so be it, but the sustaining, lasting recovery from depression happens with you alone. This is easier said than done, for when you're in depression, you're at your lowest. Don't be wise, in moments like this. In those moments, just suffer through it. It's a big part of depression.

Will we anger the world with this? Perhaps a little bit. But depression is your soul frozen, and often the result of a sadness long suppressed. Your sadness has collapsed in on itself, your soul began to froze. This was the emerging feeling of depression, which, as we've stated before, is the feeling of „not feeling". Meaning, paradoxically, it's a feeling which is characterized by not feeling anything. Or it's the felt absence of feeling. This is another way of putting it. The lack of motion and reaction of the soul toward anything. It's almost like one's body moved but one's soul no more. It's like having a rigid, stiff core, which no longer interacts with the world. Most shockingly not even with yourself. It's like touching a dead body. Your soul doesn't respond to your mind anymore. This is why you feel alien. You feel like one part of you is dead and the other part looks at it constantly. This is your mind looking at your frozen soul. It's quite close to what's actually happening. Your soul is a little dead, and your mind looks at it in disbelief. But this is only supposed to be a temporary state, and it can be fixed. You must know this, that it definitely can be fixed. It's fixed, in the abstract, by making this dead soul of yours move again. Easier said than done, but still, that's the process. Remember, your soul is not dead, she just plays dead. It's that stiff, frozen core of yours. And depression, as we've said, is the feeling of not feeling. What feels like it's dead, is not really dead. The dead feeling is your soul feeling dead. But when your soul's feeling dead, your mind's feeling debt, and rightfully so, for it has abandoned her. This is why depression occurred in the first place. You must feel the deadness, the numbness of your soul. But it is hard, very hard, for you will feel devastating nothingness. Accompanied by a distraught mind, which no longer finds purpose or joy in anything. It's a tough state to be in, and especially to willingly stay in. The harder part is not to enter the depression, but to persist in it. One must feel the frozen soul again, or one must feel as a frozen soul. This frozen soul is you, make no mistake. We're talking very picturesque here, yet it is you that we're discussing. You are feeling frozen, and you think about that, yet you cannot do anything about it. And how is this fixed. In the abstract, it is fixed by feeling frozen. It's beautifully simple, yet horribly hard. However, it comes down to that. To overcome depression, one must feel one's depression. One doesn't fight it, it's a flawed concept of handling depression. You cannot fight it, for you're fighting yourself in it. He or she fighting their own soul, will never be happy, they will always be depressed. With or without medication. Depression is the result of segregation, or separation. The mind has separated from the soul. The soul has needs and requirements which have not been met. The mind has abandoned the soul, and you feel the separation. This condition is fixed by undoing the separation. Mind has to return to soul. Depression must be sought, not fought. It's counterintuitive, but it's the way to overcome it.

Don't worry, though. Believe in this. Depression is not supposed to be a permanent affliction. Unfortunately, in reality it often is. And this is because people run from it. But when you run from it, you know who you're running from? Your soul. And she's always coming along. You cannot escape her. What do you do? Distract yourself? Your soul remains present. The entertainment ends, the distraction ceases, and she'll continue to haunt you. Do you really want to live like this? On the run from yourself? But if you're desperate, and you think, I will no longer live like this, then let me tell you this: you shouldn't. Yet of course, the solution is not what you're thinking, it's something else. It's to fully enter depression, and to feel it throughout. Like taking the deepest breath, or like drinking a whole bottle of water in one go, one must fully immerse into one's depression. But one must not be afraid. For this violent, shaky motion of the mind, the despair, the existential dread, it's all part of it. One must be brave in the face of depression. The depressed are inherently brave people, and everyone who's dealt with the subject knows this. Depression cannot be avoided. As little as cancer can be avoided, once you have it. You can either leave it untreated, or you can fight it. But the way to fight it is not the way you think. You don't push it back, you don't distract yourself from it, you don't drown it out or expel it from your thought — spoiler: this never works anyway. No, you do the opposite, and this may seem paradoxical to you, but you fight depression by capitulating to it. I know this seems like the complete opposite of what should be done. It certainly is the opposite of how we deal with it in society. But how well is that working for you? The medics call depression a state of the brain, a brain disease, and they give you medicine, and what not. It works to contain it, to control it, but I doubt it made anyone less depressed. It just made them less anxious about their depression. We let this point linger, for I'm sure many will disagree. Back to the matter. You must capitulate to it, but not for good, and not to give up on life. But in order to go down the valley. You capitulate to it, which means you allow it to unfold. Depression is like your mortal enemy, strolling around your house, trying to get in, and you are sitting inside, all scared, hoping it will not find a way to enter. Is this a way to live? Tell me this. Do you want to live like this? What I'm saying is, do the counterintuitive. Open the door, let the guy in. How much worse can it get? And I tell you this. It will feel pretty bad. It will feel like you want to die. It may feel even worse. But remember this, and only this: It's not an abyss, it's only a valley. There is a plateau, you just don't see it yet. Have faith, the plateau will come, and you will notice. And how will it change. I will tell you all about it. You will reach the plateau, and finally you will feel that the worst days are behind you. It's not getting better yet, remember it's a plateau, it's not going up yet. It's just not getting worse. That's the first step. At some point it will not get worse. It may take a while to get there. But you must go there. One day you will reach the plateau, and this will already present you with tremendous relief. For finally it's not getting worse. You can work with this. Perhaps it may get temporarily worse, but it's all part of it. No matter how the journey goes, it's never an abyss. Depression doesn't send you down into death. It only sends you down into feeling dead. There is a big difference. Depression doesn't end you, it's the feeling of having ended, and this feeling initially increases the more you reintegrate your soul. Basically, the more you feel your soul again, the more you feel her frozen state. This produces the somewhat terrifying impression that you are getting worse. In reality, the soul felt like this all along, and you're just feeling her again. You must feel her before you heal her. Otherwise the soul will stay frozen, and depression persists. In any case, once you reach the plateau, embrace it, and be happy that you've seen the worst of it. At this point the soul can slowly start thawing. This only happens once you've reached the plateau. Before that, the soul is still frozen, and you feel more frozen the more you approach her. Once you reach the plateau, you've become one with your frozen soul. Your thoughts are in the void, but from here it goes up. Your mind has at last become one with your soul. When the mind thinks, it represents the soul again, a state which for the longest time had not existed. What the soul feels, the mind conceives, which is looking at the same thing from the other side. Essentially mind and soul are one, and remember, they're still depressed together. This is not a happy state, that I'm describing, it's still a depressed one. But it is the basis of re-integration. Over time, if mind and soul continue to behave as one, as they're meant to, the soul will start moving again. It will rid itself of the ice, and the mind will mirror her motion. Remember, depression is the feeling of not feeling, and here, when the soul moves, she finally starts to feel again. She feels again! It begins slowly. The day is beautiful, is it not? For the first time in so long, you've had this thought, and you feel it. You see a friend or family, and you feel that you love them. You knew this always, but now you feel it again. You could cry, and perhaps you should. Isn't it beautiful to cry again? Oh how long it took us. You feel that you love them, and you cry, and they may also, for they see that you're returning to them. Perhaps you go out, but the world is a little slower now. The rush and the panic, it's still happening all around you, but you feel no longer part of it. How beautiful. You feel like you've left a world you hated so much. Now you realize it. Now you do. How much you hated all of this. How miserable it made you. And how good the depression was. How grateful you are that it came. It came to save you. This was its only mission. What a plot twist, right? Depression is the soul whispering that she wants healing. She wants to exist, for she is you. It's yourself screaming at yourself: I don't want to live like this. Your subconscious to your conscious, your Self to your I. Don't live this way, she says, and you must listen to her. Don't get me wrong, depression is a monster, but this is largely because of how we deal with it. We fight it, we repulse it, we deny it, we distract. But depression cannot be escaped. Those who are trying to, get ready to be disappointed. Depression is here to stay. To surpass depression, there is only one way — through it. If you run from it, it will never leave your side. You will never be happy. Depression has brought down a great many of us. It's not to say that they're to blame. No, they're never. Depression is the worst, no one should be blamed. But our way of dealing with it, is wrong. You cannot get away from it, and you do not negotiate with it. You capitulate to it, you accept it unconditionally, you allow it, and you are strong while persisting in it. Think of depression this way, the soul has died. But she can be revived, by devoting to her. The mind must sacrifice to bring her back. Depression is the result of the mind no longer associating with the soul. The soul is defiant, and she protests by discontinuing her vital motion. She becomes still, and unresponsive. The mind has done a terrible thing, it has detached from the soul. Bear in mind, we're talking about you. You have detached from yourself. You must return to yourself. And this is done by the mind sacrificing itself to the soul. In fact, this is a good description. The mind must sacrifice itself fully, because this is the only way that the mind collapses into the soul. The mind must stop thinking itself, in order to start thinking the soul. Or you must think the depression, instead of thinking against it. As long as you fight the depression, you keep the fission alive. Remember that depression is your soul, it's not an alien in your mind. It just feels that way, because you've alienated yourself. To fix this alienation, one must reintegrate the soul. And one does so, by not actively fighting depression as if it was an intruder. For this person creeping around your house is not an enemy. It's yourself. Your other half. Before you've opened the door you didn't even know you weren't complete. See, this is fission. To think yourself full, when you're only half. To turn one half of yourself into a stranger. To treat that stranger like an enemy. This was a long report, and I shall finish it like this. Depression is supposed to be temporal. It's a signal from your soul that she is no longer willing to live like this. She freezes to ice, and that's the sickness. The mind is the only medic who can cure this. But this is the good news, too, for you can make it happen. You must dedicate yourself to your soul. Do it by feeling her depression, don't fight it. You must enter depression like a dark forest. You must go into it, you cannot lurk around and see it from a distance. Once you enter it, you must be brave, but always remember this. You do this for the reward. One day you will be better. You must have faith. Faith that it gets better. It's not the depression that kills us, it's the desperation over our depression that kills us. Depression is a disease of the soul, but it's the mind that creates suicidal thought. It's more about how the mind responds to the soul's affliction. But this can be managed, and this can be changed. Faith is vital when it comes to depression. You must have faith that it will get better. Even better if you become proactive about it. Feel the depression, and have faith that you won't feel it forever. The soul's aim is not to make you depressed forever. It's to make you depressed for a while, and intensively so. Because by that, you will feel her again. This is the first time in a while that you feel your soul again. It's her last-ditch attempt to get your attention. The soul freezes when the mind no longer attends to her. The mind needs to return home, and feel the depression. The soul depresses you, not to kill you, but to revive herself. You must revive yourself by suffering the pain. And if you do that, if you enter it, and remain in it, brave and courageous, then, eventually, she will start to move again. The ice will melt. In all of this, we must be careful. People are different, and there are no quick fixes. For some people it takes long, and for others even longer. Sometimes we need the medics, and sometimes we need distraction. There are so many exceptions to the rule, as there are people in depression. Be easy on yourself.

Depression is like a fever, you need to sweat it out. Don't take my word for it. Listen to yourself, and set your own pace, but don't be afraid. Depression is a temporary state. The fact that for most people it doesn't seem to be of temporary nature, is due to us treating it wrong. We treat it like an enemy, when we should treat it like a friend. If we pull off the unthinkable, to become friends and even intimate with our depression, depression will eventually leave us, and for good. Because depression is not a thing in itself, depression is a state of our soul. Perhaps it helps to think of it this way: Replace the word „depression" with the word „soul". When you feel depression, you feel your soul. And your soul doesn't feel anymore. You don't feel anymore. This is the condition. And it's fixed, in the simplest terms, by feeling again. But to feel again, one must first feel the depression. One may have to feel it for quite some time. But one must enter it, and remain in it. One must learn to love one's depression, as impossible as it may seem. Loving your depression is a way of loving yourself. It paradoxically begins with hating yourself. But why is that? Because you made your soul hate you. She said, you know what, do what you want, I'm done. And she froze. The soul hated this, the life you led, the ideals you pursued, the priorities you set, pursuing dumb relationships, and money, and a career, what does that even mean, a career, do you think a career is worth anything, it's not worth a dime, your soul hated this, all of this, she hates you, and rightfully so, even I hate you right now after what I just wrote. All of this led to her depression, and she froze. And this is fixed how? By managing to love that hateful frozen soul of yours. Hate the soul that makes you miserable, for you made her miserable first. Once you do, there is hope for you. It may be hard for you to love your depression, but try it, it feels surprisingly good. When you're physically sick, you don't get on with your life, instead you lie down on the couch and eat baby food, right? Right?!! Let's forget I said this. With depression it's similar. You can't go on, you must pause. Only by loving your depression you can get better. I'll be honest, I tried wrapping this topic up around five times, and every time I kept writing. My experience tells me I will not manage to wrap this topic up, so I will just end it abruptly now.

Beauty is hard to capture. And that's because beauty is an impression. To capture an impression is difficult. One must somehow capture the thing that produces the impression in a way that the impression is reproduced in the recipient. A painter, when he or she sees the world beautifully, needs to not just capture the world, but the beautiful impression of it. This is difficult, and it requires you to know what you find beautiful about it. However, not in an intellectual sense, but rather in an intuitive sense. One reflects on the impression and is able to reproduce it in one's art. There are a couple of criteria that have to be met. First of all, the thing considered beautiful has to actually be beautiful. For example, if I find the grey January sky beautiful, I'm probably alone in this judgement, and even if I managed to capture it, it would not be considered beautiful by most people. There seems to be some sort of objective beauty to things, or better put, a collective impression of it. A beautiful wide sky in the summer is more beautiful, at least many feel that way, and the chances of this being considered beautiful are higher. The next hurdle is that one must be aware, not consciously, but intuitively, of what's beautiful about it. Beauty is not objective, it's subjective, or it's the beautiful impression of a world not inherently beautiful. Beauty is to see a thing beautifully, or to make it beautiful by looking at it. Picture the most beautiful scenery, the landscape is paradise, the sun is drowning the skies in a beautiful orange, lighting the Earth and the woods and the forests, the mountains and the seas stand pure as they are, but now picture this scenery, before man, picture it on a planet with no living beings on it. Is this still beautiful? You say of course, but you say that because you're perceiving it. You make it beautiful by contemplating it. Now picture all of this away, and reduce it to the fact. There is a sunset, the orange light, the mountains, but in the absence of anything contemplating it. How could this be called beautiful? It's just a fact of nature. It needs the seer, the perceiver, the receiver, call it what you want. This shows that beauty is created upon perception, or we create beauty upon sight. And we, by finding it beautiful, make it beautiful, it wasn't beautiful before, for no one found it so. When you find something beautiful, you must realize that it's an event taking place within you, and you need to capitalize on it. The perception, this fickle layer put on top of the thing perceived, is like an invisible veil your eyes have placed upon the thing observed. You need to intuitively be aware of what it is. I keep saying intuitively, because consciousness and intellect do not capture beauty, they rather destroy it, by drowning impression in expression, and feeling in thought. Beauty is not a thought, it's a feeling, and feelingly we must conceive it. Or we must conceive it with the heart, not the mind. It's our soul that sees beauty, not our mind. Therefore, one must protect the soul aspect of beauty, and subject the mind to it. The thin layer, the invisible veil, that the beautiful eye adds to the observed object is the most important thing in an artist's conception. It has many names, inspiration, muse, love, it doesn't matter. It's about what you see in the thing observed. Now a thing considered beautiful is often just something that many see beautifully, or it produces a similar impression of beauty in the many. That gives it a sort of objective beauty, but once again, it must be stated that beauty requires the presence of the admiring subject. If the artist is able to capture the beauty well, it will produce a similar impression on any other admirer. One can then reproduce beauty multifold, or create the sentiment of beauty in the many. Art should not be mistaken with thought, yet it can be compared. Art is received by the soul, thought by the mind, but the principle is the same. One captures something, which reproduces an impression in another. To capture this is difficult, and delicate indeed. To capture the evanescent world, the fleeting beauty of things, to hold it tight, to solidify it, or to internalize it, to externalize it, in order to eternalize it, to make it reproduce in the mind and soul of others. This is as close as we can come to the divine. On these earthly lands of ours, this is as close as we get.

Beauty is the impression, which we draw and add, for this is no longer a case of „either or". It's something immediate, and intuitive, nothing ideational, let alone intellectual. Beauty knows no theory, it only knows practice. Beauty has to be practiced, and exercised. For beauty does not exist in the realm of the theoretical. To explain beauty theoretically is foolish, for beauty loses all its qualities once it becomes an idea. Beauty is never an idea, it's an impression, and they who think it a concept, think it wrong. Beauty must be felt, or it won't be perceived. Only when the feeling is captured in an idea which then reproduces the feeling, beauty turns into a concept in the mind. By then it's most powerful. Picture the power of this: An idea, an alignment of letters and words, producing the feeling of beauty in your soul. Isn't this divine? I find it divine. It is powerful, to capture beauty in the written form. Only few have succeeded at this. The issue is that words often destroy beauty. Words are inherently ugly, everyone knows that. The written word is good for thought, but not for beauty. But every now and then a word strikes the soul, and impression is produced upon thought. This is so rare, and hard to achieve, that a true artist would spend his life trying to accomplish the effect. It goes beyond the power of mind. One must feel and think at the same time, which makes it so very hard. To think a feeling, to feel a thought, one must be in touch with oneself. There must not be any layer between mind and soul. Perfect harmony, and unity, is the condition for this sort of creation. But when the mind expresses the soul, the rewards are limitless.

Beauty must be perceived. If someone finds your beautiful work not beautiful, then beauty has not been created as an impression in the spectator. That doesn't make your work not beautiful, but at least in this case the effect has not been achieved. The aim is twofold, to feel the impression within, and to capture it without. Without object that is, for the true item of beauty is the invisible veil on top of the world. Or it's the layer which we don't see, for it's not a physical layer. To capture the impression, which is invisible and unphysical, is mastery, and only the truest art can accomplish this. One must be very fine, in senses and perception, and just as fine in the reproduction of it. It's a difficult endeavor, to capture this fleeting impression, to sense it well enough that one can pour it into one's art. Beauty is an adverb, think of it this way. You see and experience things beautifully. Beauty doesn't exist as a physical item in the world. It's added to and drawn from items. It's a way of perceiving things, or embellishing them through experience. Without the experience, beauty is is only a word. Therefore beautiful words which lack substance produce not beauty but boredom in us.

Beauty requires the beautiful eye. An ugly eye would not perceive beauty upon sight. It would perceive nothing. I rest my case. You must feel beauty to see beauty. The sentiment creates the perception. Beauty is motion, rather than matter. Beauty is the living essence of a still. When beauty acts, the world is eerily moving and still at the same time.

To describe beauty is often misguided. Beauty should not be described, but painted and reproduced. Too many words destroy beauty, in fact any words destroy it. Beauty is that which cannot be expressed in words. Or beauty is fleeting, by its very nature. To capture it is difficult. For capturing is a process of halting something, and beauty is alive through its vivid impression. The goal is to capture beauty in a way, that the vivid motion is repeated upon sight. Beauty cannot be contemplated, for contemplation kills the impression, and in beauty, the impression is everything.

Beauty is an introverted experience. The impression may live without its expression, but never the expression without the impression. When it comes to beauty, we're all impressionists. Beauty is something we experience first, and only then understand. Before we know something to be beautiful, we already feel its beauty. All starts with the impression, and only then makes its way to the expression.

Beauty is only denied by those who don't feel it. A dull soul could never well perceive it. It will deny it, but only because it lacks the sentiment. Yet those, who truly feel it, in their souls, will gladly turn it into a religion. Beauty is a religion, and a higher religion at that. One can truly fall in love with the beauty of the world. Yet those, who don't feel this, see right through it. They think us aesthetes, but they're wrong. Beauty is intuitive, and beauty is immediate. One finds something beautiful not upon reflection, but before.

Beauty is only a word — said no one who ever experienced it. It's the dull and vapid that speak this way. Beauty, when experienced, is the most precious thing in the world. A true artist would give his life for it. For beauty is fleeting and it passes quickly. But art isn't fleeting, and it doesn't pass. This is the artist's calling. To capture beauty. Think of the timeless nature of a beautiful piece of art. How very divine. To put the immaterial beauty of things onto the material. This is art! And the true artist lives and breathes, dies and decays for his art to be immortal. Art can never die, for once produced, it's beaten the evanescence of the world. The artist proves his artistic worth, by capturing the fleeting emotion of life. Not to speak of the physical, but of the unphysical, yet in a way that produces physical reaction. This is divine, this is artistic, and art, after all, is the religion of the beautiful.

To understand beauty, one must understand that there is nothing to understand about beauty. Beauty can result from thought and reflection, from objects and things, from nature or people, as well as from sentiment, memory, or experience. In all of this beauty is the qualifying statement of the soul. It's her way of approving of something. When she finds it beautiful, so do we, for the soul determines how we feel. Beauty is a sentiment, not to be grasped intellectually. Those who talk about it, without feeling it, are among the lowest class of people. It's the *bavardeurs*, one should carefully listen away, for they're constantly spoiling our senses.

This world no longer values beauty. Or let me rephrase it. It only values outside beauty, physical beauty, material beauty, and honestly, is that even beauty? In any case, this sort of beauty vanishes quickly, and is often accidental. I prefer inner beauty. Beauty as a sentiment. To feel the beauty of things, whether they are beautiful or not, this to me is the definition of beauty. Beauty must be felt, and in that case, it doesn't matter if it corresponds with any beautiful object.

It's nice to be illogical. For example, one should walk into a field, until the middle, then turn around one's axis, until one gets dizzy.

This is a pathetic attempt to find a new topic, but these attempts always start pathetic. Now you may say they also end pathetic, but this is uncalled for. I find that before one has an idea, one has no idea, so one has to elaborate in the no-idea-state first. You have to try to create an idea out of mere words. This is an important discipline as an artist, to not just work from inspiration to form, but also from form to inspiration. One first pretends to express something, and then, as part of that process, discovers something to express. So far I haven't found anything but I want to prove my point. It's important to work from the empty form, all the way back to a particular impression. It's easy to be inspired and create. It's much harder to create in the uninspired state. Yet this is the craft part of an art. To make it a habit to say nothing and find something on the way. For otherwise you depend on your inspiration, and inspiration quickly runs out. A great artist is not victim, but master of his inspiration. It's not about being in imagination and creating from that. It's about *not* being in imagination and getting yourself there through creation. People often mistake this. They think you must be inspired to create, and since they're never inspired they never create. In truth, even the inspired mostly start their work in the uninspired state. Inspiration then occurs in the process of creating while being uninspired. Inspiration is typically an effect of creation, not its cause. To stare at a blank page and wait for inspiration, is silly. You have to write, until something sticks. It can be a thought, a sentence, or even a word. All my thoughts on grace started with me writing down the word. Inspiration is not something that strikes you. It sounds illogical, but inspiration is work. Work creates inspiration much more than inspiration creates work. And see, now I have turned this pretty insight of Oscar Wilde's into a different form. I didn't anticipate this five minutes ago, when I wrote that this was merely a pathetic attempt to find a new topic. I'm not saying this was a brilliant revelation, I was simply trying to prove my point that most of my thoughts stem from nothingness. And now you say, they also end in nothingness, but this is a mean thing to say, and it made me sad. You made me sad now, I hope you're happy.

I got myself into the strangest situation. With a bunch of people, I ended up in the flat of a girl, who was a self-proclaimed influencer. Or I guess not self-proclaimed, we call 'em that, they have other names, which I always forget. Whatever she was, besides obnoxious, she showed us around.

We walked around in socks, which is so strange. I hate walking in socks in other people's apartments. Everything feels twice as awkward due to the fact. I did not care to learn about her cooking routine, and yet I did. She showed us the oils, can you believe it. We were moving around, and she commented on everything as if it was worth knowing. Like fyi, my long johns are in the bottom drawer. She had a room for dressing herself, which I know many have, but I cannot express how silly I find this. I know, live and let live, but still. I looked at this cheerful 25 year old influencer girl who smelled like a box of strawberries. I asked her about her books and she looked at me, somewhat panicked, for the last book she read was probably her own diary. In any case, she opened a bottle of bubble water and the misery continued.

I'm almost always amazed by these online people when at some point they withdraw into a hut in the countryside for two weeks, and then they return saying things like: In the seclusion and isolation, first it was strange and quiet, but after a couple of days, I almost felt like the thoughts came by themselves, it really changed my perspective, to reflect on things and life, and to see things from a different angle. Yeah, it's called thinking. Ideally you do this all the time, wherever you go, and whatever you do.

One has to get accustomed to the void. All good thoughts stem from it. Silence is the necessary condition for beautiful thought. Before every beautiful thought, there is beautiful silence. If the relationship with silence is damaged, words become chatter. Words must express what we experience in the void. Only when words reach deep, they deserve to be spoken. It's easy to forget thinking over speaking too much.

The void is a state, rather than a place. A state of mind. Not to be empty, but to be devoid. To be free of alien thought. Distraction operates this way. It comes in and intrudes. One must protect the barriers of one's mind. It's easy to get flooded with alien thought. To keep the mind clean. This is important, for otherwise you're thinking somebody else's thoughts. Our mind is a sacred place, and we must protect it.

The void of mind is not nothingness. This is a misconception. It's idleness. The mind idles, it no longer thinks of anything in particular. This is an important state, which is, however, threatened these days. People always think of something in particular. But how are you supposed to think of something new, if your mind is made up? You must make sure that at times it isn't. When you enter the void, your mind finds the old places long forgotten, and the new places it dreams of. Words must result from silence. If they result from other words, they're idle chatter, and they must not be spoken.

I love the void. One can think freely in it. It's good to let the mind wander. In order to think, one must learn to not think. This is just as important, for intensive thinking often takes away our clarity of thought. You can easily think about something too intensively and lose sight of it. One must think intensively or not at all, intermittently. Most people think more or less the same way all the time. This is not, I repeat, not the way a thinker should think. A thinker must think intensively when he does and not at all when he doesn't. The off-times are just as important. During those hours the mind relaxes, and when it returns it sees the world more clearly. Those who always think are almost as foolish as those who never think. There is a time to remember and a time to forget. Judgement and experience tell us which one is which. A great thinker is not born, he's made, and he mostly makes himself. Or she herself of course. A thinker is not born, he gives birth to himself. You have to bear the thinker in you.

Thought is evanescent. It slips from our grasp. But it can be captured. The number one distraction of thought is the spoken word. One must speak little, to think a little more. Speech doesn't express thought, it mostly expresses itself. The contents of speech are words, not thoughts. When we think, we are no longer able to speak, and we shouldn't be. Good thinking is a serious matter and one honors it by not speaking of it. Only fools speak their thoughts. The wise only think them. Thoughts are to be thought. And how to express them? Not in the verbal. For they don't belong there. In a world full of chatter, it's wasteful to join in with thought. Talk in chatter, think in thought, that's the way to go.

Thought is a serious matter, much more serious than talk. Talk should be done lightly, but never so thought. A wise person is one who thinks seriously and speaks lightly. They're also the most pleasant kind. But this is a world that produces the opposite type: people who think lightly and speak seriously. That's why it's so hard to listen to people these days. They have so little to say, yet they don't realize it. because they think lightly. To treat a puddle like the Pacific. Pretend they're super duper great. Yet the thought is so transparent. I see my reflection in it, so shallow is it.

Thought should be serious, talk should be light. The world practices it the other way around. Everyone thinks lightly and talks seriously. To talk seriously about light thoughts is such a drag. It really kills my soul. They don't realize how light their thought is. When all have light thoughts, light thought appears like deep thought. And what about deep thought? It's no longer understood by the light-thinking people. They call it obscure, abstract, abysmal. Their talk is different, too. For they speak seriously about light thoughts. Meaning not only do you have to share their light thoughts, you also have to share their serious way of talking about them. But to talk seriously about light topics, is the greatest threat to real thought. My mind becomes depressed just thinking about it.

To talk seriously, is bad enough, if the topic is serious. Even then it would suit us well to speak lightly about it. One should not make the words heavier than the experience is. Weight is transported through the manner of talking, not through the words selected. The words can be light, if the meaning is felt. To talk seriously about light thoughts, is painful, and no sound mind will deal with it lightly. Talk must be light, thought serious, not the other way around. The good thoughts are born in silence, never in conversation.

Thought doesn't begin as soon as talk ends. It takes a while for thought to return. In fact, I'm pretty sure there is a relationship between how long one talked and how long it takes for thought to return. This is why it's better not to talk a lot, or at least take regular breaks. People protect their homes, but who protects their thoughts? Anyone may enter, pour it all in. This is why our minds look like dumpsites.

I was in a grocery store, standing in line behind a guy. He was so neat. I admired him. Guys like this are always dressed for the occasion. I don't know what occasion, but it must be important. They always make an extra effort. Like they're trying to get a date with themselves. Meanwhile I stand behind him, looking like a zombie. Hood so deep in my face, it covers my eyebrows. I walk not like an Egyptian, but like a mummy, more dead than alive. I'm still tired from being asleep. Sleeping is so tiring. Yet he is perfect, and so is his haircut. There are no spots on his face, he's perfectly shaved. He must be one of those guys using aftershave. Finally I understand the target group. Meanwhile, whenever I shave, I still look like the polka dot jersey from the Tour de France. Everything about this guy is near perfection, or I should say near completion, because that's how it feels with these guys. As if they're trying to complete this mission called life. Then they get the equally generic girlfriend, and live in one of those soulless city apartments. This guy has skin like a baby, clearly an attractive fella, he wears one of them dark bluish suit jacket coats, whatever they're called, the casual business attire. He smells good, too. It's the generic smell of business men. The ocean smell, the ocean cave, watery, blue, fresh, oceanatic, oceanesian, oceansian smell, this ocean paradise, blueish freshness, oceanematic smell. He exchanges a quick word with the cashier, and he's off. Farewell, Mr Rockefeller, may God bless you on your way! Sometimes I overhear these people in restaurants. I should say fewtimes, for we normally don't frequent the same places. They go to expensive restaurants, I go to none. But if and when our paths cross, I hear them talk to their equally neat and generic girlfriend, and I don't believe my ears. I can't believe that you would spend your entire life on this superficial level. It's like living on the surface as a creature of the depth. And you may say, you don't know that, maybe they're different when it's just the two of them. But it is just the two of them. They don't know I'm holding my breath, to suck in every single word they're saying. I'm studying man and woman in their natural habitat. And these soulless people really talk about their soulless work. I don't even talk about my work when I'm at work. They talk about it in their spare time. Or perhaps this is a business meeting. One is always surprised to find out what these people expense. But here they are, discussing these things, and I'm passively bored into a minor stroke. It hurts me physically to listen to this. I want to shake them violently, and say: stop this charade, this needs to stop! Talk about real things! But they are doing that. Those are the real things in their world which amazes me. Do you not see the giant elephant in the room, which has „boredom" written on his belly and is about to collapse on your table. When I die, I would love to collapse in a restaurant onto a table of strangers, right into a big bowl of crap soup. It would do justice to the big bowl of crap soup that was my life. I can't believe these people exist. Then they go home into their city apartment, you know these soulless city apartments where a straight hallway leads directly into a great living room with a built-in kitchen. I don't understand the concept of kitchen islands. They're always in the way, are they not? Then there is the balcony, allowing you to look at the other 250 apartments which have the exact same design and people in it. And then, to have the audacity, to feel unique, is amazing to me. The fact that these people don't realize how generic they are. But it makes sense, when you consider it from their perspective. They obviously don't view it from mine, otherwise they would come to the same, correct conclusion, that they are generic. From their perspective, it all makes sense. They are not generic, in fact they're unique. Because their variety is not a variety of thought and sentiment, it's one of hobbies, and interests, and possessions, and favored cuisines, and used apps, and the gym they go to, and the company they keep, and whether they add coffee to their milk, or milk to their coffee, and what trip they're planning next, and how they really want to go diving, and skydiving, and skidiving, and all of the above, and that's really their horizon. I find this fascinating, and I wonder how they feel about me. They must find me strange. For I don't do any of these things, and they don't understand what I do then. What it is that makes me an individual. Which is just so ironic and funny, when you think about it. These people come to the same conclusion about me. And since the world is made of people like them, they are right and I am wrong. I am the strange one in their world. Which is crazy, because they are strange, and I am not. Well, maybe a little. But it's interesting how they don't see these things, because they really think this is individuality, when one's favorite color is orange, and the other one favors green. For me they're all the same, and I'm happy to remain anonymous to them. But in the restaurant it becomes painfully obvious how generic they are. They talk about work, their friends, their plans, this sort of thing. Not that I listened to the whole conversation, I went to the bathroom twice. But I don't think I missed a lot, for it really seemed to be more of the same. Imagine you're trapped in this life. I'd rather be deep in hell than shallow in heaven. I am more than glad to not function in their world. Yet when we stand, side by side, he's deemed a winner, and I'm the loser. I'm not bitter about it, more amused, and quite indifferent. I'm just amazed that these people are supposed to carry us as a civilization from this point onwards. No wonder we ain't going anywhere. Be that as it may, I paid for my salad and water and left the place. And yes, this was a scenario in a scenario in a scenario. Welcome to my head.

People who think are inherently more beautiful. It's good to get into the habit of saying little, for the little you say, will carry more meaning. One should always feel bad while speaking. This is a good way of building a threshold that only meaningful talk will cross. Too little meaning contained in too many words, this is my diagnosis of modern man. And woman, for we don't discriminate. They both talk too much. If it was meaningful, then I wouldn't mind. But it seldom is. One cannot talk a lot, when one talks meaningfully. Meaning is that which sums up the message naturally. The longer the message, the shorter the thought. As long as thought is disordered, it hasn't reached its natural conclusion. One must keep thinking and wait for meaning to emerge. This doesn't happen, when thought is prematurely shared. Talk destroys thought, and those who speak prematurely, speak foolishly.

Sometimes I remember a detail and I fall in love with her all over again. It's the way she held her tea cup. So strangely beautiful. So beautifully strange. It's always the details. How she would look at something, and decide. She would inspect it with her eyes, without saying a word, until she decided. Then she would look up and smile. I had watched her all the way. She did everything beautifully. I remember the little things, and whenever I do, she's back with me for a moment.

My disposition toward her was odd. For it combined two emotions so distinct. She protected me from the world. Yet I also felt protective of her. But these were distinct feelings.

She expected me to change like she did. From sad and quiet to cheerful and bright. But I didn't, and I didn't think she was going to. I really feel it was her who behaved unexpectedly. She was disappointed that I remained who I was all along.

One of the difficulties is that I must protect her image. I don't talk to my friends because they tell me reasonable things. How I took care of her for months, and when she got better she seemed to forget all about it. I know this. I just prefer not to know it. I'd rather think of the way she held her tea cup. She held it like an elderly Victorian age woman. I joked about it at times, and she would blush a little. She would try to hold the cup differently and it would look even worse. I would laugh and so would she. She would say, she was never going to drink tea in my company anymore. I would say, how about you drink it from a glass. For surprisingly she managed to hold a glass like a normal person. I loved her strangeness. If you think me strange, you should have met her.

Experience has tormented me more than it's taught me. I should've just had none of it. One must forever stay a hopeful youth. To see your dreams fade, yet to stay loyal to them. I wish I still believed that life was a dream, and that the world was a realm, and that I was free in it, and hopeful. Naivety makes people much happier than clairvoyance. I never wanted to see the world clearly. I prefer it unclearly.

Oh how I wish I could have stayed an innocent fool. I was always wrong and always happy. This is the superior way of existing. Imagine you're always right. What a drag. To lose belief is the true tragedy of man. One must do everything to keep it from happening. I choose to believe. In the untrue. The soul never makes us unhappy, the mind all the time.

I was happy, when I believed in these illusions of mine. I didnt even wonder about their truth. They felt true to me. Truth is that which feels true, in the realm of the subjective. It's strange to expect scientific truth in the immaterial world. There are no material things in the soul, hence no objective truth. All truth is subjective in the soul. In matters of the soul that which feels true, is true. Truth writes itself in spiritual matters. By feeling a truth, one proves it to be true.

How beautiful the world appeared to me. I loved it very much. I still do, but experience drags me down. Memory is the enemy, one should never indulge. I wish I remembered nothing. If only I could go back to being an innocent fool. I still am, but sort of a wise and older fool. I want to be an original fool again. I want to believe that if only I get the girl, I'll be fine. I no longer have this luxury, for now I know, it will just be more of the same. One more thing I can no longer believe in. I wish I hadn't learned anything. I should have continued dreaming. Dreaming about a life I was never to embark on. I should have kept my naivety. When we are young we want to get rid of it. Then we get older and we want it to return. I wish I could tell this to my younger self. Don't be foolish, be it a little more. One must be naive in young years. I want to go back and fall in love with the unattainable girl. This is my favorite activity in hindsight, I should have done this more often. It was so pure and beautiful. I would adore her, while she wouldn't even know my name. This has classy written all over it. I wish I could be like this again. Today I don't bother. It's because I realize that these things don't change your inner disposition. They are just shadows after which you chase. It's this realization, I wish I never had. I should have never gotten the girl. It was much better when I couldn't. This was the supreme state, for it had the beautiful sadness that I long for. Oh how foolish I was to flee this state, which was such an artistic blessing. People think I'm joking but I'm not. It's the supreme way of loving someone. It always gets worse, once it becomes real. It doesn't get better at all. But if it never begins, it's beautiful.

One pays attention to every single detail. You put your heart into it. All of this is silly, and one is well aware of it. But it doesn't matter, life is silly anyway. Love is like a permission to dream. One enters a realm of beauty and sadness. It's incredible to muse in that realm. For most people this is a fleeting moment, and they barely experience it, let alone capture it. To love like this shows you the world in a different light. Your eye picks up on things. Your thought becomes personal, strangely personal. You notice things differently, there is a particular quality to it. It changes your thinking, and it gives you sentiment. All of this is indispensable if you have any artistic or even intellectual ambitions. One must feel to think, otherwise it's all empty and theoretical. Thought in itself is not beautiful, it only gets beautiful when sentiment is expressed. Unrequited love gives you all the sadness, beauty and love in the world. If you have the virtue, and the soul for it, you can become a master in your realm.

Sadness is my friend. We are almost brotherly, or sisterly, for I'm sure that sadness is a woman. I like sadness. One can so beautifully engage with it. It becomes like a fog in the mind. I like it when I don't see clearly. To see clearly is overrated. One must make sure to always see the world subjectively. This alone lends it a personal touch. To see the world differently is not a flaw, but a privilege. We should protect this ability in our children. The subjective view on the world is what makes life unique. If you see the world objectively, you're like a calculator, or an antenna. What's the point of being alive, when you look at the world as if you were dead. To see the world objectively is such a waste of subjectivity. Subjectivity is the true purpose of life. To eliminate subjectivity, is to suck the soul out of the body. We should be more subjective, not less. But the objective people dominate the world. With their science, and maths, and what not. We should never listen to them, for they are wrong. To see the world objectively, is to be existentially wrong about life. One must see the world subjectively, for this is the right of passage. I have no idea what the right of passage is, but I've always wanted to use this term. The subjective way of seeing the world, is what makes it beautiful. Everyone can be objective, but only one can be subjective. Beauty is subjective, and that's because it takes a subject to perceive it. Two amber stones, as beautiful as they may appear to our eyes, are not beautiful to each other. A subject is needed, or beauty will simply not occur as an impression. Those who see the world objectively, could not appreciate its beauty. Even the mathematicians perceive beauty subjectively. Symmetry for example is not beautiful in itself, it's only beautiful in our perception of it. Therefore it's important to see the world subjectively. Yes, objectively, too, they're not mutually exclusive. But in a way they are, for there is constant pressure on our subjectivity. The subject is drowned in the objective world. We must make sure to stay afloat. Don't be one of the objective people, for they have lost an essential part of life. Life is objective, but living is not. Embrace the subjective, and if necessary, fight the objective. It constantly wants to overrun us, it's violent toward us. The objective wants to annihilate and absorb us as subjects. The subjective must not allow this to happen. We must fight back. The objective is to subject the objective, to become subjective instead. The objective must not reign our souls and minds. We must not invite it back for dinner, if it keeps throwing the food at us. This is not appropriate behavior, in our houses the subjective reigns. We must, by all means, remain subjective.

It's ridiculous to believe in illusions. But if you truly believe in them, at some point it stops being ridiculous and it becomes almost tragical. I think I have reached that stage. I believe so wholeheartedly in my illusions that people no longer call me ridiculous. But I don't care if it's true or not. Belief is greater than wisdom, for wisdom is relative, and it changes with the times. Yet belief is absolute, it never decays.

The way she looked at me was truth. She was my truth. I believed in her unconditionally. When I felt she was uneasy, I would have moved heaven and earth for her.

To love her in silence. To love her without burdening her. To let her be happy. To give her up and accept. To remember her grace. To reminisce over it. To accept that some things are just not meant to be.

I saw a girl the other day. She reminded me of her. I was in a salad bar in a shopping centre. This was in itself a curious situation. But then I saw her, a girl, a woman I should say, wherever the cut off is. She was exactly like her. She had her mannerisms. I was struck, like a tree by lightning, almost tumbling. Inside that is. I was seated, so it didn't show. I wasn't close to falling off my chair, in my defense. I ate the whole salad without paying attention to it. I had blindly ordered „the salad of the day“, which means that I have no idea what I ate. I wonder what was in that salad.

Time is strange, isn't it. When you've amassed a little bit of life, it becomes increasingly strange in the rearview mirror. It almost collapses into one collected past. The memories are no longer distinct. As if they're no longer in a timeline. Five years ago feels like an eternity ago, and ten years like a different life. One always complains that time passes quickly. Yes, one year does, and two. But then, the past is so long ago. Everything that felt true, is no more valid. One is confused about the realization, that one was neither wrong nor right. One was just different. This is puzzling. One always ends up somewhere else. Things change so unpredictably. The dreams I've had seem so strange to me now. And reality, so real to me then, so frail to me now. Only memory reminds me of it. Besides that no trace. If I forgot about it, it would be as though it never happened. And eventually it will be that way.

Evanescence makes me sad. Not my own, but in general. Young children growing up, just to grow down again, into old age, and eventual death. Whole generations have risen like the sun, and set just alike. Along with them, their dreams and afflictions. All gone for good. It makes me sad. That I never got to talk to them. To befriend them. To help them. Or to congratulate them on their happiness. Life cannot be captured. That's the beauty of it, but also the cruelty. Life is beautiful, one should be able to capture it. To capture the beauty of life, that would be the perfection of art.

Time is strange when you look at it. It becomes stranger, the longer you live. The past is not linear like the future. It follows almost a sinuous line. There are moments in my distant past that feel a lot closer to me than the near past. Something which happened only recently feels like a long time ago. Other memories are vivid to me, even though it has been decades. Time becomes strange, once you leave it behind. It's no longer a succession of moments and events. It's a strange and vast expanse. Moments in time feel like points in space. Some are weirdly connected, while being years apart. Others are not connected at all, even though they happened at the same time. I remember being there, but how did I feel? Memory and sentiment don't always match. Some things seem illogical in hindsight. Other sentiments only make sense today. Sometimes you recognize yourself in an action. The instinct was always right. Other times you're confused by how hard you worked for something, which made you miserable. Couldn't you have foreseen this? Apparently not. But at the time, it all seemed crystal clear.

It's interesting. Often you are miserable, before you understand why. Misery indicates that something is amiss. That's why I'm saying one should befriend one's misery. It's in times of bliss that we should be skeptical. Bliss so often lies to our face. It's a beautiful lie, that eventually collapses.

Time is strange, it looks so different in hindsight. You can hardly make sense of it.

It takes time to formulate one's dreams. One must live a little, to dream a little better. Our early dreams are often not our own. Fate means well, if we miss our early dreams.

Many people never fail young. They end up failing old instead. That's a lot worse, because it's irreversible. If I could hope for one thing that all youths should go through, it's failure. Failure tests our assumptions. It's good if your early dreams don't come true, for who knows if they were yours. Challenge your dreams by failing them.

When I was young, I thought about older age. I thought: Will I have this and will I have that? The answer is No and No. But it's the best thing that could have happened to me. It's one of the birth flaws of man. He always knows the answer before the question. We must be careful getting what we wish for. Our wishes are often misleading. To question our wishes takes experience. One can only later on reassess one's wishes. In the meantime one must try to fulfill them. But one must always reassess. The ability to self-assess is one of the most important abilities in life.

My past is like a collection of moments. I inhabit them, I revisit them, but they don't feel dynamic to me. I saw things differently back then. My dreams didn't come true, but I'm not sad. And if they had come true, I wouldn't be happy. So innocent I was, thinking life is determined by circumstances. Life determines itself. It's true what everybody said. I was the worst when I was young, for the young always know better, but I knew best. We all did, but I thought for me it was different. Which also, we all did. In any case, I come to a similar conclusion. Life does what it wants. It's hard to prepare and impossible to predict. One must allow it to happen. But I shall never tell the youths anything. They must go through it, and find out for themselves. Who knows, perhaps they arrive at a different conclusion. Life humbles you, like nothing else. You start at the top, slowly you go down. You're disappointed at first, but quickly relieved. It's good to grow older and get rid of some of your ambitions.

I saw a boy today, who was sad. I talked to him, for he was clearly in need of a friend. He was a little shy at first, but then shared his sorrows with me. He was in dire times, as he felt he didn't belong anywhere. He told me he was new in the city. He said that he had no friends and he felt lonely. I told him, that he shouldn't despair. He told me that he studied to be an architect. How beautiful, I thought. It's a worthy profession. He talked about buildings, and bridges. I'll be honest it went right over my head. But he was excited, and I was happy for him. But also sad, that no one had an ear for this excited young boy. He told me that he spent the nights alone, and the mornings, and the evenings. I told him not to despair, for many youths are lonely, I'd argue most. He said, why, and looked at me in a devout way that moved me. I was now the older brother I never had. I took it to heart, and for once let go of my nonchalance. I answered in earnest. I said,

I believe that the youths are finding it harder to engage with the real world. The world is becoming larger, and more technical, and increasingly abstract. It's hard for the youths to find their place, it always is, but for today's youths it's even harder, for the connections get lost. They spend a lot of time on the internet, and physical connection suffers from that. There is a whole layer of human relationship that's fading out. The youths feel increasingly detached from each other. Everything has become virtual now, and digital. None of this was a genius insight, but I never laid claim on that.

He said to me, that he never sees his friends anymore. He's only chatting with them. I said, yes, it's all become virtual. I asked him how he felt about virtual reality. He said he didn't know, and asked me how I felt about it. I said, I thought it was pretty dystopian. He asked me why I thought the youths are getting lonelier. I said, I think it's tough to be young. It always was, but it's getting tougher. The world is becoming more abstract. He asked me what I meant by abstract in this case. I was trying to think of a concrete example, which was of course ironic. I found one when I said that people get to know each other before they meet. That's a strange reversal of the natural process. Normally you meet before you get to know each other. He nodded. I said, now everyone is getting to know everyone, but not really. The youths never meet, but they already know each other inside out. Of course this makes them anxious. For they are an open book to strangers. You should never be an open book to a stranger. We must open up to those who we trust. But to share anonymously into an unknown crowd. To personally expose all your thoughts and dreams to people who you're not familiar with, is a strange reversal of the natural process. It makes our relationships abstract, for we are not dealing with people anymore, but with ciphers and profiles. The youths, however, form all of their relationships like that, platonic as well as romantic. He asked me what platonic meant, and I explained that it meant „in friendship". He asked me why it was called platonic, and I was at an impasse. I added that the youths share everything, so they become open books to each other, and at the same time quite invisible. Invisible in plain sight. Which is strange. Everyone sees everything about you. But no one sees you truly. It's strange, for the natural course is opposite. You see someone first, you get to know them, then you share with them. This is how relationships form. You cannot reverse the process. Because in that case the relationship never really forms. It becomes a hollow, abstract relationship. You cannot know the person before you meet them. This is a strange reversal which doesn't work naturally. It's like marrying someone before you date them. It won't make you happy, and it won't work. You must go naturally, from one stage to the next. The youths of today find themselves in reverted circumstances. They know each other first, only then they meet. This makes everything odd. For you don't really know them before you meet them. You know them in theory, but in practice they're strangers. You cannot bond with someone before you know them. True connection is formed from one person to another. Otherwise it's just not a real connection. But life has shifted from the real world to the internet. It's hard to be young these days. On the internet, everyone fights their own battle. To share becomes a necessity. One must find a way to form these connections in real life. How, he asked me. I said, you know, that's the hard part. But you must try, for otherwise you'll regret it. I told him that I believed that his generation would be the first to one day regret having spent too much time on the internet. I told him, the internet is a place one should consult. To learn and to be entertained. But it doesn't replace the real world. One must go out, into the real world, and get one's hands dirty. Living is hard when you're young, for you've done so little of it. But it gets better, over time, however, not by magic. It gets better only if you get better at it. I told him that he shouldn't worry about his feelings being legitimate. For many youths feel lonely, and even I did at the time. It's natural to feel lonely when you're young. It's hard to make it in the adult world. There is so much to learn, and so little accomplished. But it's all part of it. Don't rush it, for one day you'll regret having rushed it. You will look back and think if only I had that freedom again. I told him that he was free, and to be lonely means to be free. It's just a different way of looking at it. Many people wish they were lonely at times, for they are very much stuck in their lives. Once you enter the adult live, you'll never exit it. To be lonely can be a good thing if you use it productively. One must explore, and be held back by nothing. I told him he shouldn't settle too soon. He should try to embrace his loneliness and try to live with it. In this state, you can accomplish beautiful things. It's often a curse in disguise to become happy too young. It's a blessing in disguise to stay unhappy a little longer. But part of this experience is the loneliness. We're all lonely before we are not. And I told him this. Never forget, that all the people that are known were once unknown. Every family you see out there started from two lonely people meeting. Every child is the synthesis of two lonely souls. They stopped being lonely when they met. Things are not before they are. This is not a truism, you must take this to heart. Just because something doesn't exist today, doesn't mean it won't exist tomorrow. The things that exist tomorrow, do often not exist today. They are being made, and created, by people like you. Don't worry about the present, it won't last forever. If you're sad today, do not despair. One day you'll look back and see all the good in it. You will be happy, you just need to have a little faith. And keep going, always keep going. I told him that it's good to be lonely, for loneliness is the capacity to form a real connection with people. This capacity will one day swing into action. Should he be patient or impatient, he asked me. I told him that this was an excellent question. He added more, saying, he heard different opinions on the matter, good things comes to those who wait, say some, and others say, one must go for it and never settle. I told him, that in my opinion, one must act impatiently, yet stay patient in the process. All the things you imagine can come true. They will probably just take a little longer, and it will be a bit harder than you imagine. But they can come true, and I believe they will. Don't overthink it. Go first, think second. I told him that. Bottom line, I believe it's better to be impatient than patient. Or differently put: one should be impatient about the present and patient about the future. One must wait for things to come, but not by waiting, but by moving toward them. They are probably farther in the horizon than you think, but make no mistake, they are there and you can reach them. Stay impatient, but don't despair on your way, for your time will come. I told him, that loneliness is natural, and nothing to be ashamed of. He should be straightforward about it. He should be the person he'd want to meet, as a friend or partner. If he felt lonely, he should not pretend otherwise. He should not do what he doesn't feel like doing. If he's lonely, he must not try to meet people online. He must try to meet them in real life. How that is possible? Well, you have to figure it out. This is how life works. Learning by doing. The proactive way is always better. If you go forward, always forward, you'll find good things on the way. Keep an open mind, and an open heart. Whatever makes you unhappy, discontinue doing that. If you have to do it, distance yourself from it mentally. Be on good terms with yourself, be emotionally healthy. Always be honest, and never lie to yourself. I told him, don't be afraid to live, never be. Live, and you'll find out soon enough. Life becomes estranged when it becomes theoretical. Don't live on the internet, for that's not living. That's just waiting to live while not living. Life should never happen in this theoretical fashion. You must practice life like a craft. You must do life. Life wants to be active, and so do you. Be active, be bolt. Whatever you want, go for it, and never buckle. Chances are you won't get it, but it's not about that. It's about going for it. Don't wait for something to happen. Make it happen. This sounds simple but it's very important. Anything can happen if you make it happen. Nothing will happen if you wait for it. Loneliness is often the sentiment of helplessness. You have to help yourself and you better start early. To help yourself is one of the most important skills to learn in life. If you're lonely and it bothers you, help yourself. Meet the people you want to meet. Ask yourself: who do you want to meet, who are they and where? Then go there, say Hi, and meet them first. You cannot know someone before you meet them, and you shouldn't attempt to. Meet them first, know them second. Simple rule of happy relationships. With most people you meet, you probably don't want to know them. You should only know the people you like. And only they should know you. It's called friendship, and later on family. The social life is not a numbers game. One friendship is worth more than a hundred acquaintances. The lonely are in the majority, there are many like you. And once you meet them, you will find a true friend in them. It happens all the time. Don't be discouraged. You mostly hear from the people who are unhappy. You never hear from the happy ones. But they exist in abundance. You shall be one of them. And even if not, you'll have something to tell. Look at me, I'm not happy, but what I got is even better. This sad little wisdom of mine. Do not despair, your mind is in the right place. It's hard to be young. Only the elder idealize the youth, for that's all we have. We think ourselves back into better times. That were never any better, for I remember your age, and I sure don't want to go back. But the advantages are numerous. You have nothing to lose, don't live like you do. You have time. Use it wisely and use it unwisely. Become the person you want to be. Things are not as bad as they seem in the moment. Believe me, my life was at its lowest point — around 50 times. I have gotten used to these moments, they don't shock me anymore. The low points will not hurt you as much as they do now. You will learn and grow from them. Life becomes better when you're active about it. I told him that, and much more, for he kept asking questions. I hope he's alright, but I'm sure he is. If not today, then tomorrow, or in a year. It's good to have your identity crisis early, for everyone has it sooner or later. Most people have it later in life, which gives them less time to change.

I remembered a detail today. I had given her a key to attach to a key ring. I had failed the task. She took it — and did it in one go. It was elegant. It took her two seconds perhaps. She handed it back to me, and looked at me with her noncommittal smile. I loved her very much in that moment.

I like the days when I'm sad about her. It means I haven't lost her yet. It's the days when I forget her that worry me. I assume that this is how I'm going to lose her. She'll slip from my memory, every day a little more. I catch myself actively thinking of her to avoid this. Then I think of her, I get sad again, and a little merry, for I know I haven't lost her yet.

Are dream and life incompatible? Most people stop dreaming eventually. Are there people who do the opposite? People who stop living instead? They must be a handful at best. To say no to living, and yes to dreaming. This seems like a good choice to me. When you're young, you dream, for you barely live yet. But then you start living, and you stop dreaming. We thought we could have it all. But we couldn't. We had to decide. And that's when we abandoned our dreams. Not suddenly, rather silently, it happened almost unnoticed. Until we were dreaming no more. Now we look back and wonder: was it the right choice? For life is good, but so was dream. How sad it is that we no longer dream about life. That we have to live it now. How much better was it when we only dreamt about it. It was limitless. To dream and to sacrifice living. I don't think many choose this path. In dream we are souls again. In life we're merely bodies.

I will never forget a particular thing about her. It's the calm she made me feel. When I was with her, my world was perfectly calm. There were no questions anymore. It was like the universe had come to a stop. But it wasn't just silence. It was the feeling. I felt perfectly calm. I had never, not once, been this calm. That's the one thing that sticks with me today. When I was with her, my world became calm. It was strange, and incredibly beautiful. I had never experienced anything like it. It wasn't love, even though there was a lot of love for her right from the start. But even beyond love, this perfect calm. Everything was simple when I saw her.

It was one of the strangest, purest things I've felt. It was not a common experience at all. I don't say this lightly, but it was almost religious. If anything could make me religious, it was this moment. It was in no way a physical experience. I doubt the brain could produce anything like it. I am not a believer, but this moment was peculiar. It was the one time in my life, when I seriously wondered, while awake, if I was. It was like a massive tree had collapsed onto me, and I had crawled out from underneath it. I remember walking outside thinking: I'm about 80 % sure this is real. „80". That's not a number you want to hear in those circumstances.

There is a lot of good that came from this calm. I do not fear death anymore. I picture it to be this exact calm, just without noticing. And who knows, maybe we don't have the full picture. It's very likely that there is more to the world than we grasp. Let's give it the benefit of the doubt. Maybe when life is over, we return to dream. Maybe it is similar to this calm and beautiful state. Maybe the world has arisen from dream. Or maybe life has. Maybe the world is just a sphere in space, but life isn't. Perhaps there is more to life. Something which connects all living beings. Maybe life is a substance after all. Maybe life is the dream, realizing itself in the body. Maybe the soul dreams the body. Maybe we are dreamers thrown into existence. But maybe we return. Who really knows. I'm not saying Saint Peter is waiting at the gates. I'm just saying there is no need to be all nihilistic about it. Nothingness may await us, but nothingness doesn't hurt anyone. It was pretty before we were born, it will be pretty after. I don't fear death, I never have, but after experiencing this calm, I feel good about it. I think it will be most relaxing. Finally no strange thoughts anymore. That's what I hope for anyway. Imagine I die and everything is gone, except for my strange thoughts. Imagine my wicked mind somehow doesn't die. Oh boy. Now I'm really scared of death again.

The problem is that my mind is too strong. I can't even go insane in style. If my mind was any less strong than my heart, I would have long departed to the hopeless land. Unfortunately, this is not the case and I'm still here. Perhaps this is my mission, to tell the tales of madness, while staying somewhat in the vicinity of the real world. Let's see how it develops, I might make the transition after all.

I talked to an older man today. He gave me a lesson in how to behave. Not that I misbehaved. He lectured me anyway. Something must have irked him. He was frustrated with the younger generation which, in his words, always knew better. I listened carefully in order to prove him wrong. I ended up learning a wholly different lesson. To never become like him. A cynic. I find it pathetic when the old mourn about the young. How can you so plainly forget about how it was to be young? Don't you remember how it felt? No. You only see yourself. I'm very disappointed with the older generation in our day. They seem particularly cynical. I pledge to never become like them. Then again, it is easy for me to say, for I don't plan on reaching old age. If I see the young I shall try to understand them. One should always try to understand everyone, and make it one's duty to do so.

I was silly again. I talked to a stranger, and he thought I was genuine. The problem is, once you start, you are committed. You cannot discontinue half way into the conversation. Since they get to know you as the person you are not. I thought he was going to bore me. He ended up being a good guy, and I felt bad. Now you may say, that's what you get from talking nonsense to strangers. But the real tragedy that occurs much more often is that you speak genuinely with boring people. This sort of thing, talking nonsense to a good guy, is a collateral. It happens. This is why I let people talk first, so I can assess the situation. He started the conversation by saying his name was Kenneth, and that settled the question for me. I should have not made my decision based on his name. I was stuck in this discussion, and I felt bad.

I like hospitals. They are generally nice places. I like the variation of colors in the interior. It's got everything, a little bit of that cream white, as well as the greyish white, not to mention the white white. Hospitals are funny. Why not make them warmer. They're pretty depressing places, let's face it. Why do they have to look depressing? Why not design them more like furniture stores. There is no need to not have a single piece of fabric in the whole building. A hospital doesn't need to be stale and cold. It is, though. And the same applies to the people in there. The doctors match the walls, and the ceiling, and the overall vibe. It's almost like they're made from the same material. I like hospitals, no wait, let me rephrase this: I don't like hospitals. I don't understand why they are not comfy. Just put a couch in the room, or a plant. Why not. Hospitals are like factories for people. In a factory, you work on things, while in hospitals you work on people. We all know that, but does it have to feel that way? We could pretend it was a nice place. When you step into a hospital, you always feel like you're doing so for the last time. I have never entered a hospital not thinking I was about to die. Even as a visitor I feel that way. I always feel like when I visit at any moment a doctor could drop in and say: by the way, since you're here, you have cancer. That's why I never do health checks. I have the strong position, that if I'm sick, I don't wanna know. I just want to die. Ideally without pain. If I end up dying in pain, because I didn't check up on me, then my strategy backfired, but I'm fine with the inner logic of it. I still prefer this to the constant anxiety of thinking I'm sick when I'm not. It's better to think yourself healthy when you're sick, than to think yourself sick when you're healthy. For to think yourself sick is worse than actually being sick. The latter tortures the body, the former the mind. I'd rather not be tortured. But if I am, I dont wanna know. My goal is to wholeheartedly believe in my health until I drop dead. Hospitals always feel like the final chapter of your life. Every time you go in there, it feels like you'll never be out in the fresh air again. It always feels like the final breath on mother Earth when you enter them. It's sort of strange to work in a place like that. The truly sick are not lying in the beds, but standing beside them. This is not a life friendly environment, get out while you can. I wonder, do doctors feel more comfortable as patients? For them this is routine, isn't it? So maybe they feel at home. I wonder how their houses look. Do they have sickbeds? „Honey, I feel romantic tonight, let's push our sickbeds together!" Imagine your bed has wheels. Do sickbeds have wheels? Not really, do they? What am I thinking of? Rollerblades, I guess. The lighting in hospitals is strange, too. It's almost like when the hospital was first built, they consciously went for the most depressing light. The hospital light. I know it serves a function, to light up the room and make the sick visible to the naked eye. Yet have they heard about a welcoming atmosphere. I for once would love a pretty floor lamp. Or some LEDs. A light show would be cool. Imagine doing surgery in a light show. Or dying in a light show. Imagine you're dying during surgery, because the doctor put on the pink light. Or neon light. This reminds me of those night clocks that throw the time onto the ceiling. What's the point of that? Why would I want to know that at night. It really serves no purpose. The purpose of a clock is not to reflect the time onto every surface available, but to look at it specifically, if and when you need it. Back to the important part: my thoughts about hospitals. Hospitals always look like the homes of a future species that has replaced man. These are not buildings in which we should live, let alone die. There is something so depressing about hospitals. It might be connected to the patients, but in my opinion it's connected to the doctors. The doctors fill the room with a cold, so present, that I shudder and shiver, just thinking about them. However, I do like how doctors talk. To the point. Sometimes they even seem human to me but this is a false impression. They are clearly different. Their studies have dehumanized them. And it's important for one must dehumanize the man to operate on him. Imagine you're thinking this during a surgery: I'm operating on a soul, on a child of god. I would get a nervous breakdown. It's good to think of man as a machine when you have to remove his appendix. A doctor sees the mission, not the man.

Hospitals are a scary place. I'd rather die outside than survive inside. It's strange when you think about it. Hospitals are the two limits of your life. You begin in them and you end in them. That's scary of course. For they remind you of your mortality. Doctors scare me, for they have such a range. They are capable of the best things, but also the worst. Most professions don't have this ethical range. Doctors can be saints or monsters, it all comes down to their morals. Yet in my experience, morals are not their strong part. They are a very technical bunch. Often when they talk, it reminds me of speaking chess computers. „Pawn. To. C9". This is how they sound. „You. Have. The Cancer." Well I don't, luckily, but they sound like this. I always feel uncomfortable around doctors. It's not their job of course to make me feel comfortable. But you know how they say some people have such a warmth about them. Well, the doctors have such a cold about them. Doctors need to be cold, for they need to detach from what they see. But I am afraid of their range. I always feel like they could do terrible things, if one had good arguments in place. This is what I mean by range. They can heal you as well as kill you. That's too much range for one human.

Doctors really scare me. To a point, where if only they could save me, I would think twice if I wanted to be saved. They are a scary bunch. It's their language. They're so technical. I always feel like talking to a dictionary, i.e. one that thinks by itself. They have all the words available, yet few emotions. But it must be tough to be a doctor. Imagine you go from one sick person to another. That's depressing. I would also start to dehumanize the situation. You talk to sicknesses, not people.

And that's probably good, for that's the point of why you're here. You're not here for a good chat, you want to be fixed. And they fix you. I still think it's preferable to avoid it. Hospitals are always reflecting the atmosphere. They are cold sterile places. I mean they should be sterile, but must they be cold? Why not make them warm sterile places. In any case, I respect the doctors. I just hope I don't have to rely on them.

This reminds me of something I read in Kierkegaard where he says that he never calls for a doctor and he makes sure to stick to this principle, because the doctor, while able to fix him, might end up harming him rather than helping him, considering that the doctor's help would be in violation with his aforementioned principle. I think both the logic and the message are impeccable, and I couldn't agree more.

I hate being a visitor in a hospital. I always feel like I'm one false word away from being placed alongside the patient. That's why I never speak in hospitals. I'm afraid that I say something like: Excuse me, where is the toilet?, and the doctor would respond: When have you last checked your bladder? And I would go: yesterday, in fact, this morning actually, and then I would run away to the toilet, escape through the window, run all the way to the mall, to get a big bowl of ice cream, and eat it, while weeping and humming melodies. It's safe to say that I'm easily excitable. But I always feel like this in a hospital. Like I'm supposed to be a patient, and I would be, if the truth came out. What truth? I don't know. That's why I don't go to the doctors. I'm 90 % sure that I will die a preventable death. In fact, I'm sure I will die of something that could have easily been fixed by a doctor, if I had seen one. I'm scared of doctors. They always know, don't they? I don't want them to know me.

If the truth came out, I would be lying there, right alongside the other patients. That's my feeling in the hospital. When someone says they're a doctor, I choose my words carefully. I always fear that they detect sickness in my speech. So I speak very carefully. Which ironically leads them to assume that there is something wrong with me. Yet if I spoke carelessly, who knows what diagnosis they would make.

One should always talk to a doctor like a border guard. Don't give them the benefit of the doubt, give them the opposite, whatever the opposite of benefit is. Give 'em that. It's important that you don't tell your doctor the truth. Tell them the untruth, for the truth may result in surgery. This must be avoided, as it's better to die in the unoperated state. Trust in homeopathy, for it never lets you down. Or am I wrong? Has it ever hurt you? Has it ever killed anyone? See. That's why I trust in homeopathy. Doctors are dangerous, they put people to sleep and then they kill them.

I trust in homeopathy, and the good spirits. I think this is the better way of healing, for these are warmer people. I put my fate into the hands of the homeopaths. They have positive messages, and positive vibes. I trust them much more than the doctors. Who are cold creatures, who say bad things. If the truth is bad, it must be omitted. The homeopathic people are your friends. Just consider how they talk to you. They address you by your first name. The doctors never do that. So that's one-nil for the homeopaths. The situation is warmer, too. Have you been to a homeopath? It's beautiful. They have couches, colors, sometimes they have butterflies and birds painted on the walls, or the windows. They offer you tea or coffee. None of this happens in hospitals, for the hospitals are evil places. And how nice it is to talk to the homeopaths. They listen to you, they nod and smile, they engage with you on an emotional level. The energy is different, too. It's a warm energy. Yes, it's warm. And positive, reassuring, that's what I like about homeopathy. Compare this to the doctors who are cruel creatures. They do none of this. They don't want to hear about you, and your experiences, and your afflictions. They only care about your material disposition, and physical condition. They see you as a thing, and this is how they talk to you. I love going to the homeopaths. They reaffirm my humanity, they know what it means to be human, something which can not be said about the doctors. The homeopaths are very much in connection with their own humanity, and therefore with yours. This is how they heal you. By introspection. The body can only heal, when the soul is healed, and they embrace this wisdom. Wise, yes, the homeopaths have this superior, spiritual wisdom which the doctors don't possess. I went to many doctors, none of them wanted to hear about my soul. Every time I would talk about my soul, they would reject it, and ask about my body instead. Their fixation on the body needs therapeutic intervention. It's clearly pathological. That's why I like the homeopaths. They always agree with my intuition. When I elaborate on my afflictions, the homeopaths smile and confirm that my judgements are correct. The doctors on the other hand are rude, they say I shouldn't diagnose myself. But I believe that a human always knows best what affliction he has. A doctor couldn't possibly tell this. They are often wrong. For example about medication, and also injections. I don't believe in injections, for who knows what they put in there. I only believe in the healing powers of self. One must be in touch with one's feelings. If one has this connection, one can heal oneself. It's important to heal from within. It's a myth that sickness can be cured from the outside. And that's why the doctors have it all wrong. They try to fix something that cannot be fixed by another. Man can only heal himself. The homeopaths share my views. I can tell from their demeanor, that they understand my words. They feel them, within that is. Doctors always stay unpersonal, and distant, they would never share anything from their lives. They are inhuman in this regard, very stale and standoffish. The homeopaths on the other hand always share about their personal lives. I find it very comforting that they tell me what they are personally struggling with, and the afflictions they have. It's good to be positive in light of the negative, and this goes for sickness, too. One should encounter sickness positively, not negatively like the doctors do. It's only negative when you view it as negative. If one is positive towards one's sickness, the sickness will eventually disappear. This is the wisdom of homeopathy, and it's a higher wisdom. I learned this from my homeopath, who is my friend. She is in her sixties now and a rather confused character. She is very positive and always reaffirming. Her name is Agnes. Agnes told me this, and I do not claim credit, it's all her words. One must view the human holistically. Mind, body and soul, they need to heal as one. You cannot heal them separately, that's what the doctors got all wrong. She really is a treasure, I owe her everything. Especially my health. She has a cute little sausage dog, which sometimes barks from outside the room. Her place is beautiful, it has pictures hung up, which her grand children painted for her. Her grandson is called Nicolas, he is 9 years old. She told me about him the other day, which proves my point. What doctor would tell you this? They're inhuman, and that's why I'm skeptical toward them. My homeopath, she is different. She told me about a man that she healed from affliction. All it took was a spiritual intervention. Some people just need to talk, she said, and she's absolutely right. There are many people dying from cancer every year, which shows that traditional medicine has its limitations. She's always happy when I enter her practice. She does everything by herself, the reception, and the appointments. She practices with me a holistic approach, which tackles my afflictions on all levels. It's energy, she said. It's all energy. Isn't this what science tells us, that the universe is nothing but energy? And this energy can be channeled and tapped. Sometimes the energy flow within us comes to a halt. There is a whole new science of energy in the making. She gave me books to read, and I devoured them. They made a lasting impression on me. For it's all connected, it's called the body-soul-connection. The brain channels the energy which we receive from outer space. Her practice is warm, and this is my point. How stale and cold hospitals are, and how warm her little practice. It's embedded into a residential building actually. She lives on the second floor. When you enter her practice, she makes you a tea and you can play with the sausage dog. I wonder if sausage dogs are happy being called that. It's a pretty ugly name for you as a species. Then again, they're rather ugly specimen. In any case, her sausage dog is called Hugo. Hugo loves a good stroke. But you only have to wait briefly, for she makes sure to only accept one appointment at a time. That's what she says anyway. I once saw her calendar by accident, and a lunch date with her friend was suspiciously visible. Be that as it may, you enter her practice, and she often begins the conversation in a warm way. She talks about her own life a little bit, and how little Nicolas is turning 10 soon. It creates a warm and welcoming atmosphere, which is the basis of all medical recovery. Then she asks me how I feel today. I tell her about my afflictions, and what concerns my soul. She then asks about my soul, and see, this is the difference: no doctor has ever asked me about my soul. They never want to know how you are spiritually, or energetically. They don't even care about it. My homeopath, she cares very much. Sometimes all we do is talk. We talk for 40 minutes straight, while the session is only 60 minutes long. I wonder, what else we would accomplish if we didn't talk so much. Agnes says that talking is a big part of the healing process. And yes, it helps to talk, we often lose ourselves in it. When we talk, we're immediately immersed in the conversation. She has a great capacity to care and listen. And she always asks, as if her particular aim was to keep the conversation alive. As long as we talk, the healing advances. She says that in her view, and it's her particular conviction, that it's all energy. I remember when she first said this to me. She paused, and looked at me triumphantly. She portrayed such wisdom, such spiritual insight at that moment. I agreed, but I was also a bit mesmerized. It's so simple, isn't it? The simplicity of it struck me. It does make sense, that it would be energy, that makes my body sick. And in order to make my body healthy again, I must tackle that energy. She said that, one must get rid of the sickening energy within. I asked her if in her view it was a physical energy. She said, it's all energy, and once again I was struck by the simplicity of it. She then talked about channeling the energy. She explained that there is energy running through our body, we are almost pervaded by it. And that this energy, when the flow is interrupted, tends to make us sick. And that we must reinstate the energy flow, for if the energy flows, we will be fine. I felt the energy flow through my body, when she said it. I knew I had to reinstate the flow of energy within me. My inner balance was clearly out of sync. I asked her what she would recommend. She gave me an abundance of advice. She said I must pay attention to my soul. The soul must be, she says, we cannot live without her. I asked her if there are any people who are physically sick, despite perceiving their souls. She says, none that she knew of. We consider extending our sessions. For they have clearly cured me within. If I ever get sick, I will not go to the doctors. I will go to Agnes instead. For her and I have a close relationship, and I'm sure whatever afflictions fall upon me, she will heal me from them.

Her words still resonate with me. She's right, it's all energy. Why have I never, not once heard a doctor talk about my energy? Why do they never mention the spiritual aspects of a disease? Why is it that they don't practice a holistic approach to body and soul. They always focus on a particular area of the body. This is another aspect in which the homeopath is superior to a doctor. A doctor is specialized in a particular region of the body, whereas the homeopath is a specialist for the entire body, as well as the soul. I'm always impressed by a homeopath's ability to know so much. It seems like they have superior knowledge, or their knowledge transcends the body in a way that it doesn't even apply to it any longer. Their wisdom has transcended the body. It has become a separate wisdom, in the realm of the spiritual. Their whole discipline and intellectual work deals within the spiritual realm, which is why they perceive things that doctors are oblivious to. Energetic, atmospheric oscillations, and the inner channels that connect the whole body. The spiritual which lives inside us, and the energy that flows through us cannot be captured through the purely physical. The spiritual must be included. The doctors are hopelessly fixated on the body, and under the erroneous assumption that the body's afflictions should be healed by fixing the body. This is very shortsighted, and expressedly unholistic. It completely dismisses the energy aspect of it. The doctors only see a part of the equation. They treat the sickness as if it was merely a broken part of a functioning machine. Clearly the broken part indicates that the whole machine is broken, and must be worked on. But this includes the energy, which flows through us. It's all science, isn't it? We are beings of energy, and the spiritual is our consciousness of this energy within. It's all connected to quantum physics. We must trust the homeopaths, who approach our afflictions holistically. I dream of a society where homeopaths are the established doctors, and the doctors are no longer en vogue. I find it very telling for a society that it trusts the narrow-minded view of the medics and doctors. They are clearly materialistic, by only caring about the body. We need a society shift, and it starts with replacing our doctors with homeopaths. And then, perhaps, our hospitals will be warmer places. And perhaps I will not feel like I'm sick, when I go there. I want to feel validated and welcomed. But as long as the doctors continue their psychological reign of terror, things will never change. We need to think big, and we shouldn't be afraid of big changes. The doctors don't care about our souls and energies, so we must create new doctors. Medical studies should start and end with the science of human energy. Doctors need to take emotional care, before they take physical care. We need to humanize the profession. Doctors must care about us as human beings. They must approach us holistically. I dream of a world where there are no longer any surgeries. Surgeries are simply not necessary, they don't fix the problem. If the energy flow is interrupted, the problem will return. Hospitals should be happy places. They should make the people happy, one should want to go there. I dream of a less materialistic society, or a spiritual society, with spiritual hospitals, which heal us spiritually, and by that physically, for once the spirit is healed, so is the body. I learned that from Agnes.

I read a letter from Baudelaire, in which he wrote this: „It is said that there have been poets who have lived out their entire lives with their eyes fixed on a cherished image. I do indeed believe that faithfulness is a sign of genius. You're more than an image I dream about and cherish – you are my superstition". I, too, felt this way about her. A genius I am not, but faithful I am. I know she was imperfect, but she was perfect to me. I let her do and be whatever she chose. The girls I see today are mostly images of her. But she was not an image. She was real. And I loved her. So I guess she wasn't my superstition after all. She was my faith. My love for her wasn't irrational, though. It was rational. I loved her for a reason, for all the reasons in the world. If she had wanted me to give her the reason why I loved her, I would given her all of them. I believed in her, most faithfully.

But I was cautious with her. I protected her from my images. I knew she was too delicate. I spoke to her normally. I never thought to her. She was too precious for that. I made sure she didn't get tangled up in these storylines of I. I was always afraid that I was messing her up in a way. I mean she was pretty messed up when I met her so the stakes weren't exactly high. I was still careful with her. I always felt she was fragile. I didn't want to burden her. I wanted her to be light. So I made her light, and I was quite good at it. She got rid of her anxiety, and soon enough her sadness, too, faded.

They say you should move on, but first I couldn't, then I wouldn't, now I should, and probably will. Yet it makes me sad. To know that soon she'll just be another thing of the past. I just wish it wouldn't feel so final. I feel like I'm letting her down personally. As though I didn't love her enough to love her forever. I know it's for the best. It's dangerous when you fall in love with being in love. It can turn into an addiction. I feel the world drying up on me. Like I'm seeing normal again. It's like being healthy after long sickness. There is some good in it. But I'm also missing it already. To see illusion like reality. I was so immersed in this inner state of mine. As if I had plunged into a bucket of paint. And perhaps I shall see it like everybody else again. In any case, I feel it coming. I'm not even sad. I'm rather tired. Tired from my own madness. I loved her very much. I shall think of her every now and then. Perhaps she will think of me, too.

Dream has freed me from the freedom I dreaded. Man needs necessity, without it he becomes disoriented. And lifeless, for one cannot live in the abstract. One must plunge into existence, head first, and never come out alive. Life should not be contemplated, it must be lived and lived only. One should only contemplate it after the fact, hence never.

I don't want to go back to the dreamless state. It was a flat existence. Stuck on the x-y-plane, which I couldn't escape. I would travel in both dimensions. Yet the third I had lost. The dreamless state was tedious. It gave me little to chew on. I was never in dream at the time. But then I was, and it was with her. I remember how the world changed in front of my eyes. She was the color, and the pictures, in this new world of mine. Her presence changed the heavens above. And the earth below. It became so utterly beautiful. She was the painter that painted my world. I stood in awe, I couldn't believe. How beautiful she could turn this world so bleak. This state I call dream. I am still in it, albeit sad, for the true artist of mine is no longer with me. I only hold her piece of art in my idle hands. I adore and admire a little longer.

I reminisce about this paradise lost. I wish I could re-enter. But she holds the key, and she's no longer here. I have lost my permit of residence. I still live in dream. Although my dream is not as colorful anymore. It's painted in a dark blue. But blue is beautiful, too. It's better than grey, and certainly better than transparent. I used to see right through the world. My glance never reflected from anything. The world was objective, and so was I. Everything I looked at, I looked right through. Now I realize how unhappy I was. This is why I'm a jokester. I cannot stand this transparent society. There is never anything that our eye picks up on. I just want to sit at a table of ten people and cry. Just to make it a human situation again. I can't stand the artificial nature of man in society. We are not supposed to be like this. It's a superficial existence, and it concerns us all. I hope it bothers us all, too. There is no beauty in it. There is never any depth. It's shallow conversation. We should all lie a little bit more. Too much honesty kills the soul. There is a time to be truthful, and a time to be generous with the truth. At times we should go for the untrue version of events. As well as speak a little less. People always say what they think. I wish they would keep some of their thoughts to themselves. It's not good to know a person inside out after thirty minutes. It shows limitation of character. I'm never interested in people, for they are never any interesting. They lay everything out, right in front of you. I wish there was some mystery surrounding them.

One time we were in a supermarket, and I made her read the nutrition facts of a can of peas. She laughed at first, but I said, I'm not joking. She was in good spirits, so she did it. I watched her while she read out calories, sodium, and what not. She was beautiful when she did it. I almost didn't notice when she had finished. People must have thought we had lost our minds completely. I did anyway. She was laughing, like a little girl, her sweet way of laughing. Yet when she spoke, she was assertive. Her voice so soft, but set, I loved that about her. She had a way of being firm about things. The way she opened a window or a door. She did it with beautiful precision. She never had to do anything twice, she did everything at her first attempt. We had beautiful moments. I was the kind of person that would prompt others to say: well, he's a strange one, but if she's with him, he can't be that bad. She made me appear normal to the world. It's strange, when you're different, you know, not least because everybody tells you. Nobody means any harm by it, but still everybody tells you. They don't know everybody else told you already. With her, I was almost vindicated. She excused me in the eyes of the world. I made her laugh a lot. In fact, I probably shouldn't have made her laugh so much. It ended up driving us apart. Because she believed my laughing indicated that I was happy. Little did she know I laugh because I'm not. It's easier to laugh than to cry for a boy. Never trust the laughing boys, for they're often the saddest. Not in a girl, at least in my experience. My accumulated life wisdom leads me to the conclusion, that women, when they laugh, are happy, and when they're sad, they cry. This is very confusing to me, as a boy, who is not used to these strange ways of showing emotion. She, in any case, thought I was getting happier. I remember how sad she was at the end. I had made her happy, and she didn't understand why I wasn't happy. I tried to explain that I never was, nor would I ever be. And this is how we drifted. She was disappointed. But she also realized that I was right. We both did, and that was the sad part. I loved her very much. I loved the way how I could tell from her necklace that she was nervous. She would always breathe without any noise, was she nervous, or relaxed, you could never tell, except for her necklace, it move up and down, and I could tell she was breathing faster. Sometimes when she was anxious, she would brush her fingers over her clothes, as though she was straightening out a crease. But there was no crease, and she knew it. She had a lot of these subtleties, which fascinated me. Now you may say, what's wrong with you, who pays attention to these things? But I loved her, so I did. They made me see all the beautiful in her. I know that this cannot be understood by the more superficial kind, but to spot details is beautiful. You start to see it in all the people. Sometimes she brought me something. Then she almost sung my name, with her beautiful voice, and she would say: ‚Look, I brought you something'. Isn't it incredible that women do this? They think of you randomly, and they bring you something. Now this really does fill my eyes with tears. Perhaps I was judging prematurely. Men don't do this, do they. Do we bring stuff? Randomly? Well, I don't. But she did. And it would always be something cute and thoughtful.

I was strange. She was quiet. And we were beautiful together. Sometimes she was in good spirits, and more forthcoming. I always tried to complement her behavior. When she was quiet, I was more active. When she was in good sprits, I held back. I thought that made us a pretty pair.

These isolated memories always make me sad. When she was quiet, I was active, and I asked her questions. She would smile and answer. When she felt better, I would be silent and let her shine. On her better days she owned the world. She had her plans, and I would always say Yes to them. I was happy when she wanted something, because for the longest time she had never wanted anything. She had a puzzling personality. She had great and outgoing days. On other days she wouldn't say a thing. There was no rhyme or reason with her. Especially no reason. But I was fine with it. I really didn't mind. I found my happiness in hers. The truth is. I'd rather idealize her and see her the way she was in the beginning. Rather than, you know, how she was at the end.

I write for the silent people. The loud don't understand me. The loud don't understand anything that's not shouted at them. They always expect you to say everything you think, and ideally put the emotion on your face, so they don't have to guess. There is no subtlety with the loud people. Everything is explicit. I have silent contempt for them. They have no beauty, and no style. They only have words and syllables. I do not seek to entertain the loud people. For in order to entertain the loud people one must be loud as well. The loud are never entertained by the quiet people.

The loud people always tell you what they think. Where's the beauty in that. The mystery. I like it when I don't know everything. There is a particular beauty in a person not speaking up. Of course, they are encouraged to. But some of them simply don't want to. It's for those that I write. They resonate with my own unwillingness to speak. How nice it would be to never exchange a word with the girl you love.

The loud people always give everything away. They never hold back, or restrain themselves. Then they say: it's my personality, it's just who I am. This is not a good enough reason to behave like this. You cannot just say, I am like this and then be obnoxious. If you're obnoxious, it's your number one duty to no longer be obnoxious. Everything else comes second. But the loud are always obnoxious. They have this compulsive need to share their thoughts and feelings.

The loud people are a strange bunch. They of course call us strange. As they say, history is written by the winners. The loud people win, because the quiet don't fight. We capitulate and abandon the quest. The loud are in the majority, so they are calling the shots on what's normal and strange. Normal is to be loud, apparently, while it's strange to be quiet. How strange. To call the normal strange and the strange normal.

The loud people expect us to be loud. We are to speak our feelings and thoughts. They encourage us to share. Yet never in their obnoxious minds do they find this simple thought. That not everyone wants to share their thoughts. That some people just don't care to do that. They don't grasp the possibility. For them the matter is clear. We don't speak up, because we don't feel encouraged, or we are shy. And this makes them even more obnoxious. Not just that they are loud, but also that they want everybody else to be loud.

And then they start whining, like babies, when it's quiet. The loud people can't stand the quiet, they require the noise. And we all suffer from this. We always have to deal with their neuroses. When it's loud, the loud are happy, and when it's quiet, the loud are sad. The loud want us to be loud, whereas we want them to be quiet. The quiet have been coined the losers, and the misfits of society. But how much prettier we are than they will ever be. The loud will never be pretty. They simply have no relationship with the sentiment.

The loud always have ideas and opinions. They always feel in a particular way, and they will tell you in what way. I wonder. Do the loud ever think, that it might be better to be quiet. That there is some good in the quiet? No, because the loud don't think like that. They live off the noise. They must continue to be loud, for they don't feel alive without it. And so we must play the game by their rules. We must be loud, or we don't get acknowledged. Who talks about our misery. We, the quiet, don't want to be loud, why do we have to be.

‚Tell us something about yourself'. How about not? How about I don't do that. Not now, not ever. Never. Never ever. How about that? Is what I want to say but never do. That's why I make up stories. It's the only way to navigate through the situation with my dignity intact. I hate when people ask me questions. Why can we not talk about neutral things? Why is it always so personal with the loud people? They always want to talk about themselves, and then they want to know about yourself. I care for neither one. Can we not talk about amber stones, or, I don't know, dragonflies?

The loud people get happy in conversation. I get miserable in conversation. How can people be so different? Whenever the loud people say they have a hard time being alone, I shake my head in disbelief. How can you not possess this basic human skill. To be alone. Perhaps you should learn to be quiet then. There is a time to be loud and a time to be quiet. I wish all the times were the latter, and none the former.

The loud are full of despair, when they cannot be loud for a change. You see the life draining out of them. They can't stand it. The inability to make noise. They're very physical creatures, too. They always touch you, and hug you. They always eat. They're always snacking. And while they're snacking, they continue to talk. They don't even pause then. While snacking, and talking, they're laughing and coughing. In everything they do, they manage to create noise. It's almost something to admire again. Only almost, though.

The loud are desperate when they're left alone. When there is no noise, and no one they can touch and caress. They don't know what to do in those circumstances. It's like the suffering of Christ. The only thing missing is the cross they're not bearing. In fact, the quiet is their cross. It pains them, it burdens them, they can't stand it no more. It's been two minutes, why is nobody saying anything? The loud are almost collapsing when the silence begins. Yet they call us strange. These strangest of people.

It's their world, and we accept it. We don't fight it, for we don't fight. There is nothing prettier than a dignified defeat. One should never engage with the loud people. One cannot win this battle. They're much better at being obnoxious. It's impossible to beat them on their home ground. One must stand back in defeat, and continue to be quiet.

The quiet have been defeated by the loud. We don't mind, for we never engaged in the fight. We would have lost anyway. But now the loud are teasing us. They want us to speak up. We shall never! We must remain right here, in the beautiful land of silence. You will never enter, for you will never shut up. So we find some wisdom, that you will never get your hands on. We are safe here. Far away from the loud people.

We must not be changed by the loud people. They're a manipulative bunch. They want us to play the game by their rules. We shall never. For our rules are much prettier.

The loud want the quiet to share. The quiet want the loud to not share. Let's agree to disagree. The loud never cease to amaze me. You've known them for five minutes and they tell you about their birth stone. But since the world belongs to the loud, they make the rules. All of this is considered normal. Yes, I know, right? *This* is considered normal. When are the aliens finally coming to finish our misery. I hope they take out the loud first so we can have one final moment of quiet. Imagine this, the whole planet quiet. How beautiful it would be. We would hear the animals again. We never hear the animals anymore. They make noises, but we don't hear them. It would be nice to hear the planet again.

The quiet must remain quiet, for they made the right choice. They chose dignity. One should never become like the loud people, for they have abandoned their dignity. They tell everyone about every little detail of their lives. It's very ugly to have no secrets in front of strangers. The true masters are those who have secrets in front of their family.

We are quiet, and not unhappy with it. The world is made for the loud people, because it is made by the loud people. The loud have made a society for themselves. And what do we do about it? We don't despair, for it's still our choice to remain quiet. We must not become loud, for we are really poor at it. Almost tragical. We'll turn ourselves into fools trying to compete with the loud people. We will be awkward and uncomfortable, and obviously we will fail. Then we'll return to the quiet, but with painful memories. Do we want this? Do we really want this? So. We must remain quiet.

We must never compete with the loud people. They're a long way ahead when it comes to being obnoxious. We couldn't possibly catch up. We'd just make ourselves look foolish in the process. If the loud want us to be loud, we tell them that we want them to be quiet. We don't say it in those words, for the loud people dictate the terms. It's considered strange to not share intimate details about yourself with a stranger. What a world we live in! Quiet people, never change. The loud are just a temporary failure of mankind.

We are the quiet, and we're proud of it. You can talk to us, but you can also not. In fact, it would be preferred if you could not. Or how about we talk about something else. Something which is actually interesting. How about you don't tell me how you felt this morning. And why don't you just not show me these pictures of yours. You know these pictures that you are currently showing me, just show them to me not. I don't think the loud people are right. I think they're wrong. The quiet people are not as wrong as they're depicted to be. It's unfortunate that society treats us like we were dropped on the floor as babies. But we must not despair. It's only the loud people who don't understand us. The quiet understand each other silently. Therefore we should unite. In silence, which is our natural shield against the loud people. It's like with some animals that don't see you if you don't move. The loud don't spot us if we don't make any noise.

The quiet people are my friends. I love them dearly. I shall be their brother. Or son, or uncle, father is a bit too much, but everything else is fine. I shall be family, as they are mine. The quiet people must stick together. Just remember to never become like the loud people. They are too many already, and they're getting more by the minute. Let's not give them the gratification of changing for them. We must stay strong. When you encounter a loud specimen in the wild, endure it bravely. Don't stoop down to their level. Stay quiet, for your quietness is beautiful. The loud are ugly, never forget. To become like them is to sacrifice your beauty.

I saw a homeless man today. I don't know if he was homeless, I confess that I base this on visual inspection. Then again he was barefoot, and this seems like good enough evidence. He was sitting cross-legged in front of a brightly lit advertising pillar. He mumbled: ‚I apologize for talking to an advertising pillar, but I'm a drunk, and the drunk always talk to those who can't escape." I thought that what he said was generally true. We always talk to those who don't run away. Most people flee from us, it's their natural agitation. It's rare to meet a person that halts for you. Sometimes you're so disoriented that all you need is an advertising pillar to stabilize your view. Something that is solid in this vertigo state of yours. I tried to explain before that she had this effect on me. When I saw her, my view stabilized, on her that is. So I understood the man. He was looking for something stable in his unstable life. And his unstable view, for he seemed really drunk. He was humble — in front of the advertising pillar, which moved me. I wanted to go talk to him and become his friend. I didn't, though, for you have to draw the line somewhere, and I draw it at barefoot.

The more time passes, the more I realize that we never had a future. Circumstances brought us together. But circumstances are a bad foundation. In fact, the worst. If circumstances bring you together, circumstances will drive you apart. Love must happen despite the circumstances, not because of them.

She said, you only liked me when I was sad. I said, that's not true, but thought to myself, it wasn't exactly untrue either. When she became happy, for as much as I loved her, I loved her a little less. She became a better and happier person, yet also more different from me. We were close for the longest time, until we weren't. It was like losing her in real time. She said, why are you not happy? We should be happy, she said. I wasn't sure what to say. She said, I would make her unhappy again. I said, perhaps. She said, you will drag me down. I said, I wouldn't. Yet I wasn't so sure myself. She had a fragile temperament, and she was always prone to becoming sad again. She was vulnerable to other people's emotions, and mine were weighing heavy on her. It was strange how quickly we fell apart. We were at the highest heights, but we had gotten there too soon. Love must be stable, it cannot be volatile. If love is volatile, it's just not meant to last.

What we ended up being, in happy times, almost made me unhappy. I cannot explain it well. But it's true. I no longer felt myself. I tried to explain it to her, but I didn't succeed. Her and I understood that her and I simply didn't understand each other. Some things cannot be understood because they cannot be explained. Other things can be explained and they're still not understood. We were the latter. I explained it to her, she heard me well, yet she didn't understand. And maybe I just ended up choosing myself. Maybe that's what disappointed her. Even though she wouldn't have wanted me to choose her over myself. She wanted me to choose the both of us. But I realized, that we couldn't have both. Her and I in misery would have been my bliss. Her and I in bliss turned out to be my misery. I am to blame, I even told her that. I said I was sorry, yet not able to change. I couldn't let go of myself, that would have devastated me on a whole different level. It ended up being a choice between her and me. From an outside perspective, I am to blame, yet from my inside perspective, I assure you it all makes sense. Some things can't be explained very well. They must be felt. I did not feel myself in this new world of ours. I receded and returned to myself. One cannot live without the feeling of self. It's impossible to be happy as the person you are not. It's not your happiness then. It's being unhappy while playing the happy person. She was sad, and so was I. But I also told her, that I loved her, which she didn't like to hear. She was upset with me. If I understood it, why couldn't I change it? Well, I couldn't. You can't change everything. You can't change the way you feel. That's just not in our power. It was a fact, almost a natural fact. Like the weather, I simply couldn't change it. I didn't want to drag her down. She looked at me, disappointed, I'll never forget. She wanted me to say: I'm coming with you, or at least: No, don't go. I couldn't do either one. I could not come with her, nor could I ask her to stay. For she was actually miserable. When I met her, she was broken. There was no happiness in her. I made her laugh, and I made her light. I did that. So she didn't understand why I couldn't come with her. But she wasn't similar to me in this regard. Her unhappiness made her unhappy, and her happiness made her happy. So very strange. I never expected her to understand me, but I tried to explain myself. It just wasn't me. The sadness and the misery are deeply embedded within me. They're in my soul, in my childhood, in my every experience, and in my thought. I can be happy, but only with my sadness intact. With her, it went into a different direction. She eliminated sadness from our lives. And in a way she eliminated me in our relationship. I saw myself fade. It wasn't her fault, it was perfectly healthy what she did. I never expected her to play this broken game of mine. I never even mentioned it. I mention it now, for it makes it easier to explain myself. It didn't make any sense from the outside. But it does from the inside. To one who feels like me, it would all make sense. One would see the inevitability of it all. I let her go, without a fight, because it was me against her. I couldn't make her decide for me and pull her back into my misery. Would she have done it? I'm not sure. She would have probably not allowed me to. Which is good. I don't think she would have let me. I never considered it, so it's pointless to speculate. The alternative was to follow her. Into the day, and a new life. I didn't want that. And so it was decided. I think of her a lot, but I never really regretted it. I have lost her, but I have kept myself. I would have kept her perhaps, but lost myself. This would have been worse for me. I remember how disappointed she was at the end. It seemed so pointless to part ways, for I feel that we both loved each other. It was truly the way she looked at me, which still resonates with me. She was blaming me, for choosing me over her. And to be honest, it's what I did. It was choosing her or choosing me. And so it happened. We never spoke after this, it was too sad for the both of us. I felt that she had to forget me, and I supported that. I would have made her a mess again, eventually I would have. I only made her happy when she was sad. I stopped making her happy, when she was better. I felt myself, subconsciously, making her unhappy again. I was so repulsed by this, that I stopped immediately. But then I felt like life was draining out of me. It was all very strange. Yet I didn't choose it. There was no element of choice, or the choice had been made, once I realized its implications. To choose her and to lose myself, or to lose her and to choose myself. I didn't want to lose either one, but I had to. And I just couldn't choose against myself. So I guess she was right. My own heart was more affected to my own face than to hers. I loved hers very much, but mine a little more.

When you despair, think of this. Your soul is disquiet, and you cannot change that. But your mind is disquiet, too, and you can do a lot about that. You can quieten it. You do so, by not despairing over your despair. For almost nothing is as grave as it seems in the moment. Most things can be fixed. To be serene is not to omit a reaction to your despair. To be serene is to be serene despite your despair. To allow the despair, yet to stay composed about it. To tell yourself it will be fine, because it will be. Despair is the landslide of the mind. But the slide will end eventually. Despair lives off our reaction to it. We shall not grant it the satisfaction.

When anxiety strikes, and you feel your mind sliding, remind yourself of serenity. Serenity is the mind's confidence in itself. Despair, on the other hand, is the mind doubting itself. To control the mind in despair is not done by facing the despair head-on. During times of anxiety this makes a bad situation worse. It's only recommended once the anxiety has settled down. When anxiety strikes, in the heat of the moment, one must not face it. Instead, one must face serenity. It is as though you turned your back on your anxiety. Serenity is the blue sky, which makes you forget that you're walking on a soil full of snakes and insects. This is how it feels in anxiety. The ground underneath you is creeping and crawling, and it's very uncomfortable. Don't look down there, when anxiety strikes. Look up to the beautiful heaven instead. For there she is waiting on you, serenity in all her might.

Anxiety strikes unexpectedly. The feeling is accompanied by anxious thought. When the spiral begins, you must not face it. Whatever makes you anxious, shall only be looked at later on. In rational times face your anxiety. In irrational times don't. Instead, look up to this beautiful heaven of yours. The mind can think itself unquiet, but it can also think itself quiet. It's not a one-way-street, and if you experience it like this, then you haven't practiced serenity. Serenity is the ability to soothe your mind, any time and any place.

When anxiety strikes, don't think of it. Easier said than done, I hear you say, and you're right. That's because, it's a negative disposition. It's negating one thing, without positing another. Which makes it hard to follow up on. That's why I'm telling you to think of serenity. Don't think *serenely*, for this will not help you in times of despair. The mind will do its landslide motion anyway, and create enormous turbulence in the process. In this condition you cannot think serenely. Instead, think in your irrational, turbulent fashion, but think of serenity. Remind yourself of it. In anxious times things don't seem as they really are. They seem distorted. To look at them serves no purpose. They just show you the grinning mask of madness. Don't be afraid of it, but don't look at it either. This is only a mood and a moment, it's not real. There is no monster inside you, you must not be afraid. Remind yourself of serenity, for serenity will stabilize your mind.

When despair strikes, don't despair. Instead remind yourself of serenity. Serenity is the calm and soothing voice of reason. The mind may be turbulent now, but all turbulence stops eventually. It's good to not despair over your despair, in fact it's vital. When turbulence hits, let it hit you, don't think about it. It's important to not engage with the storm while you're in it. Anxiety is like the sun, you should never look straight into it. But this is often difficult in anxious times. Therefore, I'm not telling you to not think of your despair. Instead, I'm telling you this: think of serenity. Despite your despair. Don't try to shake off your disquiet, for this is a way of looking straight into the sun, acknowledging your anxiety. The problem with anxiety is that it gets stronger as you acknowledge it. It's a common misconception, mostly created by people who don't know the sentiment, that anxiety fades when you face it head on. This is only a good strategy in rational times, when anxiety and despair are not present, or not presently active. In the heat of the moment, you must not acknowledge your anxiety. Don't reflect on your anxiety, reflect on serenity instead. You'll still be anxious, and think anxiously. Yet you will think anxiously of serenity. This will stabilize your mind, and before you know it, your mind will be soothed. The mind is in control now as it should be.

When anxiety strikes, you will think anxiously, and nothing will change that. The soul seems to have that power over the mind. Don't fight the emotion, instead try to flow with it. Allow the emotion instead of resisting it. Control your mind, but let the emotion be. Emotion must flow, it's your mind that you should get a firm grab on. Strong are those who have strong emotions, while being in control of their mind. It's not recommended to strong-arm your emotion. The mind should not control the emotion, it should only control itself.

When anxiety strikes, think of serenity. This is not about *how* you think, it only describes the object of your thinking. And this can be controlled much more easily. Instead of struggling with the sentiment, we all know and hate so dearly, find a fixed object that you can direct your thought to. This object is serenity. And if it begins by only being a word, then we're off to a great start. Serenity is the beautiful sky, and the quiet seas. The green of the forest and the white of the mountains. Serenity is beautiful reason. You remind yourself of serenity, and it makes you calm. It distracts you from your anxiety. Anxiety shall only be looked at in its absence. In its presence don't look at it. If you do, don't worry, it's not lethal to look at it. But if you continue to look at it, you'll increase it. Anxiety lives off your attention to it, and it increases as you face it. When anxiety breaks out, make sure not to look at it. Instead look at serenity. Serenity is the soothing voice of reason. Desperate times do not call for desperate measures after all. Desperate times call for reasonable measures. You must fight despair not with further despair but with reason. To remind yourself of serenity doesn't mean you're calm. It means you're thinking of the calm. There is a difference, for when despair breaks out, it's impossible to remain calm. You are by definition in the disquiet now, and you will have to accept that. But what you can control is what you think of while being disquiet. And I'm telling you to think of serenity. Make serenity the object of your thought. This is the most effective way of making your anxiety fade in the background.

Serenity is the gentle voice of reason, within this anxious commotion of yours. Serenity says things like this: It's only a phase, it'll pass soon. Those are wise who can laugh in the face of their anxiety. Cute little anxiety, you have fallen upon me many times, yet I've always come out on top. To not be scared of one's anxiety is the most effective way of getting rid of it. Another surprisingly effective strategy is to get bored with it. At some point, it just gets boring. But chances are, you haven't reached that point. It's said that you should be rational, but in times of anxiety, this is the first ability you lose. Anxiety is very effective when it comes to dismantling your ability to be rational. In fact, anxiety is probably best described as the decay and collapse of rationality. That's why I'm not telling you to be rational, or even serene. Instead, I'm telling you to think of serenity. Make this the object of your thinking. Think of the quiet, and the calm, and the fact that things are not as bad as they seem. Anxiety doesn't describe your environment, it only describes your perception of it. Remind yourself that this perception is volatile. Anxiety is the turbulence of perception. This is not to be addressed by calling things turbulent. It must be addressed by reminding yourself that things are not really turbulent. Perception and sentiment cannot be controlled, they must be endured. You can only control your mental disposition, or your assessment of the situation. Anxious perception must be met with serene intervention, and it's done by reminding yourself of serenity.

Anxiety is the turbulence of the mind, and it must be met with serenity. For serenity is the stability of the mind. But since a turbulent mind cannot easily stabilize itself, otherwise anxiety would be a trifle, it must remind itself of serenity. What you should not do, when anxiety strikes, is to make anxiety the object of your thinking. By doing so, you will aggravate your situation. A fear, they say, must be met head-on, but fear is not anxiety. Anxiety must not be met head-on. One must turn one's back to it. It's irrationality trying to pull us down into the abyss. We fight this best by reminding ourselves of serenity. When you feel anxious, remind yourself, that you should not face your anxieties head-on, for it only makes them worse. Anxieties are irrational, they speak untruth. It's the soul in commotion, she's shaking your mind violently. See. The mind is being shaken, and that's why you're losing faith. But this violent shaking of the soul cannot be controlled or discontinued. It will discontinue by itself, just give it some time. Until then, make sure not to indulge in your shaken thoughts. Instead think of stable things, for they tend to stabilize your mind. When anxiety strikes, don't think of your anxiety. Easier said than done, I know. It's like flying on a plane that enters heavy turbulence, and trying not to think of the turbulence. In this analogy, though, remind yourself of serenity. The plane is fine, turbulence is normal, the pilots couldn't care less, they're thinking of what they'll grab to eat at the airport, the stewardesses are joking around in the front, currently thousands of airplanes are in the air flying through turbulence, none of them go down, etc. etc. This is thinking of serenity. The plane is still shaking, and so are you, but you're stabilizing your mind, and things are looking better. Now take this picture into your chambers at night. You've had an eventful day, your mind can find no rest, you cannot sleep, your thoughts keep you awake, and you are in disquiet, your soul is not resting, your mind is shaking violently, you feel anxiety creeping up on you, the despair is emerging, there it is, the feeling of panic, and if you panic once, it becomes a domino effect. This is the malicious cycle, the spiral of anxiety, and it gets worse by the minute. What do you do? Don't participate in it. Deny it. Don't face it, for it speaks untruth. It lies to your face. Yet you're no longer able to tell it's lying, since the first thing anxiety dissolves is your ability to reason. You don't recognize the lies as lies, you consider them true, and this stimulates your anxiety, which tells you more and more lies. You must break this pattern, by facing something else. Face serenity. Things are not as they seem. Your mind is just doing its thing again. In fact your soul is. Your soul is shaking your mind. Remember that what appears to be true is an effect of your shaken mind. The truth is not really dissolving, it's just destabilizing. This is anxiety taking over your mind. You fight it by not fighting it. Remember that. You cannot win the battle against your anxiety. You can only lose it. The only way to win this game is to not play it. But here is the good news: you are much more powerful than your anxiety. It depends on you, you don't depend on it. You face anxiety best by facing something else. Serenity will stabilize your thought. It's just another evening, and the world is fine. Tomorrow I shall get up and have a coffee or tea. Yes, my mind is shaking, and yes, I'm feeling anxious — you can still acknowledge this, for you shouldn't develop fear of fear, you should simply not dedicate your time and thought to it —, so yes, I'm feeling anxious, but it has no connection to how my life is going, for these two are unrelated. The way things are, not anxious, and the way I feel about them, anxious only at the moment.

Anxiety doesn't survive on its own. If you deprive your mind of it, it can no longer sustain itself. Anxiety needs your attention to exist. You no longer suffer from your anxiety if you no longer think of it. Think about that. The tricky part is that anxiety is so dominant, that it's almost impossible to not think of it. Anxiety is like a hundred red alert signals flashing onto you from all directions in space. This is why I'm not saying: don't think of your anxiety. Because you'd probably go: well, that's brilliant, thanks for that! And rightfully so, for it's virtually impossible to not think of your anxiety when it strikes. Instead I'm telling you this, and you see what I'm trying here. Conditioning you into remembering this. When anxiety strikes, think of serenity. The quiet, and the stable, the simplicity of things. I could tell you to be reasonable, but this would be a poor piece of advice, for the first thing we lose in anxiety is our rationality. Anxiety is almost a function of the irrational. It describes the degree to which irrationality has crept into our rational minds. Therefore it's misled and misleading to advice rationality to those who suffer from anxiety. For the very fact of their anxiety determines their inability to be rational. In anxiety, the way we think is slipping out of our grasp. We are no longer able to stabilize our thought, as it's violently shaken by our anxiety. We must not fight this losing battle by trying to stabilize the violent motion, as this is a way of facing the anxiety head-on. You can hyperfocus on the violent motion which will only make it worse. This is why trying to being rational produces the seemingly paradoxical effect of making us even more irrational. Because to focus yourself on being rational, is to focus on your way of thinking, which is irrational now, due to the anxiety, and this is a way of confronting your anxiety head-on, by trying to wrestle it and to beat it. But anxiety is always stronger. It will dissolve our rationality completely and pull us down into the abyss. It's important to remember one thing: The soul is stronger than the mind. She has this deep-rooted, original force over us. When we fight our soul, we always lose. We must allow her to do her thing, while staying in control of our mind. This is why I'm saying, don't try to be rational when anxiety strikes. For this will, seemingly paradoxically, yet in truth logically, make you even more irrational. Again, remember this, anxiety is your irrational or turbulent way of thinking. This is not overcome by confronting your way of thinking, for this leads you to acknowledging and engaging with the turbulence, which in return spurs and fuels your anxiety. To break this spiral, you must not hassle with it, and wrestle with it. Instead you must think of — well. You get the drill. Don't try to think serenely, for this is the same flawed way of reversely acknowledging your anxiety by fighting it on its home ground. This always ends in defeat. Think of serenity instead. Or think anxiously of serenity. This expresses the point I'm trying to make. Don't acknowledge your anxiety, just accept it, while reminding yourself of the serenity that you're actually in.

Man is always somewhat an unreal version of himself. There is something in his development that makes him not become who he is right away. Only if he's lucky he will notice in time. Most men never get to that point so they remain a version of themselves. Why this affects men more than women, I'm not sure. But it does. Men never become themselves right away.

In sadness, man no longer entertains a version of himself. Until now he thought it was him. It wasn't, and he's starting to realize it. This is often traumatic, which is why man has a difficult relationship with sadness. It opens wounds which he didn't know existed. For the first time he realizes how little he has lived. How much he's only played the man. In sadness he realizes, almost suddenly, how wrong everything is.

Men suffer differently from women. Women always suffer a little, and sometimes a little more. Men don't suffer at all, but once they do, all hell breaks lose. Men suffocate their suffering, until their suffering suffocates them. They battle it. Women have a different disposition toward their sadness. More accepting. Less aggressive. Men, when they experience suffering, try to make it disappear. For man suffering is a traumatic process. He's just not any good at it. When the suffering came, it almost instantly overcame him.

Why is it that men suffer so differently. Is it because of society? Men are not supposed to suffer. A suffering man is a failed man. Says society anyway. And treats him that way. Suffering to man is an existential threat. It's not just a bad day, or a difficult phase. It questions him existentially. It pulls the rug from under his feet. Men therefore never develop a healthy relationship with suffering. They never suffer, until they do, and then they suffer really badly. This is why I'm saying men should become more like women. There is a lot of good on the other side. In many regards it sucks to be a man. Everything intuitive has long disappeared. Everything is rationalized. Nothing is ever confronted. When one looks in the mirror, one sees the neighbor next door.

Men are not happy with this. Make no mistake. They are miserable about it. The lesson here is to become more like women. To not worry about what other men say. For they are probably in the pre-suffering phase. They will get there. And once they do, they'd love a friend like you. We should not be concerned with being men. We should be concerned with being human.

It doesn't make him happy. To live like this. His life is so solid, yet so fragile. It's the condition of man. One must always keep going, and for what. Men should look at women and learn from them. In suffering man realizes who he truly is. More often than not it has little to do with what he portrays. Man should welcome suffering. Suffering leads him home, if only he trusts. To kill suffering within you, is to kill your soul. For that which suffers in you is what you stopped being. When you became somebody else.

Man has a tendency to become somebody else. Why that is? I'm not sure. It's said that women have better instincts and a stronger sense of self, and that's certainly true. For men, the self is more of an abstract thing. Acquired rather than experienced. Men acquire a self, and almost always another. Abandoning their true self in the process. Why do men not stick with their true self? It's hard to say. They create a self, rather than discover their own. All of this is why I'm praising women, and why I believe we should be more like them.

I don't know why men develop another self. To women this happens, too, but differently. Women often go through the experience of adapting to society's expectations, and adding them to their own personality. Eventually they shake them off, realizing how little they had to do with them. How they should have spoken up. Or how they should have said No, when they ended up saying nothing. Yet in all of this their true personality is present. It's more suppressed than absent. For men this is different. They really manage to completely abandon their true self. Then they develop a different self which makes them miserable. Their suffering reminds them of that, yet instead of fighting their alien self, they fight along their alien self against their suffering self. This is why their suffering continues in silence. A woman's true self is always present in one way or another. This cannot be said about man. He really manages to completely dismiss his natural self, which he then replaces with an artificial self that he identifies with. This is a miserable way of existing, make no mistake. It's easy to say that men dominate the world, but at what price is this accomplished? Often by replacing the true, vulnerable self, with the facade of a man.

One must realize that both man and woman suffer. They should be friends. It must be possible. Women suffer from being oppressed, and belittled, and objectified, so they suffer from being subjected. Men, on the other hand, suffer from being alienated, from being homeless at heart, lonely within their souls, and ultimately trapped in somebody else's life. Men are always performing. To a point where they have forgotten they're playing a role. All men are method actors. They play themselves in a role. And why is that? I don't know. Men are not to be their natural selfs. For their natural selfs would probably be a lot more like a woman's self. We're all human after all. It has to be asked, to what extent the distinction between man and woman is produced by society. Probably to a larger extent than we care to admit. In any case, if men kept their natural selfs, they'd be a lot more emotionally intact. Instead they abandon their self, for they learn early that the world doesn't care about it. The world cares about the self they create. What a miserable world.

Man doesn't develop his natural self. He abandons it. And then he puts another on top. This is the self he creates. Now everyone praises man for his ability to create. But he should be pitied, for he created an artificial self. We only have one self after all. This is why ‚self' is in the singular. The one self we have is our natural self. To abandon it, and to replace it with an artificial self, makes for a miserable existence. The majority of men suffer from this. They get used to the suffering, within their artificial self. Like clothes that are itching, man wears his artificial self under visible discomfort. He would love to get rid of it, once and for all. Yet he's gotten used to it. To a point where he mistakes himself with it.

Man must learn to rediscover his natural self. It's hidden well below his artificial self. Focus on the suffering part, it's that which speaks the truth. The part that comments on it and fights the suffering — he's probably the liar. After all, you mistake yourself for him. Trust the suffering, for the suffering never lies. Those who suffer will be greatly rewarded. Suffering is God's test of our will. We shall show ourselves worthy by suffering like Christ. Or like any other prophet, or good fellow man. Whatever you believe in, shall be your truth. Let's not argue about who speaks the truth.

Well below the artificial self, which man has created for himself, he finds his natural self. This is why suffering is often traumatic for man. It's his natural self suffering from his artificial self. Or in other words: the self he feels suffering from the self he identifies with. The traumatic part is that they're not the same self. Yet he doesn't realize this, and unfortunately commits to the artificial self. The artificial self lectures itself about control, and power, and strength, and then suppresses the natural self further. The alien in me kills the human in me. This is how men suffer, and it's very sad. It's mostly men who suffer from this. And they're alone in it. When I think of it, I want to be their brother, and friend. I want to give them a hug, for we both know he needs it.

Man is very restrained in the emotional regard. It's torture that he endures, as he plays the part that he never consciously signed up for. Had you asked him, do you want to become an artificial self, he would have said No. But nobody asked him. And so he abandoned his natural self. Which is now suffering within him. He feels his natural self, yet he doesn't recognize it anymore. He thinks with his artificial self, and he fights back his natural self. Which, after all, seems alien to him. When the I identifies itself with the artificial self, the natural self is referred to as an „it". „It" tortures me. „It" makes me sad. But this „it" is you. Man has lost his path. He's the sheep off the flock. He shall be returned. To his natural self that is.

The I, which is conscious, separates from the self, which is unconscious. They are no longer one. They have become two, mind on the one hand, soul on the other. Women have many advantages over men, one of the most striking ones being their almost always intact mind-soul-connection. Compare this to man's mind-soul-connection, which is almost always broken. Men have to speculate about their soul's disposition as if their looking into space trying to find exoplanets. It's a most technical enterprise, which involves a lot of observation and theorizing. Women, on the other hand, know themselves intuitively. Their mind and soul are like two best friends who tell each other everything. In men, it's more like one guy sitting upstairs on the couch watching football for hours without saying a word, while there is a skeleton buried underneath the house that has been lying there for decades, unbeknownst to everyone. It's safe to say, that men do not have a functioning mind-soul connection.

And this shows how far we've come, i.e. how far off. We have committed to the wrong path, and we've been walking on it for centuries. You gotta respect our commitment. Men are very committed to keeping their artificial self afloat. Women on the other hand, as soon as the painting that is their soul is hanging crookedly by only a margin, will feel the urge to make a life-changing decision. „I'm going to Australia!" „Why is that, honey?" „I don't know, I just feel like I *have* to do it". Men, on the other hand, live a regular life, for 25 years, then collapse over a trifle. That's a man's specialty.

Men abandon their natural self to create an artificial self, and then they live a whole life trapped within that artificial self. This is nothing to envy. It's a lonely existence. Men need to be encouraged to not live like this. That's what I've been saying all along. Be more like women, we have a lot to learn in this regard. We should not waste our lives living as artificial selfs. This is a sad development, for the natural self is who you truly are. You must find it again, it's still there, within you. It's probably a bit cranky due to the way you've treated it. Yet suffering is healthy. I would go as far as to say that even depression is somewhat healthy. I stand lonely with this opinion I'm sure, but I think there is some truth to it. Because who is depressed? Our natural self. And what is it depressed about? Our artificial self. What does it aim for? To get rid of our artificial self. And what do you want? To be yourself. See, your depression and you, you are not so different. Good things come to those who are depressed.

Women, too, suffer from this. But men are more prone to it. The thoughts that lead him away from depression are the thoughts that lead him away from himself.

When I like a sentiment I make it prettier. I quickly forget about the reality of things. Reality is but an impetus. It's like lighting the match. But the flame is within. And there I shall exist. I should have never idealized her like that, yet I'm glad I did. I found beautiful things on the way. Among them, her. I would have never loved her the way I did. I would have loved her prosaically, and how boring it would have been. It was a lot better like this. The delusional element made our love beautiful. It always does. One should not love rationally, for nothing kills love better than reason. Unreasonable love is beautiful. The fewer reasons can be named, the more reasons you have to stay. It's beautiful to love illogically. One should never try to rationalize one's sentiments.

Dream changes the world from within. It makes the world unique. Unique to you, as it should be. Life must be lived in the unique fashion. It's an amazing feat to change the world with your eyes. It's like the world has plunged into a fog. You see the world as if through a mist, your eyes no longer clear.

When dream is present, our souls are applied. When dream is absent, our souls are denied. In dream we apply our soul to the world. And the world to our soul. It's genuine interaction. Deduct the world from the picture, and you have — pure isolated soul. This is why dream is important, for dream is the soul in action. The soul produces our pictures.

Dream is the subjective world, or the world turned subjective. This is often belittled, but it's important that we see the world subjectively. Modern times lay an unhealthy emphasis on the objective view. Yet the objective view makes the subject superfluous. Dream is the world through the eyes of a subject. When you deduct the world from it, you reach pure subjectivity. It's like seeing your soul through the world.

Make sure you pick up on the changes. For it's your soul that applies them. When the objective starts to look subjective, then your soul is applied. This is important. Nobody wants to live in a purely objective world. It would turn life into a most lifeless endeavor. And the subject into a conscious object. Do you want to be that? An atom with consciousness? Or do you want to be a living, breathing soul?

When dream is present, the soul is applied. Try to understand what she is telling you. The things that appear desirable in dream are the things she desires. Everywhere you go, you see truth and untruth. To desire, to wish, these are not bad things. It's much worse to have lost one's desires. In dream the world is seen through the eyes of the soul.

Most people are no longer able to enter this state. Their eyes are wide awake. If there is no refraction of the world, if you see it as it is, then you are not in dream. You are wide awake. This means that your soul is not applied. She is denied, and you don't lend her your eyes. And so you see the world, in the wake state, but this is a state in which the world becomes dull. The dream is not present, for you are present in the world. You should be present in dream instead.

To be awake means to see the world objectively. Your eyes do not see dream, they see reality. Modern times glorify this state, which explains our misery. Don't get me wrong, you should not lose the ability to see the world objectively. But you shouldn't lose the ability to see it subjectively either. It's important that you allow dream to take over at times. Love, for example, is dream in its purest form. You see the beloved subjectively, not objectively. Ideally you're always in dream, not just as a lover. One must not depend on love to enter the dream. Ideally one dreams in order to love. The reversed dynamic is possible, but it requires practice. One must learn to think of the world like the thirsty sailor of potable water. Once you introduce this dream-like thirst into your view, you see the world subjectively. It's a much more immersive and intensive way of living. It's not for always, and ideally it's controlled. You should learn to turn it up and down.

You must keep the ability to see the world subjectively. For everything that qualifies the objective world is subjective. The world is not joyful or hopeful, it's what you add to it and draw from it. But this is the layer that the soul introduces.

When the dream emerges, our soul floods the world. This is the privilege of being alive. To experience this. It's not about seeing the world objectively. The subject is not a living object. Even though that's what modern times are trying to tell us. That we're just moving objects, and not even alive, for even life is just the motion of matter. Silly, silly, three times silly. This is not what life is. It is confusion, ethical, spiritual, divine confusion, and we must not partake in it.

Of course it's dangerous to take a grain of truth and create a whole landscape of illusion from it. But I'm intrigued. I like the sentiment. The thoughts I have in that state are quite different. I call the state dream, and the sentiment love. And the thoughts? I don't know. But I like them. I feel like they are new thoughts, that haven't been thought, at least not by me. It's dangerous to cultivate an image which corresponds to no reality anymore. I'm sure it's not recommended, which is why I don't ask for advice. I'm simply walking on that path now, trying to find out where it leads. You can't deny the beauty of a new path whose destination is unknown.

Misery is powerful, and often underrated. It's an incredible state to be in, artistically speaking. Never will you see the world in a more personal light. Albeit not a pretty light. But it's your world now. Nobody else sees it this way. Misery turns the world into your own little piece of fabric. You can change it around, in the strangest ways. The world becomes an impression, and every detail a piece of that impression. There is an intensity, an impression in misery which cannot be denied. Memorize every little detail. Take it all in. Don't memorize it with your mind, take a snapshot with your soul. Take a photograph, but one that captures the sentiment, the impression and the intensity. For this is later on lost, and you must remember it in the moment of artistic creation. The moment of misery is not the moment of creation. It's your material. One day, soon enough, you'll draw from it. You will relive the misery. And if you're gifted, if you're skilled, you can turn emotion into characters, speech and plot, onto the canvas, into colors, and shades, or figures, into shapes and forms, interactions, connections, prayers and verse, into empathy and emphasis, into love and affection, affliction and pain, it is everything, most everything, but it is necessary that you capture the impression. You must have lived and suffered, to become a unique artist. Else your art is shallow and dull. The greatest writers have always been the tormented souls who went through many hardships before they picked up the pen. The greatest painters have observed the world before they started capturing what they felt. The greatest musicians have had melodies long before they've had scores. The great builders cannot help but to admire shape and form, design and alignment, they see these things like we see the normal world, they see visual patterns and their effect on the surroundings, every room and building has a soul, and they see it. All of this is necessary, you must see in order to create, and this means you have to live, and experience, and the wider the range, the better, it will all come in handy. You have to inhale the moment, you have to live for the intensity, for the artistic expression is nothing but the echo of human impression. Focus on that, gather impressions, live in them, devote to them, capture them, with your soul, and one day, you shall express everything and anything, for you will find it all within you.

One should die an unobtrusive death. This is a civil duty. Other people shouldn't be involved in your own demise. We are all drawn to the disappearing people, are we not? They fascinate us. There is something which holds our soul in awe, when we consider them. They are simply gone one day. Part of us wishes we could join them. Or we could join their fate. Isn't this a beautiful day — to disappear into the night. Never to be seen again. Not to start a new life, but to fade out of this one. To leave, as though you're falling asleep, silently vanishing from the face of the Earth. There is so much beauty in that concept, and such a strange allure to it.

To not just be oblivious, but to be the object of oblivion. It's beautiful to be forgotten. It makes for a beautiful existence.

One can exist truly and beautifully, until one day — one disappears forever. How poetic. Life is poetry which humans don't know how to read. They lack the heart. But I find life very poetic. The fact that it ends makes it a most poetic experience. And that the mind recognizes it, and that it can still touch on the eternal, that makes it a highly spiritual experience. All in all, life couldn't be any better. Imagine how dreary it would be if it lasted forever. I can barely stand it as it does. I look forward to entering this beautiful land called oblivion, from which I set and to which I'll return, and in which, even in life, I am closer to than reality. Oblivion is my home, oblivion my aspiration. Oblivion is where I belong.

I talked to a guy today who was full of it. I knew it when I saw him. His beard was too immaculate. Men who take extra care of their beard must be avoided. They want something, and it's never what you expect. I also saw it in the way he laughed during our conversation. He observed me and whenever I laughed, so did he. But the way he laughed gave him away. A natural laugh is a succession which begins in the eyes, goes via the face, and then the mouth. First the eyes laugh, then the face, then the mouth. A fake laugh does all of this at the same time. It's like turning on a light switch. He had the light switch smile. It wasn't natural. It was obvious that he took special care of his appearance. This is always a bad sign in a man. It shows his priorities. On the plus side, he wasn't a sociopath. He lacked the personality for it. His haircut made me skeptical, too. It was the haircut of a man who wanted to stand out without standing out. Here was the kind of guy who would hold a book in his hand once and later on call it his favorite book. The kind of guy to claim it all, having delivered none. Too many people like this in the world. At first he thought he could play his dirty tricks on me. Unfortunately, these guys are very clever in the practical sense. They know who to do it with. He realized quickly that I wasn't material for him. You can't play tricks on someone who sees through you. He became rather passive, and receptive. He couldn't play the cultural guy, for the guy he claimed to be was facing him. If I had been a dummy, he would have played me for a fool. He would have tried to make an impression on me and probably succeeded. Oh does it get any lower than men like this? A guy like this doesn't react to your words. He reacts to the face you make while saying your words. If you look sad, he'll mirror it. He reads your emotion, and responds in whatever fashion that will secure him admiration. He is a chameleon, he has multiple personalities. Unfortunately he doesn't have one. But credit where credit is due. You cannot play a player. He knows if he can his play his tricks on you. It's like in the animal kingdom. They not only sense fear, and weakness, they also sense character, and conviction. I'm mentioning this, because I always spot the fraudsters, but they always spot me, too. I can never lead them on. Ironically, they can tell if someone speaks genuinely. Or maybe that's not ironic, maybe that's the whole trick. When they sense that someone speaks falsely, they recognize themselves in it. And as though a sixth sense kicked in, they withdraw. They notice that you are like them. Which means you are different, and probably a lot cleverer than you appear. They notice this, because it's the game they are playing. It's like an alert is being triggered. And they do not carry on. They don't play their game with you, because they know they can't. I have often tried to defraud the fraudsters. They're always a little better than me.

It's often called absurd what I say. And that's because it's often absurd what I say. I get bored easily, that's my main problem. I try to be serious, but I only pull it off for a couple of seconds. One absurdity sneaks in, and another, and then it's each for himself. As soon as I say one nonsensical thing it's like my soul is grinning devilishly. She wants more of it and so do I. I get bored by conversation, and who doesn't. I'm always surprised by the fact that I seem to be the only one who is bored by it. People really seem to enjoy it. They talk about banality, with serious tonality. It puts me well in agony. Indeed I find it hard to pretend I care about something so trivial. Everyone is pretentious these days, and that's why my attitude stands out. Which annoys me because I'm not trying to make an impression. Sometimes I share, but it always backfires. It never goes well. When I'm saying, I don't enjoy talking about myself, then they think I'm shy or cautious. No, I'm not. I just don't like talking about myself. It's a boring kind of conversation for me. Then I say, I don't do any of these hobbies that you're talking about. I don't go on them online dates, I don't have a bucket list, and I'm not into mindfulness, it just hasn't been a big topic in my life. They do a million of these things, and this is how they've come to define individuality. Sometimes I'm honest, it's often after being worn down by conversation. Then I say things like: I really don't care about these things. Or I don't care how I look. Or men who care about their looks are useless. It gets more eccentric, the more tired I get. And then they think I'm a strange fella, or perhaps arrogant, or just different, if they mean well. But this is also not an impression I was trying to make. I wasn't trying to make any impression. In fact, it was my particular intention to not make any impression. But this is not understood by people who only ever think about the impression they're making. And how am I supposed to talk to them? Anything I say can and will be used against me. There is nothing that connects us. Yet they continue to ask me questions. They're trying to domesticate my autistic soul. I came here for idle conversation. I simply shouldn't have come here. I always regret sharing about myself. My goal is not to share with these people anymore.

People love talking about themselves. I hate it when they do. It's never interesting. Who gave the boring people the idea that they're interesting? Someone must be held responsible. One should have intervened early on. One should have said: this is not interesting. This is boring. Please don't be boring. If you have the urge to be boring, fight it. Fight it with all your might. This should have been told to the boring people right from the start. Yet today, the boring deem themselves interesting. And we all suffer from it. There is nothing like listening to a boring person telling her boring tales as though they were interesting. It's a most painful experience. One must pretend one is not dying inside. The boring always compensate for their boringness with their excitement. They will tell you all about it. They recently tried meditation, they are going to yoga now, they are planning a trip to Hawaii, ahhh Hawaaii?, ahhh Hawoow! They recently read a book — doubtful — about how to stop procrastinating. There is this place, at Kings Square, which sells fried chicken peas. ‚It's sooooo good, you have to try it'. They have a lot of curiosity for the world. They want to travel, the boring always want to travel, for they need the stimuli. The boring get cranky when the stimuli stop. That's why they don't understand people like me. If only I could not understand them either. Unfortunately I do, one sees right through them, and one is so terribly bored. The boring are never silent. It's always the interesting people that don't speak. This is a tragical, yet logical fact of the world, and it's logical because interest grows in silence. The boring could be interesting, if they learned to be silent. It's the compulsive need to speak, that kills all personality. One must develop in silence, or one doesn't develop at all.

You can joke yourself through an entire evening. In those situations you should never fall silent. If you fall silent once, you won't speak up again. It's for this reason that I never stop drinking during the night. One must not allow doubt to creep back in. It's about believing in what you do, no matter what it is. They say you must be convinced to convince. And there I convince myself to be convinced. To joke is a secure way of making sure you're never spotted. You can hide in plain sight, right under the eyes of the people. One should never allow one's true personality to shine. Only the shallow do this, and they are silly to do so. Personality must be hidden during conversation. One must adapt to the circumstances, and speak to please. Only a fool would speak naturally in artifcial circumstances. A fool or one who naturally thinks like the crowd they're in, but they're fools in their own way. In conversation, the goal is not to appear as the person you are, but as the person you are expected to be. One must give the people what they want. I remember a remark from Pessoa, that he appears as a nobody at work and takes particular pride in being misunderstood there. This is the way to go. One should appear as a different person among people, in order to protect what's valuable. This is easily lost in the crowd, and even a crowd of two is a crowd. One must keep to oneself, and share only the inessential. To share the essential with people who we barely know is utter confusion. Those who speak their minds among people are hailed and praised by the crowd, but they're also destroyed by it. It's a curse in disguise. One must speak the inessential to people, never the essential, for the essential belongs to us alone. One should say the inessential, yet in a way that makes it appear essential. This is the easiest way to avoid suspicion. For if the crowd suspects foul play, it will double down on you. They want the essential from you, and they're not satisfied until they get it. You must present the inessential like the essential, while keeping the essential to yourself. This is not being secretive, it's being protective, for you protect the essential from the greedy hands of the many. They like nothing better than for you to become one of them. That must never happen. We shall be individuals, to the bitter end.

In conversation one should only share the inessential. Yet the others must never suspect it. If the many sense that you're not sharing the essential, they will drill for it, until they find it. They shall never, for they have no business finding it. The essential belongs to you alone. The inessential is our shield, as well as our weapon. The others want our essential. We shall feed them the inessential instead. For that ensures a safe distance. It's not recommended to appear your natural self in artificial circumstances. When the conditions are estranged, we must estrange to the conditions.

We shall keep the private private. The transparent society is a nightmare, we should not participate. We must be true to ourselves and to the ones we love. We must never expose our soul to the world. The soul is vulnerable, she easily hurts. In company, one must use the mind to protect one's soul. The soul has to remain hidden, understood only by the mind. The mind will then consolidate, and carefully weigh its words.

It's a common myth that we should be truthful to strangers. There is no obligation. Society is an imposition, we didn't ask for it. We don't owe her anything, we can do whatever we like. To be truthful in conversation is setting oneself up for failure. One almost begs to be taken down. Society is a threat to each one of its members. We shall never allow company to do our thinking. One must ensure that the others do not impose on us. The inessential serves as a protector and shield. We must deny the others access to our souls. In conversation, one should never speak truthfully. Instead one should say anything, whatever, just not the truth. The truth has no place in conversation, for it has no bearing in it. The truth is ridiculed by the presence of the many.

The point is not to deceive the company, but to deflect it. From your essential self, and onto your inessential self, which you can easily get rid of. Just watch them operate on your inessential self, and see how much they influence it. One must never slip, and fit in one's essential self. This always ends in agony, and embarrassment. The essential self gets confused by the imposition of others. The others don't know us, how could they comment on us? A conversation requires you to be untrue, for the untruth protects your inner truth from the violence of your company. Your company threatens your essential self, and this happens in more subtle ways than you can imagine. They change you silently, you won't even notice. This needs to be prevented by all means.

To be truthful is setting oneself up for failure. Your true self, once exposed, becomes an object of amusement for the others. You have turned your soul into a pawn in their hands. Oversharing is overcaring, and you will get vulnerable under the eyes of the many. Your inner truth should not depend on the judgement of others. It should depend solely on you. To expose yourself in such a manner, is dangerous. They call it opening up, but this is nothing to be valued. One should never open up to a stranger society.

I only live on paper now. It's strange. Writing used to be a medium, or a way to express myself. Now it's become my primary mode of thinking. I believe it's a writer's dream to think like that. I think by writing. At the same time, I feel increasingly empty when I don't write. I barely survive a five minute conversation. My thoughts require the written form now. Otherwise they remain unstructured. I used to be a good thinker and a poor writer. Now I'm an okay writer but my thinking degrades. Or maybe not. Maybe I'm just changing. I used to do everything in my head. Now I do it on paper. It brings some relief. Yet it's strange, everything else has become more tedious. I cannot hold long conversation anymore. I cannot bear to say a word about myself. I even repulse from introducing myself. I wish I never had to say a word anymore. I shall communicate in the written form.

One should never find out about other people. It's better to imagine their personalities, rather than finding out who they are and be unimpressed. Information limits imagination, which is why information needs to be limited. Information is like salt, you need a little or the dish is inedible, but add too much, and the dish becomes inedible again. There is a fine margin for salt in a dish, and so there is a fine margin for information in imagination. Too little and imagination has nothing to chew on. Too much and imagination becomes redundant, as it's replaced by information. You only need a grain of information for a bowl of imagination. Information must be carefully controlled. Modern relationships in which both sides know everything about each other are pathetic. They have completely eliminated the element of surprise. It's important that there are things you don't know about each other. This spurs the imagination in ways unimagined. It's generally adviced to share as little information as possible. If your significant other thinks you're a whaler from the South Asian Sea, you have done well for yourself. Unless, of course, you are a whaler from the South Asian sea, in which case you have done poorly for yourself. You have overshared about your life. I am not sure there is a South Asian Sea, but it sounds like the sort of sea that would exist. On that note, one must always sound confident in the face of ignorance. The more ignorant one is, the more one must compensate with the display of confidence. If, by any bad luck, you encounter an expert in a field which you pretend to be an expert in, you must match their confidence and simply say they're all wrong about it. No one would think that you would continue your act after being found out. They would think that by this stage you would break down, and since you don't, it's proof that you're an expert on the matter. E.g. when they cast doubt on your whaler story, saying there are no whales in the South Asian Sea, you ask them how in God's name then he would explain the fact that you've been hunting whales there for what in October will be 15 years. See, this is so specific, that no one would think you made this up. They will probably counter it with some factual arguments and logic, and this is not an area you can compete in. Cobbler, stick to your trade! Don't enter this slippery slope of arguments and facts. Instead argue with pure invention. When they say there is only a South China Sea, you can say that maybe they have only been to the South China Sea, and that you recommend they go to the South Asian Sea, for the South Asian Sea is further away from China. When they say that the South Asian Sea is actually the Pacific, or the Indian Ocean, or whatever it is, for God knows what we're talking about, then you say you'd love to invite them on your cutter to cast out a rope or two. A rope, he says? Yes, you say, for you have been practicing whale roping, a technique discovered by the Oceanic people, which includes the baiting and catching of whales by one strong aluminium rope made of copper and steel. When they laugh at you, saying: ‚an aluminum rope made of copper?', you say, without blinking an eye, yes, it's a chemical compound. When they say: what's your equipment, you say this: we bring a crew of 30 to 40 men from the mainland. We bring provisions of two thousand steel tin cans for nutrition, as well as all the equipment necessary to land one of them big eels. When they say, tin cans?, what century are you thinking of?, you say, look man, it's the South Asian Sea, it's a rough terrain down there, the waters are relentless, they never tire of tiring you down. Then you fall silent, and this is called a dramatic pause. When they ask you how 40 men fit on a cutter, you say she's a strong lady indeed, she's seen many a battle with many a whale, and you nod affirmingly. When he says, a small cutter in the middle of the Ocean?, then you say, not the ocean, the South Asian Sea. When he says, what is the closest mainland to the South Asian Sea, you say, we usually debark from a place called Atamahang'ha located on the crisp of Micronesia. When they ask you what „on the crisp" means, you got them, since they obviously don't know jargon, and this is the nail in the coffin of their ignorance. It's clear for everyone to see that you are the expert. I wonder, how did the nail get in the coffin, and more importantly how did we find out? If the nail is in the coffin, and the coffin is closed, we should have never found out. Yet we did, for otherwise we wouldn't have this saying. Somebody must have re-opened the casket. Who was it and why? Imagine you're that particular nail. It's such a mind-blowing fame for a nail to achieve. To be the nail that started the saying. You're the one nail that made it into the human world. Yet no one knows about it. Not even in the nail world. It must be terribly frustrating. To know you're one of the greatest nails of all time, arguably the greatest, yet no one will ever find out. He must be the Jesus Christ of nails. Yet no one knows. Even in the nail world, he's just another nail. I wish I could find that nail and console him. I'm sure he is sad. Or she. It might be a she. In any case, when you say „on the crisp", you've got him. Victory is yours. But take it with dignity. It's good to stay humble in times of success. For all victory is temporary, and the fraudsters will attack again.

One must act on one's decisions like a dancer going through their motions. Not consciously, but unconsciously, yet with consciousness present, based on experience and training, and always action-oriented. A dancer doesn't think he or she will slip, and neither should we. The most important thing is to decide. The true failure is to stay passive in the face of decision. Any decision is better than no decision. One should always go for the seemingly impossible. The real danger lies in skipping the decision part, pushing it in front of us, just to realize one day that one should have decided a long time ago. Decisions are often considered to be definitive, when in reality they're not. In most cases decisions can be adapted later on. Also, new decisions will follow from the present ones. Life is a sequence of decisions. There is no destination, and no destiny either. It's about the way points, and there is no finish line. At some point the path will just end. Midway. One must navigate through the way points and realize that it's about making your way. To walk the path of the many is not commendable. It's usually a sign of cowardice and fear. To walk the path for oneself means to make decisions. And to keep making them. To never be afraid of making the wrong decision, for the next decision will come and by then we shall be wiser. One decision seldom ruins the path. Indecision often does. It leads you nowhere, for you are standing where you should be walking. This is why we must decide. The more the merrier. Decision is everything. The bad decisions tend to be our best teachers. For the good decisions are tied to the item we decided about. Whereas the bad decision is solely about us. We understand in hindsight that we decided incorrectly, and it makes us self-assess. One must always reflect on one's actions and decisions. Yet not in anticipating fashion. One learns to live by living, not by learning. A culture of indecision will nurture a generation of weaklings.

Indecision is the true danger of our time. We are constantly debating decisions, yet we seldom decide. To not decide in order to avoid a wrong decision is foolish. Indecision is a worse decision than the worst decision. This is not to say, that one always has to act. You can decide to do nothing about a matter, and that's also a decision. But to remain undecided, for a long time, is dangerous. One must decide first, and then correct, if necessary. This is a good, healthy way of living, for it teaches us to be the architect of our own fate. The more you decide, the better you will get at it. ‚Learning by doing' is everything when it comes to decisions. To ponder a decision, yet to never decide, is a risky business. Before we know, a year has passed, and we're at the same point. You must own your fate, you must not be owned by it. Decisions are only decisions if we make them.

People fear decisions because they think there is a definite outcome to them. Yet that's typically not the case. When good actions meet bad decisions the future may be bright. When bad actions meet good decisions the future may be grim. It's not our decisions that decide our fate, but our actions. Life is a sequence of decisions. Will we continue on our path, or will we change direction. One decision leads to another, and the road always continues. That's why we must learn to decide early. The ethical danger of our time is that the youths are not allowed to make decisions anymore. They are held, not in captivity, but in passivity. And they remain in it for a long time. No decisions are made, and if they have to be made, the young feel overwhelmed, for they learned to contemplate decisions instead of making them. They never get into the vital habit of making decisions. And so they are stuck, in their development and on their maturity level. We are raising a generation of eternal adolescents. Decisions must be taken, by all means, and at all costs. The more you decide, the better you will get at it over time. As Emerson says: „The years teach much which the days never know“. We must decide, and we must not be afraid. Decisions lead us to our true self. The good decisions as much as the bad ones. The one thing that keeps us away from our true self is indecision. If we never decide, we'll never find out. For we only find out in action. You cannot find out in contemplation. Take a word of advice from a not so young soul anymore. The intuitive decision is almost never wrong. The youth has good instincts, while reason tends to interfere. In this scenario, trust your instincts more than your reason. Give them the benefit of the doubt. Reason is more often wrong than you think. It produces a surprising amount of bad decisions. Instinct on the other hand is the silent hero of decision-making. For some reason, our instincts are mostly correct. And even if they're not, you will learn so much. An intuitive decision teaches us a lot about life and ourselves. For whatever we decide on intuitively has immediate, empirical value for us. We feel the results of our decisions. This feeling for one's decisions and their results will provide you with valuable insight. Decision is not a purely logical process, it's located somewhere between thinking and feeling. One should never let reason alone decide. One must feel and think about the decision ahead. If thinking prevents you from acting, stop thinking, start acting. You cannot think yourself out of a dilemma if thinking got you into it. When decision seems impossible, decide anyway. If you can't decide for the best, decide for the next best. To decide is almost to live. Many people regret their decisions, but all people regret their indecision. Indecision is the silent killer of our souls. Spiritually, ethically, it suffocates us. We must be free from the shackles that society puts on us. When we decide, we shall not stick with the decision stubbornly. We shall decide again, and correct, if necessary. Wrong decisions nurture good decisions, if you reflect and assess. Every man and woman needs to develop an individual culture of decision. Deciding is like breathing, one simply needs to do it. What initially is conscious and tedious, will become instinctive over time. But this doesn't happen automatically. It only happens if and when you start deciding. You will get better at it, and ultimately masterful. Those who never start deciding, will never stop doubting. They remain in agony, fearful of a life they feel not in control of. One overcomes this state by starting to decide. Later decisions are wiser than early decisions. The younger you are, the merrier your mishaps. But this is good. Decisions shape your character. Not good decisions, but all decisions. It's all about deciding. We must never let indecision creep into our lives.

Happy love is aesthetically disappointing. One has quickly seen it all. It makes for a happy life, but it kills the poetry. Unhappiness and love are like hydrogen and oxygen, they make life. Those who are happy should not create. They may procreate, as happiness works well for this. Creation must stem from misery. Otherwise where is the creative release?

This reminds me of the time I went to a restaurant abroad. The waitress had her problems with the English language. I was not to sit in the front, so she led me to the back, stating that „this area is for people". Now I'm not sure what she intended to say, but I was a bit confused for up until that point I had considered myself „people". I got takeaway, so I guess she wanted to say that the front area was assigned to guests who were eating in. In any case, I wondered if there was a slight chance that she knew exactly what she was doing, and that she was offending me, pretending she wasn't. Because that's the sort of thing I would do. Maybe she was playing a twisted game with me. If this area is for people, and she's leading me somewhere else, does it mean I'm not people? I thought about this, and one consideration led to another. I had lost all my faith, when she brought my food.

All the hopes that people put in me. I reckon they were never mine. Yet I could have fulfilled them. There was so much I could have done. Now I am tired. I won't do any of these things. People believed in me. They shouldn't have. I only let them done. Year after year, I let everyone down. When all is over, whatever remains. Whatever remorse, I have at this moment, I shall not have it forever. I will also let it down. The only thing I have delivered on is to not deliver on anything. At least I'm consistent at failing. I wanted it all, and what's the yield? I have remained at zero. I'm zero, will always be zero. Some people are just not made to last. Not everyone can be saved. When the rain is falling, the sky is crying. And so am I. We shall weep together.

The lack of personality always depraves the room of its oxygen. It becomes suffocating to stay around. Personality is said to be common, when in reality it's rare. People have two dozen hobbies, five dozen friends, and all of that becomes their personality. Then they ask about your personality, which is a lot less social in nature, and they simply don't get it. They think it's your angle, or you're trying to be interesting. Which makes it extra annoying, when the shallow people treat you like a fake. It's not even ironic. It's just annoying, honestly. And in order to avoid this situation, one pretends to be like them. And then it all makes sense to them, and they start liking you, which is just so straight up dystopian. I'm not surprised that all these people on social media are depressed.

Personality is everything. It's easy to judge based on looks. But then you sit down with someone, and they start talking, and if they have no personality, you become suicidal within minutes. It's a drag to listen to someone without personality.

Personality can make someone beautiful in an instant, and just as quickly spoil the person. If personality is absent, we want to be absent. It's a painful experience to be around people who compensate for their lack of personality with an excess of excitement. Instead of developing their personality, they treat it like a shopping basket, and they add more stuff to it. It becomes a bouquet of flowers and happiness. It's painful to witness, for the absence of personality ironically always shows up. When personality is lacking it's usually carried by a variety of superficial items that are supposed to carry the personality which clear to the world doesn't exist. There is nothing wrong with being boring. Not everyone has to be interesting, and ‚interesting' isn't even well defined. In any case, one doesn't need to be interesting. If you're boring and you're true to it, it makes you a pleasant person. On the other hand, are the boring people, who desperately try not to be boring, and unfortunately they're in the majority. There is an epidemic of the boring people flooding the realm of the interesting people. It's hard to cope with this. The boring always have dreams, and goals. They are often writers, creators, artists. Yet none of it is interesting. Just be true to yourself. Have all these hobbies, do whatever you want, but don't play interesting. One should always own one's personality with all the flaws that come with it. We're all just passing the time. In any case, personality is rare, and most people don't have one. „„Who are you to say that these people have no personality?“ Look, personality is a real thing, and these people just don't have one. It's clear to the world.

Someone with a personality is all we need. In that case the social setting becomes the best setting. Personality has become rare in a world that revolves around creating fake personas rather than developing the true persona that we are. Personality cannot be imitated, and it cannot be forged. It can only be discovered. The beauty of it is: everyone has one. But most people dismiss it to create a new one. It's those created personalities that bore me a great deal. It's like talking to a How-To-Human. The conversation is artificial, the contents are, everything is strangely limited, the scope of the conversation, and the sentiment that accompanies it. People make up personalities, and then they get sad, that they feel invisible. Well, you should have known better than to do that. By turning your profile visible, you're turning your personality invisible. You become something generic and artificial, while what you truly are, is quickly forgotten about. You are not supposed to create yourself. You're supposed to be yourself. And that is difficult enough, it requires years of practice and experience. To become somebody else is utter confusion, and it needs to be prevented from happening.

I recently discussed something, which the guy I talked to called a „non sequitur“. He had obviously made this term up, as I always do, and I liked where the conversation was headed. He tried to play his tricks on me, but I saw right through him. It allowed me to stay in control of the situation. He said a „non sequitur“ is a logical fallacy, when one makes a false assumption based on a correct premise. I nodded, to defraud him into thinking I was agreeing with him. He said, an example would be this: ‚All fish live in the water. The creature lives in the water. Therefore, the creature must be a fish.' I didn't follow for it seemed perfectly logical what he said. I looked at him with a blank face expression. He said: ‚You see, this is a non sequitur, because the fact that all fish live in the water doesn't mean that a water creature is a fish." I was confused, for in my opinion that was exactly what it meant. If A equals B, then B equals A, this is logical. I replied: But you said that the fish live in the water. He said, yes, but that doesn't turn every creature in the water into a fish. I said, but if they're in the water, then it must mean they are fish. He was hesitant. I felt I had to clarify my thought, so I did. I said, if, as you say, all fish live in the water, then the creature which lives in the water, will be fish, for it's fish that live in the water. He looked at me funny, and I got the impression he was questioning my intelligence. But he didn't give up yet. He said, ‚yes, the fish live in the water, but there are other creatures that live in the water, not just fish'. I said, yes, I know, for example crabs and lobsters. When I said this, my thoughts veered off, for I thought „craps and lobsters", if I ever have a restaurant, I shall call it that. But then I was back to my argument, and I said, crabs and lobsters and others, but technically they're all fish. He frowned at me. I said, for example „jellyfish", it's even in the name. He said, it's not about the definition of what fish is, it's about the lack of logical connection between the two statements. Now I frowned at him, for what he was saying now made no sense to me. He said, okay, let's try this again. Which annoyed me slightly for he was pretending I was the dumb guy. He talked extra slowly. He said: aaaaall fish live in the sea, alright? He looked at me expecting some sort of visual cue that I followed. I nodded to indicate that I did. He continued, even more slowly, emphasizing every syllable: a particular creature lives in the sea. He once again waited to see my reaction. I said, what creature? He looked at me funny. He said, what do you mean? I said, why do you say particular creature, just say what creature it is. He seemed annoyed, but so was I, for I didn't understand why he was talking funny like that. He said, that's not the point, it's just not the point. And I felt him giving up a little. I said: Why do you use funny words like this? „Particular creature" who talks like this? I was thinking to myself what a fool, but of course I didn't say it. He said, look, let me finish, okay? I said, alright, and waited to hear what funny thing he would say next. He said, all fish live in the water. I said, yes, alright. He said, a particular creature lives in the water. I nodded. He said, even slowlier now, ‚Logically, this particular creature must be a fish'. I said a long stretched, emphatic „exaaaactly." He buried his face in his hands. I said, what's the matter, are you sad? I felt he was getting sad, and it made me sad, too. But I'm not good at confronting reality, so I got a little confused. I said, did I make you sad? He looked at me, and all hope had vanished from his face. I said, what happened, you look terrible. He said: you really don't understand this? And I don't think I have ever heard a man more broken than him. Except for me in my thoughts of course. I said, I do. He said nothing in return. I said, and now I spoke extra slowly, aaaaaall fish live in the water. He nodded, and I could tell he was gaining new hope. I said, a particular creature lives in the water. He nodded again, and the mercury in his hope barometer was rising. I said, therefore, logically, this creature is a fish. He looked at me in disbelief. I said, what? He said nothing. I said, this creature that you talk about lives in the water, yes? He sighed and said, yes. I said, and all fish live in the water like this creature? He said, yes, but it doesn't mean that the creature is a fish, it could be another creature. I said, but all the creatures in the water are fish. He had regained his strength and said: No, see, this is exactly what it doesn't mean, not all creatures in the water are fish, just because all fish live in the water. I paused and thought about this for a second. I felt as though a truth was dawning on me, yet I couldn't quite grasp it. It was there for the taking, yet I couldn't take it. I said: all fish are in the water? He nodded. I said, and this creature is also in the water? He nodded again. I said, and this creature, you say, is in the water, but it's not a fish. He nodded euphorically, and I'd never seen a more hopeful man. I paused again. Then I said, so why did you talk about fish then? He looked at me confused. I said, the fish did not add anything to the story. He said nothing. I said, the way I see it, there is a creature living in the water, correct? He nodded weakly, for life had drained out of him. I said, so why mention the fish? He didn't respond. I said, once you mentioned the fish, I assuuumed the creature must be a fish. He said, rather whispered: this false assumption was what it was all about. I said, yes, but you should have just omitted the part with the fish and it would have never come to this. He said, I don't know what to say. I said, yeah, just don't say the part with the fish. He had mentally checked out of the situation. I said, this whole misunderstanding could have been avoided, if you hadn't mentioned the fish. I said, if you had started with the second precedent, that the creature lives in the water, I would have never assumed it to be fish. He whispered, premise. I said, pardon? He said, never mind. He was about to leave the table, so I had to resolve the situation. I said, relax, I know you made this all up. He said, what are you talking about? I said, I do this all the time, when I get bored, I make things up. He said, what do you mean ‚make things up'. I said, like you did right now with this Nonsensical. He said, „Non Sequitur". I said, yeaaah right. He looked at me and shook his head. He said, you are a strange guy, you know that, right? And then he left my table. Which, in his defense, had been his table, before I invited myself to it. I wonder what happened to this guy. I would have loved to be his friend, for his Nonsensicals would have stimulated mine a great deal. His game was close to perfection, and I aspire to his level of mastery. In any case, I hope he's still fooling as many people as possible.

There is a sense of alienation when I'm among people. I feel alien. Even to myself. It's like the film resumes and my life accelerates. As though I normally lived in slow motion. My dream is like a still image of reality. My life is very slow. When I look at people, I feel like a single glance captures them forever in my memory. People look at me differently. I'm paying attention, so they pay attention to me. If only for a split second. The world belongs to the two of us, though we remain complete strangers. There is beauty in that, I cannot describe it well. I wonder if I remind people of the slow life. I'm like an anchor to their turbulent day. There is a brief moment of recognition, so beautiful, considering that we don't know each other. I don't live in this moving picture of theirs. I live in this still picture of mine. As though I took a photograph of the world just to live in it. I'm not moving with the world, I'm moving in my picture. Time slows down, until it stands still. Picture this, your reality comes to a halt, everything is still, and quiet. This is how I exist. My world is quiet and beautiful. I look at details all day long. When I see a person that my eye picks up on, I study her detail, her expression, her glance. The way she moves, I pick up on that. Her eyes flicker a little as though she recognized something. I study her still image, she doesn't move in it. Or she moves very slowly. Picture reality coming to a halt, picture the quiet and the calm, the dominance of impression over everything else, picture how unimportant language and expression become. An impression full of sentiment. This is the world I live in. I don't live in yours, I live in mind. Now of course the world carries on as usual, the world doesn't slow down. It's rather that the moment which eludes others, becomes eternal in me. I can revisit it, and I often do. My memory remembers like a camera taking snapshots. My soul photographs the moment. It's when her eyes meet mine that she's special, and I'm obliterated by her overwhelming perfection. I remember the moment, not a sequence of moments. My memory is mute, there is no sound track. This explains why the image is so important to me. Where other people remember words and events, I remember the impression, and how I felt in that moment. How I thought she was beautiful. I live in slow motion, and this is how I capture my experience. In all of this, I never try to capitalize on my impressions, for I know their particular value vanishes once they're set in motion. The images need to remain still, and it's in them I realize their perfection. To capture the beautiful moment, to hang on to it, to re-create it with words. To paint my books. The world has seen impressionist painters, but I aspire to be an impressionist writer. I don't care for the exterior form, I only care for the interior. When a word creates a sentiment, the word has been mastered. It's the rarest form of writing. One must master the sentiment through the written word. This is a skill that only the fewest possess. To experience the world in slow motion is a rare gift and it needs to be cultivated. It's easy to call me a dreamer and a fool, but the ability to capture a moment is not learned over night. It takes years of training, and desperation, over the girl that one wants, but not really, for she's not really real. She's unreal, and it's all about the slow moving frame of yours. When the impression strikes, the world decelerates, and eventually halts. It's here that the eye can study her image. One must not flee the impression, one must flee toward it instead. You must make the impression God in this universe of thee. The impression needs to reign silently over your expression. To brush over these moments, to go with the fast moving time, is a clear sign of artistic inaptitude. An artist is he or she who can halt the time. To be rushing with the world around, shows lack of concentration. One needs to increase and decrease the speed of life at will. In the crowd all people follow the same speed. This is why it's such a disappointing way of living. When I'm among people, my picture resumes. The film continues, and I get bored. The impressions degenerate into expressions. Those people will never understand me.

Time comes to a halt, when there is something my eye picks up on. I capture the moment. Like a snapshot. The picture involves the impression, the image itself, every detail of the image, the scenery, the colors, however, no noise, for the image is silent. It's a piece of eternity, and I immerse in it. My mind is powerful, it can create a world from an image. I see every detail, and I study it carefully. When my eye is still, my soul is distant. To see everything, to show nothing, it comes down to that. I capture the moment, and I re-visit it. I make it more beautiful, every time I do. I discover new details, I embellish it further. One takes reality as inspiration, but one creates something more beautiful from it. It's true, the artist is everything, the muse is nothing. The muse must be used, not amused. An artist must love his art first, and nothing else second. He shall focus on the final piece, and everything else to the devil. When a society creates art, art becomes shabby. Art is the privilege of the few. It's the few that possess the ability to create. One must re-create the moment in its most majestic form. One trains the imagination by imagining. The more one imagines the more powerful one becomes. The ability to capture the moment, the impression, the sentiment, the atmosphere of that moment, to capture it without a word remembered, without any movement taking place, to capture a moment as though looking at a painting, to take that moment and create an image of perfection. An artist must nurture this ability. Whenever the impression occurs, it must be halted, then studied, then re-created.

The quiet are often overseen in a world governed by noise. When noise becomes the door policy, it excludes a whole lot of people from entering. The quiet do not attract attention. I reckon they are the best our species has to offer. If one feels bad for speaking, one's speech will be elegant by nature. It's rare that a quiet person speaks up. When they do, you must listen well. The word of the quiet is rare, it's the rarest of all elements. The quiet are respected by allowing their quiet.

Love is just another word for dream. I wonder if this may express something greater. Obviously this would be denied by those who reduce emotion to mere physiology. At the very least I find that debatable. In any case, when we experience love, we should feel particularly physical, i.e. „in the body". Yet never do we feel more out of it. Deep emotions feel very unphysical, in fact the deeper the sentiment, the less we feel home in our bodies. We feel as though we have become thin air, or mere life within the body. Sentiment has no location in the body, and in essence no physical quality. It manifests itself in the body, but I find it questionable that it originates from it. It makes no sense for the brain to feel love, and even less sense to produce an emotion as overwhelming, as strictly unphysical as love, and how matter is supposed to produce it, remains a questionable concept altogether. In any case, wherever it originates, and of whatever nature it is, love introduces the dream into our lives. When in love, we dream the world, rather than seeing it clearly. Life becomes a dance, we no longer feel our steps. Love is the return of dream into a dull and bleak reality. But I'm convinced that the dream is there anyway. We've just gotten rather poor at living in it.

It's funny, I told him. When I was young, I thought I could go straight to success. Instead I went from failure to failure. I didn't do a lot of things wrong. My failures most notably include the times in which everybody called me a success. Jobs that paid me well and dressed me better. I was a success to the world but a failure to myself. This was not an option I had considered when I was young. So I told him this, don't think about life before living. You cannot understand things beforehand. You must experience not just the situations, but yourself in those situations. Truth and untruth are not universal. One man's truth is another man's untruth.

I also told him that I'm happy I didn't know what was coming for me. It's good to not know when bad times are ahead. It would make them twice as bad. If they are to happen, so be it. Let's deal with them when the time comes.

I told him that he should be careful with the compliments the elder give. They tend to praise the youths if they act like an adult in young years. However, this sort of maturity is often pre-mature. The youth has become an adult too soon. He or she will notice later on. They will realize that they were „finished" at a time when they should have been developing. It's dangerous to be finished too soon. By all probability you're not really finished. You've just finished developing. Which leaves a lot of you undeveloped. Or underdeveloped. Later on, this will come back to haunt you. You will feel regret about the youth you no longer are. The elder praise the youths when they see themselves in them. It's all vanity, and nothing more. In reality, a youth should be praised for being a youth. It's good to be a youth, and act accordingly. You will mature, don't worry. Don't rush into being an adult. Youth never returns. Many people wish it did, but no one has ever recovered it. An adult you'll be much longer than a youth. Youth is short, adulthood long. The praise of the elder is often poisonous. In fact, if they criticize you, you're probably on the right track. Because it's surely your own track, not theirs. The elder praise what they understand. If they don't understand it, then you're outgrowing them. In your own way that is, which is a good thing. In young years we're susceptible. It's easy to get misled by those who have lost their youth. They don't remember how it felt. When they had the strength to move mountains. When they wanted to change the world. They want you tame, but you must not be tame. Youth is your fuel. It will inevitably run out. Let it power you for as long as possible.

Dream is an untruth that feels true. Reality, in return, is often a truth that feels untrue. Dream is lying to us, but it doesn't pretend otherwise. Which makes it almost a truth in itself. A lie is only a lie if it claims to be true. If a lie admits to being a lie, it becomes a truth in its own way. People seek truth, as though it was an objective thing, when clearly it's subjective. People who found truth couldn't point their finger at it.

I think it's pleasant to not amount to anything. You don't feel the pressure to please. After all, nobody cares. It's nice to get on with it. I like it when the skies are grey, and nothing happens. Nothing is as pretty as a cold February afternoon. One always pretends until all hope is lost. It's then that we finally see ourselves in the true light of things.

The problem with optimism is not that one is positive, but that one is passive. One assumes that things will turn out alright. But in order for things to turn out alright, one has to make them turn out alright. One should neither be an optimist nor a pessimist. One should simply act and save the thoughts for later on. But thinking is also acting, this is commonly misunderstood. One should not ponder the future, instead ponder the present and progress in it. Thought should focus on the path, not the destination. Optimism can be a curse in disguise. Which is not to say that it isn't allowed. But one must act. If optimism isn't a driver, if it becomes the game plan instead, optimism will lead you nowhere. It makes you passive in the eyes of your own fate.

Optimists are often naive, and that's because they anticipate a positive outcome. One should not anticipate any outcome, and instead work toward it. The future is born in the present, and it's the present that we need to affect. Hope has to be made redundant in the process. The best reaction to hope is to not require it. When asked if you think it will be alright, you should say that this depends on your actions, and it's not yet decided. The future is not determined as of right now. There are hundreds of potential futures ahead of me, and I myself choose which one of them is going to happen. There are plenty of potential futures, but only one actual future. By one's actions, one decides which one it will be. Hope should have no place in this, for instead of making the future, the future will make us. This is a liability, which we must avoid by taking action. Action is not always manual labor, it can be thought and reflection. Sometimes it's a pause, or a step back. Those are still decisions, and actions, for which neither hope nor optimism are required. While there are factors that we cannot influence, there is no point in despairing over them. Things that cannot be changed by us, must not be considered by us, but simply accepted. All other things, and they will be in the majority, must be affected through our decisions. Hope makes us unhappy with regard to the things we cannot influence, and passive with regard to the things we can. One should not be an optimist, not a pessimist either, and not even a realist. One should not reflect on one's fate, and instead create it, develop it, own it. The future is not determined, one must always remember that. Right now it's completely unclear what will be in five or ten years. As this is only determined in the next five or ten years.

Success cannot replace life. If success feels lifeless, it's just glorified failure. People connect through their failures, they disconnect in success. Success is a border, failure is a land.

He asked me if I didn't feel alone. No, I said, I'm not alone, for I'm always accompanied by the voices in my head. He looked at me strange. I looked at him stranger. I said, there's Samuel. I paused. Then Vinegar. He said, Vinegar? I said, yeah one of them is called Vinegar. I said, there is Tomboy. And then there is Fabricily, she's a woman. He was confused by what I was saying, but it was in a therapeutic context, so he acknowledged it. Oh yes, I should have said this first, he was a therapist. Maybe I started the whole story wrong, let me go back to the beginning. I was bored again, so I figured this would be the right time to go to a therapist. Of course I had no intention to talk about myself. Only obnoxious people do that. Whereas I belong to the classy kind of people that never says a word and one day just vanishes to the surprise of all. I was, however, intrigued by the thought of pretending to talk about myself. I love doing that for I feel it's the appropriate response to the oversharing society I'm trapped in. Imitation is the highest form of mockery after all. So I booked an appointment to finally free myself from all these inhibitions and hidden truths that I was only to learn about as part of the session. This is, after all, how therapy works.

You learn things about yourself you didn't know before. And before I had entered that room, I certainly did not know about Vinegar and Tomboy. I was excited, as this was a good test of my abilities. I intended to start by building trust. I had to say genuine things so he didn't see the disingenuous parts coming. I started off by saying. Why I was here, and what it was all about. And who I was, and where I was going. I wasn't genuine, but I sounded genuine, for I didn't insert any nonsense yet. I gave the usual answers. And then I had this sudden flash of genius. I was going to introduce the voices in my head. I had tried this before, in a civil context, and there it hadn't worked. It was too outrageous, even for me. With all my oddities personality-wise, I'm just not the type. People didn't believe me, which disappointed me at the time, but it also prepared me for my big moment. Here we were, Dr. Craig, who of course has a different name but I don't want to call him out, for I feel he did me no harm. I said, Dr. Craig, you see, I'm never alone, I'm always in good company. He said, who's keeping you company? I said, there is Samuel. I paused. Then Vinegar. He said, Vinegar? I said, yeah one of them called is Vinegar. I cheered inside, for I knew I had him hooked. He started asking about the voices, and I gave the right answers. Right answers as in vague answers. You cannot be clear in those circumstances, you must be vague, for the whole experience is certainly vague. I said, Fabricily is more active in the morning, while Sam and the boys become more present in the afternoon. Every time he pronounced „Fabricily", like I did, „Fa-bree-sea-lie", I had to keep myself from laughing. This was one of my proudest moments. I had completely made this name up on the spot, and when I first said it I almost burst out laughing because of how ridiculous it sounded. But I have been blessed with a great ability to compose myself. The depression helps. In any case, I talked about Fabricily, and that she always told me that things will be alright and I should hang on. He said, Fabricily seems like a good friend. I said, indeed, I cherish her, and I always listen to her advice. He asked about the boys. I said, the boys are a little rougher, they give me a hard time. I said, there is Sam who calls me a sissy. He said, a sissy? I said, yes, I think this may be connected to my father who had always wanted me to be a boy. Dr. Craig was confused, but he brushed it off. I said, Sam is a good guy, he's just a bit too direct at times. I said, Tomboy is rude, he always laughs at me. He calls me a loser. Dr. Craig was clueless, I could tell. He wondered if I was a fraud. I wondered if he was. So far he had done very little for his hourly rate. He said, how do you feel about that. I thought, brilliant question. I feel humiliated, I said. He said, by Tomboy? I almost burst out laughing again. I nodded for I couldn't speak. There was this devilish grin creeping up on me. I felt like Dorian Grey's painting. I said, Tomboy takes away my confidence, he always says that I amount to nothing, and that I am worthless. Dr. Craig was in thought. He pretended to listen but I'm pretty sure he thought about something else. He didn't seem as emotionally invested as I was. I started to doubt our relationship. He interrupted the silence by saying: and then there is Vinegar. I said, yes, Vinegar is nice sometimes, but rude other times. He said, is there a pattern? I said: no, it's arbitrary, sometimes he's nice, but then he's rude again, like the other boys. I said, and then there is the green man. He said, the green man? I said, the green man, yes. The green man appears every once in a while and he never says a word. He said, he's wearing green clothes? I said, no, and I said it emphatically. I said, he's an actual green man, he looks like the traffic light man. He said, the green traffic light man? I said, yes, he appears randomly, and he seems to interact with me, but he never says a word. I said, my impression is that he's either good or evil, I don't know which one. He said, the green man doesn't speak? I said, the green man is just green. Dr. Craig nodded. It was a concentrated nod, the sort of nod that wants to appear grave in order to mask confusion and helplessness. He said, does the green man interact with the voices? I was excited about the vivid nature of this nonsequitur we were engaged in. It was as though it really happened. The nonsense of one had become the reality of two. How beautiful. I said, no, when the green man appears, I don't hear the voices anymore. He said, hm, that's interesting. I said, isn't it? He said, what do you think it means? I was thinking, I would love to have this job. I always have to listen to people talking about themselves and I never get paid for it. I said, I believe the green man wants to save me. He said, he saves you? I said, yes, he's saving me from my own demise. I said, I believe the green man is myself. Dr. Craig agreed. I also agreed. I was surprised by how coherent this incoherent rambling turned out to be. I said, I believe every once in a while I get reminded of who I really am, and then the voices disappear. He said, it sounds plausible. I said, I struggle a lot with these voices in my head, and I get confused by them. I said, sometimes I wish I was simpler, and that I wasn't so different. I said, people always call me different, and that hurts. He said, why does it hurt you? I said, because I know I am, every second of every day, I know that I am different, I've always been different. I said, I'm never like anyone I meet, people ask me if I'm not lonely, I say, I'm lonely among people, because they show me how different I am, and how there is nothing that we share. I always play by their rules, I think their thoughts, and I fake their sentiments. I'm always in their world, never in mine. I don't share about myself, for it always bears the same fruit. When I pretend to be like them, I get miserable, when I come out genuinely, they call me strange and different. I hate this. Every truthful thing I say is met with the same reaction: you are different. I can't hear it anymore. I can't deal with it. I don't want to explain it, I don't want to justify it, I don't want people to approve of it, or to disapprove of it, I just want to be who I am, but they always comment. Their voices get in my head. And then I don't hear my own voice anymore. I hear theirs. I go to these places, I meet these people, and again, I shall be generic. But then I get miserable. Every second passes like an eternity. I want to leave, leave and never go back. Any boy I call my friend in theory, becomes an unbearable burden as soon as I talk to him. Any girl I could like in theory, I just want to run away from her within minutes. There is nothing, I say nothing connecting us. They say, I'm different, but they're also different from my perspective. They are just in the majority. It's how the world works. They are many, I am one. So they win, and they call me different. But I don't hear this once. I hear it every single time. I hear it from everyone. And I don't want to hear it anymore. They're rude without noticing it. I know that I am different. I don't need to be told. There is something crushing about this sentence. It's like a reiteration, or reconfirmation. Every time I try, every time I fail. We're just too different. We don't need to say it. Some things are so obvious, they don't need to be told. You see, I get criticized for saying nonsensical things, but this is the only way I can cope. If I'm genuine, I hate myself and I don't want to hate myself. Only when I make things up, I don't hate myself anymore, I entertain myself, and at the same time, I'm more or less getting along with these people. It's my way of connecting with them. I paused. He looked at me and said, that's what the green man is all about? I said, the green man? He nodded. I had come to my senses. I mumbled, yes, the green man, alright. And then I got sad. Really sad. Sad about everything. Sad about the stupid tricks I had played on this kind man. I asked him if we could terminate the session, and he was fine with it. I said, I was going to book another one, which obviously I never did. I came here for a joke, not for this. I pledge to never go to a therapist again.

Life is a distraction from thought. One should live as little as possible, in order to think as much as possible.

The idea that one has come full circle. It is perhaps the most dangerous idea. The motivation to carry on reaches its minimum. Things could have happened your way, but they didn't, so they won't. The future becomes irrelevant, for it has ended in the present. You are reduced to your past and indifferent to the future. You accept what you should change. But there is only so much power you can invest. At some point you run out. Don't we all have this dream of being broken by life, so we don't fight fate anymore? No? Well, I do. I wish life would make the decisions for me. It's decision fatigue. I believe they call it that. But there is an existential decision fatigue. The eternal and never-ending decisions we have to take. I wish I didn't have to take any decisions. It's so tiring to just carry on. It's not a net zero to exist. One must exercise a great deal of energy every day. Freedom can become a burden, for it always requires our input. We always have to use our freedom, we can never let go of it. I want to be passive. I really truly want to be passive. Until I am, and then I want to be active again. We are never happy with anything. I wonder if I could give up my freedom just a little bit. I wish I didn't have to decide so much.

The quiet people belong to themselves. They are proud, albeit in their own way. They don't tell you things. In a world that talks incessantly, the quiet keep to themselves. They don't want to conquer the world or be known. They want to hide and disappear. And that's what makes them pleasant.

The quiet people are not shy, or even anxious. They just keep to themselves. Not everything must be shared with the world. In fact, most of it can be omitted.

This is a time which is hostile to the quiet people. We do not breathe well in this atmosphere. The quiet are forced to speak up, or they remain invisible. There is no forum for the quiet people. Yet they exist in abundance. It's a society which rewards the loud. And this is what you reap. A society of loud people who never shut up. How do the quiet react to it? They accept it. For the alternative would be to be participate in the turmoil. And the quiet are simply not interested in that.

The quiet are not visible in a society made by the loud. The loud people create a loud society which in return creates loud people. One would have to be a madman to participate in this. The loud have turned society into a human pyramid. Everyone is an artist now, but only the loud ones prevail. And the loud ones are usually the bad ones, too.

What about the quiet art, and what about the quiet people. What about the quiet work, and how about the quiet thoughts? They never take place anymore. Not because they're not produced, but because they're not received. No one pays attention to the quiet people. They live well below the surface of our attention. I wish I could see their art, and hear their thoughts. The quiet people are beautiful. While the loud people have no beauty at all.

The quiet people are my favorite people. I consider them my friends. I don't know them of course, but this is what the loud people don't understand: The quiet understand each other intuitively. It's in the way they behave, and act. You can tell right away, how they feel. Their resistance to speak speaks volumes. You understand them based on the way they compose themselves. The quiet have an intuitive connection. This connection is not social or personal, for these are traits of the loud people. It's a connection of character, and of disposition. The similarity is intuitively understood by both sides. Who respect each other by not personalizing the situation. The loud people think that the quiet open up now and become loud, too. This is not what happens. The discretion remains, yet a connection is formed.

The quiet people don't speak up. They keep to themselves. It's a gentle way of existing. One doesn't impose on the others. To be discreet, to let other people be. To not confront them with your issues. In all of this, the quiet are treated as if they suffer from psychological trauma. What a strange society that stigmatizes the quiet and glorifies the loud. The loud should be stigmatized. They're obnoxious. It's madness that to be quiet is considered a character flaw. For the quiet people, it's always assumed that they want to speak up, yet for some reason they don't. First error. The quiet people don't want to speak up. There is no want, neither hidden nor unhidden. Not everyone wants to share about themselves. Yet the loud have seized society, and they're presenting the norm. The loud say, a healthy person is a loud person, so whoever isn't loud, must be scared, or shy, let's encourage them to speak up. Isn't it enough that the loud speak all the time, do they also have to make us speak? Unfortunately, the answer is yes, for the loud have this obnoxious trait that they only feel alive when there's noise. They live off the interaction and the voices. Humans, they say, require social interaction. But that's just the loud people, that's not all people. Yet the loud think that all people are loud, some are just a little better at it. They think of the quiet as inhibited loud people. And this wouldn't be so bad, if society as a whole wasn't created by them. Which means that society puts a stigma on the quiet. And the laurels on the loud. It treats the quiet people like failed people. Like people who should have been and could have been, but somehow ended up in their flawed condition from which they need saving. There is something so irritating about the loud people's ignorance in the face of the quiet. They mean well, yet they do so very poorly. The quiet should not be encouraged to speak. They should be encouraged to remain silent. It's how the quiet people speak after all. Only the loud speak in words. And if only they used fewer of them.

The quiet people have no representation in society. The many participate in the chatter and noise. Society as a whole becomes like a crowded marketplace. The quiet are asked to participate which goes against everything they value. Either the quiet become loud or they become invisible, they have to choose. Most of them choose invisibility, for the quiet are a proud people. Much prouder than the loud who are vacuum cleaner salespeople. They will say anything if it gets them the attention. Attention is the first thing the loud people want. It's also the last thing the quiet people want. The loud seek the attention that the quiet people flee. To seek attention is so much stranger than to not seek it. Yet we stigmatize those who don't seek it, and we glorify the others. What a pathetic society that is driven by attention. Attention should be paid, not sold. It's much better to do without attention. To not attract it, to keep a low profile. Yet this is a world that treats attention like the holy grail. The pathological behavior of seeking attention becomes a society norm. Society strives for attention, and it fears the lack of it. When no attention is directed toward you, there must be something wrong with you. The quiet become the failed people of this attention-seeking society. Yet the quiet are the healthy ones. They do not require anybody's attention. Meanwhile society has decided that attention is everything. Those who want it are normal. Those who don't are not. This is the fate of the quiet people in an obnoxious society. They are invisible, and when they make an appearance, they are pitied, diagnosed and stigmatized. The loud people are greedy for attention, and call this behavior appropriate. The loud people create a loud society, in which attention is the currency. Normal means that something is a norm. Most people adhere to it. In this regard, the loud are normal. In every other regard, they're not.

I went to a tailor today to have my trousers fixed. I had lost a button. Or I should say my trousers did. For I still had the button. I entered and said this. Good man, would it be possible for you to re-attach this button to my trousers? He said that indeed it would be possible and that he always went to great lengths to ensure his customer's satisfaction. I replied that while it was very kind of him to go to great lengths for it, whether it would be possible for him to do it right here, as I was in quite the hurry. He said, of course, he would fix it right here. I said, you are my savior, you are the light in the dark. He chuckled, for he thought I was joking. I wasn't. It was my favorite pair of trousers. It was a beautiful evening blue, and the fabric was exquisite. It was a delicate mix of linen and straw. Yes, you heard right, it had elements of straw in it. For this was a pair of trousers which had only been produced a handful of times in a stable at the foot of the Sierra Nevada. More is not known, and idle speculation. In any case, I was one of the lucky few to possess a pair. I always wore them when I had to make an impression. And today was one of those days. I had a job interview. The tailor saw to it, and before long he had finished the work. He had done an excellent job, for the button was now attached to the trousers again. I was ready to wear the pantalones for my future deciding interview. I was interviewing for a job in a furniture house. I wanted to show that I was wearing the pants in that fickle relationship called life. I wondered if I could insert this smart remark into my interview somehow. I changed in a nearby restaurant. When I exited the place, I felt that everyone was looking at me. It had been long since I'd worn my pantalones. When I wore them, I would always feel special. I walked with confidence, and people respected me. They liked the confident young man in his evening blue trousers. When I reached my future employer I was ready in every sense of the word. The pantalones would carry me. I entered, and I felt good about myself. My first question was: when do I start? The man liked my proactive attitude. But more importantly he was impressed by my pantalones.

I went to a job interview with a man. I didn't go there with a man, the job interview was with a man, that's what I meant. The man was hiring, and I was trying to be hired. This seemed like a great fit, and I figured it should be rather easy to agree on the fine print. I was confident that this was indeed my new employer. I had prepared everything, my CV, and my pitch, as well as answers to all the questions that employers typically ask. That he ended up asking other questions was unfortunate for I had not prepared for those. I wish he had asked the questions I had prepared for. For example, I could have described where I saw myself in five years. I would have also been able to share my thoughts on what I consider a welcoming workplace. Unfortunately, he didn't ask about any of those things. The job interview was for a salesman in a furniture store. It was a rather small shop, focused mostly on beds and couches. He explained this to me, and I was quite surprised about it, for I didn't know furniture shops specialize. If I was a furniture shop, I would offer everything. And this is because if you're looking for one furniture, you're probably looking for another one. Nobody looks for only one furniture. You either look for none of them or all of them. So I would try to sell all of them. You have to strike the iron while it's hot. I pitched this idea to him, which he wasn't excited about. I had thought that perhaps he would like my entrepreneurial spirit. Perhaps he saw his successor in me. I could smell a career in furniture. In any case, he asked about my previous experience. I thought this was a rather uninspired way to conduct an interview. I thought we were here to discuss the big picture. The roots of the company, and the vision. The present and the future. I wanted him to engage me in the shared vision of the Miller Furniture company. So I said that I had indeed worked already. He asked, as what. I said I had been working for multiple months on finding work. He didn't find this very funny at all. So I added that I had worked in a small grocery shop. He asked what duties I was obliged with. I said I was obliged with checking the best-before dates of products as well as replacing old products with new products from the warehouse. He asked me how I performed these duties? I said, I performed excellent, which is confirmed by the fact that they had me do this exact duty for years. For years, he said? Yessir, I said, 4 years in total. He said, you were replacing products for 4 years? I nodded proudly. He said, they never let you work the counter? I said, I wasn't ready. He said, ready? I said, I respect the numbers. He said, what do you mean? I said, it's a lot of responsibility to handle cash. He said, you have a cash register that calculates for you. I said, no, we didn't, we were supposed to do all the math in our head. He said, it's not exactly higher maths. I said, my maths are pretty low. He said, what makes you apply here? I was cheering inside for I had prepared for this question. I said, I believe in furniture. He looked at me puzzled which prompted me to carry on. I said, where would we be as a society if it wasn't for furniture? Where would we sleep if we didn't have beds? Where would we sit without couches and chairs? Where would we put our clothes if we didn't have wardrobes? Would we put them on the floor? And where would we work if we didn't have a desk? Where would we eat if we had no tables? Furniture is the backbone of society. When flats are empty, so are our hearts. We need furniture more than it needs us. We need to give something back to furniture. We must show our appreciation, we need to devote to it. I was finished. He seemed confused. He said: are you having a laugh? Now it was my turn to be confused. I said, what do you mean? He said, I'm asking, are you having a laugh? I said, I don't know what that expression means. He seemed annoyed. He said, are you joking? I said, no, why would I be joking? I did not understand the man, nor did I understand his sudden mood change. I said, I'm fascinated with furniture. I would love to come work for your company, mister. He said, look, lad, I don't know what's going on here, but I'm looking for a sales person in our furniture shop, we are selling beds and couches, not dreams and schemes, I cannot have an employee say these things to a customer. I said, what things? He said, that we should devote to furniture, and that furniture is the backbone of society. I said, but it is. He sighed. I said, think about it, if your flat was empty, you couldn't live there. Furniture is vital. It's indispensable to a civilized lifestyle, no one could do without it, don't you see, I'm not having a laughter, mister, I am most serious about it. He didn't know how to deal with the situation. I said, Mr Bossman, please give me a chance, I will sell you beds and couches like you ain't never seen it. I will show you that I have heart, and passion, and faith. He said, see, this is my point, you need none of these things here, you need to show up at 8 square and work your shift, you need to be there for the visiting customers, assist them with their questions, but they won't ask about any of the crap you mentioned, they want to know about measurements, and materials, and warranties. I said, Mr Bossman, just give me a chance, and I shall make you proud. He said, please don't call me that, and there is no need to make me proud, you just need to make your quota. I said, I will do whatever it takes. He said, look, you are a strange fella, but I'm willing to give you a shot, you start here on Monday and you show me what you got inside you. I said, I will, I will, you'll never regret this, Mr Bossmann, I'm sorry, I'm not supposed to call you that, how am I supposed to call you, should I call you Dean? He said, my name's not Dean. I said, okay, what do I call you then? He said, get out of here before I change my mind. I said, thank you, mister, I'm very grateful for this opportunity, I'll be here on Monday, 8 sharp, and I won't let you down. He said, alright, and he even chuckled a little. I left, and returned on Monday. The job turned out to be a drag, it was very different from what I imagined, so I quit in my first week. But I did cherish the experience, and I often think back to the good man who took a leap of faith with me.

A sadness that can't be shared is a sad thing indeed. The sad people must be consoled. And yet it's difficult, for the sad are good at hiding. There are plenty of people who have no one to confide in. Sadness requires an outlet, and the longer it's stored, the greater it becomes. You reach a point where your sadness becomes overwhelming, and you're starting to swallow it. It's similar to swallowing water in the open sea. You can no longer support your sadness, so you start drinking it. People who drink sadness are the people who most need our help. They often drink their sadness because no one was there for them. The sad can only support themselves for so long. At some point the sadness becomes too much and they collapse into it. One can be engulfed in flames as well as in tears. The sad live within their sadness, and it's hard for them to leave this place. Once the sadness is internalized, it becomes the blue blood running through their veins. Sadness is no longer an item distinct from you. You've taken its form. Those who have been sad for too long, have the hardest time speaking up. No one is sadder than the silently sad. They have reached the bottom most level of sadness. They fall into silence as into a gorge. They live down there in silence now. You call them, but you receive no response. The sad can no longer speak, for sadness is drowning them from within.

There is an overwhelming sadness which makes them unable to communicate. It's not that they don't speak because they don't want to. It's because they can't. It's very hard for the sad to speak up, for they are so used to being silent.

When sadness is internalized for too long, it becomes almost impossible to share. And yet it's very apparent. One can tell right away that herein lies a sadness, well within thought, yet well without language. When the sad cannot speak, sadness becomes madness. One is sad beyond expression.

Sadness should never be carried alone. I want the sad people to be my siblings. My beloved siblings. I want to take care of them. I want to give them what they need. Mostly attention. One must pay attention to help the others. Sacrificing instead of victimizing. I always get sad when I see a sad person. It's in the way they talk and behave.

I have read Simone Weil. She is the most perfect mind I have encountered. If only I could be as perfect as her. The fact that she led such an absurd life, and she dedicated herself to it. This is what she wrote: „Those who are unhappy have no need for anything in the world but people capable of giving them their attention. The capacity to give one's attention to a sufferer is a very rare and difficult thing; it is almost a miracle; it *is* a miracle." Isn't this the most beautiful thing ever written? They say, a man can do everything that a woman can do, but that's not true. Man could not have written this. Man doesn't see. He's too busy being seen.

When sadness is kept private for too long, the ability to share turns into an inability. This is a desperate state, that requires our intervention. We need to intuit the sentiment in order to share it. But the truly sad no longer speak. When you sit with them, they don't tell you about their sadness. Mostly they say nothing. They don't have the words for what they feel. You can learn to speak but you can also unlearn it. If you never speak your heart, eventually you won't be able to. To share is something that needs to be practiced in order to remain an option. A sadness that cannot be shared anymore is usually a sadness that wasn't shared when it still could be. The sad are those who no longer know how to communicate their sentiment. When you meet them, it doesn't pour out of them, it stays hidden, deep inside of them. While you engage them, trying to make them share, they are simply not able to. You need to allow them to be silent, and if they speak up, listen with all your heart. If they don't speak, allow them to be silent, and help them with your presence. Your presence helps them more than you think. Remember that the sad often feel that they have no options anymore. They have lost their belief that things can change. But your presence is availability, and availability is possibility. By being present, you're already helping them a lot. Sadness, once internalized, becomes the opposite of an activator. It becomes a passivator. Sadness makes the mind passive. With your presence, you show them that there is indeed possibility. Your presence allows them to remember that they were active once. Over time, they shall regain their ability to speak. Be present, that is one of the most important things that you can do for them. The sad need to be reminded of their ability to speak. But this is done gently, very gently, and never recklessly.

Nobody should be alone when they're sad. It's a tragical circumstance, which requires our intervention. We must be there for the sad. But this is the beauty of the written word. It's always intimate. One writes and one reads. The writer and the reader are always à deux. There is no other person involved in this delicate relationship. This is how one can console the sad. If there is a saint who came to save us, he would surely be sad. The sad are the true lovers of the human species. One of my favorite saints, a sad one, too, will always be Lincoln. He had such beautiful width, he spoke human, as silly as that sounds. I read his letters, and how beautiful they are. I cannot fathom how anyone could be so good. He wrote for example this to a sad person: „Perfect relief is not possible, except with time. You can not now realize that you will ever feel better. Is not this so? And yet it is a mistake. You are sure to be happy again. To know this, which is certainly true, will make you some less miserable now. I have had experience enough to know what I say; and you need only to believe it, to feel better at once." We need the sad people more than anybody else. Their duty is to remind us of our humanity. The sad have a power which the others don't have. It's the power to make people good.

The sad people shouldn't feel alone. They should feel in good company, for they are. There are more sad people than sand people on the planet. But this is rather easy because there are no sand people on the planet. Still, there is an abundance of sad people, and they should know that they're not alone. Yet there's something tragical in the fact that the beautiful souls never get together. The sad and the sad never meet, just like the quiet and the quiet. It's only the loud people that meet all the time. And now we're all supposed to become like them, but we don't want to. So we stay quiet, and reserved.

The plastic men have everything. Nay, they are everything. For one should not reduce them to their looks. They always laugh, and how beautifully they laugh. Their eyes twinkle, and their teeth are wonderful. Oh if only I had wonderful teeth like the plastic men. The plastic men are engaging, and they're good conversationalists. They never shy away from shining a little light on the people around them. They are in the center of every group, it's their appearance, they can't help it. One feels drawn to the plastic men. The plastic men are witty, and they have an inviting personality. They are family men, too, of course, they never shy away from human connection either. The plastic men are everything, handsome, engaging, smart. If only they were a little more plastic.

I admire the plastic men. I wish I was one of them. They are so neat. When I stand among them, I feel apologetic, for I am clearly not worthy. They are too good, too handsome, too intelligent. And now you may say, isn't it unfair that these perfect people are also intelligent and charismatic. And I say, yes, it's unfair that they have everything and we have nothing. Yet if you judge the plastic men by their appearance, you judge them falsely. For in reality there is a lot more to them. They are not just handsome. They are also charismatic and charming, and intelligent. And even funny, they're also funny. They are so funny, that sometimes I forget to laugh. I'm too busy admiring their humor. The plastic people admire each other, but they never admire me. I am sad because I also want to be part of the plastic people. I want to despair over a minor detail in my appearance. I want to hide my superior intelligence behind my superior looks. Oh how sweet it must feel to be one of the plastic people.

I went to a reception, or I should say: I went to something which at the time I didn't realize was a reception and if I had known that, I wouldn't have attended. But this sentence is too long, so let's stick to: I went to a reception. I arrived, and right away I realized what I was walking into. Here were the people I dreaded the most. The plastic people. Every party is full of them, but some parties are a bit fuller of them. It was one of those. Parties like that terrify my soul. To talk to the plastic people is torture of a different kind. It really is psychological torture. The plastic people always strike the eye, don't they? The men are handsome, they dress well and they smell good, they are attractive, and so very appealing. They are slim built, yet athletic. The plastic men are a special breed. If only we could all be perfect like them. The plastic women are the women's equivalent of the plastic men. The plastic men and the plastic women get along well. They are on the same wavelength, one could say. They are charming, interesting and attractive. It's a match made in heaven. I'm so jealous of the plastic people, for not only do they have the looks and the appearance, they also have the rounded personality. Yes, round, a very round personality. I'm more of a zigzag personality. Naturally, there are some translational difficulties. I like to listen to the plastic people, for they have many interesting things to say.

I listened to a plastic man conversing with a group of plastic women. I was allowed there, I wasn't being weird. I was sitting with them. But I didn't contribute anything to the conversation. I was so enchanted with what I was witnessing. The plastic man told the plastic women about his recent endeavors. Apparently he has a bucket list and he has ticked off another item. The plastic women were impressed. And so was I. The plastic women were as enchanted with the plastic man as I was. They loved him, and I got a little jealous, for I loved them all, both the plastic men and the plastic women. The plastic women were clearly into the plastic man. The plastic man was equally into the plastic women. I was also there but I remained unnoticed. The plastic man sensed that he was in demand. The plastic women got a little worked up about everything, and they got extra playful. I have never experienced this behavior first hand, so it was interesting for me to see. How the world could be if I was a plastic man. The plastic man was a fine man indeed. He had it all, and I admired him. But don't dismiss the plastic women, for they were also exquisite. They had the wits, and the charms, and the brains of course, for this has to be said, all women are intelligent, especially the plastic women, and whoever doubts that is just a horrible, horrible human being. The plastic people are superior in every way. Not just visually. The plastic women engaged the plastic man in further conversation. They asked him questions, which this was also new to me, as I have never heard a woman ask me any questions. The only time they question me is when they question my questions. The plastic women were interested in the plastic man's love life. This was convenient for the plastic man was also interested in his love life. The only one who wasn't interested was me. But I was interested in the plastic women being engaged for I had never seen them converse in real life. One of the plastic women touched the plastic man's arm, which the other plastic women didn't like. I made a note to myself that this was probably a sign of minor romantic interest. The plastic man was sharing that his love life was not a great success. The plastic women commiserated, for this resonated well with their own experience. The plastic women then hated on other women to cheer up the plastic man. The plastic man was cheering, too, for I'm pretty sure this was all part of a routine. The plastic man and the plastic women got along well, and the conversation continued. I got up from my chair and no one even noticed.

When I think, the world appears simple to me. I don't have to deal with human reactions. One observes the world, without saying a word. There is something so delicate about it. I prefer to leave people alone, for I don't know if they want to be bothered. One must think to people more and speak to them less. To think to people is a beautiful way of engaging with them. I think to the people who move me, and to the people who interest me. Most of all to all the pretty girls I don't speak to. I also think to the people who make me sad, yet I don't know if they're really sad, so I leave them alone. One should not intrude into other people's lives. It's better to spare them. One must not get carried away by one's ideas of someone. People are mostly different than you think.

I like to think to people. There is a lot of beauty in that. Most people are hiding things from the world. But when you think to them, they reveal them a little. They think to you, all the things they cannot say. Not to you, but to anyone. They share in silence. When you think to someone and they pick up on it, they think back to you. This is not a situation in which anything is communicated. Both sides remain vague, even to themselves. It's more about what we would say if we could. But we can't, so we won't. We only think to each other.

I like to think to people, for that's when they appear in their truest form. People never lie when they think to you, and that's because they don't convey anything. Those who don't convey have no need to conceal. The true poets are those who appear as completely different people to the world. People intrude each other's lives all the time. While people like me, who don't participate in this, are considered strange. I am strange, but not because of this. I think it's good to respect a person's privacy. To think to them is an alternative.

I always think to people, but I don't think particular things. Speech is precise, it has a medium and a message. Thought is different. In thought you can communicate all sorts of things, yet nothing precisely. That's the beauty of it. Thought is richer, wider, abler than speech. Its potential is unlimited, for it's never limited by particular speech. We all know that reality is a disappointment. All romance goes down the hill once the first word is exchanged. It's better to stay in the realm of the hypothetical. To keep the love pre-realized. This is a love which is rare and rarely appreciated. Most people can't wait to speak the first word to their beloved. I can wait for it. If possible, forever. In the realm of the hypothetical, in this pre-realized form of love, I shall love her, and be desperate that I cannot have her. Yet I also have no intention of changing that. This is the beautiful enclave in which love becomes art. You have to love her desperately, and you have to desperately want to speak to her, but then you may never say a word. This is the place in which you create. All beauty, all love and all sadness are here for the taking. The lover speaks to his beloved, while the poet only thinks to her.

It's often spoken, somewhat disdainfully, of puppy love. One must grow up and love like an adult. But I'd rather go with puppy love. I don't want my love to grow up. My love shall remain youthful and innocent. If I manage to continue loving like the child I am, then I have succeeded. My goal is to fall in love many times, and always unhappily. I want to hang on to my puppy love. It's silly, yes, but there is something so pure about it. The hopeless nature of it, the foreignness.

Details are everything, and one must train to spot them. Without details one quickly loses interest. It's the details that revive the picture. Every time a new detail is noticed, the picture appears in a different light. This is how you discover the same picture multiple times. The picture first strikes the eyes as an entity, or I should say as an entirety. It's the ensemble that catches you. But then you start noticing details, one by one. And these details add to the picture. Every time you go from a detail back to the ensemble, the picture appears a little more perfect to you.

There is poetic justice as well as artistic justice. Artistically just is that which pleases the eye. In the arts a truth felt is a truth proven. The general view sees the ensemble, but the artistic view sees the details. A painter doesn't look at a painting like we do. He or she sees the details, which are the signs of the art performed. An actor sees the details in acting, and a musician hears the details in music. A writer doesn't read text, but sees text. Sees every word, every comma, and every period. The value of art is hidden in the details. Whenever the eye picks up on a detail, the creation is relived.

One must pay attention to the details. And this has a lot to do with paying attention in the first place. One must engage with a piece of art in the most intimate way. One should be intimate with the art one is engaging with. Only the trivial minds care about the artist behind the art. The artistic mind focuses on the details of the art. A piece of art can be penetrated, further and further. But most art is shallow art, it ends right beneath the surface. If a piece of art possesses depth, you can discover it in the details.

The process of spotting details is intuitive, it's not academic. The details are lighting up in front of you. One develops a pattern, a rhythm in appreciating the art. This rhythm must be created by the artist. Most art has no rhythm. It's simply a stated fact in the artistic form. There is no movement, no melody contained in it. Good art has a rhythm, and the trained eye will mimic it. There is tremendous beauty in recognizing rhythm in a piece of art. It is aesthetically, almost spiritually pleasing to engage with it. To look at a fine painting, to read a fine book, makes it all worth it. If I had to choose anything to live for, it would be art. Many may not understand this but they are not the like-minded. They feel nothing when they encounter art. We feel everything when we do. Art is proof enough. To spend your life on art, is a great way of living. It's using your life spiritually. The true privilege of human life is consciousness. It's true, sometimes it burdens us, but it's still the unique privilege we have.

One must learn to see the details, for the details are the atoms of art. Every detail tells a different story. The ensemble makes the artistic simplicity, but the details make the artistic complexity. Art is the synthesis of simplicity and complexity. It's complex in the making, but simple in its final result. The artist goes from the complex to the simple, but the observer from the simple to the complex. This is the difficulty, for both the artist and the observer. The complexity that the artist faces must be simplified without being lost in the process. Complexity is not to disappear from the picture, it must be incorporated into a higher simplicity of form.

He or she who wants to be an artist must engage with the details. Long before one produces them, one has to perceive them. An eye for detail is a skill rather than a talent. It has to do with paying attention. It's the ability to perceive and to participate emotionally, or to spot something which creates an echo in you. It's not about describing the details. It's about perceiving the picture in front of you, while slowly moving from detail to detail. To see one thing and another. To always return to the picture. To make the picture greater in your head, and your heart. To devote to it, to succumb to it. The picture has to live within you. You must lend your life to it. Fill the picture with life, and it shall return life to you.

While working, he asked me if I was from around here. I said, no, I've come a long way, both physically and mentally. He chuckled, and said, that's life, isn't it? I said, indeed, and we had an uninterrupted spell of silence. He proceeded by saying that he had been located in this right spot for three decades, and he enjoyed the contact with people. I couldn't relate to this at all, yet I said I could relate to this.

In any case, he was working on my trousers and we had an awkward silence. I'm always unsure about professionals working in silence. Do they want the silence to focus on their work, or do they feel the same way as I do, struggling to find a topic to discuss? In the latter case, I should like to say something. In the former case, I should not. So this is quite the predicament I am in. For this reason I never talk to the driver while the car is moving. I make sure to wait for the red traffic light. Then again, falling silent mid sentence as soon as the car starts moving again has produced one or the other odd moment. But I commit to my silence for I don't want to get into an accident. Where was I? Oh yes, the tailor. He was either looking for a topic to overcome the silence or looking to work in silence. I didn't know which one it was. So I took a chance and chose a topic. I said, you know what's funny about the Streisand effect. He said, without looking up: what's that? I said, the Streisand effect, do you know what it is? He looked up slightly, glancing at me over his glasses. I felt like a right fool, and I cursed myself for speaking up. But now I had to commit to it. I told him that the Streisand Effect was named after a mythological figure, a barbarian named Streisand, who had a secret house which he wanted to keep hidden from the world. But the more the barbarian tried to hide his house, the more it became of interest to the aforementioned world. The world focused in on the house as a result of the barbarian's effort to keep it hidden. So the barbarian's efforts produced the opposite effect of even more attention than would have been given if the barbarian simply hadn't mentioned his house in the first place. This is called the Streisand effect. While I said all of this, he was stoically working on my pantalones. I was now about 90 % sure that he had been looking to work in silence. He only responded with an uninspired: ‚ah yeah?' I said: yes, and that's what I've been thinking about. I made a dramatic pause to bring home my point, which I knew to be a safe bet, for it was a good point I was about to make. I said: I thought about the fact that the Streisand effect has now doubled, and probably increased exponentially. I waited for him to show interest, which he never did. I said: There is basically a new level to the Streisand effect now, or a meta, which has been created due to Streisand effect being called that. And this is because originally only the people who didn't care about the barbarian's house showed interest in it. But now a whole new generation of people who didn't even know the barbarian are getting interested in his house. I waited to give the good man a second to breathe. I added: And that's because people want to know what the Streisand effect is, or why it's called that, and where the term comes from. And they all learn about the barbarian's house. Before that, they had no idea the barbarian, let alone his house existed. Now they do, because they inquire about the Streisand effect. Which means that additionally to attracting those who inquire about the barbarian's house, it also attracts all the people who inquire about the Streisand effect. It's a double effect now. The Streisand effect has become a Streisand spell, or a Streisand spill. It just spills now, like a flood, and it cannot be stopped. I took a pause to see what the man would contribute. He contributed nothing which was disappointing, but it didn't discourage me. I said: ‚I wonder what the next stage will be. I think naturally we have to reach a point where the effect detaches from its name, in a way that people will ask about the barbarian's house without the Streisand effect even being mentioned. The lexical ‚Streisand' would have to detach from the name, that is from the effect, and develop a life on its own. And this would happen if Streisand becomes a word in the regular English language. Do you follow?' He looked at me skeptically over his glasses. I said: ‚Basically, what I'm thinking is we need to overcome the ‚effect' and isolate the ‚Streisand' lexically. We need to turn it into a verb or adjective, or a noun. ‚To streisand someone': to draw the attention to someone or something against their will. Or to shed a light on something that was to supposed to be swept under the carpet. To streisand, or even better: to strise — 3rd person singular „strises", he / she / it strises. Present participle strisening, past participle strised, pronounced like fries or lies, so with the ‚eye" sound in the middle, or wait — strose, strose is better. Examples from common day language: ‚Jesus Christ, why would you strise me like me that, now everyone is looking'; ‚whenever I ask him not to make a big deal out of it he strises me in front of everyone'; ‚I tried to close the window, but I strose it instead by tearing it wide open'. ‚The man froze when his wife strose him in front of everyone; ‚When the tides have risen, the stakes have strisen', this means the bigger the attention, the more you can expose yourself by saying or doing something incorrect. ‚I have been strising this issue for as long as I can remember, management just doesn't care; I have been strising this by stressing this and training this to straining this, and strengthening and lengthening, and hardening and gardening, and yet, despite my many tries, all I hear is alibis, I never should have strisen this, now gone and broken are my bliss'. These are some examples from common day language. At this point the good man didn't even look at me anymore. He was almost finished with the work, so I wanted to bring home my argument. I said this. ‚And since I'm a visionary, I already see what's coming ahead. Which is a prefix. Yes, you heard right. I want the str-prefix. The str-prefix, pronounced straprefix, emphasis on the first syllable, and I'm sure once the Americans get a hold of the word, it will become a „strapifix", which, you know, we shouldn't judge, language is organic, it's all about being able to look at yourself in the meer, ex cetera, and after all we wouldn't want to strise our own imperfections. In any case, this is my vision for the stretomology. And yes, this was the first example of the strapifix. The strapifix has a simple meaning and I shall explain it now. It's not what a word means, but what a word aims for. It's used in the present tense, signifying a future not yet realized. It's a future subjunctive essentially. It's a futuristic meaning of something that is in the present not yet realized, only verbalized. It's vision and pioneering turned grammatical. One doesn't use the word in the existing sense, instead one uses the existing word and by adding the strapifix one implies and implores a change unrealized in the present. I shall go ahead now and give a couple of examples for the strapifix: ‚I strathink we should behave strabetter as a society.'; ‚The man and the woman stradreamed of a future together but that was before his affair'; ‚My favorite ice cream would be strastrawberry, if it had more strawberry in it, but since it doesn't, it's straciatella."; ‚One day the world strashall be a strabetter place'. And so on, you get the picture." I paused, but the man didn't react at all. I felt that I had stratired the man with my visions. It was clear that he didn't share them, and I didn't want to strise the fact any further. It had been strisen enough by the silence which my ideation had strum. I kept silent for another couple of minutes, until he was finished with his work. He did not dignify my explanations with a single word. He let me pay and leave. I felt humiliated, for once again I had strisen to the occasion.

All the things I dreamt of. None of them came true. I'm not saying they generally don't. They simply didn't for me. I have no regrets. For during the few times that what I imagined came true, it was never any special. Things are always more beautiful in imagination than in reality.

To realize that some things are just not meant to be. They say fortune favors the brave, but it mostly favors the fortunate. One should not despair over fate, for it's mostly our expectations that are disappointed. Neither the good nor the bad was destined for us. There was no destiny, and we're just here to learn. Things happening for a reason is of course not true. It should be said that things make sense when you make sense of them. The reason is added in hindsight. Things are neutral until they're experienced, that's a better saying.

I was young and I had dreams. Now I'm no longer young and I no longer have dreams. It's the way the world works. And yet I miss my dream, more than I miss my youth. I'd rather be an old dreamer than a young realist. Realism is the real disease. One should stay unrealistic for as long as possible.

We shall be happy with or without our dreams coming true. Often there are clear signs that our dreams are not for us. We tend to dream the dreams of others. It's tragical to realize your dream, just to realize that it wasn't yours. This is why we should focus less on our dreams and more on ourselves. In success we develop a blindness, which is only overcome in failure. One should seek failure as a way to readjust. Life is unique. We cannot repeat it. We must be careful not to become somebody whose success is truly our failure.

I thought I wanted to be happy. I realize now that I have to find happiness within my sadness. You cannot become happy as the person you are not. It makes you unhappy by default. There is existential misery in becoming trapped in a happy character. It's easy to be caught up in the life of another. This is why it's imperative to not enter that life in the first place.

When we're young we're prone to adopt the dreams of society. In that case, it's better if your dreams don't come true. Dreams should only come true if they're certain to be yours. But how to assess this? By relying on yourself, rather than your dreams. You should be flexible about your dreams while strictly adhering to yourself, not the other way around. Don't change for your dreams, change the dreams for yourself. Our personality is often only discovered in the process. One should not hold on to one's dream no matter what. Many people hang on to dreams that no longer match their personalities. To make your personality fit your dream is an uncomfortable way of living. You must allow your personality a maximum amount of freedom, and your dream should adapt to your personality, not the other way around.

Early success is the worst that can happen to a young person. Mundane bliss kills the poetry within you. This is why most poets don't make it past 30. They do, but their poetry doesn't. One must be generous with failure, but extra careful with success. Most people believe in success unconditionally. We shouldn't believe in success at all. We should be very critical of it. Failure is a fact, and it always speaks truth. Wise are those, who have failed most repeatedly. Their success is not a moment in time, or an isolated achievement. It's their accumulated personality, steeled by repeated failure. Failure will humble you first, but then build you up. You can be a giant failure, and yet become the ultimate success. And just like that, you can succeed and still feel like a failure.

This is why I'm saying, don't trust your dreams. Trust yourself instead. Put all your trust in what you are, and be skeptical about what you want to be. Always make sure that this hypothetical future you're hoping for corresponds with your present personality. For your present personality is a much safer bet than your future personality. What I considered to be my worst moments in hindsight turned out to be my best. What I considered my low points, I now regard as turning points. The path to yourself leads through your failures. It's only the successes that lead you astray. No one told you this, so I'll be the one. You should trust your failures much more than your successes. Nobody lies more blatantly in your face than the success you achieve. For every person thats regrets their failure, there is one that regrets their success.

There are many people in the world who feel like they don't fit in. These people must be encouraged. Not to try and fit in, but to not mind it. To not fit in is often the genesis of fitting in somewhere else. Otherwise do you really know where you belong? You may have just settled for the wrong thing. One can walk in darkness on the right path as well as in daylight on the wrong path. You never know who you are until you know who you are not. Many people realize this way too late in their lives. They reach their 50s, 60s until they find out. This is why it's good to not fit in. At least you won't commit to the wrong cause. We should all try to fit in less, not more. Fitting in leads to a loss of self, while not fitting in leads to rediscovery of self. We should not try to fit in. We should fit out instead. Be grateful that you're a mismatch. Mismatches may not match society, but at least they match themselves.

It's interesting that the night sky is the real sky. It's during the day that the sky appears in alien form. By day, the sky is like a lid put on Earth. At night the lid is removed, and we see the actual sky. Essentially, we live on a dark planet. Pictures of Earth always show us the bright side. But that's only half the planet. The other half is dark. So it's not really the blue planet, is it? It's the half blue planet. Half blue, half black. The black planet sounds cooler, too. I would love to live on a black planet. It would resonate well with my black soul. Black and bleak, yet powerful. At night we live on a black planet. And the light we see is not our own. It's the light from far away. Others wouldn't see us. We are as black to them as the night is to us. I like this very much. To be invisible, on a black planet. I'm never scared of the night. The night is our protector. It protects us quieter souls. The only thing I dread is the arrival of dawn. I would love for the night to continue forever. I'm at peace whenever the blue planet turns black.

People who talk slowly. Drain. My. Soul. They talk so slowly, so very, and even verier, slowly. There are no developments in their speech. It always stays on one frequency, and one message level, which borders on being without message.

Intuition is immediate wisdom. Nothing can be said in favor of the truth perceived, and yet it's like a proven fact.

Intuition is wisdom, yet not wisdom after the fact, but before the fact. One knows before one should logically be able to know. It's not that one doesn't have all the facts. One has no facts, and yet one knows. Intuition starts with the realization and it works itself backwards to the argument. It reverses the natural process. You don't analyze in order to come to a conclusion, you start with the conclusion and you analyze how you came to it. Intuition begins with the answer.

When intuition strikes, it's as though our soul said Yes. ‚Yes to this'. The soul is never wrong, she knows things. How she knows them? We don't know. She just does. Intuition is our soul relating to the world around us. She pulls or pushes, attracts or repulses. Intuition is not the same as instinct.

Instinct is the animal in us. Intuition is the divine. It connects us with something higher, be that what it may.

Intuition is our organ of truth. It's our soul applying herself to the world. She says, this is true or untrue. It's rare that we perceive our soul, for she usually stays hidden within us. But she is there, when we intuit. She enters unannounced.

Intuition is a primary condition. It's like being reminded of something, yet not something we experienced. Like a memory of something that never occurred. Or remembering something that we shouldn't be able to remember. A memory from a primary condition. Memory of dream perhaps. Intuition is like dreaming while awake. It's a dream state, not a wake state. And yet, interestingly, we experience it in the wake state. Intuition is like the memory of a dream, which we remember in the wake state. Or intuition is the dream's way of knowing. The moment of intuition is always strange. We feel like we're dreaming while being wide awake.

Intuition is how we exist in dream. It's as though we were being led by something that knows the answer already. We never feel this way in the wake state. Yet when intuition strikes, we do. Intuition governs the dream. It's beautiful when it strikes in the wake state. Suddenly we intuit, and we know what to do. We are guided, but what guides us? We don't know. We say soul, but what does it really mean?

There is something primal about intuition. It's so strangely unfitting. In a world of reason and rationale, intuition is beautifully different. It seems to only have two phrases which it operates, it says True and False, and we feel this statement. Our soul says ‚Yes' to this and ‚No' to this. Intuition is this qualitative statement that we feel. Yet we never quite grasp it. It's not a thing. It's a mode of feeling about something.

Right away, you know it's true. Intuition is immediate knowledge. All doubts disappear. There is no layer between us and the world. There is no reflection, or analysis. What we experience, comes to us as truth. It makes the world simple. No need to think, for the verdict has been given.

And yet, it cannot be described what intuition is. It's like a rush of self. We return to who we are, we are no longer distracted. Intuition is the sentiment of truth. We feel something to be true, yet why, we can't tell.

There is something beautiful about almost knowing someone. You look at each other, and society dictates that you are now to say a word. But you don't. You remain silent. All you exchange is a brief look. It's a strange sort of intimacy, to know someone without knowing their name.

Man becomes animal, when he reverts to the physical. That must never happen. Man must be spirit. To stay pure, even physically, it comes down to that. We must remain in the realm of the possible. The physical touch is inferior. One must skip it, and instead commit to the idea of touch. The idea needs to be strong, yet the touch may not occur. In the spirit, we shall be lovers, but not in the flesh.

The hypothetical is where dreamers fall in love. As soon as they try to translate this into reality, they fail. The dreamers are simply not good at living. Consequently, they are not good at loving either. They're good at imagining life, and imagining love. It's their privilege, as well as their burden. The realm of the possible must not be left by the dreamers whose duty it is to protect this realm. Reality should not be sought after, it has nothing in store for souls like ours. Dream protects us from the afflictions of reality. After all, those who never try can never be hurt. We shall be happy, but only hypothetically, never actually, for actual happiness kills hypothetical bliss. Aspiring to dreams which never come true. Nothing as pretty as the thought of the unhappy dreamers. It's in dream, not in the world, that we create pretty thought.

Dreamers never speak up. Every word distorts their beautiful soul. Words you feel straight come out twisted. A dreamer always sounds like a fool. But this is because he's not used to talking. One must live in the hypothetical for a long time to become a beautiful thinker. The dreamers are simply not able to create the right words for their sentiment. Yet make no mistake, they have very intact sentiment. Intimacy is not supposed to be physical anyway. Physical love is animal love, and it must be avoided at all costs. True love is the love of souls, not bodies. We shall be lovers only in thought.

Intimacy is the love of souls. To translate it into physical love is an incorrect handling of the sentiment. Intimacy must be protected from physical love, not translated into it. It only realizes its full potential if it remains unphysical. There are those who think intimacy is physical, romantic in nature. I think we can all agree that they are wrong. Physical intimacy is almost the opposite of intimacy. It's a sellout of intimacy. One sacrifices intimacy in the physical touch. Therefore, all touch must be avoided. To translate intimacy into physical form is to deplete it. When the physical is introduced, intimacy is outroduced. Love must be spiritual in essence.

The dreamers don't live in the physical, for their bodies are weak. They don't possess reality, they only dream about possessing it. Nothing ever solidifies under their imaginative touch. The mind speaks, yet the mouth remains shut.

Intimacy should never materialize, for the body is inferior to the soul. One must allow the soul to love, but not the body. The body is a thing, it doesn't deserve our attention. The less we think about our bodies, the more effort we can put into our souls. Intimacy is the soul's way of loving. If it becomes physical, we've made a mockery out of the sentiment. We must protect the sentiment from our physical ways. We must dwell on the feeling, instead of expressing it physically. Physical love is not worthy of us. We are hypothetical creatures, we live in the ethereal. Intimacy is our silent plea for a life never lived. And yet it must be protected, because all attempts to translate intimacy into reality leads to its destruction. The feeling fades, and intimacy is lost. There you are, reduced to idle physics, and how ugly humans are. Don't you think? They only become beautiful when they become mind and soul. This is where we should love. In the mind and in the soul. Never in the flesh.

I was talking to a man in a newspaper shop today. He told me about the things he experienced on a daily basis. There was an elderly woman, he said, who always dropped in at 7 sharp to get the morning paper. I said, so she always knows about the news first. He said, yes. I said, which means that during these brief minutes and hours, she knows more than the rest of us, but then her wisdom levels out throughout the day. He nodded. I said, that's interesting. He said, he likes to chat with his customers. I said, you must meet a lot of people. He said, loads. I said, what? He said, yes, many. I said, I understand. He said, it was important for him to be in the shop, for his customers were loyal to him. I said, that's odd. He said, why is that? I said, because they're buying the newspaper. He said, well, they're buying it from a known face. I said, what's got the face to do with the newspaper. He hesitated. I had struck a nerve. I said, they are buying the paper, not the known face. He said, it's all part of the experience. I said, that's a big word for buying the morning paper. I said, isn't it possible that they're only coming here for the newspaper. He looked at me, unsure as to what to say next. I said, would they come here if you sold soap? He said, soap? I nodded. He said, I guess not. I said, you see my point. And he was sad. I felt I had saddened the man, so I said, I guess they would come for you. He said, I would hope so.

I would love to be a private detective. I think I would do pretty well. I already know all the tricks, for I watch a lot of detective shows. It's amazing, if you spend some time doing research on the internet, you can become an expert on anything. I think I would make a good detective. I would chase after someone in secret. I would make sure they don't see me, for this is I believe an important aspect of it. One must be undetected. In life I'm very good at this, why should I not be at the job. I would always present myself as a detective as this would give me authority. People would know that I'm smart, for only smart people are detectives. I would introduce myself as a private investigator. This sounds even better actually. I would love to be a private investigator. I would investigate the most exciting cases. I would present myself by tapping two fingers against my head, this would be my tell-tale sign. I would go to people and offer my services. I would always offer to work at half the rate.

I would love to be a private detective. I thought about it the other day. I have everything that is needed to excel at the job. I am a rather invisible guy, and people don't notice me at first. They don't notice me later either. This is perfect for I believe a private detective has to avoid detection. I'd always engage with people in the most inconspicuous way. I would approach the main suspect, and engage him in conversation. Lovely day, innit? Yes, indeed, he would say. I would question the witnesses, by writing them threatening letters. You'll be next if you don't tell me all the details. By this clever method I would gather all the evidence. I would of course not use my own handwriting, I would cut out letters from the newspaper. It's cute when you think about it. Serial killers do this. They cut out letters from the newspaper and glue it onto a sheet of paper. It's such a childish, innocent activity in such a horrible context. I would send the letters to the witnesses to collect data. Once I have all information, I could connect the dots. This would be my way of solving the crimes. If I was a private detective, I would pretend to be the killer. This would be so baffling, that the suspect could only react in one of two ways. Either they are appalled, so they must be innocent. Or they are not, which means they are guilty for only the guilty party could know that I'm not really the killer. Even more than a private detective, I would love to be a fraud detective. I would play the detective, in a most convincing way. I would pretend to have cracked the case. Or I would like to be the actual perpetrator, investigating my own case. I would commit murders that I would investigate. This is my way of ensuring my own business.

I would love to be a private detective. I really think I have a talent for it. I would walk in on a crime scene and introduce myself as a friend of the family. Once in, I will tell the family that I'm a state detective. When the detective returns, I will say: Detective, may I have a word. And then I would act as a member of the family again. This would be my way in. I just have to avoid that the two parties talk to each other in my absence. For this I have a third plan. I will tell the detective that I'm not just a member of the family but also the family lawyer, and that I ask to be present in all conversations. Then I would return to the family and tell them I'm a state lawyer, and I was going to represent them legally. Now this is near perfection, and I'm in. Talk about a perfect crime. Here commences my real plan. Unbeknownst to everyone I will investigate the crime scene with my eye for detail. I think I have shown more than enough that I indeed possess an eye for detail. I would investigate how meticulously the crime was planned. If the crime scene is a mess, it means it was staged, and it was a well planned crime. If everything is clean and tidy, it means the crime had to be done in a hurry, for the perpetrator had no time to mess up the place. I would look at the body, extra carefully, for it's not every day that you see a dead body. It's not voyeurism if you feel bad about it. In any case, I would continue to investigate. I would look at the surroundings to see if anything strikes the eye. Besides the poor choice of interior of course. I would engage the coroner in conversation for you never know when he might come in handy. I would look at the body, shake my head, and say: no, this is not a suicide! The coroner would say: nobody said it was. I would try to pick up on small clues that the other detectives didn't spot. The way the body is positioned is suspicious. Why is that, the coroner would say. I would reply, it's almost a perfect 45 degree angle to the kitchen entrance, this can't be a coincidence. He would nod in agreement. I would investigate the body to see if there are any bite marks. If there are, I would try to identify the animal. Was it a dog, or a bat. Or perhaps the worst animal of all — man? I would nod to agree with my own statement. It wouldn't fail to make an impression on the coroner. I would return to the family and ask, did he have any enemies? They would say, none. I would say, that's not true, is it? They would say, what do you mean? I would say, he clearly had at least one. They would say, do you think this is funny? In that moment the other detectives would return. My Ponzi scheme about to collapse, I would have to think on my feet. I don't understand this expression, for I tend to be on my feet when I think. In any case, I would react swiftly. I would say, this is clearly a homicide. This is a great sentence as it makes sense from both perspectives. The detectives would say, it appears to be so. I would say, what are the next steps? This is another clever question, which works either way. The family would understand me as one of the detectives, while the detectives would think of me as one of the family. The detectives would say, we'll inform you when the time comes, but for now you may take your time to grieve. I would turn toward the family and nod in agreement. The detectives would give me a funny look from the side. They would say, what are you doing? I would turn back to them and say, what do you mean? They would say, why are you nodding as though you were one of us. I would look at them in terror. Then I would look at the family in terror. And then I would run away as fast as I can.

I would investigate the whole apartment. Nothing would escape my vision. I would even crawl into the doghouse, for you never know what you may find in there.

I would look at the diseased to find clues. Political correctness really has gone too far, he's clearly not diseased, he's dead, just call him dead already. I would look at the dead body to find some additional clues.

I would comment on the crime scene. I would confidently say sentences like: this must have been a .22 caliber. The coroner would look at me funny and say, the man was stabbed 38 times. I would say, well, time will tell. I would look at the body and make educated guesses. I would say: time of death between 4 AM and 6 AM in the morning. The coroner would say, not even close. I would look at him upset and say, who cares, the man is dead, give him a break. I would ask the family, how long the victim had lived in the house. They would say, for years. I would say, how many? They would say, they didn't know exactly. I would make a mental note: Suspicious. I would ask, if the diseased had any run-ins with the law. They would say, a couple of parking tickets, nothing out of the ordinary. I would note down, yes. Here we had a man who troubled the law and lived in isolation.

It's said that good things come to those who wait. But what about those who wait in vain? How can you tell if good things are coming for you? The answer is probably that you can't. It may be better to lose interest in the good things altogether. It's depressing to always think about the things that you don't have. It makes you unhappy. And if you had them, it wouldn't make you happy either, or not for long. Hope is not about having something, it's about not having something. And this is not related to the things we don't have. For there are a lot of things that we don't have. Once we have them, we will feel that we are missing something else. Hope makes us think that once we have what we desire, we will be happy. But if we can't be happy without it, we won't be happy with it. I hear a lot of praise for hope, and how you need to keep your hopes up. But I'm not sure about that. In all my years, hope has never failed to let me down. It disappoints us more than it rewards us. Which is ironic, because hope is supposed to save us from disappointment. But more often than not it just delays the disappointment to the future. By hoping for a different life, we devalue the life we currently lead. I'm not saying we should love what we have, for I think this is silly, too. It's the other extreme that I don't agree with. I think one should move forward, but hope is just not the right tool for it. Hope devalues the present, and it paints a future that will most likely never occur. It's too hypothetical, and this is saying something coming from me. Even when my hopes came true, they still let me down. I was still unhappy, only different now. The grass is always greener, as they say. The things you want appear in different light once you have them. It's more about the chase than the catch. And it's more about the escape than the chase.

Hope is a concealed disappointment. It's the pre-realized form of disappointment, or a present disappointment pushed into the future. It's said that hope is important, but I wonder, what good does it do? It makes us unhappy with the present, and happy about a future that will never be. To hope means to want something that we don't have. The key part is the „don't". It's the disappointment of not having. Hope provides an outlet, but an unhealthy one. It redirects our attention to a future, in which we might have what we don't have today. Hope presents us with this particular item, or experience, or person. But hope doesn't relieve our disappointment, it only dresses it in external form. Our disappointment must never be externalized like that. We must face it head-on, and understand why we feel the way we do. This is why hope is often misguided. When hope is directed toward the future, we should ask ourselves: what am I missing right now? Toward that our attention should be guided in the present.

Hope is a way of moving our present disappointment into an unknown future. The „unknown“ is a big part of it. There is a disappointment in us which we ought to know about, but we prefer to „unknow“ it. We unknow it by moving it into an unknown future in which the disappointment is resolved. But while the future is uncertain, the present is not. The present is here, and it needs to be understood in the present tense. Hope is not a strategy to cope with disappointment. One needs to face things head-on. Hope is a way of escaping the afflictions of today. But the afflictions of today will be the afflictions of tomorrow, if we don't face them in the present tense. Hope assigns therapeutic functions to external things. We should never externalize our disappointment like that.

I hear a lot of positivity about hope. That we must never lose it. But I have been my happiest when I gave up my hopes. Contrary to what the world says, this has not disappointed me at all. It's presented me with moderate bliss. My hopes were devious, they always made me want the world different from what it was. It's good to have an impact on the world, but hope should not be involved in this. I am not saying we must be grateful for what we have, for I think this is also an extreme position, namely one of stagnation. I believe in a healthy unhappiness, one that drives us to achieve what we aim for. One must, to some extent, be happy with the things that one has, but at the same time work toward whatever it is that one wants. Hope should have no place in either of this. It is destructive in regard to the present, which it devalues and empties, as well as passive and weak in regard to a future, which only exists in your imagination.

Don't lose hope, they say. But maybe you should. It doesn't mean that your dreams won't come true. It just means you're no longer tortured by them. Hope makes you dependent on external things and that is a terrible way of living. We should avoid hope altogether. We should go, not hope for things.

I've heard this sentence a lot: don't lose hope. Every time I didn't, I felt good in the moment and terrible in the long run. Hope is like a drug, it gives you a kick, but you always regret it later on. To lose hope is a necessary detox. One should detox from hope, and never touch it ever after. Hope has an incredible lobby, but we must see it for what it is: a drug. I find that the less I hope, the better I do.

Hope won't get you anywhere. The only thing that will get you there is yourself. Hope is malicious, it controls your way of thinking. You become passive in the eyes of your own fate.

There are things that you hope for, I am well aware. I'm not saying you shouldn't go for these things. I'm saying you should. But going for them and hoping for them are two different things. One is active, as in: you are moving toward them. The other is passive, as in: it's moving toward you. In the former you are moving, in the latter you're sedate. Things will never come to you in life, you must come to them. Good things come to those who wait simply isn't true. Good things come to those who move toward them. Steadily, yet patiently. Their waiting is a waiting in motion. It's persistence, and tenacity. It's not waiting around until something happens. Yet in the moment of hope, this is exactly what happens. Rest will never get you there, for the goals are not moving toward you. You must move toward them. Hoping doesn't take you there. You are just stopping in the middle of the road, looking at the horizon. The horizon isn't moving toward you, and you are not moving toward it anymore. Hope undermines your endeavors. Motion is everything, rest to be feared. Hope can be an indulgence. You can have a hope day like a cheat day. But that's it. Never incorporate it into your actual strategies.

Hope never gets you anywhere. It's you that gets you there. You get there effectively by going for it. Going for it means you'll fail forward while living in the present. Hoping for it means you'll fast-forward to the future without living in the present. One should never forget to live in the present, for this is the only time we actually live in. Everything else is just a way of not living, and rejecting the life we lead. This should never be an option, yet hope is all but based on it.

Hope doesn't deserve its good reputation. It makes you stand still in the present, yet you're not even living in that present. Instead, you're living in that hypothetical future, which has no connection to the present. To live in a time that is not and therefore not to live in the time that is, can only be called confusion. One must live in the present and move toward the future, not sacrifice the present for a hypothetical future. Hope is hostile to the present, and to the life we live. It's hostile to us essentially. To what we are, and what we've accomplished. Hope is the one thing that I pledge to abandon from my life. Hope makes me passive, and I don't like that feeling. It's not about being weak and strong, it's about being passive and active. You can be actively patient and passively impatient. It's about controlling or being controlled. It's about being in charge or being in chains. One must be an active dreamer, but emphasis must lie on the active.

They say dont lose hope, but I say do lose it. It's liberating.

Good things come out of bad things. This is one the things that the years teach which the days never knew. When you're young, you're thinking straight-forward. Good things come out of good things, bad things out of bad things. Years go by and you gain experience. Gradually you realize that life is not that simple. It's true that people make their biggest mistakes in times of success, and that's because they stop analyzing. They ride the wave. Which is often preparing their own downfall. Bad habits solidify, and they are not replaced by better habits. On the other hand, bad things tend to bring out the best in us. In failure you question everything, and there is no wave to be ridden. You start from scratch, but this time in healthier fashion. Before you know it, a better version of yourself arises. It's often surprising how quickly this happens. You can be the happiest you've ever been within months of being the unhappiest you've ever been. It's a humbling experience to realize how quickly things can turn around. At your lowest you think you're forever doomed. Two months later you're essentially fine. It's remarkable how little your circumstances actually determine how you feel. You grow older and you realize that the road is not linear. Life is less about what happens to you, and more about what happens to you when it does. The way you feel remains the variable, however, one that can be understood. The circumstances should be secondary, as they are. How do we feel when our dreams come true? We'll find out when we get there.

To believe in pure thought and art. To obtain that perfection. It's a beautiful thing to aspire to. Perfection is unattainable, but one should make an effort anyway. It's the high point of your existence that defines you. Thought is comforting, and it's always there for you. Isn't it beautiful? Thought is like a friend who never leaves our side. I think we should return the favor and be a friend to our thoughts. People invest in their possessions, but who invests in their thoughts? The beauty of mind is a beauty underappreciated. People don't understand beautiful thought, for they don't think beautifully. They barely think at all. They comment on what they're doing and call it thinking. But thought is another world, separate from the one we all inhabit. It's the world of spirit that one enters by the act of thinking. The more one thinks, the more one discovers this beautiful place. Most people live on the surface of the mind, they rarely immerse. But some people bring their goggles, they go right in, and the lucky ones never resurface. This is the true privilege of being human. To think. As far as we know, nobody else does this. The ability to not just live, but to understand. This can be your purpose. The eyes only see the world from one angle, but the mind sees it from all of them. There are countless ways of viewing things, and the mind can discover them all.

Most people don't think at all. Of those who do, most people think more or less the same. It's the remaining few that think differently. To think as an individual is a gift that should be nurtured, not suffocated in the young. We kill unique thought, and we replace it with generic thought. But thought must never be generic. The mind must be as unique as the soul. Else, can it even be called a mind? The beauty of mind is the queen of all beauties. Sensual beauty, physical beauty, natural beauty, none of them compare with spiritual beauty. A beautiful thought is immortal. Once expressed, it's forever. To touch on the eternal by thinking, allows us to overcome our mortal condition. We will die, but our thoughts will never. It's the chosen few that enrich the world. Give me his thought, and I'll give you the man. Or woman, of course. The greatness of any human is determined by their ability to think. And to think independently. There is no one who deserves our admiration but the human who thinks. Those who don't, to the devil, we must not be sad about them. Only few in this world that have their own thoughts. It's to those that we ought to listen. One should dedicate one's life to thought. Thought is elegant. It's not bound to the flesh, nor imprisoned by it, for I think we can all agree that humans have an ugly form. It's nothing to be proud of, to be human, I mean visually. It takes some imagination to find humans beautiful. But thought is different. Thought is the divine language, and those who speak it, remind ourselves of the divinity in us. When thought is expressed, the divine enters the world. Thought is not limited by the physical. It transcends time and space, which it strictly speaking never enters. It's an unphysical world that exists nonetheless. It's a world stripped of all the ugliness that we introduced into it. Nature is beautiful, but thought is superior. In nature, beauty passes. In thought, it never. You can create a whole kingdom of thought, and live in it eternally. And yes, eventually, you'll leave this Earth, but your thoughts will not. Isn't this beautiful? That you can create something eternal during your finite lifetime. I find this beautiful, almost magical.

Thought is the most beautiful thing there is. It exceeds any other beauty. Natural beauty is ephemeral, spiritual beauty is not. Once it's there, it will be forever. Long after you've passed. And it's not bound to humans either. It's only bound to itself. Humans will pass eventually, but thought will never.

I dream of creating a modern religion, which takes place in the spirit. There are no rules in this religion, for the spirit is limitless, and we shall be limitless in it. I want to believe in spirit, like others believe in God. When I die, I want to think of spirit one more time and leave with a smile on my face. For I know that while I die, my thoughts will not. My thoughts are forever, they never decay. I've lived in the spirit and I shall die in it. Isn't it beautiful to find faith in the act of thinking. When thinking has the same beautiful quality of praying. Wouldn't that be a beautiful religion. In the realm of spirit, the act of thinking is an active prayer. Thought becomes testimony to your faith. The spirit is not something, let alone somebody. The spirit is the infinite expanse in which you're set free. To live in this expanse, and to believe in it. That would be a beautiful religion. But how, I hear you say, can you have faith in something as unphysical and intangible as the spirit. Well, I'd hate to talk to you about God. To believe in something, not with your mind, but with your soul. To give yourself up to it and let it guide you. You can believe in the spirit in this exact fashion. Thinking gives you peace, and it consoles your heart. Isn't this a beautiful way of finding faith? To not believe in something physical, like man or the Earth, instead to believe in the spirit. To go there as often as possible, to stay there as long as you can. This is the beautiful thing about thinking. The more you do it, the more intriguing it becomes. This is why people are so ugly these days. They never think, and when they do, they repulse their own thoughts. They are confused by what it all means, and they feel uncomfortable with the unphysical nature of it. Then they drown their confusion in living physically again. One should never live like this. To live spiritually is the most beautiful way of living. One must never withdraw from the spiritual life. One should withdraw from physical life instead. I dream of a modern religion, which returns faith to man and woman. Faith in the spirit, faith in beautiful thought. It's a religion for the quiet, a beautiful religion. I dream of creating a religion, in which spirit becomes God. Until they all listen to me, then I'll replace the spirit with myself, and I'll turn it into a cult. Well let's see how it pans out. It depends on my agenda when the time comes. One should always be humble, for one never knows how one feels in the future.

They called me absurd which I took personally. As I consider myself most unabsurd. I think I'm moderate, in my own way of course. I'm moderating my lack of moderation. But I don't consider myself absurd. To me it all makes sense. To them it doesn't. But that's just a difference of opinion. I am always confused by this. Normal is that which most people agree on. But who says that most people are right? For large parts of history, most people were wrong.

I saw family today. I should say „a“ family, for it wasn't mine. I saw a family today. It was in the park. I was walking by, when the little one of the group made contact. It greeted me most merrily. I greeted the child back and asked where it was hailing from. It pointed to its family who was having a picnic nearby. They were a cute little family. A young father, a young mother, and their two children, who were anything between boy and girl. I am not sure, for both children had long hair and the face of an infant. In any case, I was walking by and saying Hello. They were having all sorts of things there, including bread and water. It was like The Last Supper with infants. The outdoor version. This observation made me think. How did Jesus come up with the table setup. Not just that they made the table long, while it should have been a roundtable. But also, that they're only sitting on one side of it. This is by far the worst setup for conversation. I wonder. Did Jesus have the same aversion to small talk as me? Cause this is exactly what I would have done. In fact, the more you look at the picture, the more it makes sense. All the disciples seem to think just that. Why did he seat us like this? The guys on the left are going: „Alright, Mr. Big Shot doesn't want to converse, it's his world, we just live in it.“ The guys on the right, are still trying to convince him: „Should we not sit in a roundtable, or at least face each other, it's our last supper after all.“ The guys on the far right are complaining the most, you can see them saying: „Geez, what's wrong with this guy!“ A long table is the most overrated table setup. Why is it still around as a social design. It should have long died out. Any other setup is better, really. At a long table, everything is inaccessible, while your immediate neighborhood is way too close. If you're in a group of 50 people, you don't hear from 45 of them ever, not once, and with the other 4 you have to converse for hours. It's the worst of both worlds. The others are at the same time too close and too far away. And not just the people. The food and drinks are also either inaccessible, or they are right under your nose, so you have collective responsibility for everyone. You cannot pour your own drink, without pouring an extra five cups first. It's too social in the immediate vicinity, and too little social in the broader scheme of things. You have to make small talk with a handful people all night, and you never even say Hi to everybody else. It's a terrible table design. No one can make small talk for hours. This is torture for the soul. What are we supposed to say after 30 minutes of sitting there. Everything is awkward. You are too close to the people next to you and across from you. It's too intimate. And the people just slightly further away, it's also awkward with them because you have to half-scream at them. And then there are cross conversations taking place. Everyone is laughing and smiling. This is how it must be in hell. I think this was Jesus' wisdom. He created the perfect table setup. He did not want to socialize so he decided against the round setup, and went straight for the linear table design. But he also skipped the part where he seated people across from each other. He seated them next to each other, so people would have to turn left and right to converse, which is annoying to a point where we just stop doing it. He was wise, he truly was, by choosing this table design. Of course he calculated without his chatty disciples, who got up from their seats to converse anyway. But Jesus didn't, so it worked for him. If I ever get married, I will choose this table design. Now all I have to do is get the girl, the marriage, and the friends. And the table of course. Where do you get a table like this? Is it one table or many tables? I never thought about this. Is this an industry? There must be a long table lobby. What are their interests? What's their big idea? What's their vision for long tables. What's the long table of the future? Anyway, I think I'll go for a long table. I will seat everyone left and right, and when people talk to me, I'll just look straight ahead and pretend I didn't hear them.

When you're young, you see everything for the first time. The boy looked at the crane, which was currently in motion. It was doing this thing, where the horizontal was rotating, while the vertical was still. The boy was fascinated with this. He opened his mouth, and his eyes were wide open. So very cute. I wanted to think it from his perspective. I watched the crane. It was rotating, ever so slowly. I understood the little one. Construction sites are a place of wonder for a young boy. He thinks construction site workers rule the world, and that they are the kings and queens of the free West. He's in for a surprise. If I was a construction site worker I would get all my confidence from the children's admiration. If they admire me, I must be an admiral. An admirable anyway. And so I would present myself. As an admiral, master of the cranes. Proficient in the use of tools and instruments. A craftsman indeed. I would step on the crane, and put on a show. I'm always surprised that not more buildings collapse. I feel like the structural engineers are underrated in our society. They should be our heroes. A boy can admire the construction site workers, but a man must admire the engineers. If I was to design a building, I wouldn't know where to begin. Probably at the base, though. I would work myself from bottom to top. It would be cool to have a house in which each story would be built by a different architect. Diversity of people is all very well, but we need diversity of building. Structural engineers are the coolest people, yet we never hear from them. They are one of those huge population groups that you never encounter anywhere. There is no connection point between society and structural engineers. They work in the shadows, and they never show their faces. I demand that they do. Enough with the secrecy. I don't want to live in a society in which the structural engineers can do what they want. I'm sure they have a lot of skeletons in their closets. Or perhaps in their walls. Maybe there is a whole society of skeletons that's been surgically worked into the structures of buildings. Maybe that's where all the missing people are. Are they dangerous criminals? We wouldn't know about it. They might be strange people. I'm sure they are. Who decides to pursue a career in structural engineering? What's the decision path, or the decision tree. Where do you even study that? Who are the experts of that industry? And how is it represented in politics? Where is the political ministry that oversees the structural engineers. And who designed their building? What was first, the buildings or the engineers? Who built the first building? There is a whole industry I know nothing about. Whenever I catch a glimpse, it ends up being a lot of physics and maths. But who created the maths? What are the maths of structural engineering? Who are the pioneers of this field? Who first came up with the equations? And how many people had to die to find out that the equations were wrong? Imagine you die because someone came up with a wrong equation for the building you live in. That would be an annoying cause of death. „Shoot, we forget an x on the right side of the equation, now 78 people are dead." Imagine you're a genius in the field of structural engineering, and the world admires pop stars and actors. Then again, I don't think they mind. They're probably a pleasant kind of people. Or maybe not. Now that I think about it. It takes a certain kind of character to devote your life to buildings. I mean buildings, come on. That's a rare answer when being asked about the purpose of life. To build and to create, yes, but not literally. The purpose of life cannot be to literally build a building. I wonder what they dream about. Do they have nightmares about their buildings collapsing? Is it like a stab in the heart, every time they see a building go down? Or do they find a perverted sense of satisfaction in it? Maybe they too have a death instinct. Do they talk to their buildings? They must, right? It's strange to have a personal relationship with a building. Do they humanize buildings? Do they give them names? Do they sometimes think of their buildings when they're with their loved ones? Is there physical attraction toward the buildings? Has any of them betrayed their lover for their building? Is there erotic tension between the building and them? Is there more in the room than meets the eye? Buildings are only buildings to us, but to structural engineers, they are much more. It must be like giving birth in a way. Anyone that creates can relate to the feeling. One has a personal, almost intimate relationship with one's creation. Meaning there is a whole bunch of people out there who has an intimate relationship with buildings. So what do we do with all of this? I am not sure. I have zero touch points with this industry, and a whole world of people. I would love to know more about them. Then again, I'd probably regret it. It's always weird to dive into these niche groups, that are obsessed with their own world. E.g. chess players. It's probably best to let them be. I just hope that I won't die in a collapsing building because its engineer was bad at maths.

In the pub today I had a debate with a man. I told him this. There must be a God for there is a moon. He looked at me funny, so I repeated my claim. I argued, there must be a God for there is a moon, since if there was no God, there would be no moon. He was confused, as to my flawless logic, so he made the first mistake. He engaged. He said, those two facts are not connected. I said, see, you called God a fact, you admitted it. He said, well, God is not a fact, but the moon is. I said, this is my point exactly, since the moon is a fact, so is God, for if there was no God, there would be no moon. He looked at me half amused as he was on the brink of seeing through my nonsense. I sensed the danger, but I also knew that I could pull this off. I said, what? He said, you're not serious, are you? I said, about what? He said, you know there is no correlation between God and the moon. I said, right, no correlation, but causation. I said, God must exist, for the moon does, which it wouldn't, if he didn't. He said, the moon can exist without God. I said, no, in that case, it wouldn't make sense for it to exist. He said, you know there is science right? I thought to myself, these Brits and their bloody atheism. He said, the moon was created from debris of the Earth. I looked at him all skeptical. I said, I'm not sure about that. He said, what do you mean you're not sure about that, it's a scientific fact. I said, even if it was true that the moon used to be the Earth. He interrupted me, saying that he didn't say that. I said, you did say, it was made from Earth. He said, yes, in a way. I said, it used to be the Earth then. I saw him breaking a little inside, and I felt this rush that I always feel in this moment. He said, well, go on. I said, even if the moon used to be the Earth, it still proves the existence of God. He said, how is that? I said, it's because if God didn't exist, the Earth wouldn't exist either. He said, the Earth and the moon may well exist without God. I said, that makes no sense. He said, why does it make no sense? I looked at him as though I was dwelling on the most difficult thing I had ever dwelled on. I said, you mean there is no God and the moon exists anyway. His face lit up, and he said, yes, exactly. I said, hmm. He said, it makes sense, doesn't it? I said a hesitant, yet firm: No, I don't think so. He said, what do you mean ‚I don't think so'. I said, I mean that ‚so' I don't think. He frowned at me. I said, there would be no reason for the moon to exist, if God didn't exist. He said, who says that there is a reason for the moon to exist. I said, there is a cause for every effect. He said, yes, and there is a cause for the moon's existence, but it's not God. I said, how do you know that? He said, we know this from science. I said, but maybe science is the way by which God operates. He didn't say anything this time. I bit my tongue for this was way too smart a statement for me to make in this context. Unfortunately for him, he had already bought in on the idea that I was serious. I chased it with absolute nonsense. I said, for example if there were two moons, there would be two Gods. He said, well, that's just crazy. I said, why is that crazy? He said, it just is. I said, it makes perfect sense, one moon means one God, it's not two moons, it's not zero moons, it's one moon. He started to lose his faith in me, and I had this warm feeling in my belly. He said, there is no logical connection whatsoever between the moon and God. I said, so you say. He said, no, there just isn't. I said, why would the moon exist then? He said, I told you. I said, yeah, but you're saying the moon is the Earth, which is a weird thing I have never heard of, and I do not believe in conspiracy theories. My response had the desired effect, he started to get mad. He said, it's not a conspiracy theory, it's confirmed science. I wanted to console him, so I asked him, what happened to the people that lived on this part of Earth? He said, what do you mean? I said, the people who lived on the part of the Earth that became the moon, what happened to them? He said, this was long before humans existed. I said, so how can you be sure then? He said, it's confirmed science, I cannot say any more than that. I said, interesting, not sounding so confident now. He said, I'm not a scientist. I said, that's a pity. He was about to leave. He had it with me, a feeling which I carry with me all the time. It made me warm up to him. I said, maybe you're right. He looked at me friendly. I said, maybe God made the Earth, and he made an extra Earth for the moon people. His optimism was short-lived, as he was now back to condemning me. I said, I wonder what happened to the moon people. He said, there are no moon people, there is no atmosphere there, no water, no nothing. I said, well maybe there was, and it got lost. He said, no, that's not the case. I said, maybe humans lived on the moon, and then moved to the Earth, and then died out, and then the dinosaurs came and destroyed all traces, and today we think we are the first humans, when in fact we have lived before. He said nothing. I said, maybe God made the moon as a test run for the Earth, and he was still a beginner, so he didn't do a very good job, as he wanted to create water and air, but he just ended up creating a lot of chalk and foam. He exclaimed, chalk and foam? I nodded. He said, you think the moon is made of chalk and foam? I said, it looks like that to me. He said, I'm sorry I can't continue this conversation. He got up and left. I felt exhilarated.

I read an article in the newspaper today. It was about a man who had gone to Africa to live among monkeys. I had to read it twice, for at first I had read ‚donkeys'. This had caught my attention, and I was disappointed when I read that it was only monkeys. But it got me thinking anyway. How would it be, I wondered, to live among donkeys. Donkeys are a curious bunch. They look like strange horses. They make different sounds, too. Everything is a little off with these fellas. I wonder would they accept me as one of their own? Or would they always think of me as a misfit? Would they silently wish for me to leave? I don't think so. I don't think they have the mind for it. In any case, I would do everything in my power to fit in. I think my natural personality would fit in well. I feel closer to donkeys than to humans. In the donkey world, I'd just be another specimen. I wonder if I could learn their language. I want to be a donkey whisperer. It would be interesting to hear what they chat about. What are the topics in the donkey community. How do donkeys think about the world? Do they have dreams and hopes? What is a donkey's worst nightmare? Are donkeys sad? They always seem sad to me. Maybe I can console them.

A good life is wasted. On living that is. Modesty is wisdom, for it understands that there is nothing to understand. Modesty is a rare trait. If modesty was an animal, it would be critically endangered. As time progresses, modesty fades. The beauty of the world is in decay.

Modesty is a way of not expecting the world to please you. To be unobtrusive. The modest souls never hurt anyone. Though the modest souls are often hurt. But they take it, beautifully. They represent the best in us. If humans were modest, how beautiful would we be as a species. Modesty does not exclude aspiration. One can be modest and create beautiful things.

Modesty is poorly understood by a loud society. It is often mistaken for shyness, or fear. Pretension and hubris on the other hand are referred to as courage and strength. This says a lot about our society. It's an extrovert world, we just live in it. The loud may be successful, but they're never beautiful. Only the quiet souls can be beautiful. Modesty does not exist in the loud people. We all know that the loud are obnoxious. They want everything and they are always unhappy. They are like toddlers. When they're unhappy, they start crying. And like toddlers they're unhappy a lot. The quiet people are different. They are more like spirits. They have a difficult relationship with the flesh. It bothers them more than it convenes them. One wishes to be spirit above all.

Modesty is a rare trait in a world that fancies ambition and audacity. Yes, that's what we need, another person with the ambition to make it. Good thing we only produce those. The modest are failing at this annoying game called civilization. They are not reflected properly in a society that sets different standards. Ambition evaporates modesty, which is why ambition needs to be evaporated.

Modesty makes no demands. The soul no longer wrestles with the world to make her dreams come true. She accepts that some dreams are not meant to be. Most of them actually. Dreams are guiding stars, not planets we can live on. Modesty is a way of accepting the dream as a dream. To let the world be, is an essential virtue we should all have. Unfortunately, it has become rare. Every human is a sculptor now. The modest souls do not participate. They understand that the Earth is not our creation, that we are hers. Earth and God, mother and father. We are to be, not to become.

Modesty is a sentiment. One *feels* modest above all. If one thinks it, one isn't really modest. One only pretends to be modest. Which is ironic. Because modesty is the lack of pretension. And this is the world we live in today. The loud claim all the virtues, even the quiet ones. It's the tyranny of the loud. But modesty is a sentiment and if it's not, then it's not really present. Modesty never mentions itself, for its number one characteristic is its inability to mention itself. To mention oneself requires an audacity that modesty doesn't possess. Modesty is somehow trapped in a cage with itself. The modest don't speak because they're modest. This is why, when modesty is mentioned, it's typically the exact opposite of modesty. It's pretension, and intention. The truly modest are those who don't mention their modesty. The clear sign of modesty is the absence of any clear sign. Whereas when the signal occurs, it usually signals the absence of modesty. Modesty is a sentiment whose key characteristic lies in its inability to claim itself. But every expression of modesty is a claim, namely one of modesty. One claims one's modesty by mentioning it. As modesty is the inability to claim, you would have to claim your inability to claim. Either you can claim this, in which case you're not really modest. Or you're unable to claim it, in which case you can't claim your modesty. In other words: either you are modest and you cannot say that you are, or you can say that you are, in which case you are not. Which means, if you extend this, that all people who claim to be modest are not really modest, for their alleged inability to claim is disproven by their very ability to claim that inability. On the other hand, only those are truly modest, that cannot claim their modesty, for this would require an ability to claim, which they do not possess. This leads us to the predicament that modesty is not able to express itself. Therefore, when modesty is expressed, it's not present, but absent. This is a universal rule. No truly modest people could express their modesty, for the very expression would refute the claim. Modesty is therefore an interesting trait, as it can only be disproven, not proven. Which seems paradoxical at first, but makes a lot of sense if you reflect on the matter. Fortunately, a modest soul can still be recognized. Her modesty, her majesty. A beautiful soul can only be spotted by a beautiful soul. The loud never understand the modest, for they comprehend everything based on verbal expression. If someone was to say they are modest, the loud would believe it, for they are rather crude souls. On the other hand, when the loud people encounter a modest soul, they can strictly speaking not appreciate her modesty. Which means that the modest are invisible to the loud people. They are visible only to the quiet people. But the quiet people see it in each other, and that's the beautiful part. The modest people must remain modest. If they mention their modesty, it happens at the expense of their modesty. Society is made by the loud people who urge the quiet people to speak up. But the quiet must remain silent in order not to become ugly like the loud people. Modesty is a beautiful trait, it must be protected, and it's protected by not mentioning it. One must be modest without appearing so. Instead of appearing modest without being so. Which is what the loud people do.

To be nobody is a blessing. Too few people realize this. How beautiful it is to exist in secrecy. Thrown into the world, for a brief moment only. Nobody pays attention to you. I don't know why people despair over this. It's an elegant way of existing. Going about your life, not attracting any attention. We should all be more discreet. Discretion is a beautiful trait. To leave people alone, to not impose on them. We should never digress. Discretion is a rare quality in our time. Everyone is communicative these days. Communication is the worst, I even hate the word, this is how little I think of it. To not communicate, to be discreet. Isn't it beautiful. It's not a lack of interest. It's appreciating people's privacy. This is a misconception created by the loud people. When something is not verbalized, it doesn't exist to them. This is why the loud have such a poor relationship with discretion. The loud only know one way of appreciating someone, and that is by telling them. But this is often an invasion, and it has little to do with appreciation. Appreciation is to treat people at their own accord. Treat the happy ones happily, but the quiet ones quietly. The loud never do this. They treat everyone equally, loudly that is. To be quiet annoys nobody. To be loud annoys everybody. Discretion is undervalued in an indiscreet society. Everything is shared with everyone these days. Especially the things we don't want to know about. I wish we were a discreet society. The loud think being discreet means being disinterested. They couldn't be more wrong.

Discretion is beautiful, for it leaves people alone. This doesn't mean that one is not interested in them. If they say a word, you can engage with them. This makes for a pleasant and enjoyable atmosphere. Conversation should never be forced. But almost always it is. This shows how low discretion has sunk in our day. It's barely recognizable at this point. Society has become an indiscreet industry. Everyone's industrious, everyone's illustrious. But who is discreet? Discretion has all but vanished from society. Yet it is discretion that makes a society worthwhile. It's the tragedy of our time that the loud have taken over everything. Discretion is not distance, this is often misunderstood. Discretion is attention, not inattention. It's a way of seeing and appreciating someone, and because you do, you leave them alone. Communication, on the other hand, is often the opposite. It's a way of imposing yourself on other people. It's your mood that initiates the conversation after all. There is no attention given to the counterpart. On whether or not they want to deal with your happiness. This is never taken into the equation. Communication is a lot more egoistical than discretion. Discretion focusses on the other, communication on oneself. But of course, the loud people spin the narrative. They make it seem like the discreet are only occupied with themselves which is the reason why they don't engage. Whereas, obviously, communication is a way of showing interest in the other. But that's not the case. Conversation is imposing your wishes on other people. You make them communicate because you want to. Discretion is the choice to not impose on them. It's a sign of appreciation to spare them. To appreciate them in silence.

Discretion means to not engage. Not because you're not interested. But because you don't know if they are. You don't know them, so you leave them alone. In discretion we prioritize the other over ourselves. It's a noble trait. Or habit. For discretion is not a trait, it's a decision. Everyone should exercise discretion. To never restrain yourself, and then excuse it with your „outgoing personality", is just a way of admitting that you take yourself more important than the others. There is something inherently annoying about the outgoing people engaging the quieter people in this fashion. Why does everyone have to be like them? Why are you not like us? It's unbalanced, and unjust. The quiet are always treated like flawed people in our society. Then again, this is a society which turns flaws into virtues and virtues into flaws. To be outgoing is fair enough, but just be outgoing with your peers. The outgoing people should exercise discretion with the quieter people. Yet they never do. And that's because they don't understand it. They only understand themselves. Maybe if they talked less and reflected more, they would. But it never comes to that. The outgoing people have created a tyranny, and we all suffer from it. The quiet either stay quiet and are ridiculed, or they make an attempt at being outgoing, ridiculing themselves in the process. So either way, the quiet are deemed ridiculous. Yet the truly ridiculous are the loud people and the society they've built.

Discretion is a way of letting people be, instead of turning them into a gadget of your amusement. Communication has turned into a disease. It's all connected to what I call the social disease. The social disease consists of treating private matters like social matters. Everything is verbalized these days, and what isn't verbalized seems to no longer exist. It creates a tremendous pressure to verbalize everything. But not everything should be verbalized. In fact, very little should be. You should think a lot more than you speak, not the other way around. We live in a society in which talk has replaced thought. This happens when you let the loud people reign. We should not communicate a lot, we should communicate a lot less. How beautiful society would be, if it was quiet. A discreet society on a beautiful planet. By being discreet we prove our decency. Discretion and decency are synonyms after all. And so are indiscretion and indecency.

Discretion is not valued in a society so indiscreet. When indiscretion becomes the currency of a society, we must not be surprised about society's decay. Everyone is indiscreet, so indiscretion becomes the new normal. Discretion on the other hand is out of the norm. The discreet are never praised for being discreet. They're treated like they have a screw loose. As if they can't talk, or they're shy, inhibited, whatever. Discretion is treated like a character flaw. Which is crazy, because discretion is a beautiful trait. If society was discreet, how beautiful a place would it be. No one would impose on any other. We'd be a reflecting society. A society in thought.

To leave people alone, not because you don't care, but because you do. You care about their privacy, so you don't impose. Appreciation doesn't require communication. One can appreciate without saying a word. In fact, one should appreciate this way. It's not the other one's duty to facilitate your emotional needs. Communication should be considered as a last resort. If nothing else works, you can still talk. Until then, you should try everything else. To appreciate something doesn't mean you have to communicate your appreciation. You can appreciate in silence. This is what discretion means. To appreciate by not imposing. To spare them your emotional need. You should not burden another with your own burdens. If they offer, then yes, but not, if they don't. Your burden must be carried by thee. Not by everybody else. Discretion is a way of dealing with it by yourself. This seems hard at first, but it gets easier. We must persist in crisis. We must not try to turn it into everybody else's crisis.

Discretion is a beautiful trait. Its very essence lies in the fact that you don't engage with people. Discretion is a decision not to interfere. One appreciates, yet without verbalizing one's appreciation. It's a sign of consideration to not engage.

Discretion appreciates by keeping a distance. The distance is not one of disinterest. Distance can be isolation, but it can also be space. To choose discretion means to choose another over yourself. To deprioritize yourself. We should all teach ourselves in the art of discretion. Discretion is our constant reminder that action is often misguided. To not dictate your pace to others. To not force them into moving your way. This is discretion. A way of loving in silence.

Discretion is acquired in society, or it should be, for it's not really practiced anymore. It's an action. One acts discreetly. And one does so, by not imposing on other people. It's simple actually. One simply has to skip the part where one imposes. Unfortunately, most people can't help themselves. They live in public as they do at home. Which turns society into an awful place. One that one wants to visit as seldom as possible. But society doesn't have to be that way. If we were discreet, it would be a wonderful place.

Discretion acts by not acting. To not act is not an act of discretion. To act by non acting is. Discretion is an active decision against decisive action. One's activity is reduced, in order to allow the other to remain free. To ensure the other's freedom by not engaging them. This is an important trait in social life. It's a sign of paying attention to someone. You see them, and you understand that the right thing to do is to not engage. One pays attention to them by not taking their attention away. From whatever it is they're attending to. We don't know what it is so we shouldn't impose.

Discretion must be nurtured, not suffocated in society. The state of discretion describes the health of a society. Where discretion decays, a society has lost its ways. It's become a marketplace of indiscreet individuals. We should never decay like this. We must remain faithful to discretion. Discretion must be valued, not ridiculed in a society. Discretion is not an inability to speak. It's an inability to be annoying. There's a big difference. It's a way of not imposing on the others.

Discretion is not a handicap, or a character flaw. Discretion is a choice. And the fact that so few people choose it, that people abundantly choose indiscretion, shows the poor state society is in. Discretion is ridiculed by an indiscreet society. It's treated like an inhibition of sorts. The discreet are always considered negatively. Where is this social tyranny coming from, that we all must be in constant conversation? Is the world suffering from too little or too much noise? This is called a rhetorical question for you might as well ask if the night sky is black or mint green. It's a clear and obvious fact that the world is too loud. I want to prescribe mankind a dose of quiet. Imagine how beautiful the world would be if it was quiet all of the sudden. I believe this is why people love Japan. I'm sure there are problems with their society, but it's certainly not that they're too loud. In this regard we should all be like Japan. We should japanize, not jeopardize our souls. And we do so, by teaching us the art of discretion. If we were discreet, how beautiful could we be as a species. Quiet and discreet, thoughtful and original, wouldn't that be nice? Yeah, well, it's not going to happen. For the loud people rule the world, and now they terrorize us all.

It's interesting how you don't really move on from things. You take them with you. They move into the background. Where they don't hurt you as much. And not as frequently. It's an occasional hurt. Always ready to be triggered. Yet the memory is present, and it remains fresh. You don't forget it. And in that sense, it never becomes a memory. It's a present memory. Or a memorized present. Your reality incorporates the memory. It will be different from here. But different doesn't mean bad. Life would be dull, if it always stayed the same. Change is an indicator that life is being lived. The past ended when the memory occurred. Life changed, and then it changed again. But change shouldn't scare us. Life is not supposed to be a straight line. It's supposed to be zig-zag. We should not mourn after the past. The past was necessary to get to the present. Not always is the present nicer than the past. But if the present is not nice, the future may be. Things get better all the time. It's more natural for things to change than it is for them to not change. The real anomaly is permanence. Permanence is what makes the years pass like seconds. Change is to be born, and to be born again. We need to lose what we gained, just to earn it again. What we seize, we shall lose, for nothing is truly permanent. Life is about the experience of win and loss. Of success and failure, of victory and defeat. We are not meant to keep the things we have. We are meant to lose them again. This is a way of preparing us for the ultimate loss. The loss of ourselves. At the end of the road, we will lose it all. This is engraved in the very essence of life. Things are born and things are buried. Life is not about keeping what you have, it's about gracefully losing it again. It's about saying goodbye when your loved ones are still with you. It's about treating them like we're about to say goodbye. Life is a moment, and it's all about that moment. We shall not worry about the passing of the moment. We shall love the moment, once it's on and once it's over. We must not despair when the moment has passed. Life has been lived, so it has been accomplished. Life — it all comes down to this. When life is over, we shall find it in our hearts to be happy that a life has been lived.

This is seldom mentioned. How many women in history we never learned about. They never had a chance to shine their light on the world. This is a very sad fact. It must have been terribly disheartening to realize that you're talented, but you happen to be born in the wrong gender. Which is not an unlikely event. It comes with a 50/50 probability. It's cruel when you think about it. Cruel to deny someone because they're a woman. All the talent that could have been, and never was. It's very sad. That this happened. Yes, there are problems with this in our times, too. But who thinks of all these women in history. Imagine you're very talented, and the simple fact that you're a woman degrades you under any ordinary man. Any fool is your superior by gender. To say it's not fair is an understatement. It's cruel. It was a terrible cruelty done to women, through large parts of history. All the creation that was never created. Not because they're women they would have created, but because they're human. We denied one half of humans any chance to create. This is a terrible cruelty, and it gets crueler the more you think about it. It must have been saddening beyond words to realize you cannot become anything due to the fact that you're a woman. Imagine this, you want to become a great painter, or writer, or scholar. But you cannot. Instead you have to become a house wife. You're reduced to the fact of being a woman. This becomes your sole quality in the eyes of the world. Disposed of all your actual qualities. Disposed of your character, your talent, your thoughts. Disposed of your humanity. Reduced to your femininity. I don't think this is properly understood. How cruel this is. That all times have had incredible talent, which simply wasn't allowed to be, for it happened to be trapped in a woman's body. And so you become reduced to the fact that you're a woman. No one asks about your talent anymore. For you are a woman, and that's it. The simple fact denies you everything. This is not talked about enough. Yes, sure, things have to change in our times, for many issues still exist. But for many it's over. They spent their entire lives, without ever shining their light on the world. They could have, and they wanted to, but they were denied. Man denied woman to become anything. He forced her to stay what she was, and only in his eyes. So much humanity lost. So much pain and sadness. And it's irreversible. We cannot make up for this mistake. We can only improve it from here. And yet, all I can think of is them, and the way they were denied.

It must have been shattering. The whole existence shattering. To know what you could do, if you were allowed. To realize you won't be able to. Instead of pursuing your dreams, you become what every other woman becomes. A mother and a wife. Every man is unique and a conqueror in his realm. Every woman is supposed to do the exact same thing. How cruel. That every woman should live like any other woman. To see right past her humanity, to fight for your rights while denying her any. Man can become anything. Woman can become nothing. She can only become what she already is.

Every man can live his own life. Every woman is supposed to live the same. There is no reason why this should have ever been so. It was literally a man-made situation. And it's inconceivable how only now things are starting to change. How long it took us to come to this simplest realization. That women should have the same opportunities as men. This is a sad fact of history that for the longest time this has not been a priority. It's simply been ignored. It must have been shattering to be a woman at basically any time in history. The simple fact of being a woman denied you everything.

I am sad. So many lives lived and never to their fullest. The female genius didn't get to see the light of day. They were denied. Denied to become what they were all along. For every male name written in the history books there is a female name written besides it in invisible ink. All the originality we never got to see. To be forgotten before you're remembered. To cease before you were. To become invisible because the world looks away. This is cruelty. Not injustice, but cruelty. We were cruel to these women. To all women, but particularly to the gifted women. Those that could have been what their male counterparts turned out to be.

Woman reduced to a mother, a lover and a wife. Woman not acknowledged as human. A distinction which should have never been made. All humans should have opportunity. And yet one half never had it. We only gave opportunity to one half of mankind. Mankind, but it shouldn't be called that, for man wasn't very kind. Man was cruel, and who gave him the power? He took it. It's oppression, make no mistake. The history of man is the history of oppression.

All the women who never stood a chance. They had the ability, and the will. But they were women, so they became mothers and wives. Wife to an ordinary man who could do anything. Due the fact of being a man. This is called injustice, but the word doesn't begin to express what it was. It was cruelty. The murder of minds and souls. And many of them, so many of them. Again and again, in every single one. A young girl growing up just to realize she couldn't become anything because she happened to be born in the wrong gender. Not one in a million. Not one in a thousand. One in two. Every second human. How was this allowed? Were we so morally lost? I am so sad about this. Sad about the many lives which in a way remained unlived.

It's incredibly sad, to picture this in detail. A young girl growing up. She's talented, original, unique. She's got all the thoughts and ideas, the ambitions and the plans. Just to grow up and realize she can't have any of that. She was born in the wrong gender. Instead she must live the life that all women live. She must be mother and wife. First she despairs over it. But over time she accepts. She finds her little bliss. Perhaps in her family, or her hobbies. All the dreams she had. None of them saw the light of day. It wasn't her fault. She could have done it. All of it. Yet she never did. She was denied. So she lived, and so she died. Perhaps when she was old, in her final days, she contemplated again. On what life could have been, if she hadn't been a woman. Thus she ends as she began. Invisible. This was her life now. And then it happened again. To another girl. And again. It happened all the times, in all the places. Cruelty, this is what has been done to women in history. They were denied. Denied a life, and denied freedom. They could've been human, if only they hadn't been women. Tough luck, one could say, if this was in any way related to bad luck. But it was man-made. Man did this to woman.

All the women that could have become anything. Yet they had to be women. Man became everything. Woman remained nothing. Her fate was sealed, her genius concealed. She was not allowed to become what she was all along. She had to be a mother and a wife. So it was decided by man. I'm so sorry for all these women. It must have been incredibly sad to witness this from the first person. To be that person. To be talented, to have dreams, just to be denied because you're a woman. Something which you simply can't change. A simple fact of nature. To realize that all the things you want to do will never be. We all experience this, but this is different. Here it could have been, and it should have been. There was no reason why it shouldn't have been. It would have been, if we hadn't actively prevented it. It's a cruelty done by one half of mankind to the other half. It's denying her everything for nothing. We always talk about the unfortunate in an unfortunate way. We talk about them from the perspective of the fortunate. We should take the perspective of the unfortunate. Think and feel like they do. Then it becomes a different matter. You feel at once with a heavy heart that it must be terrible to be trapped in unfortunate circumstances. To objectively not be able to navigate out of them. To be dependent, even though you have done nothing wrong. To depend on people who should have no right to make you dependent on them. And yet to be. To remain dependent, for independence belongs to the others. You can only look and ponder. How it would feel to be one of them. To have freedom and opportunity. But then it stops. Dream time is over, and it's back to reality. And here you become a mother and a wife. The dreams you had will forever remain dreams. Reality is different. But only for you. Not for them. For them reality can be anything. It's limitless. I am so sorry for them. These were real people. They were forgotten when they were still alive. One half of mankind, simply forgotten. Reduced to being woman, never allowed to be human.

All the talent, and all the minds. I wish we could repay the debt. I wish we could turn back time. Bring them back, and do better. To allow them what they weren't allowed the first time. To go back in time, and change it. To allow them what they should have been allowed in the first place. Not special rights, but the same rights. To simply allow them the same as men. To make sure they can become anything. To give them choice. Men have always had choice, women never.

Men are in debt. It cannot be brushed off like this. It must be a priority for men to own up to this. To change this, and to improve this. To make sure this is no longer so. And that it never happens again. So at the very least, there is vindication for these women. It won't make it any better for them, but at least their fate stops being pointless. And yet, even this feels wrong. For once again, it's the simple fact that they were women, and namely oppressed women, that makes them change the world. And this should have never been so. They should have changed the world as humans. They didn't want to change it as women. They didn't even care about being women. We did. We reduced them to that. We allowed ourselves all the sweet freedoms of a human life. We considered us human, and so did they. Yet we told them, you are not human, you are woman. You shall be woman, only I shall be human. We must make sure this never happens again. Not once is it allowed to happen again. Every human must have opportunity and choice. Where choice is denied, freedom ends, and oppression begins. We must make sure that every human can do whatever. Man and woman should not fight, they should unite in being human. Humans must be free, and free to choose. There should obviously not be a distinction made between man and woman.

I talked to a young man today, who told me that he felt lonely. He asked me if I felt lonely, too. He was genuine, so I abandoned my nonsensical approach and instead „decided to practise my new, normal personality on this man", in the words of Sylvia Plath. I told him that I did not feel lonely, but that's because I don't have the personality for it. If anything, I felt lonely among people. He said, that's interesting, for he felt the opposite. And this made me think. How strange it is. That some people get lonely when they're alone and they blossom when they're among people. Whereas I get lonely among people. It made me think of the nature of loneliness. Loneliness is not the same as aloneness. You can feel lonely when you are alone. But you can also feel lonely among people. It's not about the objective fact of being alone. It's about the subjective feeling of being alone. In aloneness we are objectively alone. In loneliness we are subjectively alone. Often these two correspond, which means that we feel lonely, when we are alone. The feeling is tied to the fact. However, when they don't correspond, we may feel lonely, while not being alone. This is more paradoxical, but only at first glance. Because then you realize, it's a sense of isolation, or unconnectedness, if that's a word, and perhaps disparity. It's the feeling of not being alike. But with whom? It has to be asked. You can be among people and feel like the loneliest person on Earth. So when we feel lonely, it means that we feel our isolation or distinctness, if that's a word, distinctly, and I know that's a word. We feel distinctly that we are distinct. If we don't feel this, we are still distinct, but not lonely. Our objective isolation doesn't subjectively strike us as an isolation. There is a feeling of connection despite our isolation. But connection with whom? When we are alone, who could we feel connected to? There is nobody here. Well, except for ourselves. This is Ockham's razor applied to the situation. When we feel subjectively connected despite being alone, there is only one person we could feel connected to. And that is our own person. Which means that loneliness describes our connection or lack thereof with ourselves. If we feel connected to ourselves, we are not lonely, despite being alone. Whereas if we feel unconnected to ourselves, we feel lonely even among people. And this is interesting, isn't it? It means that we're mistakenly assuming loneliness describes our connection with others, when in reality it describes our connection with ourselves. In other words, loneliness is a one-body-problem. Which is a different takeaway from the matter. Most people try to cure their loneliness, by seeking connection with others. Loneliness, however, is not a lack of connection with others, but with oneself. Meaning one must must form a connection with oneself to overcome it.

Dark, they said. He's a dark character. Which I don't agree with. I may be a dark soul, but my character is pretty bright. I'm a bright character in a dark soul. I'm like a black sun. I shine in darkness. No one is safe from my darkest rays. A ray of darkness is a beautiful thing. It's like a shudder. But there is truth in darkness. Darkness strips you of your appearance. You become impearance instead. You appear to the inside. This is what I call impearance. An appearance within. It's beautiful to be in the dark. To not be aware of what's going on. One should always aim for the least amount of information. Knowledge has never made anyone happy. The wisdom of unwisdom, is to not possess any knowledge. To know not even yourself. To know nothing. Isn't it beautiful?

To walk between dark places. There is something poetic about it. When you walk at night, from one place to another, and everything is empty, and dark. Darkness is made for people like I. Darkness is vile, but caringly so. It never tells us any lies. A truth not felt at night is only a disguised untruth. The night validates our truths. If at night we don't feel, what we do during day, it's during day that we lie to ourselves.

To walk between dark places. Everywhere you go, darkness awaits. To have a dark soul is not without its benefits. Most people don't live intensively. Their lives lack in substance. Yet the dark soul experiences the world intimately. The sky is hanging a little lower. It's like you carry it on your back. Your feet touch the ground a little more. Your thoughts are big in your head like the Hollywood sign. Human contact is curious, too. There is an element of distance, as well as an element of proximity. You walk past the others, without seeing them. But then you do, and you see them a lot more intimately. It's like falling into their souls. You can get trapped in another quite easily. You close in on them by increasing your distance. It's like a vanishing point that falls toward you. As though proximity became the vanishing point. There is a strange distortion of reality, when your soul becomes dark. To walk between dark places means to walk back and forth between a distance closing in and a proximity falling away. The near can never be touched, for it's out of our grasp. While the remote can be touched as though it was here. It's strange. How much reality can change, based on your perception of it.

Darkness distorts your view in a particular way. It estranges you from the world, but it also personalizes your relationship with it. While the world becomes more distant, it also becomes closer in a way. You become close with the estranged world. Your proximity is far away, but that distance is experienced more intimately. You become intimate with your own estrangement. It's a strange way of turning the world on its head. When previously you felt close to your proximity, and distant to the distance, you feel the opposite now. What is close to your body is remote to your soul. But this remoteness is felt intimately by your soul. Your soul feels close to the distance. Proximity becomes a burden which only distance relieves her from. You relieve yourself by distancing yourself. Closeness becomes a casket, you cannot bear it anymore. You must be remote, for this is what your soul wants. The soul has a desperate wish to escape her vicinity. She longs for the remote. She wants to remove herself from the body. The body and the soul move against each other. What the body touches, becomes remote to the soul. But this remoteness is felt intimately. This is not closeness, it remains remoteness. The remoteness is felt like a closeness of sorts. Or the body's closeness becomes the soul's remoteness.

You can experience the world quite differently. A distortion is often not perceived. It stands firm as an objective reality. You don't see your eye broken. You only see the world broken. What you see, appears to you as true. One never notices this sort of thing. It's imperative that we understand people from their perspective. To understand them from ours, is to not understand them at all. For not only their view is distorted, but ours is too. Subjectivity is a realm, whose surface refracts the entering light. It always looks different from inside. One source of light, but countless impressions of it. Every eye distorts, for there's a soul waiting within. The subject remains the variable. To understand the objective is of little help. The subjective is tied to the distortion which takes place at the surface of the subject. This surface is often the eye. Literally, when it comes to the world, and figuratively, when it comes to the mind. There is an entrance point, or an intersection, between the objective and the subjective.

We distort the world by looking at it. There is no such thing as an objective view. Every view, by the very fact of being a view, is subjective. Only a subject can view the world after all. One must understand the particular distortion of the subject. It takes fine senses to grasp the distortion of another. Once this is accomplished, which only happens to a degree, support can be granted. You can analyze the distortion, and where it presents a problem, you can help fix it.

I disagree that beauty is truth. The aesthetes say this. They identify beauty with truth. But if anything, beauty is untruth. Beauty is not seeing the world the way it is, but the way it is not. This is beauty. To see the world differently. To fill it with meaning. To look past the objective world, or to see the world subjectively. What makes the world beautiful is that we find it beautiful. Beauty needs to be conceived in a subject. When the subject is absent, so is beauty. The artist sees the world beautiful before he or she creates a piece of art. The piece of art then represents the beauty the artist perceived. But this beauty is not objective, it was born and raised in the subject. Beauty transitions from from subject to object. This is commonly misunderstood. The capacity to conceive beauty is necessary, or beauty will not be conceived. Beauty is not truth, it's the transcendence of truth. Beauty is beyond truth. Or behind it. You must traverse truth, all the way until you reach beauty. When beauty is won, truth is gone, for beauty is untruth, and she reigns over truth. Beauty is higher and greater than truth. Beauty is to the soul what truth is to the mind. Perfection, or the criterion of perfection.

Beauty never lies, which creates its paradoxical character. Because beauty is untruth and yet it never lies. It proves itself by being conceived. Doesn't it make it a truth then? Yes, but in a different way. It's subjective truth, not objective truth. Beauty validates subjective reality, as truth does objective reality. The paradoxical stems from the fact, that these two are often opposites. To the extent that we sense objective truth, we lose our sense of beauty. On the other hand, if we sense subjective truth, it's almost a function of how little attention we pay to objective truth. Beauty becomes a function of the untruth. While truth destroys beauty in the process of being found out. Therefore, one should pick carefully. Truth without beauty, or beauty without truth. One must have a little of both. But never should truth devour beauty. It's better to go mad than to go reasonable. The truth prioritizes the object over the subject. This is a loss of beauty felt in the subject, as one is now committing to the object. If we saw the world objectively, we would not find it beautiful. To see the world like an object strips it of all beauty. In order to see the world beautiful, we must see it subjectively. This is why it's dangerous to become objective. Once we see the truth, we are losing sight of beauty. Truth is like an exotic spice. It needs to be added in small portions. One can never have too little truth in one's life, and easily too much. Truth spoils our innocence. The untruth alone has potential to be beautiful. We should go, where beauty takes us. All truth becomes irrelevant, when beauty strikes.

To be nobody is a blessing. It's much better to live in freedom, and to die in oblivion. Much better than living in unfreedom, and to die accordingly. To be hiding in plain sight. To not be spotted even though you are. It's a privilege to be nobody. A privilege poorly understood. One should always aim to remain a nobody. This ensures a freedom so sweet. The freedom of mind. And the freedom of soul. Without this freedom, life becomes tedious. To feel unfree because you know you're being watched is a terrible feeling. To be chased by other people's attention. Society is a burden, this is a natural fact. Aristotle says man is a social animal but I'm not convinced. I think we're made to be in secret. Life must never be burdened with the expectation of others. To have to live up to anyone except for yourself. We should never expose ourselves like that. We must remain invisible. Only a nobody is truly free. It's a blessing, not a curse. To be unknown is to be independent. Who would want to live any other way. Perfect freedom, unbeknownst to the world. Buds are made to blossom. But they get shy when you watch them. Make sure not to watch them. To be a nobody is beautiful.

My expression is not in my words anymore. It's in my thought and sentiment. What I write down, expresses me well. What I say, doesn't. Skill comes with practice and this is why people are skilled at expressing themselves. It's also why I lack this skill. I lack practice. An unwillingness to communicate has become an incapacity. Now I'm incapable of expressing myself. However, only in the verbal form. Because surprisingly, I still manage to express myself in the written form. When I write, I speak genuinely. It's when I speak that I don't. I need to write in order to speak. There is some beauty in that. Most people speak, even when they write. But who ever speaks in writing. The words that I write are my language now. This is why I am engulfed in silence. Written words make no sound. My speech is all but gone.

It's often mentioned that you forget a foreign language when you don't speak it. But this can happen to your language altogether. I wonder if it's possible to take this to a fault. If I continue not to speak, will I eventually forget grammar and vocabulary. That would be nice. To silence myself into idiocy. Or illiteracy. The actual inability to communicate. For now I still possess this ability. I can communicate. I'm just not very good at it. I wonder is it possible to lose this ability. To make sounds, but neither rhyme nor reason. To sound as alien as I feel. To say something which lacks linguistic coherence. To lexically drop out of society. To say something which sounds like language to me, but not to them. To earn astounded glances by those who still possess the skill. To make an attempt to say something, but to say something else. To forget how simple phrases are formed. That would be nice.

To be a nobody is a blessing, and we must never move away from it. To not draw any attention. To never be looked at. I wish I was invisible. Matter is a burden. The body is a prison. I wish I could be mind and soul. To be a nobody, this is what I aspire to. To be so hidden that people never remember me. I want to be in one place, but only briefly, so that people forget me again. I want to disappear, as I appeared, virtually unnoticed. Visually unnoticed, too, that would be ideal. I wish I could reduce myself further. I wish I didn't have to eat for example. This is a major burden to my day. I wish I could sit under a tree in a forest, and sit there for the rest of my life. I wish I could do nothing, or only one thing, which resembles nothingness more than somethingness. To live like a pillar of salt. I wish I could observe the world from one particular angle. I wish I could become a bodiless mind.

To be a nobody is beautiful. You don't owe anything to anyone. It's a beautiful, pointless existence. This is poorly understood by a society that is never satisfied with anything.

They say you can't have it all, but that's not the point. The point is you shouldn't want to have it all. For if you have it all, you'll enjoy everything a little less. It drains you to have it all. You should have nothing, or barely anything, but the little you have should be enjoyed by you. To become an expert at one particular thing. For example tying your shoelaces. To spend your life becoming really good at tying your shoelaces and forgetting about everything else, e.g. starting a family. This would be a life well lived. I want to become a master at something absolutely meaningless, but this I want to fill with meaning. I want to add meaning to the meaningless, and I'll do so by removing meaning from the meaningful first. One should never aim to have it all. A family, career, travels, it becomes too much. We should do less, but the less we do we should do more. To be a nobody is a satisfying aspiration because it's easily achieved. It's impossible to fail at staying a nobody. Unless of course you become a somebody, but this can be actively steered. As soon as you see yourself becoming somebody, you must intervene. You must avoid to ever run into a port. Whenever this seems to happen, you must steer the ship back toward the open sea. To be unfulfilled is to feel alive. To be fulfilled is to fall asleep.

It's beautiful to be a nobody. It's my new ambition in life. The good news is I already made it. I reached my goal of being a nobody. I'd like to thank my family and supporters. I wish I could hold a victory speech. Unfortunately, this would turn me into a somebody, so I have to decline. I'll gracefully accept the merits of being a nobody. A nobody is not accountable, for no one accounts him. It's called freedom. A nobody can never be stripped of his freedom. One doesn't have to please anyone, for one doesn't exist in those terms. Failed in the eyes of the world. Succeeded as a nobody. It's liberating to be a failure. It's a burden to be a success.

To be free of expectation. One can apologize for being a failure, but only once, and after that one has to commit to it. Failure is nothing to be ashamed of. It's something to be proud of. Nothing is harder than failing in style. To fail while proudly defending your ways. This is true ethical success. We should try to fail as hard as possible. It makes for the best stories. Life is like money, it needs to be spent. We spend it by endeavoring. We pay with life, and we earn failures on the way. Life is a resource borrowed, not bought.

If only we could remain a secret. How beautiful that would be. To live in secrecy. To be an absolute nobody, even in the eyes of myself. Not to become grand in my own way. To remain small and insignificant. To be little. So little that no one ever saw me. I wish I could be a flea. Or an amoeba. They are well hidden. I wish I could have the body of an amoeba and a human mind. That would be my preferred way of existing. A thinking amoeba. It must be beautiful. Unlike the word amoeba, which is ugly. I have no idea how it's pronounced nor do I care to find out. I want to be an amoeba without knowing that I am. One is so beautifully hidden beneath the world. And yet one is right in the middle of it. To become a grand mind, while hiding physically. Or to become invisible when it comes to the physical, yet sublime when it comes to the spiritual. A sublime mind in the body of an amoeba. This seems like a great way of existing. I wish I could shake off my body. I wish I could liberate my soul from it. I wish my mind and soul could go elsewhere. To leave my body behind. For the body is a prison, which takes away our liberty. I want to claim my liberty back from my body. I want to get rid of it. But I also want to keep my mind, and it seems to be a package deal. If only I could be mind and soul while leaving my body behind. I would love that.

We should not aim to please. Not to displease either. We should not aim for anything. Wisdom is to never try. Or to try with the intent of failing. That's the sweet spot. Only perfection is sufficient. To aim for something which you can never reach. To not even get close. To die prematurely.

My goal is to be a nobody. To be so inconspicuous, that people never look at me. It must be beautiful to be invisible. To be a nobody is a way to ensure maximum freedom.

I am happy now, for I'm reaching my goal. To be a nobody. I wish I could reduce myself further and further. Until I'm all mind and soul. Only the most basic requirements of the body shall be fulfilled. I shall breathe, but even that silently. I shall breathe through my teeth, I shall never open my mouth. I shall sit in the corner of a room and never leave this corner. I shall reduce myself to minimal space and physicality. I wish I could live in a way that people would forget they ever saw me. I want to move like a shadow among people. Or not even among people. A shadow in my own home. A shadow in my own body. Or I want to dissolve. I want to disintegrate. I want to fade. How much I want to fade. I want to disappear, but gradually so. To disappear abruptly causes a fuss. To disappear gradually doesn't. One has to disappear one step at a time. The word is withdrawal. One needs to gradually withdraw. This becomes the act of disappearing. One needs to disappear in a way that the disappearance never becomes obvious. Not the vanishing kind, but the withdrawing kind. Or the dissolving kind. To dissolve gradually. To do a little less every day. To reduce oneself to mind and soul. To sink down and sigh, one last time. This is a beautiful way to conclude a life. To sigh, but silently so. To sigh with the soul. To sigh without despairing. To sink down and sigh.

This is my goal now. To be an absolute nobody, and take this to a fault. I want to be the nobodiest nobody of all time. I want to be the greatest nobody who's ever lived. Does this not make me a somebody? By no means. For my essential, my only quality remains that I am a nobody. I am without feature. I have disposed myself, of myself. I have freed myself from I. And now I shall be a nobody. Isn't it beautiful. To be nothing. I wish I could be nothing. Air. Not even air. For air is still something. Air is too much. I want to be less than air. I want to be nothing. Can I be nothing? If only I could. I want to keep my mind and soul. I want to be spirit. Yes. Spirit. Beautiful spirit. Like a breeze. But not of air. A breeze of spirit. I aspire to be beautiful nothing. Nothing as beautiful as beautiful nothing. To be nothing is even better than to be a nobody. I want to have no physicality whatsoever. Not even form. I don't want to be a ghost, for a ghost is still in the physical form. Physicality needs to be overcome completely. When the body is nullified, the spirit is clear. And so I aim to become spirit. Like a breeze I want to travel the world. More importantly the minds. I shall come into every mind, and be a friend. I want to be the breeze to the minds quite alike, and quite unlike, too. Every mind shall be my world, and I shall be invited. I am spirit now. Beautiful spirit. Not to be stopped by the flesh. How pretty, isn't it? To be beautiful spirit.

The question has to be asked: What are horses doing all day? As the saying goes: „Am I interrupting something?" I never have that feeling with horses. They're always available. I wonder how they pass the hours. There is nothing happening in a horse's life. There is not even a real community. Cows are hanging around in a group, some sitting, some chatting. Cows are vibing. But horses are just there. Even when they are together, they are apart. I relate to that. They stand next to each other, but not aligned. They stand in crooked angles to each other. When horses mingle, it's always like a group of people at a party but no one speaks. There's something eery about the social gatherings of horses. They just stand there, and so randomly, too. They are not face to face. They are face to butt. Or face to hip. Do horses have hips? I mean the mid to end section of a horse. They stand like this for hours. I mean I'm guessing it's hours. I'm not watching them for hours, but they always stand there like it has been hours. When you walk past them, they barely move their head. Compare this to a cow. She will drop everything to look at you. The verve, the sway, with which a cow moves her head toward you. The anticipation in her look. Find yourself someone that looks at you like any random cow. You're always a celebrity in a cow's world. Back to horses. It's hard to interact with them because they're so distant. They seem so detached from the world. This is why I relate to them. Nay, I aspire to them. I aspire to their level of detachment.

Horses are interesting. The way they look at you all strange. I know there are ways to decipher a horse. I'm just not familiar with those ways. When I see a horse, I'm puzzled. Do they think about you? Do they think lowly of you? What's their general mindset? I wish they could talk. I guess they would talk funny. Horses do not strike me as particularly ordinary type animals. They're a different breed. It's hard to connect to a horse emotionally. Or socially. Socially is the better word. Whenever I try to make a horse friend, I fail. There is something which I don't grasp about horses. I believe it takes a particular sort of personality to connect to horses. I don't know what personality, I only know that I don't possess it. I'm not the horse personality. I'm more of a cow personality. Then again everyone is. Cows love everyone. And everyone loves cows. Cows are the dogs of the agricultural realm. It's impossible to dislike a cow. A horse is more edgy, polarizing. It's never afraid to make an enemy. A horse doesn't try to please you. It's their way or the highway. A horse never buckles. I am impressed by the fortitude of their character.

A horse registers you, but that's about it. Sometimes I walk past cows which don't register me at first, and when they do, they get startled. This is so cute, and I always talk to them in those cases. I say: no need to be startled, it's just me. I say it with a child's voice, because I reckon that cows go by the sound of your voice. All animals do, but cows in particular, for I reckon they are not very smart. Even though for every animal there is an animal expert who calls this particular animal smart. A cow always builds rapport. A cow is a people pleaser. On the other hand, it's hard to build rapport with a horse. I know, the horse lovers disagree, but I stand firm with this opinion. I like horses. No, I love horses. I think they are majestic, lovely creatures. But I'm always confused by them. They register you, but they don't acknowledge you. One has to earn their affection. You never know what they're up to. A horse could plot terrible things, and we wouldn't know about it. It's impossible to see through a horse's facade. There is an element of seclusion and impenetrability. A horse plays games with you, mind games. It looks at you with this neutral expression. This is what I find eery about them. Cows look dumb, but friendly. They react with their expressions. A horse doesn't have facial expressions. It always looks the same way. A horse is a mystery, perhaps one of the remaining mysteries in the world. What goes on inside a horse's head. Are they plotting something? They sure look like it.

When you walk past a horse, the best you can get is a slight, the slightest head movement and this means the horse registers you as „something". What that something is, only the horse knows. Their arrogant attitude is too much. What gives them the right to meet you with this arrogant demeanor. A cow is beautifully humble. Albeit because a cow is stupid, but still. A horse is never humble. Have you seen a humble horse? Have you even heard the expression? No? I rest my case. Horses have expectations. They are entitled. They look down on us. While I look up to them. I hate their arrogance. Yet I love horses. They are good creatures. They can't help their arrogance. It's genetic. Horses are genetically arrogant. And yet I don't know what they're doing. They just stand there. Sometimes they randomly break into a trot but they only do this for ten seconds or so. Then they stop, and stay where they are. I don't understand what's going on in their heads. They're just doing things. But it's a very limited catalogue of things. The day must be so long for them. It must trot on forever. And yet, when I walk past them, it should be a highlight to their day. Well, who's arrogant now, right? But I stand by it. Nothing happens in a horse's life, so if and when something does, it should be a major event. Yet they care even less about events than nothingness. They don't care about anything. They have become completely indifferent to the world. I admire that. Horses are better than humans. They have mastered the human condition. The horse condition. We should all aspire to be like horses. We must live up to them. To meet the horse's standards is to reach absolute detachment. To disregard the world and to accept the neutrality of life. To remain still like a pilar of salt. To have lived by not having lived. This is virtue. To stand still, and to observe, without reacting. This is the way to live. I admire horses. I aspire to their level of detachment. I just want to detach and stand around, and do nothing until I die. I wish I could be a horse. It must be an amazing life.